PRAI

"Blood of the Sands is an enthralling enemies-to-lovers fantasy set in harsh desert landscape filled with fearsome creatures and unbridled magic. S.C. Grayson weaves a rich tale of a deadly competition rife with betrayal and a slow burn healing love that simmers with the perfect amount of spice. An absolutely fantastic start to this series!"

Tessonja Odette, author of the Entangled with Fae series

"Blood of the Sands is a Reylo fan's dream romantasy. With interesting and complex characters, high-stakes action, and a unique world, this book was an absolute delight from start to finish. Erix is my new favorite brooding, bad boy book boyfriend and Keera is a fiesty, stabby delight. I adore both of them and cannot wait to read more of this series."

Megan Van Dyke, best-selling author of Second Star to the Left

Paperback ISBN: 979-8-9892825-7-9

Hardcover ISBN: 979-8-9892825-8-6

Ebook ISBN: 979-8-9892825-2-4

Cover design by Moonpress

www.moonpress.co

Hardcover case laminate design by Covaleinne

Editing by www.greymothediting.com

To anybody who has ever felt alone—
And turned to books to know that they are not.

BLOOD
OF THE
SANDS

BOOK ONE
THE BALLAN DESERT

S.C. GRAYSON

AUTHOR'S NOTE

This book is a dark romantasy intended for adults. As such, it contains heavy themes and intense action typical of the genre, as well as on-page physical intimacy.

If you like your conflicts complicated, your stakes high, your characters morally gray, and your romance sizzling, this book is for you.

A full list of included themes can be found on the author's website.

PROLOGUE
KEERA

The desert held her breath. She'd been my only companion for many years, and I knew her rhythms like I knew my own heartbeat—the swish of the burrowing owl's wings and the brushing of wind over sands. While the desert seemed quiet to many, it was a symphony to those who knew how to listen.

Now, she fell quiet. Even rustling of the date palm leaves had ceased and the back of my neck prickled with awareness. Something deep in my belly stirred—something that had been dormant for so long I thought I had imagined it, not yet awakening but shifting.

The desert was waiting, and I stood with her on the precipice.

Something was coming.

CHAPTER ONE
THE VIPER

Sparks danced through the air as the blade of my saber clashed against my opponent's. My blow was stronger than his, knocking his sword out of the way. He switched directions quickly, blocking my next strike before it could land.

The Lord of Clan Ratan wanted a battle with the Viper, so that is what he would get.

I pressed forward in a flurry of strikes, driving him back toward the edge of the circle of people watching us fight. His arms shook as he blocked my blows—he was growing tired.

Even as his movements became sluggish, his technique saved him from several strikes, speaking to the skills that allowed him to become Lord of Clan Ratan. I gritted my teeth at the show of his talents. He would have been useful in training the riders of the combined clans if he hadn't gotten it in his head to challenge me to a duel of honor.

Such duels could only end one way.

Finally, the lord made a mistake, and I struck with a flick of my wrist. My opponent landed on his knees, saber dropping to the sand beside him. As the tip of my blade pressed into the space below his breastbone, not penetrating him but clearly showing my victory, he snarled up at me.

I stared back down at him in a mix of triumph and frustration. Battle had amplified the voice of the desert in my head, her power pounding through my veins. With magic coursing through me, begging for blood, it made gritting out my question difficult.

"Will Clan Ratan bow to Lord Alasdar and Clan Katal?"

"Over my dead body," sneered Lord Einil.

It was a challenge, the lord mocking me. Duels in the Ballan Desert were to the death, and sparing your opponent was seen as a dishonor to both parties. My hesitation to end his life had not gone unnoticed, but I had no honor left to risk.

Before I could move, Lord Einil fell forward onto my sword, impaling himself on the blade. I hissed but did not pull away, staring into his face as the life drained from his eyes. My blood boiled at the waste of such a worthy warrior, one who could have been useful in saving the desert, but I leashed my anger through force of will.

The clans had to be united, and Lord Einil had left me no choice. He challenged me to a duel of honor as the condition of Clan Ratan's allegiance, and a true warrior of the clans could not refuse such a challenge. The shouting of the desert in my mind reminded me of the urgency of my task.

With a decisive movement, I yanked my sword free of the corpse, and it teetered on its knees for a moment before collapsing to the ground. A hush had fallen over the surrounding crowd, but nobody protested my actions. The clans of the Ballan Desert understood power above all else.

I turned toward a young woman at the edge of the crowd, Einil's daughter, who would now serve as lord of the clan. Leadership in the clans didn't necessarily pass from parent to child, with riders of the Ballan Desert valuing power over blood. The way every member of the clan turned deferentially to her though told me she had been groomed to have the strength to lead.

"Lord Alasdar will expect Clan Ratan to join him within a fortnight."

"I will see it done, Viper."

The way she spat my title spoke of more insult than respect, but I paid her tone no mind. It didn't matter what anybody thought of the masked warrior, Lord Alasdar's Viper. I had been tasked with restoring the desert, no matter the cost. If my penance should be the hatred of the clans, then so be it.

I wiped the blade of my sword on the sand, and the shouting of the desert in my mind quieted to a whisper. As the crimson melted into the golden dune, I looked up to the sky, the rays of the sun moving quickly toward the horizon, piercing the openings around the eyes of my mask and heating the stifling metal against my skin. I drank in the rare moment of clarity that came after a fight, grateful to be able to hear my own thoughts where so often they were drowned out by the overwhelming crush of magic.

My saber was clean enough for now, and I sheathed it across my back with a sigh. I was envious of the blade—it didn't have to think about its existence until it was brought out to draw blood, put away with no worries until the next fight. I needed to make my way back to Lord Alasdar.

I walked through the crowd, and they parted like water to let me through, no one daring to come too close. We were already near the edge of Clan Ratan's encampment where my horse waited for me.

Alza tossed her head as I approached, throwing her glossy black mane into my face. At least she was happy to see me, greeting me with a low whicker. I spared her a pat on the forelock before vaulting onto her back and spurring her on with a squeeze of my knees. She picked her own pace across the sands, and I didn't bother to direct her with my heels at her sides. The desert was pleased with me today and wouldn't let me wander long before she offered place to rest.

The dunes flew by, familiar only in their ever-changing ways, the landscape shaped by the wind to be something entirely different, even though I had passed this way earlier in the day. An oasis appeared in the distance, and I directed Alza toward it with a nudge. The sight of date palms rising out of the greenery indicated that this oasis had at one point supported a clan's encampment, and they had cultivated the trees to protect the water source from the wind and sands, making it a lasting haven for travelers. I could camp there tonight and let Alza drink her fill before rejoining with the rest of the clan tomorrow.

As the verdant splotch of the oasis in the otherwise golden landscape drew closer, I realized I was no longer alone in my own head again. The whispers of power in my mind returned so gradually that at first, I believed it was just the wind brushing against the sand. With each step Alza took toward our resting place though, they grew in volume until their words tumbled over each other in a violent cacophony, always unintelligible. As always, their tone seemed to suggest they wanted something, and I did my best to placate them by healing the desert the only way I knew how. By now, my annoyance with the incessant chattering was tinged dark with resignation.

I clutched at strands of Alza's mane that caught in my fingers so tightly she snorted in protest. I released her mane, but the frustration that held me only gripped tighter. Usually feeding blood to the desert bought me at least a day of peace, but this time I only had hours. Darkness whirled and eddied in my vision, and I closed my eyes, trusting Alza to lead us to our destination without guidance.

The sudden cease of motion beneath me caused me to look around, finding that Alza stood at the edge of a small pool, gulping thirstily. I jumped down beside her but did not drink. That would have to wait until I took my mask off for the night.

For now, I busied myself setting up a camp. I wouldn't need a tent as I was alone, and a small fire would suffice to warm me. It was the dry season, so the nights didn't get as cold, and Alza generated more than enough warmth if I needed it. As I collected fallen branches from the date palms surrounding the oasis for fuel, the back of my neck prickled. The ghost of a breath brushed over my ear. I whipped around, searching for the source of the whisper. Looking around, I found it to only be my own madness playing tricks on me. This was not the first time it had done so. Still, I couldn't shake the notion that the desert was stirring around me, the voices echoing in my skull taking on an excited tone. Where normally they were angry, crescendoing in anticipation every time I rode into battle, their cadence was different now.

I grunted in frustration as I waved my hand over the pile of fuel, and it burst into flame with more enthusiasm than I intended. My magic tried to slip its leash, still fizzling from the earlier battle. I dug my fingers into my palms, pushing away the buzzing power at the base of my skull that threatened to overwhelm me. I was only paying it such mind since it returned much more quickly than I was used to. I had lived with the constant voice of the desert since I was a boy, and it never truly abated. I could only hope they would calm when I fulfilled my task of healing her.

Having finished refreshing herself, Alza trotted over to inspect my progress. I lifted my small number of packs from her back so she could rest completely. While I rode with no saddle or bridle, as did all who called the Ballan Desert home, I roped supplies to Alza's back for multiday trips, much to her dismay. As soon as I released them from her back, she rolled gleefully in the sand, rubbing dirt and grime into her shining midnight coat.

I located my sleeping mat and laid it out next to the fire, grateful for its warmth as the desert air cooled rapidly with the sun descended below the horizon line. The sweat beneath my mask chilled with it, itching along my nose and jawline where the metal sat against my skin.

Looking around to ensure my solitude, for the volume of the chattering in my head somehow suggested that I was not alone, I reached up to release the catches of the contraption. The metal fell away from my face, skin greeted by the evening breeze and the grit of sand always carried along with it. It was a jarring sensation, as I never removed the covering outside of the privacy of my own tent when in Clan Katal's encampment. Out here in the dunes though, there was nobody to witness me but Alza and the desert, and they already knew of my sins.

CHAPTER TWO
KEERA

The wind pulled my hood back from my face, and I didn't bother replacing it. I was too busy thanking my luck because the desert surely hadn't brought the traveler to my oasis.

Crouched behind my rock, I could spy a lone figure silhouetted in the setting sun, moving around making camp. While it was hard to tell from a distance, the large frame suggested that it was a man, and a powerfully built one at that. A horse dipped its head to drink from the pool of water, indicating he was not an exile, just traveling separately from his clan. I tore my eyes away from the elegant slope of the animal's neck, a lump in my throat, to consider the traveler further. I couldn't see many details at this distance, but he appeared to only be wearing gray clothing with no colored sash to tell me which clan he hailed from. At least he didn't wear a maroon sash, marking him as a member of Clan Padra. Something in me boiled at the thought of encountering one of my former people. Robbing them in the night wouldn't be a great enough punishment for abandoning me.

I shoved that ugly line of thought away, despite the simmering low in my belly, in favor of considering why this man was here and how I might take advantage of his presence. After all, survival was the highest law of the desert.

It was odd to ride without the caravan of a clan, especially this far out from the Great City, but not unheard of. A rider alone was likely to get lost unless they had the favor of the desert, and it was not as if there were any map they could follow.

When I was a girl, I heard it said that those who came from beyond the mountains to visit the Great City of Kelvadan often asked for a map, hoping to trade with the clans of the Ballan Desert. This request would only ever be met with a laugh and a shake of the head. The Ballan Desert was a living thing, ever changing with the winds and her mood. Only trusting the desert with your life—or death—could bring you to your destination. Even then, journeys that took the fastest rider days could take only an afternoon for another. One time, a member of my former clan had ridden in one direction for hours, only to find himself right back where he started. The desert was as harsh as she was beautiful, and without her favor, I was forced to remain at my oasis or risk never finding my way back.

Try as they might, those who came from beyond the mountain couldn't draw a map of the Ballan Desert. So, they were forced to do all their trading at the Great City of Kelvadan. The thought of the city that could be my only haven made me swallow around the dryness in my throat.

Even when the crushing isolation at my oasis nearly drove me mad, and I considered setting out for Kelvadan—the one place I might be able to make a home for myself—I hesitated. I had been trapped here at my oasis by the knowledge of what the desert often did to those who journeyed alone. Every time desperation gripped at my heart, and I began trudging away from my oasis in search of a reprieve from loneliness, my feet became leaden. Icy fear dripped down my spine, and I would be unable to continue, despite the overwhelming need to be free of the prison of my isolation. Sinking sands or terrifying mirages that made you wander for hours awaited those without the desert's favor who set out on their own. The desert's approval had abandoned me here at the same time Clan Padra left me alone among the sands to die.

I hadn't been lucky enough to find a clan, yet alone a lone traveler, in far too long. My supplies ran thin, and without a new weapon, I wouldn't be able to hunt for much longer.

Crouched behind that rock, I watched the man set up a sleeping mat. My thighs ached from my stillness as I waited for him to sleep, but he sat staring into the fire for hours. Still, I dared not move and draw his attention, or worse yet, look away to find that he had only been an illusion—a cruel trick of the desert in the face of my growing hunger or my unyielding desire for the voice of another human. It wouldn't be the first time I imagined such a thing, although the last time I had been recovering from the venomous bite of a snake, delirious from the poison in my veins.

The moon hung high in the cloudless sky by the time the traveler lay down on his mat and I dared creep out into the open. My bare feet shifted silently over the sands; I was glad the sands cooled rapidly in the night air. My tattered sandals had given out two days earlier, and the soles of my feet already carried blisters from the heat of the sand during the day.

The man's fire dwindled as he slept, affording me the cover of darkness. The horse lifted its head with pricked ears at my approach. I froze, both in fear and in awe of the beast's beauty. Its coat was as black as the night sky, the sheen of the moon on the silky texture showing off the delicious luxury of thick muscle.

The horse blew out a breath through its nose at me but did not react otherwise. I suppressed the urge to coo reassuringly to the animal, not wanting to wake its rider. Even if I was a desperate thief, I would never harm my target's horse.

I carefully picked my way toward the small stack of bundles on the ground where I was the most likely to find useful supplies. With quick fingers, I loosened the ties to look inside. While the man traveled lightly, my eyes burned in relief at the treasures I found in the packs. Dried meat, a spare length of linen that could be worn as a hood, a water flask, and sandals four sizes too big, but I didn't care. These items would protect me from the harshness of the elements and keep me alive until the next clan passed.

I moved all the items I planned to take to one sack and quietly tied it to my back. As much as my hollow belly urged me to take the entirety of the man's rations, I left a small portion with his things. Hopefully it would be enough to reunite him with his clan.

With dismay, I realized I hadn't found a weapon. Even if the meat would last me a few days, I needed to be able to hunt. My sling was on the verge of disintegrating completely, and an eagle had flown away with the knife I needed to be able to skin a creature for a hide to make a new one.

I chanced a glance at the sleeping man, just a massive lump in the darkness, the gentle whisper of breath all to indicate his presence. Perhaps he kept his weapons closer at hand. I crept around his sleeping mat to the far side, the direction in which he was facing. I feared waking him, but the fear of starvation was even more present in my mind—a weight that rested between my shoulder blades and never truly abated.

In the darkness I couldn't see his face, but I was too fixated on what lay in the sand, inches from his outstretched hand, to care. A saber, gently curved and longer than my arm, larger than any I had ever seen, called to me. My palm itched to grasp the cord-wrapped hilt, bracketed by gently curved quillons. A knife would be much more practical for my purposes, but my hands didn't care, already reaching out for the awe-inspiring weapon. The way the moonlight reflected off the lethal edge called inexorably to me.

A rustle broke the stillness of the air, and I froze. Before I could so much as throw myself backward, the form on the sleeping mat leaped forward. His bulk bowled me over, driving me down into the sand. I kicked wildly, using our momentum to continue our roll, trying to end up on top. With his superior size and the sluggishness of my limbs, he managed to trap me between his thighs. I slapped at him ineffectually, but he gathered my wrists and pinned them above my head with one hand, the other held threateningly at my throat.

Then he stopped.

At first, I thought it was simply because he had bested me, but the preternatural stillness of his muscles and the tick in his jaw belied something else. I shuddered beneath him, a bolt of adrenaline, more intense than any I had ever felt during my struggles to survive, coursing through my body.

While he sat frozen, my muscles quivered under my skin, a feeling of life pouring through me that I had not felt in many years. Every inch of my skin felt drenched in cold water after months of drought. Maybe it was the awareness of how quickly he could kill me, my pulse fluttering wildly beneath his fingers. Or maybe it was just the touch of another human after so long in isolation, the warm pressure of his fingers so solid along the column of my throat. Either way, my world turned sideways in that moment where he held me pinned. He stared at my face as if stricken.

"Who are you?" he asked, voice raw and jarringly loud in the silence of the night.

His solid weight pushed me into the coarse sand, stealing most of my ability to speak. I opened my mouth but found my voice slow to come after years of disuse. Instead, I settled for hissing and wriggling futilely to free myself.

The man exhaled sharply through his noise, letting go of his grip on my neck. I tried to use the moment to my advantage, but in a matter of seconds he had removed his sash and used it to bind my hands. I snarled in frustration, but he ignored me. Then, he stood and unceremoniously dragged me closer to his packs and the burnt-out fire, which we had rolled away from in our scuffle. He quickly located another leather band and tied my ankles. I fought the best I could, but months of inconsistent meals left me no match for his strength, despite how energized I felt.

With me immobilized, he wordlessly turned to the fire to urge it back to life. Curiously, he didn't light it with a flint. Instead, he just held his hand over the embers and stared for a few moments. It grew beneath his palm, like a succulent after rain, until it crackled and danced as strong as ever. No wonder he was not afraid to travel alone, if he had such mastery over the magic of the desert. While several in my former clan had been gifted with her power, very few had enough to use it so casually. It made something squirm in my gut.

My captor turned to me and crouched. While it brought him level with me, the power in the pose held a promise of violence if I tried to run. With the fire offering ample light, I got my first good look at his face. His features were delicate but proud, his skin oddly sallow looking. In this light, I couldn't make out the color of the hair curling gently around his temples, although it seemed dark. His eyes were the same luminous silver as the crescent of the moon above us. My heart thundered in my chest under the weight of his stare, as if trying to remind me

I was alive after so long feeling as good as dead. It woke something else in me—a burning, roiling storm under my skin.

"Who are you?" he repeated his question again, voice low but firm.

I continued to glare, and the moment stretched between us. Then, I spit in his face.

CHAPTER THREE
THE VIPER

Spittle splashed across my cheek, and my stomach clenched in horror. The feeling of saliva on my bare skin woke me more thoroughly than the thought of a thief taking my saber, my most prized possession. Abruptly, I stood and spun away, wiping my face clean with my sleeve.

My mask lay where I left it, right next to my bedroll for easy access. I snatched it up and lifted it to my face, fastening it on with uncharacteristically clumsy fingers. The familiar weight and smell of the metal against my skin brought me back to myself somewhat, but it couldn't erase the fact that this girl, whoever she was, had seen my face. A thief in the night was the first person to see me in years.

The chatter in my skull intensified at the thought, and I ground my teeth. It only served to remind me of the moment of absolute silence I had experienced when I held the girl's wrists in my bare hands, her pulse hammering beneath my fingertips. I grabbed my gloves and slid them on now too, before turning back to my would-be thief.

She sat sprawled on the ground where I'd left her, tilting her head at me curiously even as her odd golden eyes continued to glitter defiantly in the flickering flame. Looking at her face more clearly, I found she was a grown woman, not the girl I had originally thought based on her slight build. In fact, it was hard to tell with her on the ground, but with the length of her legs, she would probably stand taller than most women in Clan Katal. She only seemed small due to her emaciated state, wrists so thin they bent like reeds in my hands.

I took a step toward her, and she sidled back, although her eyes stayed fixed on me. I broke her gaze, not that she could truly meet mine in my mask and cast around for where she might have come from.

"Where is your horse?" I asked, since she was reluctant to tell me who she was.

The girl opened her mouth, croaked, and then licked her lips before trying again.

"I have no horse," she said, voice raspy as if she were unaccustomed to speaking. Still, despite the thinness of her tone, she spoke the words like a challenge.

It was my turn to tilt my head in curiosity, and the woman scuttled back as far as her bonds would allow at the gesture, seeming to find it menacing. Only exiles didn't have a horse, and they rarely survived more than a few weeks. Many took their own lives in preference to dying of thirst or starvation or out of shame for having their mount taken from them.

"An exile," I observed. The woman made no move to deny it.

I bent to pick up my sword where it lay in the sand, unsheathing it with a swift motion. The chattering in my skull intensified in response to the metallic sound that rang through the air as the blade came free. I pointed it at the woman.

"An exile won't be missed," I said, taking a step forward, the tip of the blade landing in the hollow of the woman's throat. It bobbed as she swallowed.

My wrist tensed, ready to spill the woman's blood on the sand. It might even be considered doing an exile a kindness, and my offering to the desert would buy me enough peace to sleep through the rest of the night. Besides, the memory of my face would die with her, making it as if she hadn't seen me at all.

The woman snarled at me as if daring me to do it, and to my great

shame, I hesitated, my blade hovering at the woman's throat. It went
against everything Lord Alasdar had taught me: that strength was the
only rule in the desert and feeding her the blood of the weak was the
only way to calm her overwhelming power. Maybe it was the woman's
defiance, or the quiet of the desert, or how unbalanced I was by involuntarily revealing myself to stranger. Maybe it was the moment of unprecedented stillness I experienced when my skin touched hers.

I lowered my sword.

"The lord of Clan Katal has been looking for a sacrifice for the new
moon." I stared up at the sky where the moon shined a waning crescent.
It would be fully dark within a week. "Thank you for volunteering."

Turning my back to the woman and her scorching glare, I took in
my situation. There would be no more rest for me tonight, especially
not with a prisoner likely to slit my throat with my own sword the
moment I closed my eyes. I hated to push Alza through the night, but if
we left now, I could be back at the encampment and put this mess
behind me before the heat of midday. It had only taken me a day and a
half to reach Clan Ratan, and I hoped the journey back would be similarly quick.

I bent to pick up my bedroll and packs, finding my things to be out
of order. I quickly spotted the other pack, fallen where I had pinned the
woman in our tussle. I made short work of rearranging my belongings
back to their original state before turning toward Alza.

She had watched the happenings with interest but made no sound.
Now she whickered in disapproval as I approached with the packs and
rope. Still, she rose when I clicked my tongue and dutifully let me ready
her for travel.

Then I turned back to my new charge, who watched me warily but
had not attempted to escape yet. I approached once more and scooped
her up off the ground.

As soon as I touched her, she began squirming so forcefully that I
nearly dropped her before slinging her over my shoulder. Banging on my
back and kicking her feet, she fought me, even going so far as attempting
to bite my shoulder blades through the thick layers I wore. Her struggles
ceased abruptly a moment later as I threw her over Alza's haunches. A
soft *oof* escaped her at the impact, then she stilled. Taking advantage of

the moment, I tied her on tightly so she wouldn't slide off as we rode. With as slight as her weight was when I moved her, it would not slow down our progress.

Then I launched myself astride Alza's back, who obediently set off into the night.

CHAPTER FOUR
KEERA

I was riding a horse. I could hardly believe it. Perhaps riding was a strong word for being unceremoniously tied across its hind quarters, but the feeling still froze me in place. A silky tail tickled my face, and muscles shifted under me as a powerful body propelled us across the sands. Tears pricked my eyes, but I did not let them fall, as I couldn't spare the moisture.

I had dreamed of riding a horse so often for so many years, it seemed the cruelest of ironies that I would finally touch one again as it carried me to my death, instead of to the Great City as I always dreamed. Although maybe it was a gift. I had fought to stay alive for so long, although for what, I did not know. Perhaps it was so I could ride a horse and hear the voice of another human one more time before my blood was taken by the desert.

The man paid me no more mind than if I were another supply pack, quickening the mount's pace. With incredibly long legs, the horse easily lengthened its stride. The constant bouncing drove the horse's back into my abdomen, and I would have retched if there had been anything in my stomach. We rode until the sun dappled the horse's side. It was all I could see at this angle, my neck too stiff to raise my head and see where we were going.

We had to be far from my camp by now, farther into the unforgiving desert than I had ever made it on foot. I couldn't tell which direction we were going, and I was sure the desert would not guide me back to the safety of my oasis. I had only found it by chance before and hadn't left sight of it for years, knowing I would never find my way to it again.

The relative safety of my prison was lost forever, but I felt strangely calm. Perhaps I was no longer afraid to die after so many years toeing the line of survival. The newly found flame of life in me protested at that line of thinking, but I did my best to smother it. It seemed that the sands would claim my blood soon, no matter if I wanted to live or not.

I tried not to dwell on it, instead thinking only about the magnificent animal beneath me. As the heat of the desert sun began to burn the back of my neck, the horse pulled to a stop, the change in momentum driving my side against my captor's back. He paid me no mind, dismounting and walking out of my eyeline. I couldn't see him at this angle, but I could just make out soft murmuring, surely meant for the horse, because he had barely spoken to me.

Gloved hands pulled at the ropes holding me in place. As they loosened, I tried to control my slither to the ground, but ended up falling gracelessly in a heap. Laying on my back, the hood fell from my face to pool around my shoulders, and I stared up at the cloudless sky, a washed-out shade of blue from the unforgiving intensity of the sun. I couldn't retie my hood with my hands bound, but what did a little more sunburn matter if I was to be sacrificed when we reached our destination? I had been living on borrowed time anyway.

I twitched in surprise as my captor hauled me to sitting, half expecting him to leave me as a forgotten bundle on the sand while his horse rested. I had used the last of my strength to fight him during the night and had fully intended to lay completely still. Even the disconcerting energy I felt when he touched me faded, leaving me a dried-out husk. My lips cracked, and my limbs trembled constantly. Now, I wavered as I sat, staring at the dark shape of my captor. He stood stark against the dunes in the distance. Sweat dripped down the back of my neck, and I hadn't had water since the afternoon before. With gloved hands, he pulled up my hood, securing it around my head without touching me. I stared at him in shock, opening and closing my mouth a few times.

My captor tilted his head as he looked at me, the meaning of the gesture unclear without the context of an expression. The mask that covered his face was an odd thing, made of a solid sheet of silvery metal, absent of features or adornments. The only deviations from the solid surface were several small holes where I imagined his mouth would be and slitted openings for his eyes, the shadows too deep for me to make out the gaze I had met the night before. It looked like armor, although the rest of his garb was dark cloth with no other protective gear. The only other piece of clothing designed for combat where the leather tabards over his shoulders.

"What's your name?" he asked, drawing me from my contemplation.

I croaked, but my voice stuck from dryness and disuse. I licked my lips and tried again.

"Keera," I rasped out.

"Keera," he repeated thoughtfully, the voice of a young man at odds with the fearsome, masked creature before me. My name on his lips, hidden as they were, made me shiver. I couldn't remember the last time anybody had spoken my name. I couldn't even be sure there was anybody alive besides myself who remembered it. Hearing him say it, even if he was the one bringing me to my death, felt like a gift.

"What's your name?" I asked, voice rougher than the sand I sat on.

He didn't answer, instead reaching for his belt. Before I could react to his reach for a weapon, he pulled out a water skin. He lifted it toward me, and I didn't care about his name anymore, instead pitching forward to fasten my lips around the opening. I gulped greedily as he tilted it back, a few drops escaping to run down my jaw to my neck.

After a few swallows he pulled the skin away, standing abruptly and turning around. Then he stalked away, leaving me to stare after him in confusion.

The second part of the journey passed as uncomfortably as the first, although this time I occupied myself with trying to puzzle out the man in the metal mask. I hadn't seen someone wearing one like it before, but it had been many years since I had been among a clan, and things changed.

Just as the sun reached its zenith, if the burning on the back of my neck was any indication, the wind carried voices to us. They grew louder as we rode, and my heart hammered. Never had I approached a clan in the light of day, and the growing sounds of life being lived nearly overwhelmed me. The man in the mask rode his horse into the clan, ignorant of my racing pulse. I craned my neck as best I could, only managing to see the bottom edges of tents staked into the sand. We passed dozens of them, my head spinning with the idea of this many people.

"Viper," greeted several voices as we rode past, but I couldn't twist enough to see their faces. Their tones were deferential, as if he were the warlord of the clan, although they did not address him as such.

Eventually, the horse came to a stop, and my captor dismounted. His heavy black boots tromped across the sand through my line of vision, but he didn't move to release me. A whisper ran through the nearby people before a hush fell over the camp. I ceased my squirming at the thought of all the watching eyes.

"I bring a gift, Lord Alasdar," came the voice of the man in the mask.

"I hope it is news that another clan has joined our cause," responded a slippery voice that had shivers slithering over my skin like a horned viper, despite the sweat dripping down my back.

"It is, along with fresh blood to spill to thank the desert."

The oily voice *tsked* in contemplation. I itched to see the man who would demand my death while simultaneously shying away from that voice.

"Let us see this offering."

Several sets of hands pulled me down from the horse, but none of them were the gloved hands of my captor. I found myself held between two men, neither of them masked. As my weak knees wobbled, they were forced to hold me upright with bruising grips on my arms.

The dark form of my captor kneeled at the feet of another man, this one taller but slimmer—Lord Alasdar I guessed. This man was not masked, but instead contemplated me with lifeless gray eyes. The flatness of his gaze made my shoulders pull forward, as if I could hide myself from him, but I refused to cower. His clothes were lavish, loose pants and fine vest held closed by a wide sash embroidered with a pattern of snakes. A luxurious robe completed the ensemble, almost hiding the long knife shoved in his belt. As my eyes skittered across his face, reluctant to meet that calculating gaze, I noticed gray hairs peeking out from the edges of his hood and lines around his mouth and eyes.

"She looks half-dead already," he commented dispassionately.

His dismissiveness leant some fire to my blood, and I pulled my lips back in a snarl. Even if I did not have the strength left to run away, I would not die meekly or without protest. To my dismay, he smiled at that, although it didn't extend to his eyes.

"Although she has enough spirit left it would seem," he continued, raising both his voice and his arms. "Tonight, we will celebrate our new alliance with Clan Ratan and thank the desert for her gifts! With our increased strength, we will return the Ballan Desert to the ways of old and give her the battle and blood she desires."

The crowd around the clearing we stood in, which had accumulated during the brief exchange, cheered. My head swam as I tried to make sense of his words, although a grim part of my mind told me it didn't matter. I would die at their hands whether I understood their cause or not. Perhaps this was their version of a gift—to save me from years of cruel isolation before I inevitably crumbled to dust. The desert would claim my blood, as she had longed to for many seasons.

CHAPTER FIVE
THE VIPER

"Take the sacrifice away, and prepare her," Lord Alasdar ordered as the clan quieted. A shuffle behind me and the sound of feet dragging through sand indicated the riders' obedience. I chanced a glance out of the corner of my eyes to see the woman pulled through the crowd, although she clearly tried to move under her own power.

Keera my mind supplied unhelpfully. I don't know what had possessed me to ask for her name. It would only make it harder to watch her bleed out as Lord Alasdar's sacrifice. I grit my teeth, the desert in my mind growing louder as she was dragged out of sight.

"Viper, come into my tent, and tell me of your travels," Lord Alasdar continued, already turning around, clearly expecting me to follow. I stood, turning to check on Alza, who waited patiently, although her head hung in exhaustion. I patted her cheek before waving over a clansman.

"See to it she is cared for. I will check later to see that it was done properly." I let my voice pitch low, and the man scurried to obey, paling under his deep tan.

I watched him lead her for a moment, Alza's ears flicking back in displeasure at being cared for by a stranger, but it wasn't wise to keep

Lord Alasdar waiting. I turned away and ducked through the flap of fabric at the opening of the dwelling.

My eyes took a second to adjust to the dimness as Lord Alasdar kept all the flaps of his tent closed, blocking out the bright sun. A lantern on the table served to light the cavernous space. It was filled with a rack of fine weapons on one wall, fine rugs overlapped to create soft flooring, and dotted with lush pillows that served as seating. It was a far cry from my tent at the encampment, filled only with my sleeping mat and a few supplies. I supposed I could have a similar dwelling, but I didn't see the point—not when I would spend most of my nights out traveling with only Alza for company if I could.

Lord Alasdar had already knelt on a low stool on the far side of a low table and beckoned me to join him. I settled myself onto a cushion across from him, putting myself at a lower height. After all, I was no more than his sword.

"Was Lord Einil easily persuaded to our cause?" he asked as soon as I sat, pouring himself a glass of dark liquid from a cut crystal pitcher. Only a single glass was on the table, and he did not move to find another, not that I would have accepted one.

"He took some forceful persuasion," I admitted. "He was willing to fight with us, but hesitant to give up command of his riders."

"And how did you persuade him?"

"I didn't, but his daughter and heir was much more amenable to our demands."

Lord Alasdar chuckled, a humorless sound. "They do not call you the Viper for nothing."

"I am as you made me." I bowed my head deferentially, even as I grit my teeth at his casual laughter in the face of death. I pushed those thoughts down, afraid Lord Alasdar could sense my hesitance to do what needed to be done to save the desert. After all, I owed him more than my life. I owed him my sanity, his teachings and guidance giving me the only defenses I had against the voices in my mind. He was wise, and I would do what he commanded—kill those whose death he deemed necessary.

The image of me lowering my sword after pressing it to Keera's throat flashed through my mind, and I pushed it away. The exile would still die.

"And the girl?" Lord Alasdar prompted as if reading my mind. "Was she one of Clan Ratan?"

"No, my lord. An exile who I happened upon during my journey home."

He huffed. "Exile? More proof that the clans have gone soft. No wonder the desert tries to purge us so. The clans of the Ballan Desert were born warriors and gave traitors the doom they deserved. Now, the traditions of Kelvadan have made us soft, and the desert herself tries to return us to our warrior's way. The storms and thinning herds are evidence that she is not being fed the blood she deserves."

"My lord," was my only answer, having heard this tirade many times.

"There was another sandstorm while you were away. We lost two horses."

My gut twisted. That was the second one in two weeks, while the last had been nearly a month before. They were growing in frequency. Nearly every day, hunters who rode out didn't return or only stumbled back into the encampment days later on the brink of death. It hadn't always been like this, but the desert grew harsher.

"We must unite the clans as quickly as possible. You know better than any what is at stake if we fail to take Kelvadan before the desert sees no more use for us." Lord Alasdar gave me a hard look over the rim of his glass as he took a sip.

My hands balled into fists on my knees so hard the leather of my gloves creaked around them. I would not let that happen. I carried the blame for my home's unrest, and setting it right was the only way to atone—and to ward off my impending madness.

"I will ride for the remaining five clans at once," I declared, but Lord Alasdar shook his head.

"You are needed here for a little longer," he insisted. "The riders of the three clans that are already here need training and to be shown the prowess of their captain. They have sworn their allegiance, but they will not follow us into battle unless they see you as the viper you are."

I remained silent, gritting my teeth behind my mask. I didn't appreciate being paraded around as a figurehead for the united tribes of the Ballan Desert—not when I earned the title by being a lethal weapon, and I much preferred to perform my purpose in obscurity. Still, the mask helped.

I also didn't relish being in the encampment during the new moon. In accordance with the old ways, it was the time at which sacrifices were made to appease the desert, a time of death before rebirth. I had delivered the exile to her doom, but I didn't itch to witness it.

Lord Alasdar was sure to be in fighting form, preaching to the clans about the importance of restoring the old ways and the anger of the desert, whipping the crowd into zealotry. When faced with desperation and scarcity, the common enemy of Kelvadan gave the clansman something to fight for.

Where the residents of the Great City sat safely behind their walls, denying the desert the sacrifice and death she demanded in return for the life she gave, the people of the clans suffered and starved. Kelvadan had abandoned the old ways where strength and survival were the only law for a softer way of life, breeding resentment in those who still tested their mettle against the fury of the desert. Lord Alasdar played that resentment like a finely tuned instrument to gain their loyalty.

I, though, had no interest in hearing the half-truths that haunted me. I was all too aware of all that was at stake should the clans fail to unite and fulfill our mission to destroy Kelvadan. The desert's magic would rip our home apart. There would be no survivors, and the Ballan Desert would return to the lifeless land it had been before our ancestors first crossed to the ocean.

"It will give your horse a chance to rest, as I know she has been on many hard journeys lately," Lord Alasdar continued, probing at my weakness. If it wasn't for the truth of his words and the fact that I could sense Alza's weariness, I may have insisted on leaving for the other tribes in the morning.

"She has carried me across the sands often," I admitted.

"And she bore an extra burden today. The sacrifice comes at a welcome time. The sand will drink her blood in celebration of our latest step toward a return to the old ways and hopefully buy us the desert's favor and freedom from the storms for a few more weeks."

This time I did remain silent. I preferred to spill blood in battle and didn't share Lord Alasdar's fervor for sacrifice. Killing only bought me silence in my mind when it was in service of the desert. Still, the desert gave us life and often demanded life in return.

"Why don't you perform the sacrifice in a few days? As a show of strength and to allow me to honor your successes?" Lord Alasdar's expression remained neutral, but his hard gray eyes pinned me as if he could see beneath the metal of my mask, daring me to refuse.

I bowed my head in acceptance. "The desert gives and it takes."

CHAPTER SIX
KEERA

I let the men who dragged me away throw me into a tent without resistance, and I rolled across the ground. I stayed lying on my side, spitting sand from my mouth, although it was a hopeless cause. Grit always found its way between my teeth, especially when I had so little water, the stickiness of my mouth trapping the particles.

The sound of the tent flaps closing announced that the men had left me alone. I briefly considered how foolish of them it was to leave me unattended so that I might escape, before I realized I was too weak to mount much of an effort. The journey had sapped the last of my strength. They would have known I couldn't escape my bonds, let alone attempt to run, from the dead weight of my body as they dragged me across the camp.

The size of the clan's migrating encampment surprised me, at least twice the size of what I remembered of the last clan I had scavenged supplies from. The clash of swords drifted through the air, but the lack of panic spoke of a population used to the background of combat training. Even now, the metallic clangs filtered through the thick canvas of the structure around me. They must boast a large contingent of riders for such training to be a regular occurrence. The sounds of so many people jangled my nerves, at odds with the strange calm of resignation that had dawned over me.

I struggled to sit, flopping around uselessly for a few moments before getting myself upright without the use of my arms. From the baskets and bundles piled around me, along with the lack of rugs creating a floor, I surmised myself to be in a storage area. Apparently preparing me to be sacrificed included treating me as a bag of grain until the appointed hour.

I slumped back against a stack of baskets in relief, happy to be left alone and in the shade. It seemed the last few days of my life in captivity might be more comfortable than the preceding years. After all, this tent did more to block the sun and sand than my lean-to at the oasis. Instead of clinging to survival by the tips of my fingers, I could spend my final days contemplating what I was leaving behind. I almost laughed, the noise dry and strangled in my throat. Everything that a person might regret leaving—a horse, a clan, a family—they had all left me years ago. My eyes burned and my throat closed. Nobody would remember me, and the desert winds would scour away all traces of me. The only person who knew my name was the one delivering me to my doom. Maybe I was already dead, if nobody knew me, let alone cared for me. This could be a mercy.

A whispering in the back of my mind drove those thoughts away, telling me I needed to escape. I grit my teeth at the thought, recognizing the voice that had driven me to crawl to shelter each time the elements bested me, and I considered laying down and letting the sands take me. The voice always came when I was on the edge of starvation, of thirst, of delirium from the heat. It insisted that there was something worth staying alive for, although I had yet to find what it was—what purpose my existence may yet serve. Maybe the isolation had truly made me delirious. I bargained with the voice, saying I would have a better chance of running if I gathered my strength.

The whisper urging me to run died down enough for me to close my eyes and let a dreamless sleep take me.

I roused to a hand on my shoulder, the foreign feeling of human touch chasing all relaxation from my limbs, and I tensed. I tried to thrash, not remembering I was bound and only succeeding in wriggling where I lay on the ground.

"Stop struggling, or you won't get food and water," commanded a female voice, although I could not see the owner.

I froze. The promise of food and water cut through my addled brain like a knife.

With my fighting ceased, I found myself hauled to a seated position, meeting a curious gaze. We contemplated each other for a moment, and I took in her sharp eyes and freckled complexion. While her expression was hard, it didn't hold the cruelty I expected from one of my jailers.

With business-like efficiency, she lifted a water skin to my lips, and I swallowed greedily. She *tsked* lightly, but I didn't get the sense that she disapproved of me.

As she pulled the skin away, I tilted my head in silent question.

"The desert is harsh these days," she said.

I frowned at her words. "The desert is always harsh for an exile."

She ignored my answer, instead picking up a small plate from the ground next to her, holding a small piece of flatbread and a small lump of what appeared to be goat's milk cheese. I nearly cried at the sight. As meager as the clan might consider such sustenance, I had survived on little but dried meat and dates from the palms at my oasis for too long, without even spices enliven the flavor.

The woman looked back and forth between me and the food, and I fidgeted impatiently, as if the meal might suddenly disappear.

"You either have to feed me or untie me," I said.

She considered me for a moment before putting the cheese on the bread and holding it up to my lips. I didn't waste time leaning forward to shove as much of it in my mouth as possible, nearly choking myself.

"The clans don't often have prisoners," she commented, meaning clear. The clans tended to deal with enemies and criminals decisively, either by death or exile. I knew this all too well.

Still, it explained why I was shoved in a storage tent.

I didn't care where they put me, too busy leaning forward to snag my next bite of bread and cheese.

"I'm Izumi," the woman said, clearly trying to carry on a one-sided conversation while I focused on chewing before swallowing. I narrowed my eyes at her, wondering why this woman would bother introducing herself to a sacrifice.

She shrugged. The rest of my small meal passed in silence. Once the food was gone, she stood, picking up the plate and turning toward the exit.

Despite having just slept, I found myself drowsy again. The fullest stomach I had had in a while, mixed with the disconcerting lack of anything to do, made my limbs heavy. I slumped back into the sand. Before pushing out of the tent flap though, Izumi paused.

"The new moon is in three days." She didn't look at me as she said it.

I don't know if she meant it to be a kindness, warning me of the date of my death, but I oddly had no reaction. Three days or ten, it didn't matter. My breaths were numbered.

Closing my eyes, sleep claimed me before I even heard Izumi leave.

The next two days passed similarly, Izumi bringing me water and a meal twice a day, and me sleeping the rest of the time. I didn't think it was possible for me to sleep so much, but I consistently surprised myself. By the second day, I chided myself that I should be thinking of an escape plan, but something in me urged patience. An odd sense of waiting overtook me. It wasn't quite peaceful, but I was filled with the stillness of a caracal about to pounce. I was content to wait.

On the third day, the morning that would be followed by the night of the new moon, the routine broke. Izumi walked into the supply tent earlier than usual, carrying no food or water.

"The clan needs this tent today, so you'll have to stay outside," she said by way of explanation.

She hauled me to my feet, and while my legs cramped with disuse, they still held more strength than they had when I had first arrived. Waiting had done me some good. With a hand around the rope at my wrists, Izumi led me outside, and I squinted in the sudden light, looking around to get my bearings.

Based on the thin density of the tents here, we were somewhere near the edge of the encampment, as I would expect for a little-used supply tent. The center would be reserved for the living tents of prominent riders and clan members, arranged in circles around communal cooking fires and areas for people to gather and work while children played and hunting dogs rested.

Izumi led me to a tent at the very fringes of the encampment, where she motioned me to sit before tying my bound hands to one of the stakes driven deeply into the sand at the corner.

"I'll be able to keep an eye on you here, so don't try and run," she said before striding off purposefully.

I watched her go for a moment before more movement caught my eye. For the unpopulated edge of the clan, there seemed to be a large amount of hustle and bustle. Riders trickled in, horses laden with bundles and tents as if they had been traveling, although this encampment seemed to have been present for days.

It was almost as if the clan had split up, and now part was rejoining with the whole. I watched curiously, mostly admiring the horses of the new arrivals as they trickled in bearing supplies. Likely that was why I had been kicked out of the supply tent, so the newcomers' reserves could be reorganized with the rest of the clan.

I didn't mind, as it was a welcome break in the monotony of considering my impending death. I faced the appointed hour with numb resignation, but every so often the instinct to fight for survival at all costs would rear up again. The desperation to escape would strangle me until I reminded myself there was no point—no family to welcome me home with open arms, or horse waiting to be fed and pampered. Death would be a welcome respite from unending loneliness.

Today, though, I was saved from the repetitive cycle of panic and exhaustion by the chance to watch the influx of people. Even as my gaze was constantly drawn to the horses of the incoming riders, movement in the open space beyond the encampment caught my eye. I turned to find a crowd of people trickling out onto the packed area of sand, and my gaze landed on their weapons. Each carried a saber. These would be the clan's riders.

They boasted an impressive number, appearing to be several hundred strong. I had never seen a clan with such a large fighting force, although rumor had it that the Great City of Kelvadan boasted a force of nearly a thousand riders, the most formidable army in the Ballan Desert. To be a rider of Kelvadan marked you as one of the most impressive warriors in the desert, and supposedly, the world. As a child, I had dreamed of ranking among their numbers, although that dream seemed impossibly far away now.

I had only seen the Great City of Kelvadan once, camped outside its walls with my parents when I was nearly too young to remember. The haziness of childhood memories added to its dreamlike quality in my mind—the towering walls and the skilled riders on the most beautiful horses I had ever imagined. Even now I could feel my eyes widening and my jaw hanging open the sight of the Kelvadan riders in action. My parents had laughed at me when I declared that I would be a rider of Kelvadan, reminding me that we were proud members of Clan Padra. Now I had no clan, and riding for Kelvadan was an even sweeter and more unattainable dream.

The riders before me now were much more real but lacked the exaggerated prowess of the Kelvadan riders in my memory. As I watched, they formed long lines, facing off in pairs. Walking to the front, as if to lead, was a figure that caused an odd flip in my belly.

Even from this distance, I recognized the man in the mask. His unremarkable gray tabards and robes distinguished him as much as the broad set of his shoulders and something understated yet powerful in the way he held himself. My gaze snapped to him so quickly, it was like a falcon zeroing in on their prey. Perhaps it was because he had been the one to bring change to the monotony of my existence, but he had impressed himself deeply in my mind.

He unsheathed his own saber, which he carried across his back as opposed to at his hip, and moved it into a ready stance. The lines of riders copied him, but I didn't spare them a glance.

As he led them through drills of strikes and parries, my eyes remained fixed on the way the man in the mask moved. Even as his movements remained slow in demonstration, he held all the power of a coiled snake, waiting for the right moment to strike. That controlled strength spoke of danger, but there was something undeniably mesmerizing about the sight.

Like the desert, he offered both beauty and death.

I don't know how long I watched, absolutely entranced and blind to all else in the world. By the time the riders stopped training, the sun was well past its zenith and evening fast approached. Soon, night would fall and bring with it the new moon.

My last day to escape, and I had spent it in stunned admiration of the one who had hauled me across the desert to serve as a sacrifice. I grit my teeth that I had wasted so much of a prime opportunity to get away, but some strange sense of stillness still lingered within me.

I looked around, wondering if I could still take advantage of the time outside my tent, but one of the riders broke from the group, walking back into the encampment and approached me. I recognized Izumi.

Sweat clung to her hair, turning the dark brown nearly black, and she breathed heavily but seemed used to the exertion of training. Her grip still hauled me to my feet with ease as she untied me from the stake.

"The new clan should be done with the supply tent by now," she said by way of explanation, leading me back to my temporary prison. She deposited me there before scurrying away. While she hadn't been harsh with me in my days with Clan Katal, even offering me her name and feeding me by hand when I had the feeling nobody would have faulted her for leaving me to starve, she refused to look at me now.

Maybe I imagined it and she was simply tired, or maybe she felt guilty about her clan sacrificing my life tonight.

I still had a few hours before nightfall to escape, but as I collapsed to the floor of the tent, my body urged me to rest. I let darkness take me, figuring it was a better way to spend the last minutes of my life than contemplating why I had been so enthralled by the man in the mask with his saber.

Rough hands grabbed me, pulling me from the escape of unconsciousness. Not waiting for me to rouse properly, they yanked me from the tent. The sun didn't hammer down on me as we pushed through the flaps, indicating that night had fallen.

Smoke laced the air, as the dancing light from braziers illuminated the spaces between tents. The riders on either side of me barely spared me a glance as they dragged me back through the labyrinth of tents toward the large open circle I guessed would mark the center of the encampment. Catching sight of a crowd in the clearing, I began to struggle but quickly stilled. While days of sleep and shade had strengthened me, something in me stirred, telling me to be patient just a little longer. The opportune moment to slip away would come if I just waited.

I couldn't wait too long though, as it seemed my time was limited. The crowd murmured in excitement and celebration as my handlers dragged me to a wooden stake driven into the ground and pointing straight up to the sky like an accusing finger. As they forced me to stand with my back to the pole, one warrior began binding my ankles to the stake, while the other untied my wrists, currently held in front of me. A jolt of adrenaline shot through me as my hands sprang free. This might be my chance to escape. The urge to run was quickly dashed by the tight rope wound around my ankles and the throngs of clansmen blocking my way out of the circle.

Before I could consider my escape further, the guard wrenched my arms back, affixing my wrists to the pole behind me as well. Then, they left me, melting back into the surrounding crowd as I awaited my fate.

My gaze darted around my immediate vicinity; the area was more densely packed now than it had been during my day tied outside. I found myself curious after years without so much as hearing a human voice beyond my own on the occasions I had been desperate enough to talk to myself. The wave of chatter washed over me like an icy balm, simultaneously overwhelming and soothing. The general tone of the voices was that of excitement for my death, but as I listened closer, an undercurrent of something much more potent and sinister cut through —something I was far too familiar with: Desperation.

There were dozens of onlookers, but as I watched, they seemed to stay in self-contained groups, not mixing, even as they talked amongst themselves. A child with sunken eyes and tattered clothes eyed me from where he stood, clutching on to his mother's hands with spindly fingers. Usually flourishing clans boasted the highest number, but while this was the largest encampment I had ever seen, many looked to be struggling.

A hush fell over the clearing, halting my musings. The crowd parted, and a tall figure came forward, approaching where I stood bound. I recognized the cold gray stare of the man who had commanded my sacrifice, the one the masked man called Lord Alasdar. He had the gall to smile at me, although it didn't reach his eyes, before turning to address the onlookers.

"People of the Ballan Desert, we come to celebrate today's great progress in restoring our home to its rightful state. Already we have three clans together here under one banner, and Clan Ratan joined us just today."

My eyes widened as a cheer went up around me. I had never heard of clans uniting, let alone this many. The new arrivals today weren't a faction rejoining with the whole, but a whole clan arriving to add their numbers to the encampment.

"While we face the wrath of the desert for the desertion of the old ways, united we will return our people to the ways of the past, giving the sands the blood they deserve. When all nine clans of the Ballan Desert are united, we will march on Kelvadan!"

The roar that went up from the crowd in response wasn't enough to drown out the pounding of my heart in my ears. Kelvadan, the Great City, stood as the bastion of hope at the edge of the desert. A city where even an exile would be welcome if they were lucky enough to make it there and a testament to the power of the sands. The idea of violence against the only permanent settlement on this side of the mountains was unfathomable.

The lord continued, raising his arms and whipping the crowd into a frenzy with an impassioned tirade. The fervor in his eyes would have bordered on lunacy if not for the way it was mirrored in the gazes of many onlookers. It was a fanaticism that could only be bred into the desperate who saw no other options.

The clans weren't just united—they were itching for war.

"The desert sends her storms, the disease, the hunger and the thirst to punish us for letting Kelvadan make us complacent. We clansmen have always been a warring people, spilling blood on the sands so they may give us life in return. With the peace brought by a unifying city, we have forgotten that the desert demands death in repayment for the life she gives us. The Ballan Desert does not want the peace and unity promised by the city. She wants blood.

"Those of us who still live among the dunes know this, although those in the city turn a blind eye. It has not even occurred to them that we would unify and attack them! They have truly forgotten the warrior's way. But the nine tribes of the Ballan Desert will raze Kelvadan, spill their blood on the sands, and free our home from this curse. In return for blood, the desert will protect us from the storms and starvation that plague us more each day. The desert gives and it takes!"

"The desert gives and it takes," echoed the crowd, rapping their knuckles to their temples in respect for their lord.

Panic rose in my throat, choking me. Kelvadan couldn't fall. The dream of Kelvadan had always been hazy, but it still became the only real hope a clung to through the years. As my only real chance for a better life, Kelvadan was an aspiration that had etched itself into my soul. A haven from my exile, where one without a clan could still live among others. A place where it wouldn't matter that I was cursed by the desert. The vision of Kelvadan had always represented in my mind the one thing I craved more than anything: A home.

They had to be warned.

It barreled into me with the force of a galloping horse. I had to be the one to warn them. That was why I still lived.

As if my newfound drive to survive hastened my death, Lord Alasdar now turned his gaze on me, formerly cold eyes burning with the fire of zeal.

"We will start with her. A promise to the sands that we will give them the battle they crave! A gift from the Viper himself." The lord stepped aside and gestured into the crowd.

A familiar dark silhouette came forward, the backlighting of the braziers ringing the circle accentuating the width of his shoulders and his prowling gate. The flickering firelight danced across the metal mask, but the smooth surface still looked lifeless, like perhaps there wasn't a person underneath at all.

He reached up to his shoulder where the hilt of the saber I'd almost stolen rested and unsheathed it with deliberate slowness. Unlike the sabers of many riders, it was too long to be worn at his hip. The power of his limbs and the light flashing off the lethal edge screamed of violence, but something within me stilled, like a wild caracal preparing to pounce.

He stepped forward, the tip of the blade level with my throat, just inches from where my pulse hammered beneath my skin. I stared at his face, and just for a moment, the light illuminated the dark pits of his eyes, and I remembered the proud nose and angular jaw hidden underneath.

I lifted my chin. We had been in this position before, and he had hesitated, just as he hesitated now. The blade inched forward, and as the tip touched my skin, it quivered ever so slightly, scratching me. A warm rivulet of blood dripped toward my collarbone, and I became aware of every millimeter it traveled, the cold steel barely brushing my neck. I could count the grains of sand beneath my bare feet and see through the metal mask before me to the closed off expression of my captor. Time froze, sucking away the shouts of the crowd and whistling of wind across the dunes into deafening silence. The only things to exist were me and the man in the mask. The Viper.

Fire exploded through me, accompanied by a crack so loud, I was sure my skull had been cloven in two. When the white behind my eyelids faded, and I peeled them open, unsure when I had shut them, I was greeted by the sight of my hands in the sand. Somehow, I had fallen on my hands and knees.

Looking up, the crowd before me scattered in panic, mouths open wide as if screaming, but I could hear nothing as my ears still rang from the noise. I glanced over my shoulder to see the pole I had been bound to split in half, charred as if it had been burning for hours.

Lightning flashed again, this time striking a nearby tent, which burst into flame. I staggered to my feet, coming face to mask with the man who had been tasked with taking my life. He stood frozen, sword no longer pointed at me. Before I could move, he spun on his heel and dashed toward the burning tent as lightning continued to flash around us, alternately blinding before plunging the camp into chaos.

Not pausing to consider my captor's retreat, I turned and ran the other way. My bare feet churned through the loose sand, and I pumped my arms furiously, driven by a singular thought. I had to get to Kelvadan and warn them of the impending attack.

As weak as I was, the adrenaline of my escape fueled me, and the ongoing lightning strikes distracted those who might have stopped me. My sense of hearing returned, greeted by the crash of thunder and the crackling of yet another tent set ablaze. Horses screamed in fear in the distance, and I veered toward them.

Near the edge of the camp, I came upon an enclosure, horses bucking and stamping in agitation. One stood nearest the temporary fence, seeming calmer than the others, although its ears pulled back flat along its head, a full circle of white around its eyes illuminated by another bolt of lightning.

I sent a silent apology to whomever this mount belonged to as I clambered to the top of the fence. Horse theft was akin to murder in the clans, but I was already an exile, and I had a mission to fulfill.

With a leap from the top slat of the fence, I landed on the horse's back. It whinnied and bucked, but I threw my arms around its neck, barely staying on as I squeezed with my thighs. This spurred the horse further in its frenzy, and it charged toward the opposite edge of the enclosure.

Desperately I readjusted my grip, trying to center my weight more firmly on the animal's back. Fear gripped my heart as we approached the fence, but something came along with it: Exhilaration. My mount took to the air, my heart leaping into my throat as we soared over the barrier.

Then we were free, and the horse ran, me bent over its neck as it lengthened its stride. I chanced a glance back at the encampment. For a moment, a bolt of lightning illuminated a dark silhouette between the tents, but then we were cresting over a dune, and the clans were lost from view.

I didn't try to slow my mount as we put distance between us and the spot that was to have been my grave. The storm seemed centered around the encampment, and the desert around us remained dark as the lightning grew more distant. The farther away we could get before anybody tried to follow us, the better.

Not only that, but I couldn't bring myself to give up the wind in my hair, the powerful animal surging between my thighs as we dashed across the desert. I had missed this, these wild gallops under a star-spangled velvet sky. I threw back my head and did something I hadn't done in far too long. I laughed, an unpracticed broken sound, but something I couldn't stop even if I wanted to.

Who would have known that I would come closer to death than I had ever been before to find a reason for my survival? Not only that, but now I felt alive, an energy still crackling through my body as if the lightning *had* struck me, and the sparks still danced across my skin.

Surely the desert would guide me to Kelvadan when I carried such dire news. Perhaps this is why she had allowed me to scrape by all these years. So I could warn the city that was the testament of the desert's power and save it from the mad lord of Clan Katal—surely he must be mad.

For now, I let my horse carry me across the open sands, thinking of the Great City and how I had to save it.

As beams of light broke over the horizon, my mount slowed to a stop with a disgruntled snort. He had slackened to a walk long ago, and hours had passed as we traversed miles. At the stop, my head snapped up from my chest where it had been bobbing in a fitful doze.

My mount apparently needed rest as much as I did. Leaning to one side, I tried to swing my leg over and dismount, but only succeeded in sliding off and landing in the sand with a bone-rattling thump.

The stallion pranced and whickered as if amused by my ineptitude, and it surely was a stallion based on how far up I had to look to glare at him. After a moment, he settled, bending his forelegs to lay down on the sand next to me. Absently, I reached out to pat his nose, reveling in the velvety softness beneath my fingers.

I had certainly stolen a prime specimen. In the gray light of dawn, the coat that had appeared dark at night glimmered a golden chestnut.

Even covered in sweat and dust as it was now, it shone silky, with a mane and tail to match. He tossed his head and snorted, as if he could sense me admiring him. I huffed in amusement at his pride.

"What are you called?" I asked, as if he might answer. Only a few days around people, and I craved conversation again.

He flicked an ear back and bumped his nose into my hand as if wondering why I had paused my admiration.

"I'm Keera," I continued on, resuming my petting. I cocked my head consideringly. "How about Daiti for you?" A swift name for a fast mount, for he had certainly carried me far in a short amount of time.

He snorted, and I took that as acceptance.

We sat there in the sand as the sun rose, and I pulled my hood up over my head, wrapping the end across my face. I didn't speak anymore, having become comfortable with silence, but unspeakably pleased with Daiti's company. I continued to run my fingers through his mane, which he enjoyed if the way he stretched his neck to give me better access was any indication.

Soon though, Daiti began nuzzling my torso, investigating for food or water. He was right—we wouldn't last long without supplies. I didn't have anything on me right now I could use to hunt even if we were lucky enough to come across an oryx or a jackrabbit. We would have to hope to reach Kelvadan before either of us died of thirst or hunger.

The memory of Kelvadan rose in my mind at the thought, the city enormous against the backdrop in the mountains, magnified in size by the forced perspective of childhood memories. The hazy sight of the city walls and the plains beyond had only grown in my mind during exile—blown to mythical proportions. The dream of Kelvadan, as shadowy a hope as it had been, had kept me alive through many a harsh season. I couldn't let it fall now—not when I had a chance to save it.

I crawled over to Daiti's back and began to swing my leg over. He whickered unhappily at my rather undignified method of mounting when he still laid in the sand, but I slapped his shoulder lightly to tell him to get over it. None of the horses I had ridden before my exile from Clan Padra were nearly as large as Daiti, and therefore they'd been much less difficult to mount. Not to mention, I was out of practice.

While Daiti snuffled his disapproval, he suffered my clambering ineptitude before begrudgingly standing, little puffs of dust rising around his hooves as he stamped. With a slight nudge from me, he ambled forward. I didn't bother directing him, as I had no idea in which direction Kelvadan lay. Daiti's instincts would be better than mine, as I was far away from the oasis I'd called home. Besides, the sands had a way of speaking to horses, and direction hardly mattered in the Ballan Desert.

As the sun climbed higher in the sky, I squinted at the horizon, wondering if the light was altering my vision as it slowly transformed from endless golden sands to sharp rocks. My doubts melted away as mountains came into view, reaching up to the sky in jagged gray peaks. Relief filled me, palpable as cool water dripping over my burning skin. We were headed in the right direction.

After hours, Daiti's gait flagged, hooves dragging in the sand as he walked. He continued on doggedly though, as if he could sense our destination ahead.

At first, I didn't recognize what I was looking at as the city, instead just seeing an odd texture in the rocks at the base of the mountain in the distance. Getting closer, the pattern became more regular, rectangular and organized in a manner at odds with the rolling curves carved into the dunes by wind.

Squinting at the rock formation, squares organized themselves into tiers of buildings, carved from the same gray rock of the mountain. Growing ever closer, it became clear the buildings weren't just made of the same stone, but the whole structure was carved directly into the side of mountain. Dozens of buildings climbed up the face of the cliffs, stacking on top of each other in an incredible feat of architecture. So seamlessly did they fit with the rocks that it seemed they had grown from it instead of having been carved.

Even now that Kelvadan was in sight, it took ages to traverse the distance, the base of the mountains seeming deceptively close. Even as Daiti plodded determinedly along, the shade of the high stone peaks grew no closer. I wavered on his back, barely keeping my seat as the heat and dehydration clawed at me. I kept my eyes fixed on the arch in the stone wall that had just come into view, repeating to myself that if we could just make it there, everything would be alright.

What seemed like a day but was probably only an hour passed. My vision narrowed to the opening in the stone wall by the time we reached it.

From far away, it had seemed small, like the opening flap to a tent. Walking through it though, it was wide enough to fit at least five horses abreast, and twice that tall. Daiti's hooves clopped against the ground as it transitioned from sand to stone. I swayed in my seat, ready to topple to the ground as the determination of reaching my destination faded. I had made it.

I had no clue what to do next.

People milled about in a courtyard, streets branching off in half a dozen directions. My eyes refused to focus on any of the figures—where to go? Who to approach? Who would even heed my warning to in a place like this?

Daiti's sharp whinny cut the air, and he pranced sideways. I glanced down to see the source of his displeasure—a woman, with her arm outstretched as if she had been patting Daiti's withers. A burnished breastplate topped the leather tunic covering her down to her thighs, but my gaze zeroed in on the large, curved dagger sticking out of her thick crimson sash.

"Are you all right?"

I opened my mouth to respond, not sure if to insist I was fine or beg for help. With my dry throat, I only managed a croak. This was a theme as of late, a challenge of thirst that rarely came up in my life, as isolated as it had been.

I choked around the sand in my throat and hacked a cough. My eyes watered, and I began to slip sideways.

"Kelvadan... in trouble," I managed to grit out as my surroundings blurred, dismayed that I had come this far only to be unable to deliver my message.

Daiti shifted under me as if to try and help me keep my seat, but it was too late. My already tunneled vision darkened, and I toppled sideways. I was too tired to even brace for impact with the stones below but landed in strong arms instead.

Chapter Seven
The Viper

The clash of sabers drowned out any noisy thoughts, for which I was glad. The warriors of all three clans trained together now, and I threw myself into their midst. The man I faced now was a member of Clan Miran, and so I had not faced him before. I relished the opportunity to hone my skills against new foes, to practice reading the movements of somebody who I didn't already know.

Izumi was the best combatant besides me in Clan Katal, but sparring against her was rarely productive anymore, with us so used to each other's strengths and weaknesses that it became a game of wits more than a proper fight. Still, she challenged me to practice with her nearly every day I trained with the riders, so determined was she to surpass me in skill.

My opponent came at me quickly, feinting and slashing with great speed, a move that had worked on his prior opponent. His blade whistled through the air with the force of his blow. The momentum of the swing carried the blade past me as I ducked instead of parrying like he had expected. I used the opportunity to slash, catching him in the shoulder of his sword arm as he was unable to reverse directions fast enough to stop me.

He stepped back, rubbing the divot between the meat of his

shoulder and neck where I had hit him with my blunted blade. It was an unpleasant place for a bruise, but it would teach him to measure the force behind his blows. Faster was often preferable to harder with a saber.

I nodded sharply at him in acknowledgement, preferring to teach without words, and he raised his guard again. Before we could engage, he froze, eyes fixed on something over my shoulder. He dropped his blade, bowing his head.

I turned, teeth gritted as I already knew Lord Alasdar waited behind me.

"My lord," I acknowledged, also inclining my head.

"Viper, I have need of you," he announced before turning and striding away, not checking to see if I would follow.

I handed off my training saber to a nearby soldier and strode after him. He didn't slow for me, but I refused to hurry my steps to catch up with him. I did lengthen my stride though.

"You must head to Clan Tibel at once," he said without preamble.

"What of training the soldiers for a fortnight as you suggested yesterday?" I asked, trying to keep my tone free of any opinions on the matter.

"That was before the storm. We need to unite the clans sooner rather than later—before the desert tears herself apart."

"Even if all the clans agree to an alliance within a week, we will be far from ready to attack Kelvadan," I pointed out.

"It is not just a matter of invading Kelvadan, although that will certainly come," Lord Alasdar explained, stopping at the edge of one of the many horse enclosures. Alza ambled toward the fence from where she had been munching from a trough. "It is an issue of survival. These disasters will only get worse. Storms, disease, bad hunting. There is a strength to be had in numbers if we are to endure long enough to obtain our goal."

I reached out to Alza, letting her snuffle into my hand in favor of responding. Yesterday I had been anxious to leave, but now something urged me to stay. Maybe the thought of a woman riding off into the night who might come back. I shook the vision of her defiant gaze from my head, although it seemed intent on returning. The clash of swords had given me a brief reprieve from her image, but now my more idle brain brought her back.

"That storm last night was far from natural. The desert is so angry, it almost seems like she would turn her magic against us," Lord Alasdar murmured, quietly enough that passing clansmen would not overhear.

I thanked my mask for keeping my expression hidden when my face spasmed. However, Lord Alasdar would know my thoughts all too well despite not being able to see my face. While the magic of the desert that pooled within me made it easy for me to manipulate the environment around me, Lord Alasdar's gift focused easily on the magical energy of those around him. Especially on somebody with emotions as loud as mine. As much as Lord Alasdar tried to help me keep them in check, they always bubbled to the surface.

I had told him of the storms that accosted the desert when I lost my temper as a child—I'd run scared into the dunes as the lightning turned sand into glass around me, and I howled at the sky in confusion. While it had been many years since those days, the smell of magic in the air had assaulted me with memories last night.

When the first bolt of lightning struck, I almost thought I had been the one to summon it, but it didn't come with the spine-tingling awareness of the desert spread around me. I had pushed that awareness into the depths of my soul for a decade now, fighting a losing battle against being swallowed whole by that immense force. Before the storm, I had been too busy falling into the gravity of two dark eyes full of flickering firelight to dredge up that power.

"It is a shame the sacrifice escaped. Maybe her blood would have been enough to slake the desert and assuage the storm," I commented without feeling. After all, so many believed that the desert was angry simply because the unprecedented peace brought by Kelvadan deprived her of the blood she demanded.

"Or perhaps the storm interrupted the sacrifice as a sign that it will not be appeased by half measures," Lord Alasdar speculated, watching me intently, as if he could see the truth in my movements.

"I will leave for Clan Tibel in the morning."

I set out before the sun, riding in the opposite direction Keera had the night she escaped. I briefly wondered where she had gone, and if she had made it there, before turning my eyes to Alza's ears in front of me. One was unlikely to survive very long in the wilderness with no supplies, and I found myself loathe to envision the grizzly end Keera would have met dying of exposure or thirst. Driving my saber into her throat would have saved her from suffering, and I didn't know why I hadn't done it.

Alza snorted, drawing my attention back to her. I patted her neck in reassurance. Normally even-tempered, even in the face of violence, she seemed skittish this morning. Perhaps the unnatural storm had spooked her.

At midday, I pulled her to a stop near a formation of rust-colored rocks, ready to take shelter in the shade for the hottest hour of the day. As I dismounted and walked toward a pile of boulders, she pawed at the sand, making it rise in small puffs around her forelegs. She didn't follow me. I whistled for her, but Alza wouldn't budge. I hadn't put her on a lead rope since she was a foal, used to her following my direction without need for any tack or bridle, but now she acted like a willful colt, freshly caught from one of the roaming herds of the desert.

I was stomping toward her in annoyance when I caught the smell in the air. The earthy scent of magic, like the morning after a rare rain shower, had me on alert. I looked up just in time to see the source of the vibrating growl emanating from the rocks above me.

A ball of black fur leaped through the air, landing on Alza's back. She screamed in pain, bucking as claws dug into her flesh, the attacking creature hissing and spitting in fury. My dirk flew into my hand as I lunged forward, trying to draw the creature's attention without harming Alza.

My closed fist connected with silky fur as I just managed to skim the creature's flank. It rounded on me, fixing me with glowing purple eyes. The sight stunned me enough that I barely had time to raise my dirk in defense before the cat-like animal pounced.

Claws slashed at my face, skittering across my mask with a nasty metallic screech. I let the momentum of the attack take me to the ground on my back, curling my legs into me before pushing them out, launching the creature over my head at the rock wall behind me.

It yelped as it hit the boulders with a crunch, but we both sprang to our feet, seemingly uninjured. I reached over my shoulder with my offhand, knowing my saber would give me the reach I needed to keep those claws and savage teeth at arm's length.

The animal pounced again before I could fully draw my blade, but Alza leaped in the way, lashing out with powerful hooves. One caught the creature in the chest, knocking it back, but not before it viciously slashed her leg. Alza collapsed with a scream, foreleg buckling beneath her.

A growl tore from my throat, and I lunged forward, blade in each hand, to where the creature lay, belly up from my horse's attack. Before it could right itself, I plunged my saber deep into the white spot in the center of its chest.

The metallic sent of blood joined the earthy magic in the air as the beast shuddered. It whined once before going still. The glowing light faded from its striking purple eyes, still open and staringly lifelessly at the sky.

I stared at the creature now that it was still, not having had a chance to take it in while it attacked. It was somewhere between a cat and dog in shape, its fur all black except for the white circle in the middle of its chest. It was the aura of magic I sensed, like an impending storm oozing off the body more than anything that convinced me of what I saw. I had killed a Sichat, a creature of legend said to steal the souls of the dead. As far as I knew, nobody had seen one since before the desert had been crossed. They had disappeared, along with all the other magical beasts, when the Heart of the Desert had been conquered by our ancestors who journeyed across desert to the ocean for the first time. Now, the desert was unbalanced, and the creatures rose once more.

A distressed whinny behind me tore my focus from the mythical creature. Alza struggled to get to her feet, injured foreleg straining to hold her weight. I rushed to my knees at her side, shushing her with a hand on her flank. She stopped trying to stand, but her muscles shook with tension beneath my palm.

Bending close, I examined the wound. Four slashes ran horizontally across the side of her leg, just below the knee, where the Sichat's claws had torn her flesh. While the wounds were jagged, they didn't appear to be deep. Her tendons would be unharmed.

I huffed in relief as well as disappointment. Alza would recover, but I wouldn't risk her traveling for the rest of the day. I didn't relish delaying our trip, as I hadn't packed supplies for a longer solo mission. Lord Alasdar would certainly find a way to make me pay for not completing my task efficiently as well.

Alza's eyes rolled in her head, and I grit my teeth, mind made up. I urged her to her feet. She favored her injured leg, but managed to stand. I untied the small number of packs from her back, slinging those over my shoulders instead.

Slowly, we walked along the edge of the cliff face in search of a shelter for the night. Alza didn't complain, but I kept my hand on her neck, the trembling beneath her skin giving away her pain. Luckily, we happened across a break in the cliff face after a short walk. Leaving Alza outside, I pushed inside, blade drawn in caution.

The bones of dead animals littered the corners of the cave within, marking it as the lair of a predator, but it was currently unoccupied. I sensed I had recently killed the creature who had been living here. If not, I was confident that I was a more deadly predator than any that might return to their shelter.

I beckoned Alza inside after me, and she followed obediently. It took very little urging to get her to lay down on one side of the cave. While she rested, I busied myself with setting up a camp for the night, starting with building a fire near the entrance. I stoked it as hot as I could, sweating beneath my hood and vest.

Once the flames glowed blue where they licked the dry brush I used for kindling, I drew my dirk. I thrust it into the flames and held it there until the length glowed red. Turning to Alza with the heated blade before me, I approached quickly, not giving her the chance to panic. The whites of her eyes showed, but she stayed still until I pressed the flat of the blade against her torn flesh.

She bucked against me, but I laid my weight against her haunch as the fire did its work, stopping the bleeding and clearing any infection. As she fought me, I was only glad she did not have to inflict this process on herself as I had in the past.

When all four claw swipes across Alza's foreleg were cauterized, she collapsed against the rocky cave floor, sweat dampening her sides and foam at the corners of her mouth. I gave her the water left in our large water bag, forgoing refilling my skin. She needed it more than me.

As she settled down to rest, I sat beside the fire, letting it dwindle down to embers. While the desert nights grew cold, I could easily rest beside Alza for warmth, with no need to burn the little brush in the area.

My hands drifted up to remove my mask now that I was alone, but I hesitated. The magic of the desert still drifted on the air, whispering under my skin and caressing my mind, tugging at the tightly knotted ball of magic living at the base of my skull. The feeling of being watched that accompanied the sensation gave me pause, like the magic would see me for who I was, and I would be lost to the madness in my mind.

Without removing my mask or gloves, I laid down next to Alza, facing the entrance of the cave with my saber in hand.

Come dawn, Alza's wounds looked improved, but she still favored her injured leg when she walked. One more day and we would be able to travel again. I would have to go out to hunt and gather water to account for our delay.

I strapped on my dirk and saber, wrapping my hood securely around my head and shoulders before stepping out onto the baked earth outside the cave. I turned my face up to the sky and closed my eyes, breathing in deeply. As much as the feeling of magic that lingered after the appearance of the Sichat made me wary, I knew it could guide me to supplies as well. The creature wouldn't have lingered here if there was no water source nearby. I assumed even beasts of myth needed water.

I let my feet carry me away from the rocky formations forming the cliff-face behind me, out into open land. A shadow passed over my vision, and I looked up to find a falcon gliding overhead. It passed by me before wheeling in several circles and descending in the distance.

I followed its path to a rough well, the kind often dug by herds of roaming horses with their sharp hooves. As I approached, a light tinkle grabbed my attention.

The falcon I had seen before stood at the edge of the watering hole, a black-tailed jackrabbit limp in its claws. It hopped forward, and the jingling sounded again. I cocked my head at the bell tied to the hawk's leg, marking it as a hunting animal. Perhaps I was closer to Clan Tibel's encampment than I thought, or maybe a hunting party had ventured far from camp. After all, game was growing sparse, and Clan Katal's hunters roamed farther afield to feed our numbers.

Before I could investigate further, the falcon took to the air with its prize. I noted the direction it had gone before turning to the well before me. Tracks in the muddy ground, indicating this water source was frequented by local wildlife, told me it was safe to drink from. I filled the large water bag as well as my own skin before slinging both across my back and turning back to the rocky cliff where Alza waited.

Not yet a quarter of the way back, a cloud of dust on the horizon to the left drew my attention. I squinted, trying to gauge the distance to the cloud. If I hurried, I could make it back to the shelter of the cave before the sandstorm reached me. Just about to break into a jog, I stopped, catching sight of the distinctive shadows of horses in the haze of dust. It was no storm, but riders approached.

I dropped my burden of water to the ground, drawing my saber from across my back. Out here in the wilds, approaching hunters were rarely friendly. As the thundering of hooves on sun baked dirt grew louder, the glint of sharpened steel in the sunlight, blades held aloft, revealed that the riders felt the same about my presence.

They formed a wedge shape, the leader charging at me with a sword pointed forward like a spear, ready to skewer me like a wild boar. I stayed still, sword drawn at my side. Even though my eyes stayed open, the world blurred around me, sensations narrowing to the vibrations of approaching hoofbeats beneath my boots and the trembling of magic connecting me to every grain of sand in the desert, nearly overwhelming if I hadn't learned to block out most of the feeling.

I didn't move until the riders were a horse length away, but then launched myself into the air, my leap bolstered by threads of magic. Not expecting my move, the leader didn't have time to raise his sword as I flew over his head, twisting in midair to land on his mount behind him. The hilt of my saber connected with the side of his skull with a crack, and he slid off the broad back. The flame of his life in the magical landscape snuffed out as the horses trampled him. I nearly winced at the sudden extinguishing of light, but the roar of battle already overtook my mind.

The horse beneath me dug in its hooves, bucking and skidding to a halt at the change in weight, realizing his master was no longer the one on his back. I squeezed my thighs around his middle to stay on even as my hands busied themselves holding my sword and pulling my dirk from my belt.

I reached a tendril of magic out to the horse's mind, calming it—a relatively simple task given that the magic of the desert ran strong in horses as well. I had inherited a touch of influence with horses alongside the rest of my power. The stallion calmed under me, and I leaned my weight, wheeling him back around to charge at the other riders who had scattered upon the leader's demise.

I wove between them, swinging my saber and dirk on either side, bodies of my foes slipping to the earth as blood coated my blades. My breath came in humid pants through the metal holes of my mask. With each life that I silenced, the voices in my head grew until they screamed so loud, I felt my skull would split open.

A screech of power cut above the rest, and I whipped around just in time to dodge a whip of fire lashing out from the hands of one of the last remaining riders. Such power was rare outside of clan lords or their warlords. Still, it was no match for mine.

With a clench of my fist, the flames that danced in the rider's palm extinguished. He shook his hand as if trying to resummon his advantage. It was too late. I flicked my wrist, sending my dirk flying across the space between us. With a wet thud, it embedded itself right below his breastbone. The rider let out a gurgling gasp and began to slip sideways from his mount. I didn't watch, instead turning away to face the rest of the riders.

I wheeled around, looking for my next opponent, only to find a littering of slumped forms on the sand surrounded by frightened horses. I growled, ready to fell another fighter but none approached. Still, my instincts screamed for blood, a cacophony clamoring in my head, awoken by my use of magic in the fight and begging for more.

I slid off my mount, unsteady on my feet, and fell to my knees. My vision cleared enough for me to focus on the sight of my saber, shining crimson in the harsh sun. Methodically, I wiped the blood of my felled enemies on the sand, offering the desert the lives I had taken.

The voices in my head quieted from a scream to a whisper to a rare moment of silence as the sands drank up my sacrifice. All the clansmen's lives belonged to the desert, and she begged me to return them to her. I exhaled heavily as the constant threat of madness retreated.

The desert always screamed at me, as if she wanted me to do something, find something, destroy something. She only quieted to a whisper for a short while after the rush of battle had abated, and I assumed I had given her what she wanted. At least, that was Lord Alasdar's thought, and he knew more secrets of the desert than most. He alone had discovered the truth of why the desert was angry and had been able to teach me how to control my magic. I would follow his wisdom.

A jingle broke the new fallen silence, drawing my attention to the falcon I had seen earlier. It hopped around one of the fallen riders as if waiting for instruction or expecting him to lift his arm so he could perch. I rose from my knees and walked over to the body.

The blue sash around his waist, fastened with a silver pin, embossed with a snarling hyena, declared him a warrior of Clan Tibel. I recognized him as the one who had tried to burn me with a whip of magical fire. A small shard of blood glass, known to enhance the bearer's magic, glimmered on a cord around his neck, explaining some of the strength of his power. He had come to the fight prepared. It seemed Clan Tibel expected my arrival, and I was not welcome. This attack was a message, and I would send one in return.

With a decisive slash of my saber, I severed the warrior's head from his lifeless body. The falcon squawked in alarm and fluttered a few feet away as the blade hit the sand next to it. Still, it watched me with a cocked head as I lifted the severed head by the hair, more blood dripping onto the already stained sand. I carried it over to the horse lingering nearby, clearly at a loss without his master.

The mounts bore no saddlebags, signaling we were not far from

Clan Tibel's camp. They would carry my messages back to their home. The riders had been sent to tell me their clan would not bargain. The return of their heads would tell Clan Tibel that the Viper did not compromise.

When I arrived back at the cave where Alza rested, she whickered and greeted me at the entrance. I tried to brush her away, not wanting her to put weight on her leg if it wasn't healed yet, but she snuffled her nose against my clothes, smelling blood and seemingly giving me a once over to make sure it wasn't mine. I gently pushed her head away to unstrap the water bags from my back. That seemed to placate her, and she quickly turned her attention to the water, drinking deeply and noisily as I held it for her. I took the opportunity to watch how she stood. She carried her weight easily on all four legs, not avoiding the injured one. While the flesh looked angry and blistered where I had cauterized it, the wounds hadn't been deep, and it seemed it would carry her fine.

Now that I knew we were so close to Clan Tibel's camp, there was no need to delay longer. I began packing up our small camp, tying saddlebags together and making sure our fire was completely extinguished. As I approached Alza with our supplies, a tinkling caught my attention.

I whirled toward the cave entrance, dropping my burden, hands flying to the hilts of my weapons. Standing in the cave entrance was the falcon from earlier. It hopped toward me inquisitively, and I frowned.

It had taken flight as I sent the horses back in the direction they had come with a sharp tap to their flanks, each bearing the severed head of their former rider. I assumed it would make its way back to the encampment with them to be cared for by somebody else. After all, a well-trained hunting falcon could be useful for catching small prey, especially when oryx became scarcer by the day.

Instead, the bird fluttered toward me, and I instinctively held out my arm. It landed on me without further prompting, the leather gloves I wore over my tunic protecting me from the worst of its talons. I inspected the bell tied to its leg, pondering removing it and turning it free. As the bird jumped farther up my arm and made a low *kack,* I exhaled heavily through my nose.

This fellow was too domesticated to survive long in the desert, clearly seeing me as a friend and not a threat. If he would follow me regardless, I wouldn't chase him away. Perhaps I would even enjoy a little more fresh meat on my travels if I could learn how to fly him.

For now, I lowered my arm toward a pile of rocks, twisting it until he jumped off so I could finish packing up. Once my minimal supplies were secured to Alza's back, I led her out of the cave with a hand on her neck. If Clan Tibel was close, I could afford to walk alongside her and rest her leg.

The falcon fluttered toward us, attempting to alight on Alza's neck, but she tossed her head and snorted at the feel of talons on her skin. Next, he tried to perch on my shoulders, hooks digging through the material of my vest and robe. I winced at the weight and the pinch of him trying to grip me.

Carefully, I lifted him from his perch and set him on top of one of the packs of supplies on Alza's back. He settled there, ruffling his feathers a few times before deciding it was an adequate perch. With that, I led us in the direction that Clan Tibel's riders had come from.

Chapter Eight
Keera

Persistent, gnawing hunger brought me to awareness, as it usually did. My mind jumped into calculations, counting how many strips of dried oryx meat I had left to determine if I could afford to eat breakfast. While I normally liked to hunt first and save my meal for the hottest part of the day when I would hide away from the sun in my lean-to, today wouldn't be one of those days. The hollow feeling in my belly was too intense for hunting without sustenance today. As I tried to move my limbs, they sank into the soft surface below me as if rooted there.

I froze instantly. The surface below me was far more comfortable than my barren nest of pilfered cushions and threadbare rugs. My eyes snapped open, and I drew in a sharp breath through cracked lips at the sight of solid stone above me.

"She lives!" proclaimed a male voice.

I turned my head, cheek brushing against a pillow so silky, it didn't even chafe my perpetually sunburned face.

A brown-skinned man stood in my line of sight, smiling broadly at me, before my brief glance at him was blocked by a figure immediately beside me. She fell to her knees and cocked her head, her eyes unsmiling but kind. I recognized her as the woman who approached Daiti and me when...

Kelvadan.

That's where I was. I struggled to sit up, arms weak as desert grass blowing in the wind. The woman helped me with firm hands on my shoulders. The touch of human hands still surprised me, and I tensed.

"You're safe, it's all right," she insisted in a firm tone that still somehow managed to be comforting. Maybe it was the way her reassurances brooked no argument.

I opened my mouth to speak, but while less dry than it had been before, my swollen tongue still refused to form words. As I sat there with my mouth hanging open, I studied the woman before me, drinking in yet another new set of human features. Her hood now pooled around her shoulders, revealing a clean-shaven head; a single thick line was inked into her skin, running from her forehead across her scalp, the black stark in contrast with her pale skin. Her eyes narrowed as she examined me in turn, although I didn't sense malice in their icy-blue depths.

Another figure coming to kneel at the side of the low couch where I lay stole my attention. The man I'd seen earlier offered me a cup, and I snatched it from him before I could stop myself. He smiled at me, the twinkle in his dark eyes almost as bright as the light reflecting off the silver beads adorning his black braids. I lifted the cup to my lips and gulped down the heart-wrenchingly delicious water inside, some overflowing the sides of my mouth to dribble down my chin.

I yanked the cup from my lips with great effort, wanting to down it all in swallow after glorious swallow, but knowing from experience that would only end in me vomiting it all up again. I knew better than to waste precious resources like that.

The woman took advantage of my distraction to explain. "I brought you back to my home after you lost consciousness. You've only been out for an hour or so. Shade and water can do wonders."

"Why?" I croaked out. Some of the urgency from before I fainted returned, but it waged war in my chest with the wariness of strangers—especially ones showing this degree of unwarranted kindness.

"Kelvadan is a safe haven for all who travel the Ballan Desert," the man exclaimed cheerfully, gesturing expansively as if he had been personally appointed to welcome weary travelers.

I blinked. Could it be possible that this city was really the paradise I had dreamed? It had seemed rather like a place of legend as I approached the mountains, but that might have just been from my exhaustion.

"It is, and it is my job to keep it that way," the woman agreed. "I'm captain of the Kelvadan riders, and the last thing you said before collapsing was about a threat to Kelvadan."

I opened my mouth, the determination that had carried me across the sands bolstered by the reminder of my purpose. Clan Katal would destroy this wonderful place. A place that I had dreamed for so long could offer me a home.

"She will tell us about this threat over a meal," the man cut in before I could launch into whatever had been about to come spilling out of me. "She's clearly had quite a journey, and it won't do to have her collapsing in the middle of her tale."

I swung my legs over the side of the couch, turning to take in the room where I had been resting more thoroughly. Seeing rich fabrics hanging from the walls, sheer curtains looking light as air as they billowed from the slight breeze coming through the windows, I winced at the crust of dirt I currently smeared on the couch beneath me. The bright colors and variety of textures gave the modest size room a sense of luxury despite its odd construction. It was completely hewn of gray stone, from the floor to the ceilings to the walls, with no joints to indicate a construction from blocks.

It had seemed like the city was carved directly into the mountainside as Daiti and I approached, and I could see now it was true.

"*Daiti*," I gasped.

The woman shot me a question look.

"My..." I swallowed, knowing that he wasn't exactly my horse, but now wasn't the time to broach that. "My horse."

"He's in the stables right next to Neven's," she assured. "Although it was no mean feat getting him there. It certainly seems you are the only person he tolerates."

I blinked. He had seemed friendly enough to me, putting up with my undignified mounting and unpracticed riding. I hadn't seen him around other people yet. Still, I was glad for him to be cared for after I dragged him away from his home and across the desert.

"Come," the man beckoned, gesturing me over to a table he was currently setting with food. My eyes widened at the sight of fruit and roasted meat. Even bread—a rarely heard of luxury among the clans, where the nomadic lifestyle did not lend itself to farming grain.

I lowered myself to one of the cushions around the low table on shaky legs, balling my hands into fists and tucking them under my thighs to keep from immediately grabbing at all the food I could reach. My instincts told me to snatch as much as I could while it was in front of me, but it hadn't been so long since I had been among my clan that I didn't remember how civilized people behaved. Now that my brain was sluggishly recovering from my exhaustion, it latched on to the need to hide my status as an exile from these people. As far as they knew, I had a horse. I was a member of a clan. If they found I was an exile, they might ask why. If they found out what I had done, I might be cast from this incredible place.

"Eat," the woman insisted. "You look like you have had quite a long journey and could use all the sustenance we can offer."

My hand shot out and snatched the closest piece of meat, looking like the roast leg of some bird. I brought it to my mouth without bothering with the plate before me. I tore into it, hot grease dripping down my chin and my eyes stinging with unshed tears at the taste of spices and fresh meat.

"Besides, with your mouth full, it will give us a chance to introduce ourselves properly," the man cut in, thankfully diverting attention from my behavior. "I'm Neven, and this is my wife, Aderyn. She serves Queen Ginevra and has been charged with keeping the city safe. I still don't know why she agreed to marry me, a simple weaver."

Aderyn smacked Neven on the arm, her expression softening into something akin to a smile as she chewed a bite of bread. "You act as if the queen's dresses aren't all crafted of the fine fabrics you make."

"And who might we have the pleasure of having at our table?" Neven asked, turning back to me. I had already picked most of the meat off the bone in my hand, and my stomach clenched as it squeezed around the food, unused to rich fare after so much hunger.

"Keera," I volunteered, expecting awkward silence after my name where I would normally announce my clan. I considered lying and naming one, but Neven and Aderyn didn't even seem to notice. They had only given their own names too, I realized.

"And what brings you to Kelvadan, Keera?" Aderyn asked.

I swallowed, to dispel the tightness of sudden nerves in my throat. I had come this far to warn the Great City of what was to come. I couldn't fail now simply out of fear of accidentally revealing myself as an exile.

"I was captured by Clan Katal. They planned to sacrifice me to the desert to please her."

Aderyn frowned, and Neven shook his head, but neither interrupted.

"While I was captive, I heard their leader, Lord Alasdar, talking of his plans. He's... he is uniting the tribes. Once he has all nine tribes under his banner, he plans to attack Kelvadan. I managed to escape and came to warn you."

The plate Neven had been holding clattered against the table as he nearly dropped it, but the line between Aderyn's brows only deepened as she frowned.

"Kelvadan is the only place where the tribes meet in peace. He will never be able to unite them," she said, although a question in her tone betrayed her concern.

"Four clans have already agreed to his plans. I... I don't think he is giving them much choice," I admitted. The image of the man they had called captain, in his metal mask with his long saber, flashed in my mind. If he was the one sent to convince the other lords to join them, I didn't think he would stop at peaceful negotiations. Then again, he hadn't killed me when he had the chance.

"The queen will want to hear everything you know," Aderyn said, and I stiffened.

I already felt out of my depth here in Neven and Aderyn's lovely home. I hadn't worn clothes that were not second-hand in over a decade, and the cloth looked even more ragged next to the lavish upholstery in Aderyn's home. I didn't know how I could possibly face a queen.

"We will get you cleaned up, no worries. And I'm sure I can dig up something for you to wear that will make the queen want to order an outfit for herself," Neven offered.

"After you've eaten of course," Aderyn added.

The ball of anxiety in my stomach only eased slightly at their reassurances, but I nodded all the same. If warning Kelvadan of Lord Alasdar was the reason for my years of survival, then I would face the queen with all the courage I had left.

I stopped eating after another piece of bread and a piece of fruit, the likes of which I had never had. When I looked at it curiously, and Neven showed me how to remove the thick rind to get at the tart flesh within, Aderyn explained that it was from traders who came through the mountains to the city. They wouldn't venture out into the harsh conditions of the sands and chance the wrath of the clans, especially not without any way to navigate, but ventured to the city with increasing frequency over the past decades.

Even as I wiped my hands on the cloth Neven offered me, my stomach full to bursting, I eyed the pieces of bread and fruit remaining on the table. It went against my very bones to leave food uneaten, and I wondered if I could store a couple of the fruits in my shirt.

"I'm sure the queen will insist on feeding you too," Neven said, giving me a knowing, sidelong glance.

I nodded.

"Let's get you clean while Neven finds you some clothes that will fit." Aderyn led me from the room through a hewn arch of a doorway and down a narrow hall to a small chamber. The gentle patter of trickling water echoed in the tight space. Even as I watched liquid trickle down from the ceiling in a fountain in wonder, my skin crawled. After years of sleeping under the open sky, only ever taking shelter in my lean-to during the hottest hours of the day and the occasional sandstorm, being encased by stone was unnerving. The weight of the mountain I knew the house was set in pressed in around me, and it took several seconds of focusing on the sound of water to center my thoughts again.

"There is soap over here." Aderyn gestured to a ledge cut into the wall. "The water is cold, but it beats carrying buckets from the well for a bath."

I held my hand out into the stream in wonder, finding it icy as she indicated.

"It comes directly from the springs high in the mountains. The tunnels were carved into the mountain along with the city," she explained. "Not every home has them, and some people still prefer warm baths. I myself find the cold bracing."

She gave me a sharp nod before turning and leaving me to my own devices. I stripped from my clothes, nearly taking my skin off in the process as the grime and sweat clung to me. I had the delirious thought that I could peel my skin off like the rind of the fruit, so thick was the crust of dirt and sand. I stifled a choked laugh, the broken sound echoing in the enclosed space. The exhaustion that still clung to me, and the panic at being shut in a stone room, were getting the better of me, and I turned my focus back to undressing. As tattered as my clothes were after being taken from a passing clan—already well worn—I normally kept them and myself relatively clean, rinsing in the oasis every day.

Sand dusted the floor as I dropped the tunic and loose pants to the ground along with my sash and hood. I stepped under the water, and while it stole my breath with the sudden change of temperature, I didn't shy away. Aderyn was right that the cold was bracing. It soothed the sharp sting of my sunburnt skin to pleasant numbness.

Once I was accustomed to the temperature, I plucked the soap from the alcove and began cleaning. While I rinsed regularly, I rarely had the luxury of soap or water quite this crystal clear. Wiping away the layers of dust revealed tanned skin whose color I had not seen clearly in some time. I washed my hair, the dusty color turning to a dark brown, lighter than the nearly black it had once, before so much sunlight.

A knock sounded at the door, and I called for Aderyn to enter. She rounded the corner and stared for a second. I looked down at myself to see what she was staring at, before remembering my modesty. Alone in the sands, I was often naked whenever it suited me, usually only to be seen by a curious black-tailed jackrabbit or a passing fennec fox. I hadn't given any thought to my appearance in recent memory, and I wondered what she saw what she looked at me.

My hands drifted in front of me, but Aderyn shook her head.

"They must have held you captive a very long time."

I swallowed and offered a jerky nod by way of response. If she thought my sorry state was due to captivity, I wouldn't disillusion her. While Kelvadan was rumored to welcome even exiles, my lack of a clan shamed me to admit. Still, as she held out a cloth to dry myself and a bundle of clothes, guilt creeped its way into my gut. I shouldn't lie to somebody showing me such kindness, especially when my presence might be putting them in danger. It was a detail I always glossed over when envisioning building a life for myself in Kelvadan—that I would endanger everybody here just as I had endangered my clan. After several days of being around other people once more, I wasn't willing to give up company again quite yet. Once I told the queen about Clan Katal, then I would be honest with Aderyn.

After drying myself off with the proffered cloth, I shook out the clothes to reveal loose pants that tapered around the ankle, and cropped tunic that would leave my arms and abdomen bare. Both were a golden-yellow color, threads of a darker shade of the same tone forming unknowable patterns on the shoulders and at the waistband.

"These are too beautiful," I admitted.

"It pleases Neven to make lovely things." A smile tugged at Aderyn's lips and softened the lines around her eyes, an expression she only seemed to wear when speaking of her husband.

I put the garments on, unsurprised but dismayed when the pants hung at my waist, leaving my protruding ribs exposed.

"Neven will be disappointed that he doesn't have time to tailor it, but he'll make sure you look your best regardless."

Aderyn beckoned me from the room, and I trailed her down the narrow hallway, this time more prepared but still unnerved by the stone walls pressing close on either side. We entered the same room we had eaten in where Neven still waited.

He folded his arms, cocking his head to assess me. Humming under his breath, he turned to a nearby chest and dug through it before emerging with several lengths of cloth, both a rich blue the color of a night sky turned to velvet by a full moon.

"These will do for now." He approached me, winding one wide strip around my waist as a sash, securing the pants more tightly around my jutting hipbones. He stepped behind me, using the other to tie back my hair, long loose ends hanging down alongside the still-damp tendrils.

"Lovely," he proclaimed, stepping back to assess his handiwork. He grabbed a hand mirror from a nearby chest and handed it to me to admire the final result. I lifted it slowly, as if afraid of the face that might stare back at me as I had only seen my reflection distorted in the rippling pool of the oasis.

I blinked at the heart-shaped face that greeted me in the mirror. The golden eyes, set deep under a prominent brow, were darker than I remembered from my youth, and the slight upturn of my nose stood out all the more from the hollowness of my cheekbones. I handed the mirror back quickly.

"Thank you. The outfit is beautiful," I said.

Aderyn nodded in agreement. "Time to meet Queen Ginevra."

I jumped for the third time in as many minutes as a shoulder brushed against mine, my heart in my throat. It took several deep breaths before I could continue walking normally along the winding road up the mountain toward the peak of Kelvadan. I had been bracing myself for my introduction to the queen and had not expected the journey to the palace to be as overwhelming as meeting royalty might be. The walk from the middle tiers of Kelvadan (where Aderyn and Neven lived) to the peak where the palace was made my skin crawl. People were everywhere, barely having to look at each other as they went about their business in a complex choreography, coexisting but never getting in each other's way. Compared to the silence of the wilds, broken only by the rustling of wind in desert scrub and the occasional hoot of an Omani owl, Kelvadan was deafening. Voices sounded everywhere, and I found myself constantly distracted by stolen snippets of conversation, gone as fast as they had come in the whirlpool of human life around me. My heart rate jumped as somebody shouted a greeting from an open window.

We climbed through several tiers of the city, rising higher along the side of the mountain face. Finally, we walked through a broad set of metalwork gates into a much less densely populated courtyard. Across the open space stood a set of doors leading directly into the palace embedded into the side of the mountain, the top tier of the marvel that was Kelvadan, with a spire reaching high into the sky. I looked up at it, prepared to gawk at the incredible building, dotted with terraces and windows overlooking the city and the desert beyond.

Instead, my gaze caught on the statue in the middle of the courtyard. The stonework looked slightly different, as if it hadn't been hewn into the mountain like the rest of the city but added later. A man sat astride a magnificent horse, oversized saber raised overhead in a clear depiction of power. His face burned into my mind, proud, regal, and wearing a confident smile that held just enough mischief to keep the depiction from seeming stuffy. I craned my neck to keep looking at it as Aderyn led me toward the doors.

The guards flanking the entrance nodded respectfully and opened the doors for us, clearly recognizing Aderyn and deferring to her authority. Inside, I didn't know where to look, the decorations opulent yet elegant. Part of me had expected gaudy décor, but instead it spoke of understated luxury and beauty, wide windows letting in bright sunshine that gave the whole thing the feeling of being out of a dream.

Aderyn didn't give me time to admire the lush tapestries and simple stonework further, leading me up several staircases until we reached a wide terrace, set with a small table and chairs. Sitting at one of the chairs, reading something off a scroll while her other hand held a cut crystal glass, was one of the most stunning women I had ever seen.

While the lines at the corners of her eyes and the thick strands of gray shot through her brown hair indicated the years of her youth were long since past, the queen sat with an elegance that made me stand up straighter myself. The intricately woven hairstyle piled atop her head and flowing silver dress might have seemed ostentatious on anybody else, but she wore them naturally. Her poise might have made her seem stuffy if not for the genuine smile that lit her eyes when she looked up and spotted us in the doorway.

"Aderyn my dear, I didn't expect to see you until our meeting tomorrow!" She gestured to the empty chairs at the table before her gaze alighted on me. "And who did you bring with you?"

An uncomfortable silence stretched as I opened and closed my mouth a few times.

"Keera," I choked out. Hopefully introducing myself would get easier with practice, but it still came slowly to me. The silence where I would normally name my clan hung heavy in the air, but nobody seemed to notice.

"Keera came to the city from the desert earlier today, and she has some news I think you should hear." Aderyn took a seat in one of the sculpted metal chairs around the table, and I followed her lead.

My eyes snagged on a pitcher, following the path of a droplet of condensation down the outside of the blue glass vessel. The queen reached for the pitcher and poured a glass of the liquid within before offering it to me.

I blinked in shock and took it from her with a nod of thanks. The gesture of service, even from a queen, did more to unstick my throat than the swallow of sweet and tangy liquid within. I didn't recognize the flavor, but I instantly took another sip.

"What news from the sands?" the queen asked.

"Clan Katal, they plan to attack Kelvadan."

"Lord Alasdar? How do you know this?" The queen's lips turned down in a frown.

I told the queen all I had told Aderyn. When I finished, she sat back in her chair with a heavy sigh, still looking poised despite her slumped posture.

"When I heard of Lord Alasdar taking leadership of Clan Katal years back, I had hoped the position would satisfy his lust for power. After hearing nothing of him for years, I assumed my wish had come true. It seems I couldn't be further from correct." She tilted her head and observed me thoughtfully. "Did you hear how he is persuading the clans to unite? I doubt any lords would give up command of their own people easily."

"He claimed it was the only way to appease the desert and..." I chewed my chapped lips, thinking back to being tied to the stake as Lord Alasdar whipped the crowd into a fevered frenzy. The harsh metal mask as a saber dug into my throat. "He has a man. They called him the Viper. They seemed to fear him."

"The Viper? Our intelligence has not told us of anybody by that description, but our news of the clans is sparce." The queen frowned before schooling her expression back to concern. "Is the desert really so harsh these days?"

I looked down at my hands clasped in my lap, my ribs jutting out farther than I remembered even in years of exile. My struggles to survive hadn't been merely the result of my isolation. Herds were scarcer with every cycle of the moon, and even the oryx and wild boar I hunted had less meat on them than they used to. The hairs on the back of my neck stood on end at the visceral memory of lightning striking the sand in a supernatural storm. It certainly didn't take a great amount of imagination to believe that the desert was punishing those who lived there.

"The sands are not a kind place to live," I admitted. Even as I took a sip of my drink, reveling in the luxury of plentiful food and water, the words tasted off in my mouth. Survival had been difficult, but memories of my oasis—of the sun setting over the dunes, staining the whole world a burning gold—reminded me that the desert was a harsh but beautiful home. I frowned at thinking of the desert at home, when I was finally in the place I'd hoped to find belonging, but I brushed the thought away as the queen continued.

"Sands," the queen swore. "Perhaps I haven't been out of the city in too long. The Trials come soon though. They will be an opportunity to reconnect with the desert, sway the tribes into halting their aggression."

Aderyn nodded, and I filed away my questions about the Trials to ask later. The phrase sounded like something out of a memory, but there was so much about Kelvadan I did not yet know.

"You have travelled far and risked your life to bring us this information," the queen continued. "I would like to invite you to stay in the palace as a guest in thanks."

I sputtered into my drink for a moment as I choked on a response. I couldn't refuse a queen, but how could I keep my status as an exile secret right under her nose? Supposedly Kelvadan didn't turn away those without a clan, but it might lead to questions of why I had been exiled. If Queen Ginevra found out what I had done, my punishment might be worse than being sent out into the desert on my own once more. I had just been given a chance at the belonging I had always sought, and I couldn't bear to have it be ripped away so soon.

"After the trials she has endured, I think Keera would like to stay somewhere a little quieter to recover," Aderyn cut in, shooting me an unreadable look. "If she were to stay with you, I fear you would subject her to a few too many dinners with important visitors that ended in too much *laka* and impromptu dance performances."

"I like to keep my guests well entertained," the queen defended with an affronted sniff, although she did not seem truly offended. "I hope you will at least come to the festival next week then."

"Neven would never pass up having another model for his clothing."

"Just make sure neither of you wear anything more spectacular than what he has already made for me." Queen Ginevra pointed at each of us sternly.

I found myself smiling. Despite her regal appearance, the queen had a playful manner, so far from the clan lords I had become accustomed to.

Aderyn stood, and I copied her, quickly draining the dregs of my beverage before setting the empty glass on the table.

"We will discuss increasing Kelvan's security in our meeting tomorrow," Aderyn said. "For now, I should get Keera back to my home to rest."

"Of course, although I still hope for a diplomatic solution," the queen agreed, worry working its way back into her voice, a crease furrowing between her brows.

Aderyn bowed her head, rapping her knuckles to her brow in respect, before leading me off the balcony and back into the palace.

"I hope you don't mind me refusing the queen's invitation to stay on your behalf," she said once we were halfway down the stairs. "You seemed... overwhelmed."

I nodded. "I don't want to be an imposition to you and Neven though."

"You needn't worry. I'll barely be home this week as I supervise security arrangements for the festival next week, and Neven could use the company."

I thanked her for her hospitality, hoping they would not regret opening their home to me.

The following week was a mix of bliss and terror. I ate more than I had in memory, feeling strength seep into my wasted muscles after only a few days. As Aderyn left early each morning and returned late each night, Neven put me to work helping him with simple tasks in the room at the back of his house that served as a workshop. I watched him weave the most incredible textiles I could imagine, draping them into fashions I couldn't even conceive of as I fetched and carried.

He was easy and talkative, and his tendency for conversation made me wary he would pull a secret from me unbidden. Every time he asked me about myself, I deflected, asking him something about his work and setting him off on a cheery tangent for the next hour.

The crowded nature of the city also set me ill at ease. My heart raced at the proximity of strangers every time I stepped onto the street, and sweat collected at the small of my back beyond what I would expect from the dry heat. At first, I only ventured out into the chaos of the city to visit Daiti, who was indeed stabled a few blocks away.

The first time Aderyn took me to see him, the horse master sighed in relief.

"Thank the sands you're here. Could you calm him? I've barely been able to muck his stall without him trying to smash in my skull with those devilish hooves of his."

I frowned, approaching the stall. Daiti eagerly stuck his head over the gate, snuffling against my clothing and hair, although if to check my identity or find any hidden snacks, I couldn't be sure.

Aderyn chuckled. "You seem to have a well-trained warhorse. He won't respond to anybody but you."

I frowned as the stablemaster approached, causing Daiti to stamp and snort at him in displeasure. If Daiti was really this distrusting of strangers, it was a wonder I had been able to snag him from the enclosure so easily.

For now, I just nodded and continued to visit Daiti every day, bringing him samples of the strange fruit that Neven and Aderyn fed me. I myself ate so much of it that I became sick, but it didn't stop me from consuming enough that my stomach bulged after every meal. After all, I didn't know how much longer I would be able to stay here where food was plentiful. The truth of my exile hung like an axe over my head.

With the frequent walks through the city streets and my growing camaraderie with Neven, it became easier to be around people. I no longer started every time a shoulder brushed mine in the street, and I looked forward to dinner with Neven and Aderyn when she returned home.

Each night, as it grew later, the couple would shoot each other teasing looks, Aderyn's hand drifting to Neven's knee where he sat cross-legged on his cushion. Her hand drifted higher as he said something that made her laugh. I would look away with an odd pang in my chest.

I would excuse myself to go to bed in the small guest room at the back of the house, stealing myself for my least favorite part of my new routine. Lying on the impossibly soft bed, covered in a blanket with the texture of cloud, a weight landed on my chest.

Through the walls, I could hear giggling from Aderyn and Neven's bedroom, followed by a sharp, feminine gasp. Staring up at the ceiling, it seemed as though the rocky weight of the mountain above pressed down on me. From the couple next door enjoying each other's bodies to the crush of people living in every corner of this city, I was surrounded by humans. It was enough to feel claustrophobic, overwhelmed in the current of life around me.

But the worst part was not the number of people after so long in isolation. It was that it didn't seem enough to stem the loneliness that had taken hold inside my chest— as if watching friends and lovers after so long without made me more acutely aware of what I didn't have.

I didn't sleep the first night, and the second night, when my breath came in pants and gasps from the ache beneath my ribs, I sprang from the bed. Grabbing a pillow, I crept from the room and out of the house. With the stacked stone design of the building, it was easy work to climb to the roof, which was flat on top, serving as a step to the next level of the city.

There, I laid on my back, propping my head up on the pilfered pillow and looking up at the velvety sky. Warm wind brushed against my skin like ethereal fingers, the touch of the desert welcome in its familiarity in this alien environment. Even here in the city, so far from my oasis, the stars looked the same, and my breathing came easier as I counted them. Somehow, they eased the growing tightness in my chest and sleep found me.

On the third night, I had a dream of a type I hadn't had since I lived with Clan Padra, still learning what it meant to be a woman. In my sleep a man came to me and enveloped me in his arms, and instead of the feeling of too-tight skin that still sometimes overcame me at the touch of another, it felt warm and comforting. I breathed easily, but that changed when his lips met my neck and his hands drifted beneath my clothes. I tried to pull back and see his face, but the dream left me unable to move, helpless to his ministrations.

I woke gasping, just short of release, and disoriented. My hand drifted between my legs taking the place of my imaginary companion's even as I wondered what had triggered such a dream. Perhaps it was living in close quarters with the intimacy Aderyn and Neven shared. Either way, the dream had felt shockingly real, and as I gasped through my hasty pleasure, I wished I could picture the face of the man who had inspired such feelings, even if he was imaginary. Then, I shoved the feelings away, feeling lonelier than I had before, and tried to go back to sleep.

Each morning, I made sure I was back inside by the time Aderyn rose. While she looked at me oddly in the morning after the first night I spent on the roof, she didn't comment.

After being in Kelvadan for several days, Aderyn brought me to the palace once more. Infinitesimally less overwhelmed by the presence of others, I was better able to appreciate the impressive architecture of the massive structure. Located at the peak of the tiered city, multiple levels of terraces led up to a tower, many with vines of golden larrea flowers dripping from the railings. It gave the palace a lush feel despite its construction from the same grey stone as the rest of the city. At the very top, a spire pointed straight into the sky, reaching nearly the height of the mountain peak behind it.

"The queen has a few more questions for you now that she's had time to decide how to proceed with the news you gave her," Aderyn explained as we approached the main entrance and I could no longer see the top of the tower no matter how far back I craned my neck.

"I'm not sure how helpful I'll be, but I'll try." I gripped my elbows, trying to hide my consternation at what kind of questions the queen might ask. I hadn't been at Clan Katal's encampment very long, and had seen very little outside of the supply tent I'd been kept in. I wasn't keen on answering questions about where I had been before my capture either.

Today, Aderyn led me to a room instead of a terrace, and I shied away from being enclosed instead of in the open air. It reminded me of sleepless nights in Aderyn and Neven's guest room. I swallowed it down.

The queen was already in the room when we arrived, sitting at a long table strewn with papers, a man at her right. He wore a close-cropped beard, and the sharpness of his gaze combined with the high arch of his nose gave him the appearance of a hawk. As we approached, she looked up and beckoned us in. "Aderyn, Keera, please sit. This is Oren."

The man nodded, eyes darting over me appraisingly. I squared my shoulders.

"Keera, I need you to tell Oren everything you know about Clan Katal," Queen Ginevra explained. "He is going to their encampment to gather information."

I blinked. "A spy?"

"Hearing from you about Lord Alasdar's plans to attack made me realize how blind I've been to the activities of the clans. I hadn't even heard of the Viper you say is doing his bidding." the queen explained, her expression one of frustration. "I suggested once that the clans appoint ambassadors to the city, but the lords did not appreciate that, preferring only to communicate with me when necessary."

I exhaled through my nose in amusement, envisioning how the lords I had encountered would react to the suggestion of fussy diplomacy and diplomats. The clans of the desert negotiated through shows of strength and preferred to leave it that way.

The queen shot me a look, and I froze, worrying I had offended, but she raised a brow in amusement. "I see you understand the difficulty, but I'm not willing to continue operating blindly when the clans pose a threat to my people. That's where Oren comes in. Maybe if we can gather more information about Lord Alasdar's plans, we can stop this war before it even starts."

I looked at Oren once more, this time really taking him in. He met my examination with a crooked smile.

"I used to ride with Clan Ratan," he offered. "Hopefully I can convince my family that I want to join them once more, to infiltrate the riders at Clan Katal's encampment."

I nodded. It was better that somebody who had been among the clans before served as the spy instead of somebody born and raised in Kelvadan. Life here seemed so different, I wasn't sure I'd be able to explain the mindset of the clans to one who had never experienced it, or at least well enough for them to be able to join without arousing suspicion. It had been a while since I had ridden among the clans myself, but I still remembered the company in the encampment feeling different than the crush of life in Kelvadan. Among the clans, fires and stewpots were communal, where here everybody ate only with their families in their own houses. When I rode with Clan Padra, you traded what you had for what you needed, with honor and strength as the only currencies. Here in the city, Aderyn had been trying to teach me the values of the different coins and how they were exchanged for goods. Apparently, they were useful for trading with the handful of merchants who traveled from beyond the mountains but never ventured out of the city to trade with the clans.

Queen Ginevra spoke, drawing my attention back to the present. "I know you told me that Clan Ratan was the latest to join Lord Alasdar. Do you know which other clans are at his encampment?"

I shook my head. The only reason I knew of Clan Ratan's presence was that I had been present on the day of their arrival.

Oren and Queen Ginevra took turns asking me questions about the encampment, although I only had the answer to about one in ten. I shifted uncomfortably in my chair. Perhaps my lack of information would make them think that I was lying and turn me out into the desert. Maybe they would think that I was the spy.

Aderyn, who had remained quiet through the whole conversation, reached across the table and poured a glass of water from a pitcher resting between us. She offered it to me, and as I took it, she met my gaze, giving me a reassuring nod.

She didn't smile, but the firmness of her gaze settled me. I didn't know what I had done to earn her friendship, but I appreciated it all the same.

I continued answering their questions as best I could, racking my brain for any detail I may have forgotten in the chaos of my escape from Clan Katal. If I could help Kelvadan in any small way, after Aderyn and Neven and even the queen had shown me such kindness, then I would. I didn't know if there were any other exiles sustained by the dream of Kelvadan, but I would not let the potential of life in the Great City be stolen from them.

Soon, the questions turned toward Lord Alasdar himself.

"Do you know who in the clan might be close to him? Close enough to be trusted with important information?" Oren asked.

I swallowed. "There was... a man."

Queen Ginevra nodded encouragingly.

I searched my mind for the right words to describe the man in the mask. My memory stuck on the image of his strong silhouette as he led the riders in saber drills, but that felt like the wrong information to volunteer.

"He rides a black horse," I started instead, "and he wears a strange mask. I think he oversees training the riders."

"The Viper you mentioned? Do you know his name?" Queen Ginevra asked.

I shook my head. "Lord Alasdar only called him the Viper."

"This mask, does he wear it all the time?"

I nodded. I had first encountered him without it, but I had come upon him while he was sleeping. He had put it on almost immediately, and the fact that I had seen his face was something I was strangely hesitant to admit. The strange intimacy of meeting his silver eyes in the moonlight felt like a private moment, and I was loathe to recount it to anybody else.

"If he is in charge of the riders, this Viper might be a good place to start," Oren observed, running a hand over his dark, close-cropped beard.

"There's another rider as well," I spoke up. "Her name is Izumi. I don't know much about her"—I hesitated, unsure what I meant to say, but envisioning her feeding me every day—"but she is not unkind."

"Perhaps she might be helpful," the queen said.

They continued to ask questions until my head spun and my voice nearly gave out. When they were finally finished though, the queen clasped my hand in both of hers and gave me a warm smile with a sincere "thank you".

I found myself smiling at her kindness. A lord could demand answers without offering any gratitude, but her acknowledgment warmed me. A spark of happiness ran through me at the thought that the desert had spared my life so I could help save the inhabitants of this city. I only hoped that the help I could offer would be enough.

I woke up on my eighth day in Kelvadan to anticipation in the air. The excitement came in the form of chattering and music on every corner. While the residents of the city never shied away from color, today every person seemed to wear their brightest attire and every piece of jewelry they owned. The effect was as enamoring as it was dizzying as I wove my way down the block on my way back from a visit with Daiti. His presence calmed me as I worried about Oren, hoping that my warning would be enough to help Kelvadan withstand the clans. I wished I could help more but held myself in check for fear of revealing too much about my past.

"I was afraid you wouldn't get home in time for us to dress you for the festival," Neven worried as I pushed my way into the relative quiet of their residence. I blinked at the sight of Aderyn draped in pale-blue silk. A golden collar fastened the dress around her neck, the folds dripping like water down her torso to a golden belt gathering the fabric to her waist. Her arms and back were left completely bare, showing off more thick stripes of black ink tracing down her spine and down from her shoulders to the back of her hands. Even her eyes had been outlined in thick black kohl, making them stand out dramatically in her pale face.

"You look incredible," I complimented, as Neven retrieved a pile of purple silk from the couch I had woken on a week ago.

"Neven's textiles make me feel incredible, even though they aren't practical to wear during daily training or patrols," she admitted.

"And sands do you look beautiful in them, even if you hide the way they drape by strapping on a dozen weapons."

Aderyn patted the handle of the curved dagger at her waist with a smile. "I know for a fact you find the number of weapons I carry attractive."

I coughed behind my hand, and Neven peeled his gaze away from Aderyn to look at me. He shook out the fabric in his hands, and my eyes widened at what he had picked for me to wear to the festival.

He and Aderyn spent the next several minutes wrapping me in one long continuous strip of cloth, as my outfit turned out to be. I watched curiously as Neven affixed the end at my hip with a long silver pin, decorated with the emblem of a rearing horse, wondering at the style.

"I practice the sacred weaving techniques of our people, making the fabrics of Kelvadan the finest most travelers have ever seen," Neven explained in response to my curious expression. "Sometimes it seems a shame to cut and sew something I consider a piece of art in and of itself, so I've designed many ways to wear the swathes of fabric as I create them. You have to let the fabric tell you what it wants to be."

I nodded my understanding, awestruck by the way the cloth dripped over my body disguising the sharp hipbones and ribs that were already softening after a week in Kelvadan. The amethyst color brought out the golden undertones in my light brown skin. Once I was dressed, I sat still while Aderyn braided a matching purple scarf into my hair, using the end of the strip to tie it in place.

"Now you're ready to dance and drink too much *laka*," she proclaimed proudly as I laced up a pair of sandals, slightly too tight as they were borrowed from Aderyn. While she certainly outweighed me in muscle, I was taller, and my feet were larger.

"What exactly is the purpose of the festival?" I asked as we left and joined the chaos of citizens making revelry in the street, a steady flow climbing the streets up toward the palace.

"Purpose? Does one need a purpose for a party?" Neven asked with a smile.

Aderyn elbowed him, but he didn't flinch, indicating she hadn't put her significant muscle behind the action. "It's the yearly celebration of the anniversary of Kelvadan's building."

"How was a city like this built? I would think it took years." I looked up at the buildings each set into the mountainside like jewels in the hilt of a sword, the road up through the city weaving back and forth as it ascended toward the spire of the palace at the precipice.

Neven's eyes twinkled in excitement. "We wouldn't want to tell you and spoil everything. The queen recites the story of Kelvadan's founding at the palace's celebration every year, and she tells it better than anybody."

My curiosity piqued, I looked to Aderyn, but neither of them said any more on the matter. When we reached the palace, the general atmosphere of revelry was at its peak. The gates to the front courtyard were thrown open, partygoers milling about the large stone space as they joked and laughed. Aderyn led us through the crowds, past the horseback statue that served as the centerpiece. I glanced up at his face again, my eyes inexorably drawn to his strong jaw and quirked brow. He had been decorated for the festival, a crown of golden larrea flowers woven around his head and draped over his horse's neck.

At a table near the wall of the palace, Neven fetched us drinks. He handed me a mug and I sniffed curiously. Something floral and spicy met my nose, the liquid a pale yellow, almost completely clear.

"The queen always breaks out the good *laka* for the festival every year, so enjoy Kelvadan's finest while you can," Neven urged.

Taking a sip, it coated my tongue and warmed my belly in a way that wasn't uncomfortable despite the balminess of the night. The liquid was nutty and bitter, but not in an unpleasant way. I remembered nights of adults drinking *laka* and laughing in my clan, but I had been too young to partake and had never tried it before.

Aderyn and Neven milled through the crowd with me at their

elbow as I nursed my drink. Nearly everybody seemed to recognize them, and I found myself introduced to more people than I had even imagined lived in the city. I nodded and smiled at each of them, trying to store names in my already overcrowded brain and failing miserably. Just as I was about to give up on the endeavor altogether, a hush fell over the crowd.

I followed their collective gazes to the palace doors, which swung open to reveal a shimmering figure. Queen Ginevra stepped forward to stand at the top of the handful of steps leading up to the doors. I hadn't realized it when we met before, but she was short enough that even elevated a few steps, her head didn't come much higher than the taller men in the crowd. Still, with the braziers on either side of the door flanking her, firelight shimmering off her silks until she looked like a statue of molten gold, she captured everybody's attention in an iron grip.

She raised her arms, and the whispering hush turned to total silence, as if everybody held their breath in anticipation of her words.

"Nearly two hundred years ago, something completely ordinary and yet utterly miraculous happened," the queen started. "Two people fell in love."

My brows rose, and I leaned forward as if I could get closer to the queen's words.

"Kelvar was a great rider of Clan Katal, blessed with the desert's magic beyond what many had seen before. Enemies fell before him like grain before a scythe, and many came to fear his clan. The lord of Clan Katal rejoiced in the power it gave him, sending Kelvar to attack Clan Padra and steal away the lord's daughter, for he coveted many of their riches.

"Kelvar did as his lord asked, and stole away the lord's daughter, Alyx, in the dead of night. On the ride back to Clan Katal, Kelvar's mount stepped into a fox hole and injured his leg. Kelvar was so bonded to his loyal mount that he refused to end its life. Seeing this, Alyx, who was blessed by the desert in her own way with a gift for healing, tended to the horse. During their delay, they came to know each other better, and one of the greatest bonds ever known to the Ballan Desert was born.

"When they returned to Clan Katal, Kelvar told his lord that he refused to ransom Alyx back to her father and planned to marry her instead. Alyx sent word to her father as well, but both lords refused them, threatening the couple with exile if they went through with the wedding.

"Kelvar grew full of rage that the warring ways of the clans would get in the way of love, a power greater than all of them. He called upon the magic of the desert for a feat greater than any that had been seen before. At the base of the mountains where the clans had camped, the desert reshaped herself at his command. All the clans spread across the sands to the sea felt the ground shake as a city carved itself into the side of the mountain, a safe place for Kelvar and Alyx to make a life together.

"He declared the city would be a safe place for members of any clan to come together without war or violence. It was a new beginning for the clans of the Ballan Desert. On that day, my grandfather, Kelvar, became the first king of this city, which was named in his honor."

The queen flung out an arm, gesturing to the statue in the middle of the square. Looking now, I saw the same determined set of her jaw as the horseman, Kelvar, wore.

"Tonight, we celebrate not only Kelvar and Alyx, my grandparents, but what this haven they built stands for. It was carved with the magic of the desert in the name of their bond. So let us celebrate the gifts Kelvadan represents: peace, magic, and the greatest of all, love."

The crowd roared and stamped in approval, glasses lifted in the air before all drank deeply in agreement. I myself drained the remaining contents of my glass, the warmth of the alcohol drowning out the sudden stinging behind my eyes.

At a wave from the queen, musicians I hadn't noticed before at the side of the square began playing. The noise of pounding drums, overcut by a cheerful melody from a wooden flute, filled the air. If I thought the atmosphere had been celebratory before, it was nothing compared to the joy in the air as people began to dance. Neven and Aderyn quickly drifted away, her hands thrown in the air as she moved to the music. Neven's gaze seemed glued to her, his hands drifting to her waist.

The beat of the drums filled my blood as I accepted another cup of *laka,* and I found myself swaying along to the music as I watched the rhythmic movements of the sea of dancers. The sun had set, and colored lanterns and flickering braziers lit the courtyard, giving the whole place a dreamlike atmosphere.

As I finished my second glass of *laka*, a hand landed on my elbow. I didn't start like I might have, the atmosphere and the alcohol making my body molten and pliant. Looking to see who asked for my attention, I found the smiling face of a man Aderyn had introduced me to earlier. My brain was too fuzzy to call forth a name, but I remember a joke he told making me laugh.

"It's not a true festival if you don't dance just a little," he commented, talking loudly to be heard over the increasing volume of the music.

"I don't know how," I nearly shouted back.

He grinned. "Neither do I, but that's not really the point."

I found myself smiling and nodding back, letting him take my empty cup to set on a nearby ledge before leading me toward the center of the courtyard, near the statue where the dancing was most lively.

Following the lead of the figures around me, I started swaying gently to the beat. The man moved with me, and I found myself grinning, my heartrate quickening to pump in time to the drums. As we began dancing in earnest with no real finesse, I threw my arms up in the air, and a laugh bubbled up. Maybe it was the alcohol, or the feeling the queen's tale had roused in me, but I felt more alive than I had in a while —since a strange man held my throat in his hand, pinning me with an intensity that turned me to fire.

As I twirled in delight, purple silk forming a swirl around me, my eyes caught on the imposing statue once more. My gaze met his sightless eyes, and something shifted—something that had lain dormant inside me since my exile and had only began to move again recently. My partner's hand on my hip suddenly felt overwhelming once more as touch had been when I first arrived in the city. Instead of being carried away by the beat of the drums, they pushed in on me, more tightly than the thick stone walls of Aderyn's home when I was alone in the dark.

I tripped over my feet in the too-small sandals, smooth silk rubbing against my skin like hot sand. My dance partner caught me by the elbow before I fell, but I jerked away stumbling once more. He frowned, but his expression was one of concern.

"Too much *laka*?" he shouted over the crowd. "Let's find somewhere for you to sit down."

I nodded, not sure if it was the alcohol or something else entirely making me feel as if I were about to burst out of my skin. The man cut a swath through the crowd, but the dancers were densely packed, and the going was slow. Bodies bumped and jostled me, and I flinched away from each touch as if it burned. The edge of the courtyard where I spied a bench seemed miles away, and even there I would be surrounded by this constant noise.

I couldn't wait for my partner to edge through politely anymore, striking out on my own as shoved through the crowd. I needed to get out. Now.

Unsure how it happened, I broke free of the dancing horde and stumbled toward the open front door of the palace. Guards flanked it, shouting at me that guests must stay in the courtyard, but the hallway called my name as there were no revelers within.

Too-small sandals pinched my feet as they smacked against the stone floor of the palace hallway as I ran deeper. I had only made it twenty yards before I tripped and fell to my knees with tooth-jarring force. The sudden pain in my shins and palms almost ripped me from my fugue, but it was not enough.

My vision narrowed, and at first, I thought the guards shouting after me stopped, but as they barreled down on me, I realized my hearing had disappeared. Instead, I felt the vibrations from stomping feet through the stone beneath me, and the air whispered over my skin like a physical touch.

The heartbeats of hundreds of people echoed in my head, just as loudly as the shuffle of a Fennec fox burrowing in the sand miles away. My surroundings fell away, and the sensations in my mind grew until I was sure my skull would explode, if I even still had a physical form.

A blast of scouring wind and a piercing scream brought me back to myself with a snap. I was on my knees, in the palace hallway, and the screaming came from me. The guards who had chased me lay on the floor, as if knocked over by a sudden earthquake. Everything was preternaturally dark and quiet as the wind stopped, having extinguished all the lanterns hanging from sconces on the walls. The only light came from the braziers outside the distant door, barely penetrating the shadows.

As I blinked, trying to clear my head, the guards stared at me. I swallowed, my throat raw. A shuffling broke the stillness as a figure approached from the still open door.

Panic gripped me, threatening to paralyze me, but I forced myself to move. I looked up to find the queen staring down at me, eyes dark in the shadow, something unreadable on her face.

CHAPTER NINE
THE VIPER

C lan Tibel's encampment was quiet as I approached. I half
expected a greeting with more soldiers and walked beside Alza
with my saber drawn, but no riders charged me. However, the
camp was much larger than I'd expected, even larger than the one I had
left, of Clan Katal joined with three others.

Standing at the edge of the tents lining the camp stood five figures,
three men and two women, all wearing leather armor and bearing
swords, although none were drawn. They all had their hands clasped
behind their back, posture stiff. I walked right up to them, not halting
until I was a horse length away.

"I come with an offer for Clan Tibel from Lord Alasdar of Clan
Katal," I started without preamble.

"We know why you've come, Viper." The man in the middle practically spat my title. His blue sash marked him as a belonging to Clan
Tibel, and the gold inlay on the handle of the dirk at his waist made me
guess he was the lord I had come to treat with. The others all had
different color sashes, and I frowned beneath my mask.

"Then you will also know that it would be unwise to refuse me."

The falcon chose that moment to emit a soft squawk and ruffle its wings, as if in reminder of the fate that met his former master. The lord of Clan Tibel glanced at the bird, expression hardening even further.

"And you would be unwise to assume that the remaining clans of the Ballan Desert will be so easily bullied," cut in one of the women bearing the maroon sash of Clan Padra.

"The five clans of the Ballan Desert that have not joined with Lord Alasdar stand together. We do not wish to join your war," cut in another of the men, a scar running across his jaw giving him away as a hardened warrior.

I stared, realizing that the five people before me were the five lords of the remaining clans, all gathered before me in a unified front. Magic surged within me at the realization, anger that they would stand against Clan Katal, against the Viper, bubbling beneath my skin. Sand at my feet began to rise unbidden, the start of a whirlwind forming around my calves.

"If you raze our encampment, it will not sway us to your cause," the lord of Clan Tibel claimed, even as the whole group stepped back from the crackle in the air around me, the earthy smell of magic rising. They could likely sense the magic of the desert and harness it to some degree, the lord of Clan Padra better than most if I were to judge by the glimmer of blood glass on the hilt of her saber. Still, while they had the prowess to lead their clans in battle, none of them would be able to stand against my fury if it came unleashed.

I blinked to clear my vision, which threatened to blur out in the flare of magic I fought to contain. While I held the hilt of my saber in one hand, I gripped the blade in the other, squeezing until the sharp edge bit into my palm, pushing away the sensation of the desert in my mind that threatened to overwhelm me. I could not fail in this mission and destroy those I needed to be my allies.

"If you know of my cause, then you know why Lord Alasdar seeks to unite the clans," I grit out.

"We know the desert becomes harsher by the day," the lord of Clan Padra conceded, "but it could be Lord Alasdar fashioning himself as a false Champion of the Desert that has stirred her ire."

"The desert has no Champion," I spat. It was an absence felt by all the clans, but Clan Katal most sharply of all. After the last Trials, the competition held every twenty years to crown the desert's Champion, no winner had emerged.

"Perhaps that is why she is angry."

"Even if it is, Kelvadan must fall. The city has taken over the Trials so no true Champion of the Desert may emerge. The abandonment of the old ways, of the clans, where strength and survival were the only rules, has made her angry," I argued. It was the truth, but only part of it. Kelvadan had ushered in an era of peace between the clans, when the constant struggle for power was inherent to the old ways. I knew why it was imperative that Kelvadan fall to restore the glory of the desert, but that secret belonged to me and Lord Alasdar alone.

The lords before me seemed unconvinced.

"Surely you have felt the magic stirring."

The lord of Clan Padra shifted on her feet.

"On my way here, I was attacked by a Sichat. You can still see its claw marks on my horse's leg. I managed to fell it, but how many lesser riders would it kill? How long before other creatures of legend, lava wyrms and flying terrors, rise and attack the clan? We must do something." My voice remained firm, and I pushed aside the notion that I was begging. The Viper did not lower himself.

The assembled leaders looked between themselves. They too had sensed the growing sense of foreboding in the magic holding the desert together. It had begun years ago, so subtle that nobody could pinpoint the day it first appeared. Perhaps something had always been there and was just amplified so those sensitive to it could notice. By now, it was so pronounced that even those not attuned to the magic of the desert could feel the heaviness in the air, the thick sense of a threat lingering just over the next horizon.

"We will only follow the true Champion. We will not risk angering her further by uniting the clans under one who has not been victorious in the Trials," the lord of Clan Tibel declared.

I gritted my teeth. If the old ways had been upheld, Lord Alasdar would have been victorious in the Trials twenty years ago, but the weakness of Kelvadan kept him from being crowned Champion. Before the founding of Kelvadan, the Trials had been fights to the death, the duels conducted in the old ways of the clans. Now, those who killed their opponents were expelled from the competition.

"The Trials are a farce," I argued.

"The Trials are one of the oldest traditions of the clans, from far before Kelvadan was carved from the mountainside. While they may be held in Kelvadan and presided over by the queen now, if you claim to follow the old ways, you would be wise to honor them as tradition," the man with the scar interjected.

"The Trials are to be held at the end of the dry season, a few new moons from now. If a Champion emerges, we will unite in this war against Kelvadan," the lord of Clan Tibel announced.

"Lord Alasdar would not be permitted to enter." I gripped my sword tightly again, the bite of metal against my gloved palm keeping me from losing patience with the conversation.

The lord of Clan Padra tilted her head, and the hint of a smirk toyed with the edge of her lips. "You could enter the Trials, Viper. If you are as fearsome as the rumors say, then you should be able to best all the competitors and emerge victorious."

I stiffened, remaining silent. The Trials were months away and the desert was fraying faster by the day. I was wary of visiting Kelvadan without an army in tow—and without Lord Alasdar.

"These are the only terms we will accept. You must win the Ballan Trials, or we will not join with Clan Katal," the man with the scar declared. They had clearly discussed this prior to my arrival.

"Your clans will be vulnerable until then," I pointed out.

"It is why we have camped together." The lord of Clan Padra folded her arms. "Our numbers are even greater than what you boast at Clan Katal's encampment."

My gaze darted down the line of clan leaders, and I knew this was the only way forward without killing many riders who would be needed if the clans were to ride against Kelvadan.

"Then it's agreed."

I would ride in the Trials.

As much as I would have rather rode out that night, camping on my own somewhere in the wilderness, I found myself accepting the lord's begrudging invitation to stay at their combined encampment. We had settled on a truce of sorts with our agreement, and so there was a hesitant peace. More importantly though, as healed as Alza was, she could benefit from another day or two before we set out.

I spent a long while tending to Alza in the enclosure a rider showed me to keep her in. I brushed her out, ensuring she obtained arrowgrass and water, muttering praises to her under my breath as I fussed. At one point, the horse master had approached me, offering to look at the wounds on her leg for me.

Rounding on him, I glared for a moment, prepared to shoo away anybody who would dare touch Alza. I had been raised to take care of horses and knew how to treat many of their ailments.

In the face of my silent stare, the horse master began to back away, hands raised.

"Wait."

He paused. I chewed on my tongue. He would have supplies I did not carry on the road.

"I do not want her wounds to become infected."

The horse master nodded. "I can prepare a poultice to cleanse her wounds. I'll add something for the pain and swelling as well."

I stayed with Alza until he returned, taking the bowl of greenish paste from his hands. He hovered as if he had planned to apply it himself.

"She's rather particular," I offered by way of explanation.

With that, he nodded and scurried away.

"Thank you," I offered to his retreating back, and he froze as if he hadn't expected my gratitude. Then he retreated to the far side of the enclosure where the other horses gathered.

By the time Alza's wounds had been tended to my satisfaction, the sun was dipping below the horizon. I grabbed my packs, resting on the ground near the fence, and headed off to pitch my tent at the edges of the encampment. My small structure, the bare minimum needed for privacy when traveling, looked meager compared to the larger tents of families and riders—those tents had been erected for an encampment that would be in place for weeks if not months near a water source before picking up and moving to follow the game they hunted.

As I finished driving the spikes to support my shelter into the ground, the fluttering of wings caught my attention. The falcon had flown off when I entered the encampment, and I suspected it would find a new master among the clan it had once camped with. Instead, he settled near me now, looking at me expectantly. I exhaled heavily through my nose.

Before I could tell the animal that I had no food for him, and he would have to hunt for himself, shrieking split the air. I dropped the folded canvas bundled in my arms, leaving my tent half erected as I dashed toward the noise.

I found the source of the commotion easily enough. A young woman lay on the ground, bleeding out of a deep gash in her leg. A man crouched over her, long, curved dagger drawn as his eyes flickered between the injured woman and the darkness beyond the edge of the encampment.

Others had come running as well, and now a shouting mass of confusion surrounded them.

"What attacked her?" someone shouted. "Is it caracals? Red wolves?"

The man shook his head, eyes narrowed as if trying to pick out a shape in the night that had fallen around us. I looked in the direction he stared.

"It was so fast. I didn't see it. It looked like...a skeleton."

The voices scoffed in unison at his admission.

"You sneak off with a woman to steal a kiss, and it turns your head so bad you can't recognize a beast."

"Attacked by a skeleton?"

I would have been ready to join them in their disbelief if it hadn't been for the image of glowing purple eyes set in a too-long feline body. Just the day before I had been attacked by a creature of legend. Who knew what prowled the sands at night?

Turning and scanning the crowd, I found a man holding a torch. I snatched it out of his hand before he could protest. He opened his mouth to argue, but upon seeing my mask, his snapped it shut.

"I'll find what attacked her," I volunteered. The assembled crowd quieted, mocking derision turning to hushed whispers as I drew my saber. With a blade in one hand and a torch in the other, I marched out into the sands.

My boots sunk into the soft powder as I trudged, holding my light aloft. Either it would help me get a good look at my quarry, or it would scare off any lingering predators. It was odd that a caracal or a red wolf would attack an encampment, but if hunting grew difficult for the clans, then it would for other predators as well.

A muffled scuffle behind me drew my attention, and I whirled around, pointing the light in the direction of the noise. I was greeting by only blank sand. Still, the sensation of something skirting just around my pool of light persisted.

I continued further away from the encampment, assuming most animals would be scared away by the large group of people now gathered at the edge. Even in times of duress, a predator would prefer to pick off one or two individuals lingering on the outskirts.

By now, I could no longer hear the speculation of the clansmen I had left behind. Another scratching noise grabbed my attention, and I spun in a circle, trying in vain to catch sight of my prey. Seeing nothing, I stilled, slowing even my own breathing to catch any sound of it in the darkness. All that greeted me was the distinct scent of the desert after rain.

I tensed the moment before it was upon me. It wasn't enough, knocking the torch out of my hand as I used the momentum of my fall to roll out of its grasp. With the light from the flame low and scattered, I couldn't get a good look at the creature as I sprang to my feet. As I thrust my saber out in front of me, creating a barrier between me and my attacker, I got the vague sense of too many limbs and a clattering of bones.

The flickering fire only gave me the vague impression of a writhing mass before it charged once more. Waiting until the last possible second, I side stepped, turning as I did to strike out at its side. My blade connected with a thump, and a disembodied limb fell to the ground. For a moment of stomach-clenching horror, it registered as an emaciated human arm before I was distracted by another claw-like appendage swiping at my face.

The metal of my mask deflected the blow, although it screeched across the metal at a pitch that made my teeth ache. I parried the next blow, a kick from what looked like the skeletal foreleg of a horse.

The next series of blows came too fast to follow, faster than would be possible with two appendages, or even four. Still, the shape of the creature eluded me. As I backed up, unable to block or parry every strike, I tripped over a snakelike tail thrust behind my ankles.

I toppled to the ground, wind rushing from my lungs. I didn't have time to catch my breath before rolling to the side to avoid being trampled by the charging creature. As it changed course, I turned this way and that, avoiding the stomping of too many feet, one landed on my hand, knocking my saber away.

Weaponless, I cast around for my sword, but the creature drove me away from where I had dropped it. In the darkness, I couldn't spot it to make my way back to it. Instead, my gaze caught on the torch, still burning fitfully in the sands a few arms' lengths away from me. I rolled onto my stomach and pushed to my elbows, pulling myself toward it as fast as I could. I dodged quickly to the left as a whistle by my ear warned me of an incoming attack but kept my eye on my goal.

Right before I could reach the torch, a heavy weight landed between my shoulder blades. My forehead hit the ground as I was pinned down. I thrust my arm out in the direction of the torch as the force shoved me down. The wooden handle just scraped my fingertips.

With the adrenaline coursing through my veins, the leash on my magic was already lose, and the barest hint of my power was all it took to draw the torch the last inches into my hand. It was as if the threads connecting everything in the desert pulled taught to bring the world into alignment.

I swung at it blindly, and the weight on my back lifted. Not wasting a moment, I rolled onto my back, waving the lit torch before me. The creature reared back from the flames, and I got my first good look at it.

A shapeless mass of tattered flesh served as the centroid for a nauseating amalgamation of limbs. Arms and legs from every type of human and beast imaginable sprouted from the central body at disjointed angles. While some were fleshy, most were skeletal, or only had the barest hints of skin hanging from ravaged bone.

Whatever the creature was, it seemed to fear fire. It lifted many of its limbs as if to shield itself from the light, although I saw no eyes. Before I could take advantage of its retreat and scuttle the rest of the way out from under it, the creature seemed to recover from the shock of the light. It fell on me once more.

Without a blade in hand, I did the only thing I could think of. I shoved the lit torch as hard as I could through the mass of writhing limbs into the creature's center. A horrible screeching split the air, although I did not know from where, since the creature didn't appear to have a mouth. It tried to writhe away from me, but I followed it, pressing the torch into it until the stench of rotting flesh filled the air.

After an eternity of twitching, the creature finally fell limp, nearly pinning me beneath it. I just managed to pull back in time to avoid the brunt of its weight. By now, my torch was mostly extinguished, smothered by the creature's flesh and leaving me in the dark. Only the glimmer from the camps braziers a way off and the silvery moon lit my actions as I pushed to my feet. Carefully, I felt around for my saber, finding it a few paces away; I was steadied by its weight in my hand. I kept it unsheathed, not knowing if there may be more of the creatures.

Turning back to my felled enemy, I considered the lifeless lump for a long moment before bending to sling it over my shoulders. It was an awkward affair, as misshapen as it was, but I managed to load it onto my back.

With the monstrosity in tow and my blade in hand, I trekked back to the encampment.

By the time I arrived, the group I left had doubled in size. They had to have heard the creatures screeching in its death throes. At the front of the crowd stood the lords of the five clans.

I dumped the creature at their feet with a clatter of bones.

Gasps greeted the sight of misshapen limbs, all attached at the center as if by a deranged doll maker. The lords hid their shock well, but the lord from clan Padra didn't completely suppress her wince. It was not lost on me that none of them had come to aid me in the fight, although the noise of battle would have easily carried through the night to the encampment. Perhaps they thought I would be killed, and our bargain would be void.

"A bone spider," the lord of Clan Tibel observed dispassionately, although he could not fully hide the edge of concern in his voice.

Now that he said it, the term knocked a memory loose, a tale from an old scroll in a stone library. All sorts of monsters roamed the desert before the first man crossed it, claiming the magic and the right to live here for the clans. Old texts described lava wyrms and flying terrors, but the bone spiders had been hard to picture. Now I could see why: they defied explanation.

The old scroll I had come across while searching for explanation of the power that flowed through me said they were born as faceless, directionless masses of flesh. They roamed aimlessly, stealing the limbs off corpses and out of graves, attaching them to its form without rhyme or reason. As it collected limbs, it grew bolder, attacking living beings to take their limbs too, adding to the overwhelming mass of bones and rotting flesh.

Somebody at the back of the crowd retched.

"The day before yesterday I confronted a Sichat, and now a bone spider attacks your clans. Legends are waking, and the desert is angry." I stabbed my saber at the fallen creature in emphasis.

"All the more reason we must protect our own people and not waste our riders on useless wars," the lord of Clan Padra said, folding her arms across her chest.

"Perhaps the terrors will cease when a true Champion of the Desert rises." The lord of Clan Otush fixed me with hard eyes. "After all, she has been without for too long."

"The desert will have her Champion."

The ride back to Clan Katal was thankfully less eventful than the journey to Clan Tibel. Alza whickered happily, ears pricking forward at the sounds of clashing steel as riders trained drifted toward us.

While I knew Lord Alasdar would be waiting for news, especially after our trip had been longer than expected, I rode to the enclosure where the horses were kept first and tended to Alza. I wasn't willing to leave her to the horse master of the clan after her injury, preferring to tend her myself. While the man may be competent enough, my father had taught me to take care of my mounts better than most. For a moment, I could picture my father bending over a new foal in the Kelvadan stables with a fond smile on his face.

I forcefully shook the errant thought from my head and focused on examining Alza's hooves for any cracks, satisfied when I found none. As I finished unloading my packs of gear from her back, the falcon that had perched on the bundles fluttered away to hunt. I didn't pay him much mind, sure he would be back. He had flown away several times on the long ride, only to reappear later and perch on my shoulder, once with the tail of a lizard dangling from his beak.

I brushed through Alza's mane once more, and she head butted me in the chest, as if telling me to stop worrying over her and let her eat her arrowgrass in peace.

She snorted in response to my giving her nose one last pat before trudging off to Lord Alasdar's tent. As expected, he was already sitting at his table, perusing a parchment when I arrived.

"I take it Clan Tibel will be arriving in a few days?" he asked, glancing up from his table.

I swallowed. I did not take failing Lord Alasdar lightly.

"Clan Tibel was not alone when I arrived," I started, kneeling on a rug across the low table from him. His gaze snapped up to mine. He met my eyes through the slit in the mask, something very few people did, making me feel exposed. The woman, Keera, had been the same. I blinked at the sudden thought of her.

"What other clan was present?" he asked sharply.

"All of them that are not yet here. They had heard of our endeavors and joined together so they would not be intimidated by Clan Katal."

The candles and lanterns in the enclosed space all flared brighter as Lord Alasdar slammed an open hand on the table. His own magic tugged on its tether in his ire, and I could feel it thicken in the air around me. Still, he succeeded in controlling his more tightly than I did, free of the incessant whispering clouding his mind. He had taught me how to control my magic better, but I could never rid myself of the constant noise of the desert.

"Five clans would still not be able to stand against my might," he spat out.

"Nor mine, but I did not want to decimate forces we will need to destroy Kelvadan."

"So you let them defy me?" Lord Alasdar's eyes sparked. I bowed my head.

"I made a deal. They said they would follow the Champion of the Ballan Trials. I will be that Champion."

The fire remained in his gaze even as he cocked his head. "They would join with Clan Katal if you are the one who wins the Trials."

"I am your sword," I admitted honestly. If he would simply point me in a direction, I would kill whomever he wished. I was the Viper and little else. "Besides, you are the rightful Champion to anybody who follows the old ways already."

This seemed to placate Lord Alasdar, and he leaned back on his hands, although his eyes remained narrowed as he observed me.

"You will have to go to Kelvadan for the Trials, be under the queen's watchful eye."

"I will do what I must," was my only reply. I did not relish camping in the shadow of the city for the duration of the Trials, but I had endured worse. Lord Alasdar had ensured I could be strong.

He nodded, expression already shuttering off. I could nearly see him recalculating his plan, always the one who was two steps ahead, allowing me to simply be a weapon.

"You will need to continue training the riders in the meantime and shape the forces we have already into a force that can take on Kelvadan. We can't afford to be starting from scratch when the rest of the clans arrive. I expect to see you conditioning them every day until the Trials."

I understood the command as the dismissal it was and nodded my assent before departing. Alza and I had ridden all day to get back to the encampment, and now the shadows of the tents stretched long across orange-stained sands as the sun dipped toward the horizon.

As night fell, I sat in my tent, sharpening my saber and my dirk. The encampment stirred outside with people cooking around communal fires, riders coming back from a day of training to linger in groups. A feminine giggle from a joke some warrior told drifted through the fabric of my tent flap. I dragged the whetstone more forcefully across the long, subtle curve of my saber, drowning out the sounds of camaraderie with the metallic *shink*. The whisper in my mind grew louder, as if trying to call out to me even as I ignored it.

Nights like these reminded me why I preferred camping in the wilds with only Alza for company. Hearing people around me only reminded me how I was other—the Viper charged with leading the riders but never one of them.

It made me want to leave on my mask, the constant physical representation of my separation from those around me. The exhaustion from my travels wore on me, and I chided myself, unfastening the metal from my face. Tonight, I would rest, and in the morning, I would train alongside the riders of the united clans, continuing with my mission of healing the shattered desert.

Just as darkness was about to overtake me, blissfully silencing my mind, my heart stuttered in my chest. I shot bolt upright as magic surged through me, unbidden and without warning. My skull was too small for the power that surged in my head, and I plunged my hands into my hair tugging at it like it would alleviate some of the pressure.

I screwed my eyes shut, leashing my magic through sheer force of will, as if I was taming a wild horse, just as I had Alza. Pounding a closed fist on my thigh, I focused on the dull ache it caused in my flesh, letting it pull me back into my body where my mind had moments ago threatened to scatter over the desert.

As the magic receded from my body, settling back into the incessant whisper I had learned to tolerate, the stirring air in my tent from the disturbance settled. A faint taste of panic lingered in my mouth, but distant, as if it weren't really mine. I breathed in and out through my nose, pounding my fist into my thigh a few more times for good measure. Pain was one of the best antidotes to my uncontrolled magic I had found, although it had been years since I had lost my grip on it with no warning.

These days, the magic of the desert stirred restlessly, and it dragged me along with it.

CHAPTER TEN
KEERA

I stared at my feet as two guards marched me further inside the palace. Even as they flanked me and ushered me through the cavernous stone hallway, a strange sense of calm washed over me. The sensation seemed to be coming from beyond me, slowing my heart rate and breathing even as thoughts crashed through my mind.

I would be lucky to be exiled again at this point. More likely I would be killed for endangering the queen's guests, showing how the desert had cursed me.

The queen led her guards and me into a lavish sitting room and slumped down on a couch, somehow making the movement look composed even as the silks of her dress fluttered down around her in disarray.

"Wait outside," she commanded to the guards who bowed and backed out of the room.

I stood in the middle of a plush carpet, wringing my hands as I wrestled with my confusion. The queen tilted her head as she observed me, taking me in.

"What clan are you from?"

I swallowed heavily. "I have no clan."

"But you are from the Ballan Desert."

Her tone indicated it was not a question, but I nodded anyway. She paused, and the silence stretched until it threatened to snap my sanity.

"I am an exile," I explained, my voice tremulous, but it did not break.

"And why were you exiled?"

I furrowed my brow. "You saw…"

"I saw that the desert's magic runs strong in you, and you have not learned to control it properly."

I shook my head. "The desert does not favor me."

The queen raised an eyebrow. "And how long did you survive as an exile?"

"Since I was fifteen," I admitted. With no way to keep track of time at my oasis, I didn't know exactly how long I had lingered on in isolation, but I knew it had been many years.

"It would seem to me that the desert would have to favor you for you to survive the elements on your own for nearly a decade," the queen observed.

"Whatever magic flows in me has cursed me," I insisted.

"How?"

I shifted from foot to foot, knowing I couldn't escape answering but hoping the guards would come in and drag me away to spare me the pain.

"Sit and tell me how you came to be an exile." The queen gestured to an ottoman beside me. Her tone was gentle but held a hint of command that could not be ignored.

I arranged myself on the seat, pulling the purple silk around me to give me a moment to call the memories to mind, as if they weren't simply hidden under a thin layer of denial to keep me from looking at them too closely. I had cultivated that denial, both afraid of and exhausted by the anger that bubbled up in me every time I remembered the reason for my seclusion.

"When I was thirteen, and my first blood came, my father took me to the horse master to pick my first horse."

The queen nodded, indicating she understood this custom of the clans.

"Her name was Farran, and she was nearly wild still, but I loved her.

The horse master of Clan Padra said she would be too difficult for a young girl like me, but Farren warmed to me, and I wanted no other. She was so fast, we would gallop across the sands free enough that I could leave even my own thoughts behind."

I swallowed thickly. I hadn't meant to share these details, but I hadn't had the chance to speak of Farran in years. The images of her rich brown coat and the proud arch of her neck sprang forth unbidden.

"Two years later, I rode to hunt a herd of oryx. We weren't the only hunters out for meat that day, and we got into a skirmish with a mother caracal and her cubs. Farran was wounded, her leg broken, before I managed to drive off the caracal. I helped her limp all the way to the encampment—back to the horse master, begging him to help her."

I had to take a few shaky breaths before continuing.

"He said he would help me. Before I could stop him, he had drawn his blade and driven it into her skull. He said it was a mercy, that she never would have recovered. But something happened in me the moment I heard her dying scream. It was like my body couldn't contain me anymore, and the whole world began to shake. I don't remember most of it, but everybody said the ground before my feet cracked open, creating a huge crater that engulfed the horse master and several other tents. When I came back to awareness and saw what I had done, I couldn't believe it.

"The clan lord declared my sentence to be exile for murder, saying it was unsafe to have me camp in the clan. I begged and screamed for my parents to do something, to talk to her, but they only looked at me with the same fear as everybody else. The next morning, the clan rode away, leaving me behind with no horse."

My voice trailed off, and I stared down at my hands where they fisted the amethyst silks in my lap. I relaxed my fingers with great effort, not wanting to crumple Neven's fine work.

"The story of my grandfather doesn't end with the building of Kelvadan." The queen broke the silence.

I glanced up in surprise. I had expected horror or instant calls for me to be thrown from the city. Instead, she cocked her head pensively, a lose silver curl escaping her elaborate twist to brush against her neck.

"We normally only tell the first part, as everybody loves a happy ending. But the immense power Kelvar carried didn't come without a cost. He was prone to fits of rage and often fell to distraction. Still, for one hundred years, he and Queen Alyx ruled Kelvadan, granted long life by the favor of the desert. Eventually though, time came for Alyx, as it does for us all.

"With Alyx gone, Kelvar fell into a fit that he didn't come out of. He shouted in argument with imagined voices and lashed out at those around him as if he didn't recognize them. Soon, he left the city, and although his children tried to stop him, he was still too powerful for any to stand against. He took his horse and wandered out into the sands, never to be seen again."

I blinked rapidly, the tragedy of Kelvar's demise pulling at a thread inside my heart.

"The desert's magic is a difficult gift. My family knows that better than most," the queen continued. "If you carry it too, then perhaps we can help you control it."

"Why would you do that when you could just as easily send me away?" I asked. Part of me wanted to clap my hand over my mouth and keep myself from dissuading the queen from letting me stay. The other part of my mind could only see a dark chasm splitting the earth before my feet and the horrified faces of my parents. I would never forgive myself if I damaged the city of Kelvadan, the greatest monument to peace and love.

"My lineage has failed to help those burdened by the desert's gifts before. Perhaps you are an opportunity to set things right." The queen's eyes shone overbright in the flickering torchlight. "Besides, if war with the clans is coming, I would prefer to have you on our side. I'm sure Aderyn would love to have you train as one of the Kelvadan riders. Only my guards and I saw you lose control."

My throat fought me as I swallowed thickly. It hurt more than I expected to find kindness in strangers that I had not received from my own parents. If I could repay the Queen of Kelvadan by fighting against the clans that would rejoice to see the city fall, then I would gladly fight alongside the City Guard.

Neven chuckled as I led Daiti through the city streets, keeping a firm hand on his head to prevent him from lashing out to chomp down on the arm of an unsuspecting pedestrian.

"You truly have yourself a war horse," he commented when I slapped Daiti's flank as he eyed a woman carrying a basket of fruit.

"I wasn't aware he was so hostile to people besides me," I admitted honestly. "I haven't had him around others before this."

After my conversation with the queen, I had admitted my exile status to Aderyn and Neven as well, bracing for their wrath for lying to them when they had shown me incredible hospitality.

"I know," was all Aderyn had to say with a firm clap on my shoulder.

Neven piped up at my crestfallen expression. "You were so clearly shy of people, it was hard not to guess. Still, you risked yourself to warn Kelvadan, so we weren't going to press the issue."

Now, he helped me bring Daiti to the palace stables where Aderyn's mount and those of all Kelvadan riders members and trainees stayed. When we entered the courtyard outside the palace, we turned toward a row of structures to the left instead of heading forward toward the main palace. From the smell of hay and the low whickering of animals, I could tell we had arrived.

"Kaius!" Neven stuck his head through the doorway of the nearest stable and called out.

A man with tanned skin and enough lines around his mouth to show he enjoyed smiling as much as he liked spending time in the sun emerged. He wore a close-cropped salt-and-pepper beard and clapped Neven on the shoulder in an easy greeting.

"It's been too long, Neven! I'm sorry I didn't have more time to catch up with you at the festival the day before last, but it turned out to be rather eventful."

Neven cleared his throat and jerked his head toward me.

The man, Kaius, didn't miss a beat. "And there is the event herself! I was told I would be seeing you soon, although nobody mentioned such a magnificent animal."

Daiti pawed the ground and tossed his head as if he understood the compliment and wished to show himself in the best light.

"I'm Keera, and this is Daiti."

"It's a pleasure to meet both of you. I'm Kaius, Queen Ginevra's husband."

I stammered a touch before inclining my head and placing my fist over my heart in respect. "I didn't realize you were the king."

Kaius chuckled. "I hold no such title, although Ginevra would love it if I did. However, it turns out that I'm much better with horses than people. I told her I would only marry her if I could be consort and royal horse master only. She was so desperate for me, that she accepted my terms."

"That's not how she tells the story," Neven said in a teasing tone.

"She gets all sorts of ideas into her head after a few cups of *laka*." Kaius waved a hand dismissively, but his tone held nothing but affection. "Now let's get this magnificent beast settled."

Kaius reached toward Daiti. Neven and I both drew breath to warn him, just as Daiti's teeth closed around where Kaius's hand had been a moment before.

Unperturbed, Kaius cooed gently and reached out again; Daiti shied back for a moment before eventually letting Kaius lay his hand on his forelock. He patted gently and muttered a bit more nonsense. I looked on in surprise as Daiti leaned into the touch and whickered gently. While the horse had never been anything but patient with me, he had turned out to be a bit of a menace to all others.

"How..."

"You're not the only one outside of the royal family to be touched by the desert," Kaius said with a crooked smile, producing a treat from his pocket that Daiti gobbled up greedily. "Not all of us were lucky enough to have as flashy of powers as you, but having a way with horses suits me just fine."

I shrank internally at the mention of my unintended display of magic at the festival. The queen obviously told her husband what happened. Outwardly, I smiled as Daiti continued to revel in Kaius's attention, acting much more like a kitten than a warhorse.

Neven murmured in my ear, "I have to be getting back to work, but Kauis will get you and Daiti oriented and point you toward where the riders train." He set off back toward the house as Kaius led me and Daiti further into the stable.

Once he had shown us to the stall that was to be Daiti's, he went to fetch some fresh arrowgrass, leaving me to settle the horse in.

"Glad to see you well."

I started at the voice, nearly smacking Daiti in the nose as I spun around. I hadn't heard footsteps behind me despite the floor being stone, as it was everywhere in the city.

A familiar man stood in the opening to the stall, hands shoved into the sash at his waist, holding closed his leather vest. His smile was broad and easy in his round face, giving him an open and friendly look.

"I'm Dryden. We danced at the festival a few days back," he said when I continued to stare.

"I remember." I shook myself from my silence but stayed partially behind the solid shield of Daiti's body. I didn't know how to explain my behavior, and part of me hoped that if I stayed silent, Dryden would leave.

"You seemed to have a stressful evening. I wasn't sure if you would remember the minor details." A friendly smile split his face as he rubbed a hand over his close-shorn hair sheepishly.

I inched out from behind Daiti. "I'm sorry I ran away. I was... overwhelmed."

"*I'm* sorry that I was being too forward. I hear the magic of the desert can be hard to control."

"No!" I held up my hands placatingly. "It wasn't that. You were being incredibly kind. I'm just... not from the city. I've never been around so many people before. The crowd and the noise—" I broke off as his words struck me. He knew about my magic.

My wide eyes and slack-jawed expression must have signaled my shock.

"News travels fast in this city, but it's nothing to be ashamed of. Plenty of people carry a touch of the desert's magic. I'm just glad to know that it wasn't me being overbearing after too much *laka*."

"I think I'm the one who had too much *laka*." I offered him a wry smile, which he returned. I didn't tell him that I likely suffered from more than the "touch" of magic he was accustomed to. His friendly demeanor eased the tension in my shoulders a bit.

"So, you're keeping your horse in the riders' stable now? Are you joining up?" he asked, turning his attention to Daiti. The horse stamped his feet and blew a breath out through his nose.

"It was the queen's idea. She said I could start training today and that she might be able to help me with..." I gestured vaguely. It seemed almost too good to be true that I might be able to control my magic, making my hope hard to articulate.

Dryden nodded knowingly. "I'm glad you'll be joining up with the riders. I myself am in training right now."

At that moment, footsteps sounded as Kaius rounded the corner, huffing as he hauled a bundle of arrowgrass for Daiti.

"I see you've met Dryden," he commented as he set down his burden. "That means he can show you where the riders train, and I can stay here with the animals."

"Be careful, or we might start to think you like horses better than people," Dryden commented.

"I'm not trying to make a secret of it," Kaius grumbled, but his smile betrayed him.

Dryden led me out of the stable and around to a set of stairs that carried us to a large flat terrace. About a dozen others, a mix of men and women, milled about, some stretching or doing various exercises while others chatted animatedly. As I looked around to get my bearings, I furrowed my brow.

"Are we... are we on top of the stables?"

Dryden nodded. "With a city built into the side of mountain, you have to take advantage of vertical space. There's not a lot of room to spread out."

I nodded as Aderyn walked into the courtyard. She only acknowledged me with a small nod before putting her hands on her hips and looking the group over with a critical eye.

"All right, recruits, you know the drill."

At her command, the others immediately dropped into a series of calisthenics they already seemed to know by rote. I followed along as best I could, but within minutes, sweat poured off my body, dripping down my overheated skin to create a puddle on the ground around the spot I had claimed for myself. Panic gripped me at the site of so much lost moisture, but I reminded myself of the constant trickle from the spring in Aderyn's bathroom. Water was not in short supply here.

After a few more minutes, my muscles began to shake in the effort to keep up with those around me. As I followed along, using my arms to lower and lift my body from the ground, I narrowly missed breaking my nose as my arms failed to hold my weight and I pitched headfirst into the stone.

I struggled back up into the position, arms as wobbly as the legs of a newborn oryx; I looked up to catch a glance of Aderyn watching me. She offered me a brief nod and continued pacing between the rows of other recruits. Something about her stoic acknowledgement of my effort, even if I'd failed miserably, gave me the strength I needed to get through the rest of the grueling exercises. If I could prove worthy of a spot among the recruits, then perhaps I could truly find a home in Kelvadan. My time in the city may already be softening the sharp protrusion of my bones, and years of hunting had kept me spry, but my muscles still had a lot of catching up to do.

"Now that we've warmed up, it's time to move on to our forms," Aderyn proclaimed.

I put my hands on my knees and panted in despair. This was supposed to get me warmed up, and yet almost every inch of my body felt more like it was on fire.

"Dryden, go ahead and lead us through the first form. Keera, come to the front and watch. Try to memorize the movements," Aderyn barked.

I gratefully plodded up to where Aderyn stood, turning to face the rest of the recruits who positioned themselves in a ready stance. Wordlessly, Aderyn handed me the skin off her belt, and I took several grateful gulps of water as the recruits began their forms.

They moved rhythmically, looking somewhat like they were fighting although they had no weapons or opponents. Dryden, standing at the front of the group, wobbled often, but wore the look of utmost concentration. The deep furrow between his brows, and the tip of his tongue poking out between his lips as he focused, sweat shining on his deep skin in the rising sun, made me smile.

I did my best to commit the movements to memory, but they moved from the first form, to the second and the third, before repeating the movements with blunted sabers in hand. Eventually my brain couldn't hold any more, and I focused the best I could on the way each of the recruits moved. The patterns looked familiar, like something I had watched the riders of Clan Padra do when I was young and scampered off to the horse enclosures next to where the riders practiced.

After finishing the fourth form, Aderyn indicated they were going to be moving on to sparring with blunted sabers before turning to me. "The queen is waiting for you in the main courtyard. You have some other training to attend to."

I nodded before trotting off down the stairs, thinking hopefully of the cool shade of the palace after standing in the sun, still flushed from my earlier exertion. The queen greeted me in the courtyard before leading me through the grand doors into the palace. I found it odd that an exile would be treated so personally by the queen, but I reminded myself that Kelvadan was different from the clans. As we passed the statue, I looked at it again, this time in a slightly different light, knowing Kelvar's fate was to be driven mad by his power.

Instead of heading up the stairs like we had the last time I visited, the queen led us down a winding stair cut into the stone. I repressed a shiver at the weight of the mountain pushing in on me from every side.

"It looks like Aderyn put you through your paces today." The queen made conversation as we walked.

I pushed back the tendrils of sweaty hair that clung to my forehead and neck, considering how savage I must look, sweaty and panting, compared to the queen's effortless grace.

"I'm not sure I'll make much of a rider," I admitted. It was true that I hadn't even made it through half a day's training.

The queen looked over her shoulder at me knowingly. "You might surprise yourself once we get another month or two of solid meals in you. But having you become a rider isn't the only reason I asked Aderyn to train you. There is something about exhausting the body that makes learning to control the desert's magic easier."

Now we walked down a long corridor, and I got the impression that we walked straight into the mountain. Something inside me suffocated, and I chided myself for my claustrophobia. I was just not accustomed to being surrounded by stone and would get used to it in time.

Looking at the walls to distract myself, I noticed they seemed rough-hewn, unlike the flawless cuts that formed the rest of the city. I reached out and ran my fingers over the walls, finding many lips and jagged edges.

"This wasn't part of the original palace," the queen explained, seeing my curiosity. "My father, Kelvar's son, built this when he started finding the desert's magic overwhelming and feared the same fate as his father."

I tilted my head as I considered. It was odd to think of Kelvadan being ruled by one family for two hundred years, when in the clans, lordship shifted regularly as power waxed and waned. I wondered who would rule when Queen Ginevra died, as I had heard no word of her having children. Although, if she were to be blessed with the same long life as Kelvar, it wouldn't be a concern for decades to come.

At the end of the hallway, the queen stopped and opened the door to a room. It was more a stone cube than a room really, with only two cushions sat across from each other at the center. I cocked my head at it dubiously.

Queen Ginevra settled herself onto one without hesitation and gestured for me to take the one across from her. I folded myself onto it, mirroring her cross-legged position.

"My father, King Torin, built this room for meditation. One of the most overwhelming parts of the desert's magic is the ability to feel everything happening, as if you yourself inhabit the entirety of the desert."

I nodded, remembering the sudden burst of awareness threatening to drown me before I unleashed a whirlwind at the festival. It wasn't all that dissimilar to the eerie and deafening quiet that washed over me before the lightning storm at Clan Katal. That thought sat uncomfortably in my belly, but I tucked it away to examine later.

"This deep in the mountain, the stone blocks out most of that sensation, helping you concentrate as you tame the power inside of you," the queen explained.

"Do you use this method to control your magic?" I asked.

"Along with other things, although it is not as difficult for me as for some. I have not been as touched by the desert as many in my bloodline. Most of my power seems to lie in diplomacy." She gave a wry smile. "Still, my father taught me his methods in case I needed them some day."

"I'm glad he did."

"Now, close your eyes."

I did as she asked.

"Picture how you felt at the festival, before you unleashed your power," Queen Ginevra prompted in a soothing voice. "Think about the awareness that connected you to all the living things in the desert."

I pictured the burrowing fox I felt that night, and the whispering of coarse grasses. The sensations felt choked and muted, but I held on to them.

"Follow those sensations to their source, deep within you."

I did as she asked, finding the threads of sensation leading me to the part of myself that felt suffocated by the walls around me. It was a force in myself that had been asleep for years, until the fateful night the Viper came across my oasis. My breathing quickened as I prodded it with my consciousness, claustrophobia returning. I tried to focus on the queen's words and control my heartbeat.

"Once you locate that source, imagine constructing a barrier around it. Something firm and hard, to keep it from leaching into the rest of your being. Something unyielding enough to control the wildness of the desert's magic—as solid and permanent as the walls around you.

"You won't be able to build the entire barrier today, but try to create the image of it, firm in your mind."

I struggled with the queen's directions, imagining burying that seed of power within myself under a mountain as tall and imposing as the one we sat within. In protest, the seed within me started to grow, sending tendrils through the foundations of my mountain. I tried to push back but it writhed and squirmed with the fervor of a wild horse who refused to be tamed.

My magic burst forward from the scaffold of the enclosure I sought to build around it, not silent in my head this time but screaming. The feeling washed me away for a moment before something caused the tendrils of magic coursing through me to retreat. My eyes snapped open as a loud crash echoed through the room.

The door behind the queen had been blown off its hinges, cracked in two straight down the middle. The queen bit her lips, looking me over carefully.

"I–I'm sorry. Was that..." I stammered.

She quickly schooled her face into a calm smile, but not before I saw a flash of something familiar in her eyes. "My fault. I underestimated how feisty your magic would be and dove in too fast. We should just start with some breathing exercises first."

We spent the rest of our time doing simple meditations, but I left feeling less centered than when I'd entered. The muscles in my shoulders gripped steadily tighter as the feeling of inescapable rock surrounding me grew more oppressive by the second.

Even as I was glad to leave when the queen had to attend to other business, I eyed the broken door as I walked out. It seemed an ill-omen for my training.

Seeing where I was looking, the queen reached out to lay a comforting hand on my shoulder but stopped, perhaps remembering what led to my first loss of control.

"It could be worse," she assured me.

I wasn't so sure, but I decided to trust her. After all, nobody else would be able to teach me control. And without control, I would not be able to stay in the city that had offered me the home even my own parents had denied me. I would not—could not—fail.

Over the next month, my training with the riders proved to be much more promising than my work with the queen. While I knew proper rest and nutrition would change my body for the better, I was astounded how quickly I found myself able to complete the entire training routine. Muscles filled in my frame before my eyes. I would have suspected Aderyn was lacing my food with some sort of stimulant if not for her surprise as my progress.

While my body's changes allowed me to keep up with the exercises, the saber forms were where I showed the starkest improvement. My body fell into them almost as if they were a comfortable habit, even after I'd only practiced them a few times.

After Aderyn had left us to our own devices for the day, Dryden watched me as he massaged a sore shoulder, head cocked to the side as I flowed through the movements.

"I don't know why you're still practicing. You already make the rest of us look bad," he complained with no annoyance. After a couple weeks training alongside him, I learned that nothing really ruffled Dryden's feathers.

"Yeah, and you're already giving us enough bruises," another female recruit, Nyra, piped up as she put away the blunted sabers we had practiced with. Her quip held more bite.

I just shrugged as I continued moving through the third form, this one especially challenging as it involved a series of deep lunges. While I had accomplished the balance most others struggled with in this form, the muscles of my thighs still struggled to hold the positions as long as necessary. The others had an advantage over me after years of using their legs to steer and hold themselves on their horses.

In truth, I practiced because it made me feel less like I was failing Queen Ginevra, and by extension, Kelvadan. This city and its leader had opened itself to me when all others turned me away. They went out of their way to help me and gave me a place to belong—something I hadn't had in far too long. Even if learning to control my magic was slow at best, I could repay Kelvadan for opening its gates to me by fighting alongside its riders.

"Are you going to enter in the Trials?" Nyra asked Dryden as I lowered my arms with a long exhale, finishing the form.

"Of course! I know I'll get my ass served to me on a silver platter, but it might be served to me by the next Champion of the Desert. That'll be a story to tell my children."

"That's assuming you find anybody to procreate with you." Nyra elbowed Dryden playfully in the side.

"I have my charms, don't I, Keera?" Dryden retorted.

"I wouldn't know. And the Trials?" I asked, happy to deflect Dryden's flirtation. His manner was light, but I was still too busy

working out how to exist around other humans to try to decode
flirting.

"The Ballan Trials? They're being held at the end of the dry
season?" Dryden seemed incredulous that I wasn't aware of the massive
event about to descend on the city.

I blinked. I had attended the Trials with my parents when I was
small, the only time I had ever seen Kelvadan before, and the skill of its
riders were forever imprinted in my brain. My parents had both been
eliminated early, but we had stayed through the days of feasting and
watched the remaining events. It was hard to remember specifics, but I
remembered the excitement in the air, even more palpable than it had
been at the Kelvadan festival. I also had vague memories of my parents'
disapproving frowns as we rode away from the city. Perhaps they had
been disappointed to lose so early.

Apparently, that had been twenty years ago. Now it was time for
another generation of riders to compete for the title of Champion,
charged with protecting the desert until the next Trials.

"I don't know as much about them as I should," I admitted when
Dryden continued to stare at me. "I only vaguely remember the last
competition, and... we don't talk about them much outside of the
city."

"Kelvar himself was the last Champion before the Trials moved to
Kelvadan, wasn't he?" Nyra asked.

"I think so." Dryden shrugged. "Since the founding of Kelvadan
and the Trials moving to the city, they aren't quite as brutal, and the title
of Champion is mostly ceremonial. The duels aren't to the death
anymore, but the challenges are difficult enough that a few competitors
still die every time. They're a huge event, and some of more traditional
clans take them very seriously. Do you think you'll enter?"

I shook my head, although the thought of being part of such a
competition—of being named Champion so nobody could deny that I
had earned my place—was seductive. "We've barely started training to
fight on horseback. I hardly think I'm ready."

Nyra frowned. "They only happen every twenty years though, so
this might be your best chance to participate. Plus, these will be the
tenth Trials since the city was founded, and word has it that the queen is

planning to make them a huge to-do. 'A display of peace and unity' they say."

I had a feeling the queen's desire to promote harmony stemmed from the growing threat of war from the clans. The words of Clan Katal's lord were another source of motivation for my extended training.

"Plenty of people enter the Trials that don't have as much training as they would like, since they come around so rarely," Dryden added. "They get weeded out pretty early, before the challenges get really dangerous, but it's about saying you competed."

"What kind of competitions are there in the Trials?"

"They change every time," Dryden explained excitedly. "Since nobody knows exactly what the events will be, riders must be prepared for anything. All we know is that the events are supposed to test all an individual's skills, from survival to combat, even horsemanship. That, and the last event is always the same. The final Champion is decided by one-on-one duels."

"The range of events are supposed to be best to discover who truly has the desert's favor," Nyra added on.

I shrugged, feigning casualness. It still felt unnecessarily bold to join the Trials when I had only been training for months, but the queen's words about me being favored by the desert echoed in my skull. I had always thought I was cursed, but perhaps this would be a chance to prove the opposite. "Maybe I'll give it a go then. Who was the last Champion?"

"That's the thing, there wasn't one." Nyra leaned in conspiratorially. "I'm too young to remember the last Trials, but my dad says the last duel went awry, and the winner killed his opponent. The Trials are dangerous, but competitors aren't supposed to fight each other to the death in the duels. After that, they didn't crown a Champion. My mother is from the clans, and she gets upset every time they bring it up —says its bad luck for the desert not to have a Champion."

"The clans are too superstitious." Dryden waved a dismissive hand at Nyra, and she frowned at him.

I mirrored her expression. "I have to get going."

I left them there discussing the coming competition, not wanting to leave Queen Ginevra waiting. As I passed through the palace doors, one of the guards flanking the tall arch told me the queen was waiting for me up on the terrace. It was a change from the tight stone box we sat in for an hour every afternoon, and my heart lifted. I had come to dread the feeling of layers of rock pressing in around me. Following afternoons shut away from the sky, I had dropped all pretense of sleeping in Aderyn and Neven's guest room and set myself up a nest of rugs and cushions on the roof where I could see the stars.

As I pressed down rising panic every time I tried to contain my magic, I wondered if this was the only way. An image of the Viper casually lighting a fire with the wave of his hand flitted through my mind one afternoon as I attempted to meditate. He seemed able to use his power without fear, not forcing it down into a tiny box at the base of his spine.

At that thought, the image of his face came to me again unbidden— the way his eyes had gone wide, a tremor running through his body as he held his hand to my throat. The way he had asked me my name. For some reason, it was very hard to return my focus to meditating with that image in my head.

Today, Queen Ginevra sat sipping tea and reading a scroll when I finished my trudge up the stairs, my calves protesting the climb after the morning's exertion. I gratefully sat on the chair across from her when she motioned to it.

"I thought we'd try something a bit different today."

I nodded, a tendril of shame unfurling in my mind. Somehow, this felt like an acknowledgement of my failures to make any headway on the walls around my magic. While I hadn't destroyed any more doors, every time I extended my consciousness toward the wild power deep inside me, it lashed out like a mother caracal defending her cubs. It always tamped down quickly as if snapped to heel by some invisible tether, but I still couldn't come close enough to make any headway.

Queen Ginevra poured a steaming cup of tea and handed it to me. I nodded my thanks and blew on the liquid to cool it a bit. I tilted my head when I saw the liquid carried a strange bluish hue, overlaid on the surface with an oily sort of iridescence.

"It's my own special blend," she explained in response to my staring.

"It contains an infusion of the lyra leaf. While many people can drink it without feeling any change, for those with a connection to the desert, it can dull those senses."

"It's a sedative?" I asked warily.

She shook her head. "Only for magic. I wouldn't drink it myself if it would impede my ability to rule." She took a sip as if to demonstrate.

I followed her lead and instantly my features scrunched in distaste. I tried to hide the disgust in my expression, but the taste of the liquid, like pungent sulfur on my tongue, overwhelmed me.

"You get used to it." Queen Ginevra laughed.

I wiped my mouth with the back of my hand. "You drink this often?"

"Every day."

"I thought you didn't have trouble controlling the magic?"

"Usually I don't," she admitted, "but I don't like to take chances. My father preferred to wall off his magic but keep it available in case he ever needed to call on it. I prefer to take the temptation away entirely."

"The temptation?"

She dabbed her lips daintily with a napkin, making me shrink back at my poor manners in comparison.

"I have come to think using the power of our bloodline to rule the city is a crutch. I endeavor to lead by being a good queen and not let any doubt seep into my mind that I only hold my position based on the power I was born with."

I nodded my understanding even as my stomach clenched—probably from the bitter flavor of the tea slithering down my throat. Even though we had just celebrated this city's origins through the overwhelming power of the desert, I supposed it was noble to rule the city through diplomacy and intellect alone.

"Now finish your cup and then we can try something."

I gulped down the rest of the liquid as fast as I could, hoping I could forgo tasting the tea at all. It scalded the roof of my mouth, but I decided it was preferable to the flavor. Still, it sat in my gut like a nest of snakes, twisting and uneasy.

Queen Ginevra nodded her approval. "Now, reach down inside yourself, and see how your magic reacts."

I did so hesitantly, less easy about the way it might retaliate out in the open. As much as I hated being entombed in rock, it did protect others from the backlash of my magic. What I found was magic, still present but feeling languid and lazy. I reached a tendril of myself out to it and its reaction was that of a snake hissing in warning, coiled back to strike but not attacking yet.

"I think it's working," I admitted.

"Good. Now you can rest a little easier knowing you won't lose control while we work on building your walls."

I exhaled in relief that I wasn't going to cause a scene on the terrace, magic exploding out unbidden. Still, with the power in my belly as close as it had been to asleep in over a month, part of me felt... barren. Like I was walking up stairs only for my foot to fall through space when there was one less than I expected. I shook away the thought. I just wasn't used to the sensation of calm within me yet.

I stared up at the stars wheeling above me in the night sky and smiled. It took me a long moment to realize that I hadn't just woken where I had gone to sleep on Aderyn's roof, but far outside the city walls. The silence of the wilderness was deeper and held far more mystery than what passed for quiet in the city.

The only source of noise was the breathing of another, lying in the sand next to me. If I had been awake, I might have wondered how I got here, or been fearful at who had approached me while I rested, but the unknowable logic of dreams kept me stargazing peacefully.

"The city seems so different, but the stars look the same as they do here," I observed to my unknown companion.

"You never see the stars in the Kelvadan. I hate it." The dispassionate voice that responded was male. It seemed tired and... familiar.

"Do you think the stars would still look the same if you were to cross the mountains to the kingdoms beyond?" I asked.

There was such a long silence that I wondered if my companion was ignoring me.

Then—

"Do you want to leave the Ballan Desert?"

"No." The answer came before I could process his question, but it rang of truth nonetheless.

"Me neither," he agreed. "I think it would feel like..."

"The room under the mountain," I filled in. A sharp intake of breath from my companion broke the calm spell of the dream.

In the shattered stillness, it finally occurred to me to turn my head. My gaze was met by molten silver eyes that I had last seen in the pits of a mask with a sword pressed to my throat.

My eyes snapped open to stare at the same stars I had just been observing, but now the unmistakable firmness of the roof pressed into my back, and the sleepy sounds of stabled horses and the collective breathing of hundreds filled the air.

Now though, the open sky brought me no peace. It was a long time before I slept again.

Aderyn smiled at me, and my stomach sank. That grin was never good.

She might have the occasional soft smile for Neven when she thought nobody was looking, but this expression was reserved for when I was about to be pounded into the dirt. She had been giving me many more bruises since we started adding on some extra training together after the other recruits left. These extended sparring sessions had come about naturally when she had seen me stay behind to continue practicing my forms. Now they were part of our daily ritual—my favorite part, to be honest. It was the only time of day my mind found peace, unable to think of anything but countering Aderyn's lightning-fast blows, lest she dump me on my ass again.

Thankfully for my bruised behind, it seemed to be happening less often of late. In fact, yesterday Aderyn had been the one dumped in the dirt as we sparred, and I sensed I was going to pay for that now.

"I thought we'd try something a little different today," she announced, turning toward the weapons rack on the far side of the open training area. When she turned back toward me, she held not the saber that I had become accustomed to, but a sickle blade, so curved it nearly formed a perfect half circle. She twisted the handle, and it split in two, revealing a perfectly matched set of blades.

I swallowed.

"Not everybody you fight is going to use as saber." She twirled the weapons in her hands, and they blurred into perfect silver circles. "Especially if they're not from Kelvadan."

When the clans attack. The unspoken words hung in the air.

"You'll need to be able to adapt to other fighting styles on your feet."

I watched her swing the blades a few times as she adjusted to their weight in her hands, calculating my strategy. As curved as they were, she would have much less reach, but they would be lethal at close quarters. If I closed in too fast, I would lose my main advantage.

She squared off against me, and I raised my saber in an overhead guard. We circled around each other for a moment. As always, I lunged first.

It was one of the things I admired about Aderyn but never seemed to learn from her. Her patience in a fight was endless, always waiting for her opponent to move first—to give her an opening.

Luckily, I had learned through a few harsh bruises to protect myself when I attacked, and while she spun the blade in her left hand to deflect my attack, I ducked under the swing of the other with ease.

We fell into a pattern of quick exchanges, but while I never got close enough for her to slash me with the curved edges of her sickle swords, I soon discovered the disadvantage of my longer reach. While I could keep Aderyn at arm's length, when she spun the handles of her blades in her hand, they created a virtually impenetrable shield of swirling silver. I chanced a thrust of my saber at her face, thinking I saw an opening. In an instant, she twirled the circled blades toward each other, trapping my sword and stopping my stab inches from her nose. We froze for a moment, a twinkle in her eyes, before I wrenched my weapon free.

I would have to get in close to force an opening.

With a side sweep of my blade, I knocked one of Aderyn's swords out of the way, pushing in close. I kicked out, foot striking her forearm and knocking it aside to make my opening. I advanced, but she was no longer there.

Instead, she used the momentum from my kick to circle around me. Before I could turn, her blade was at my throat, her breath tickling my ear as she panted in triumph.

Raising my hands in defeat, I shook my head. "You're incredible with those."

Aderyn did an unnecessary flip with the weapons in her hand, giving them a fond look. "They're my secret skill. To be honest, I needed to break them out today for the sake of my pride."

"Your pride?" I echoed dubiously. Aderyn never struck me as somebody who struggled with confidence, her commanding demeanor projecting self-assuredness.

"You've been keeping me on my toes more than I'm used to," she admitted ruefully. "It used to be that nobody—except maybe one person—could best me consistently."

"I got lucky one time. That's hardly 'consistently besting you,'" I argued. "Besides, keep breaking out those sickle swords and you have nothing to worry about."

"My father taught me how to fight with them. He was a clan rider when he was younger, before he married my mother and they settled in Kelvadan."

I contemplated her. I knew she had been born and raised in the city, but I found myself curious.

"Have you ever considered joining one of the clans?" I asked. "With your skill, you could be named warlord."

"And leave Kelvadan? Never." Aderyn looked out over the edge of the stable roof that served as the training area.

Everywhere in the top tier of Kelvadan afforded a great view of the city...and the desert beyond. If I hadn't experienced the endlessness of the sands myself, I could almost imagine the glimmer of the ocean on the horizon.

"I would miss the people, the energy on the streets," Aderyn continued, gazing out at the buildings below, the colorful forms weaving between them looking small from this height. "Here, there's always so much to see. A neighbor to visit or a new market stall to peruse. Out there in the desert, there's so much... *space.*"

She said the final word with a shiver of disgust that almost made me laugh, even as I found it odd that she would miss the constant crush of strangers and stone around her. I supposed you got used to it. Maybe I would too, with time.

Footsteps on the stairs interrupted our conversation. I tore my eyes away from the horizon to see one of the palace attendants crest the edge of the roof.

"I'm sorry, I'll be right there," I said, hastily mopping sweat from my brow. The queen and I had pushed my lessons back by an hour for the past several weeks so I could spar with Aderyn after training with the recruits. Knowing I could swing as hard as I liked after helped me stay in check and stick to the drills during training, although everybody but Dryden still avoided pairing up with me whenever possible. Although, his persistence picked at something in me even as Aderyn would raise her brows at me over his shoulder. Her expression clearly intimated a dare to act on Dryden's flirtations, but I simply didn't have it in me—not when casual touches still had me ready to fly out of my skin. Still, I appreciated his steadfast friendship.

The attendant shook her head, bringing me back to the present moment. "The queen requests both of your presence in the study this afternoon."

Aderyn frowned. "She must have something to discuss."

We hurried to clean up and put away our training weapons. In the palace, Aderyn led us farther up the winding stairs through the center of the structure than I had been before, past the terrace where the queen and usually drank nauseating tea together. My thighs already ached from hours of training and nearly burst into flames by the time we finished our climb.

It seemed that we wouldn't be able to rise too much higher before reaching the spire at the top of the palace, but as Aderyn turned off a landing, several more flights ascended out of my view. She led me into a round room, where the queen already sat at a circular table in the center.

Around the edges were shelves, laden with scrolls, the alcoves between them adorned with stained glass windows. The bright afternoon sun filtered through the brightly colored glass, staining the room in refracting rainbows. I itched to approach each window and examine the different pictures wrought into them, but the queen looked up when we entered, and the dire look on her face stole all my attention.

She clutched a small rolled up piece of paper in her hand so hard it began to crumple between her fingers.

"Are you competing in the Trials?" she asked without prelude.

Aderyn frowned as she sat. "No. As we discussed, I thought it would be better for me to keep my undivided attention on the city's security given the current situation."

"And you Keera?"

I looked between the two women. I had increasingly considered trying my skills in the competition but kept talking myself out of it. Every time my magic lashed out, knocking over even the tiniest fence I managed to erect around it, I told myself it would be better not to risk it. As fast as my fighting progressed, I seemed to move backward in controlling the power dwelling within me.

"I hadn't decided," I hedged. "Why?"

"More is riding on the Trials than I thought." The queen pursed her lips, turning back to the note before her. "A messenger hawk brought news from Oren."

I sat up straighter in my chair, and Aderyn echoed my movement, leaning in close to hear the news from the spy.

"He has joined with the riders of Clan Katal, and he confirms that only four clans are united under Lord Alasdar's banner currently, although they are training for battle. However, he overheard the Viper discussing with Lord Alasdar that a deal has been made with the remaining five clans. If the Viper is crowned Champion of the Trials, then they will join Lord Alasdar."

My spine hit the low wooden back of my chair with a *thunk* as the breath rushed out of me. The Viper, who had taken up residence in my sleeping mind as much as I tried to evict him, would be coming to the Trials.

"You could always bar him from competing," Aderyn suggested. "Wouldn't a violation of peace like this warrant it? People have been banned from the Trials for violence before."

The queen shook her head, the action so tired I was certain she had already run through this scenario in her mind a thousand times. "At the last Trials, I refused to crown a Champion when Lord Alasdar violated the rules by killing his opponent in the final duel and exiled him from the city. Now he is the one that leads an army against us. I'm not going to make the same mistake twice."

"Then you will let him?" Aderyn asked, her voicing edging the closest to incredulity I had ever heard in the presence of the queen.

Queen Ginevra pressed her lips together in a thin white line, clearly as unhappy with the situation as Aderyn was. "The clans believe in the legend of the Champion of the Desert. As the granddaughter of Kelvar, the greatest Champion the desert has ever known, ruling the city that is the very proof of his legacy, I'm not sure I don't believe in it either. The clans, and even the people within this city, feared what the lack of a Champion would mean twenty years ago.

"If Lord Alasdar is smart—and he has certainly seemed crafty enough so far—he'll use that to his advantage to further turn the clans against me. If I interfere with these Trials, it may only turn them against us further."

Now, Queen Ginevra turned toward me, and I blinked, unsure where I fit into this discussion. We had gone far beyond the meager information I had gathered on Clan Katal during my brief captivity.

"Perhaps, the desert has chosen her own Champion though," she said, words laden with a meaning I didn't process.

Only after several moments of blank staring did the full weight of her words hit me. I began shaking my head so hard I feared my brain might rattle out my ears.

"I only just got here," I protested. While the months in the city had been kind to me, I was far from Kelvadan's Champion.

"Kelvar was only nineteen when he carved the city from the mountain," Ginevra pointed out.

I opened my mouth to protest but paused. He had been so young.

"There is no denying that you have been touched by the desert and delivered on Kelvadan's doorstep by some odd coincidence just months before the Trials that only occur every twenty years," Queen Ginevra pressed on.

"There must be somebody else," I insisted, looking imploringly at Aderyn.

Something dark and sad flickered in her eyes, but it was gone before I could even be sure I saw it at all.

"I could make it pretty far through my combat skill alone," Aderyn admitted, "but the title of the desert's Champion has never gone to one who hasn't been gifted with her power."

I furrowed my brow. "I thought magic wasn't allowed to be used in the Trials."

During training, Dryden and Nyra had been discussing the possible events to be included in this year's competition, and they had mentioned that particular rule.

"Even so, the desert chooses her winner," Queen Ginevra explained. "When the last Trials ended in upset, I thought somebody might rise to the occasion and fill the role of Champion. I was wrong. But you brought a warning to our doorstep, and with it, our best hope for preventing the clans from uniting."

I was pinned by two intense gazes, trapped like a jackrabbit in a snare. I could not let Kelvadan fall, and so I would face the Viper in the Trials.

I woke the next morning to a ball of molten iron burning in my gut. I rolled onto my hands and knees with a moan as a wave of nausea washed over to me. I feared a reaction to the liquor I shared with Aderyn the afternoon before, but when I glanced down my body, I found a far more innocent, if unexpected, culprit. Dark blood crusted the light linen pants I wore to sleep at the crux of my thighs.

Another wave of cramps shuddered through me, and I collapsed back onto my side and curled up in a ball. One of the few blessings of malnutrition had been freedom from my monthly cycle. While it had been disconcerting to be unable to mark the passage of time with my blood, at least it didn't slow my hunting or cost me precious moisture after several months in exile.

Now it seemed the symptoms returned with a vengeance. After a few minutes of clutching my lower abdomen and trying to remember how I had ridden a horse in this state while I was younger, Aderyn clambered up to the roof to check on me, no doubt wondering why I hadn't come down to breakfast.

Seeing the problem, she offered a crooked smile of sympathy.

"Has it been a while?"

I nodded, embarrassed to be laid out by something Aderyn likely walked off.

"It will get better with the passing months. Your body is just out of practice," she said with a shake of her head. "I'll have Neven bring you some tea and give the queen your apologies."

I rolled over and pulled the sheet over my head, preparing to endure the next few days.

CHAPTER ELEVEN
THE VIPER

My body rebelled against me. It was likely due to the heavy training I had been leading the riders of the combined tribes through, but my muscles ached. I hadn't hurt like this since I first came to Lord Alasdar and he taught me to master my magic through a combination of exhaustion and pain.

I looked down at my breakfast and wrinkled my nose. I had been eating more than usual, trying to keep up with the demands of increased exercise, sleeping heavily every night. Even when I was unconscious, my mind joined my body in unbalancing me, sending me odd dreams. My usual nightmares of being encased in stone had eased, only to be replaced by the face of the exiled woman I had almost killed, her defiant expression illuminated eerily by a flash of lightning. Sometimes I saw her galloping away on a too-large horse into the darkness, as I had spied her before she disappeared, a beautiful, wild thing. It was as if the desert wanted me to go after her, but there would be no point. Traveling alone without supplies, she would likely be dead by now. I shook the notion from my head.

I needed to eat, but today an undercurrent of nausea had my meal looking exceptionally unappetizing. I pushed it aside and picked up my mask, fastening it on my face, the weight giving me the separation from myself I needed to push away the unpleasant sensation.

A squawk and a peck indicated Zephyr found my meal more satisfactory than I had. I cursed internally as I found myself using the name Izumi had bestowed on the bird, despite my insistence that a name made him a pet. Zephyr had stuck, and so he stayed.

Mask firmly in place, I pushed out of the tent to greet the first rays of dawn. The riders were not required to report to the edge of the camp until the sun was fully risen, but I preferred a moment of solitary practice before having to wrangle dozens of sloppy fighters.

At the open space alongside the horse's enclosure, I began my forms, my muscles protesting the movements despite having done them hundreds of times over the last decade. Perhaps I had been forgoing my exercises more than I realized as I rode around doing Lord Alasdar's bidding. I needed to be more diligent in my practice, as they were one of the more pleasant ways of controlling my magic.

The forms were a tradition of clan riders, passed down through the generations since the first time the desert had been crossed. They were still just as essential for those wanting to hone their skills as a warrior as well as those who served the desert's will.

I finished with an exhale as I lowered my hands, the riders of the four clans congregating around the fence. I grimaced, wishing my magic had calmed more throughout my forms, but it tugged on its leash more insistently these days. It was in league with my body in rebelling it seemed. Still, I had plenty of practice ignoring the whispers in my mind, the shadows of my connection to every grain of sand in the desert, stretching from the mountains to the sea.

I pushed those thoughts aside as I approached the riders, each gathering their training weapons and mounts. They still seemed to separate into their clans, limiting any mingling to nods and glances as they pushed past each other. Such divisions would need to be patched before we could move on Kelvadan.

Izumi stepped up beside me, leading Alza as well as her own mount and echoed my thoughts. "We need to run drills as a group today."

I nodded as Alza butted my hand with her head. I leapt up onto her back using only a hand on her neck for leverage.

"We will be riding in practice meles of four against four today," I announced from Alza's back. "Each group of four will have one rider from each clan."

This announcement was met with general grumbling from the assembled group. However, it quieted quickly as I scanned the crowd. While they couldn't see my face, I knew my posture projected my disapproval.

Izumi and I wove between the riders as they milled together, reluctantly mixing and recombining themselves. A pocket of riders I recognized as being from Clan Ratan was slow to disperse, and I nudged Alza toward them.

"—let the warlords command their own riders."

One of the voices carried on the wind. I stopped Alza behind the man who had just spoken.

"You wish to offer a critique of my techniques?" I asked, keeping my tone casual.

The man spun in his seat so fast he nearly fell from his horse, having to dig his hands into the stallion's mane to stay on. The steed didn't appreciate this and stamped at the ground in irritation.

Another man in the group came forward, rescuing the rider who clearly hadn't expected me to be listening.

"The warlords of the clans know their riders best," he insisted. His posture was proud, but his eyes flicked over my mask as if they didn't know where to look. I knew it unnerved many, and I made no effort to change that.

"Did Clan Ratan not swear fealty to Lord Alasdar? I remember it distinctly." Indeed, I could feel the blood of Lord Einil dripping over my hands even now. His daughter had been quick to comply.

"We did, but the warlords of each clan should remain in command of their warriors even as we fight Lord Alasdar's war." He lifted his chin. "I am the warlord of Clan Ratan, and I would lead my own riders into battle."

"Lord Alasdar's war?" My voice dropped low, the hiss of snake hidden in its den preparing to strike. The voices in my mind murmured in response. "Does the fate of the desert not belong to all the clans?"

"If it does, then why should Lord Alasdar be the one who we

follow? And why should you be the one put in command of all the riders, when he won't even make you a proper warlord?"

A murmur swept through the surrounding riders, as all attention now gathered on our confrontation. I kept my tone even, but firm enough to ensure all could hear me.

"Because I am Lord Alasdar's fist, and I will come down on any who seek to undermine his plans. You would do well to remember what happens to those who oppose the leader of Clan Katal."

I stared down the knot of riders from Clan Ratan until one by one they bowed their head in deference. My gaze lingered on one with a close-cropped beard that I didn't think I had seen before. His eyes held something calculating just before he averted them, staring down at his horse's neck in respect. Perhaps I had been away too much recently to know the riders as well as I should.

With that, I turned away from the warlord, ready to lead the riders out into the flatter plains beyond encampment where there was more space to ride. The clash of swords would calm the clanging in my mind.

I hadn't made it more than a handful of horse-lengths away when a screaming erupted in my mind. I wheeled Alza around, throwing my arm out as I did it.

A crimson slash split the air where the warlord of Clan Ratan sat on his horse, saber raised as he charged at my back. The assembled riders watched in silence as he froze, blood bubbling from his lips and the realization dawning in his eyes that he was already dead.

Crimson splattered the faces of his comrades behind him from the force of my slash, stark against their ashen skin as their leader slid sideways off his horse. He crumpled to the ground, already a corpse, thick blood blackening the sand around him.

I looked to the sky and breathed deeply. My head swam as if after too much *laka,* drunk on the swift rush of power that came with such decisive use of my magic. The voices in my mind purred in contentment as the desert drank in her sacrifice.

"Move out." Izumi barked orders as she kneed her mount up next to me. "The horse master will handle his mount. We still have training to do."

The riders were silent as they arranged themselves on the plain for our mock battles. Izumi gave me a small nod, but her eyes narrowed at me. I just turned away from the crumpled form on the sand, trotting after the other riders.

When I walked into Lord Alasdar's tent, the dusk air was heavy. I pushed aside the entrance flap, and fragrant smoke met my senses, even as dulled as they were behind the sheet of metal.

Lord Alasdar sat cross legged by the fire, eyes closed and hands clasped in a pose of meditation. The heavy smell of incense in the air stirred memories within me, accompanied by fear and overwhelming relief.

"Your control slips today." He didn't open his eyes as he spoke.

I nodded, but he could not see me and required no response anyway.

"You killed today, but it did not bring you peace."

"The riders question you and resist joining together. Without their combined forces, we will not breach Kelvadan. I will not allow us to fail."

Lord Alasdar opened his eyes to look at me, almost luminescent in their paleness, despite the dim light. "That is not why your magic fights you, though."

I did not answer, but again, he required no reply. He could feel the roiling under my skin.

"There have been no more storms or strange beasts these past weeks. All our hunters have returned safely, not drawn astray by the desert to lose their way and die of exposure. But the magic that holds the world together seems to shiver in anticipation, waiting for something."

The fire crackled in the silence.

"We will give it what it waits for." The flames reflected in Lord Alasdar's wide eyes, making them flash a fiery orange for a moment.

The confidence in his gaze calmed me, but not as much as it normally did. We would destroy Kelvadan and restore to the desert what she had lost. Still, the closer we came to our goal, the further I seemed to slip from the peace that so eluded me.

"I can tell it is testing your control. I have felt the surges of power from you all week." Lord Alasdar's tone was sympathetic. "You have kept it leashed, but you must grow tired. Let me help you."

His hand drifted toward the fire where a metal bar already lay growing red hot. I nodded, untying my belt and letting my leather vest and tabards fall open. I shrugged it off along with my tunic before kneeling by Lord Alasdar.

The neat rows of brands ran across my upper shoulders, extending to the lower points of my shoulder blades by this point. Tonight, we would add more.

I clenched my fists on my legs to keep my hands from shaking even as my mouth grew dry. I hated that I had not yet purged the fear that came over me before Lord Alasdar's lessons. Even so, I forced myself to sit still, screwing my eyes shut behind my mask, glad for the protection from his scrutiny. I would bear the pain, and in return, I would be granted peace from the swirling awareness of the desert constantly murmuring in the back of my mind.

"Bite your tongue. I don't want to bother the camp," Lord Alasdar instructed as he pulled the sizzling poker from the flames.

I bowed my head and stayed silent, as I had for many years.

Izumi found me as I moved through my forms the next morning. My eyelids were heavy with exhaustion from a lack of sleep the night before. I preferred to rest on my back, but three new charred lines across my ribs made that impossible.

With her brown hair darkened with sweat and a sunburned flush disguising her freckles, it was clear she had just returned from her morning run. It was a ritual she had followed since I had joined Lord Alasdar, her having been a member of Clan Katal even before he rose to command.

She set her hands on her hips and observed me with sharp eyes as I finished my second form, working hard to suppress a grimace as a twist stretched the skin on my back.

"You visited Lord Alasdar's tent last night." Her tone was emotionless, but I felt the hidden question behind her words.

I only nodded in response to her observation.

"Does he have any new plans I should know of?"

And there it was, the subtle tinge of frustration that undercut so many of my interactions with Izumi every time we spoke of Lord Alasdar. She always asked me if he had any new plans, as he never called her into his tent, even though she commanded the riders when I was gone.

I never had the heart to tell her that her lack of magic saved her from the burdens of being in his confidence—from the weight of understanding our mission in its entirety and the pain of his mentorship. Perhaps that is why she ran miles every morning before the rest of the riders came to train. To hone her body so thoroughly that her lack of magic was no longer a weakness.

"Nothing of importance." I paused in my forms, resting my hands on my knees as I breathed deeply. My practice left me oddly winded today.

Izumi's eyes flashed, and a muscle in her jaw ticked. "Maybe instead you should be discussing better ways to protect us from the wrath of the desert."

I flinched. I knew the importance of our mission better than most— better than even Izumi, perhaps, but the writhing of my magic and memories of a feral exiled woman had distracted me from our recent setbacks.

Izumi glared at me now, clearly not suffering from the same distractions. While I shied away from very little, her gaze was hot enough to scorch, and I wondered what it would have been like to be on the receiving end of matching glares before her identical twin had been lost to the wrath of the desert.

"I will speak to him of increased measures to protect the clans until we can ride on Kelvadan," I said.

Izumi nodded. "Tell him I'll be happy to assist in whatever way he sees fit. I betrayed my people to make him lord because I believed he could heal the desert."

I felt the hurt in her voice in my own chest. She had marked herself a betrayer, fighting against the riders of Clan Katal that stayed loyal to the former lord when Lord Alasdar made his bid for power. After the death of her twin, I had watched Lord Alasdar easily fill her with fervor, turning her grief into anger against Kelvadan—the root of all our issues. Still, she seemed to itch for his acceptance, glaring at me every time I was summoned privately to Lord Alasdar's tent.

Words formed on my tongue.

I may have Lord Alasdar's confidence, but he is all I have. Do not envy me.

Such words were not fitting of the Viper.

"You will serve him by riding against Kelvadan with us."

She pursed her lips, and I could tell she was dissatisfied, but she let the issue drop.

I sat outside under the stars, looking into a fire. The warmth of another person radiated from one side, although they were a few inches away, just close enough that if I leaned my weight, I might brush their shoulder with mine. I rested my chin on my arms where they were folded over my knees, and after a few moments, my companion hummed.

While the melody was a familiar tune, a song often sung by riders around the fire to celebrate a victory, her sense of pitch was terrible, and it surely was a woman based on the tone of her song.

I exhaled heavily through my nose. "I've heard riders who downed an entire flagon of *laka* sing that tune better."

"Then why don't you sing it," she shot back.

Neither of us looked at each other.

"I think I would need a flagon of *laka* before doing that." Indeed, the song in question had some rather explicit lyrics that I was unlikely to repeat outside of the safety of my tent without some liquid assistance. Not that I ever joined the riders in their celebrations around the fire as it was.

The two of us lapsed into comfortable silence for a long second before she spoke again.

"You're... in pain?"

The way she said it sounded confused, as if she was surprised by the fact she could tell.

At her words, my attention drifted to my back, where I could still feel the shadow of fire pressing lines into my skin. It felt distant though, as if a veil of silk lay between me and the sensation.

"I needed it," I responded.

The words came surprisingly easy, the hazy feel of the world around me making them drift out of my head through my mouth nearly unbidden.

"Why?" Her question was innocent.

"Because it makes me strong, so I can do what must be done."

A rustling came from my side, and I looked out the corner of my eyes to see a long-fingered hand pick up and handful of sand before letting it run out between her fingers.

"I've suffered a lot in my life," she observed. "I don't know yet if it's made me strong. Is all that pain noble, or does it just hurt?"

At this, I turned to look at her fully, and met the bottomless eyes of the exiled woman who had lived in the recesses of my mind since her escape. The corners of Keera's mouth turned down as she looked at my unmasked face.

I awoke with a gasp, sitting bolt upright as my hands flew to face, tracing my bare features. My mask lay on the ground beside me, but I was alone in my tent. It had just been a dream.

I grabbed it now, shoving it on as if that might protect me from the memory of the dream. While I thought of Keera more often than I should, it had always been mere curiosity at where she may have gone or conjecture about the lightning storm that had allowed her escape. Sometimes, it was bouts of frustration that I hadn't been able to snuff out the life of the only person to see my face in so many years.

The dream left me unbalanced. Usually, my only nighttime visions were of being crushed beneath an avalanche of stone or the desert dissolving into the ocean, falling to pieces as I failed to hold it together with my bare hands. This, though—this had been peaceful.

With a groan, I pushed to my feet, grabbing my sword, and pushing out into the pale gray that came before full dawn, painting the world in tones of black and white. There would be no more sleep for me tonight.

I headed to the horses' enclosure, hoping a few quiet moments with Alza might quiet my nerves. A few whispered words with her followed by several hours with my saber in hand would hopefully be enough to free my mind from the odd path it had decided to tread.

I paused as I entered the enclosure, hearing whispered voices. The only one who ever rose as early as me was Izumi, and she normally departed on her run without a word.

I ducked behind a nearby mare that dozed standing up, head hanging partway down. Peeking out from behind her flank, I spied Izumi standing near her own piebald, head bent with another, taller figure.

Inching out a little further, I recognized the man from Clan Ratan with the close-cropped beard. He had been with the warlord who questioned me.

"—protection would the queen offer?"

My hackles rose at the mention of the queen, and I bared my teeth. Still, I quelled my anger enough to bite my tongue and listen closely.

"She is loyal to those who help her. You'd have a place in Kelvadan." A male voice drifted across the enclosure.

I would have had to suppress a laugh of derision if not for the icy feeling in the pit of my stomach. Of all the threats I had envisioned toward the clans, Izumi hadn't been counted among them.

"Meet me outside Lord Alasdar's tent at noon. I will help you get the information you seek," Izumi promised.

Before I could sneak away, Izumi and the man broke apart, and she walked toward the entrance to the enclosure. She would pass my makeshift hiding spot. Quickly, I stepped out from behind the mare, walking purposefully as if I had just entered and not been lurking in the shadows eavesdropping.

As she spotted me, she didn't even narrow her eyes at me in suspicion or seem surprised, only offering the small nod that passed as a greeting between us. I returned the gesture, not wanting to let her know I had heard her plot.

Exiting the enclosure, she set off for her run as she had on every other morning since I had known her. By the time I reached the far edge of the enclosure where Alza waited, the man had disappeared, probably jumping the fence and heading off around the line of tents on the other side.

I debated turning back and heading straight for Lord Alasdar's tent, but I didn't want to tip off Izumi or the rider by acting out of the ordinary. If they knew they had been discovered, they might flee to Kelvadan with valuable information.

Alza, whom I idly patted while I thought, tossed her head in a mirror of frustration, always sensitive to my changing moods. While the Viper did not make friends with the riders of the combined clans, Izumi at least had my trust as a capable warrior. My stomach soured at the thought of her betrayal.

She's betrayed before.

My mind offered me the thought unbidden, and I gritted my teeth. The day Lord Alasdar took control of Clan Katal had been a bloody one, in no small part due to Izumi leading the riders who would lead the former lord into a trap where I could ambush them.

Lord Alasdar, warlord as he was at the time, had been calculated in revealing the plan for grabbing power to Izumi. As she grumbled quietly about the former lord not taking action to save the desert, even after her family had been swallowed by a patch of sinking sand that appeared in the middle of the night, Lord Alasdar was as a sympathetic ear. He knew her anger would drive her to do whatever it took to right the wrong that had stolen her twin sister from her.

Perhaps that anger drove her toward another betrayal as he continually pushed Izumi to the side of his plans.

I ran my fingers through Alza's silky forelock, considering. If I could catch Izumi and the rider red handed, I could rob them of any chance to escape. Perhaps a spy of Kelvadan could even be leveraged as a source of information, or a way to feed false intelligence to the queen. After all, I had heard their plans. I would wait until noon and catch them in the act.

I left the morning of training covered in a sheen of sweat, stomping off in the direction of my own tent as I usually did. When I got there though, I lifted the back of the canvas and ducked out again circling back to the center of camp where Lord Alasdar's tent would be.

As I walked, I tugged on whispers of power running through the camp, making gazes of clansmen and riders slide over me. Anybody particularly favored by the desert wouldn't be affected by such a small deflection, but I knew that Izumi harbored no such magic. If she happened to look my direction, her gaze should skate over me as just another person going about their day.

I reached the edge of the ring of tents marking the center clearing of the encampment just in time to watch Izumi usher a familiar rider through the door of Lord Alasdar's tent. I internally scolded her for her foolishness even as I grit my teeth in anger at her betrayal. She may be high enough ranking that she wasn't questioned entering the lord's tent, but if information were to go missing, she would have been seen coming and going.

Quickly, I skirted around the side of the structure, knowing that they would likely be watching the front flap as they searched. If I were to take them by surprise, I needed an alternate entrance. I didn't want to risk going in without the element of surprise, as Izumi was the fighter who had come closest to besting me since—in a long time, and they would outnumber me.

As I approached the back corner of the tent, voices drifted through the canvas from within, but I couldn't make them out. Without waiting a moment, I slashed my saber through the fabric and jumped inside. Magic flared at the base of my skull in anticipation of a fight and fizzled in frustration when I froze at the sight before me.

Lord Alasdar sat at his table, fingers steepled as he rested his chin on them with an expression of mild interest. Izumi stood over the rider where he knelt on the rug, a bruise blooming across one side of his face. All three looked up at me as I crashed through the tent wall.

"Viper," was Lord Alasdar's only response, somehow a statement and a question, all woven together with threads of disapproval.

"He's a spy," I spat out.

"It seemed Izumi pays closer attention than you, considering she gained his trust and then brought him to me before you even put it together," he explained coolly.

I glanced up at Izumi, and although she did not smile, an unmistakable flash of pride danced along her features. So this was her bid to gain Lord Alasdar's favor.

"As I was saying," Izumi started when I continued to stare, sword still drawn, "Queen Ginevra is obviously concerned about the threat we pose and knows of our progress in uniting the clans if she sent a spy to watch our actions. I spotted Oren sending a messenger bird and became suspicious."

At that, Lord Alasdar stood and walked to stand before the man kneeling on the floor—Oren I guessed. Even as his sandaled feet stopped in his line of view, Oren did not look up, although I could see a muscle working in his jaw.

Izumi kicked him in the side, none too gently. He grunted in pain, but his eyes remained fixed on the ground. Lord Alasdar, seemingly unperturbed, lowered himself to one knee, crouching before the spy in the way one would lower themselves to speak to a small child. My stomach clenched.

With a hand on his jaw, Lord Alasdar forced the spy to look at him. Oren resisted, and Lord Alasdar's long, spidery fingers dug into his cheek.

"What have you told the queen?"

The magic binding together everything in the tent began to shudder, and I tensed against it. Izumi remained expressionless, unable to feel it as Lord Alasdar tugged on the tethers of Oren's mind. Even as Lord Alasdar focused his power on the spy before him, a slithery feeling of unpleasantness ran up my spine at this use of the desert's magic.

While Lord Alasdar didn't harbor nearly as much raw power as I, his iron control gave him skills I could scarcely dream of. I'd never reached into the thoughts of another, aside from the gentle nudge of reassurance against the consciousness of a horse, knowing I would likely shred their sanity on contact. I could barely keep my magic from ripping into my own brain, always inches from falling into the madness that would one day be my fate. My magic was better suited to wild outbursts, shaping the desert around me to its will.

Oren bit his lips as if trying to resist speaking. Lord Alasdar's eyes narrowed as his power flared and Oren began to shake.

"The Trials," Oren blurted out as if saying the words were both pain and relief. "I told her that if the Viper is crowned Champion, the clans will unite."

"What else?" Lord Alasdar's tone was as casual as if he were asking about the weather.

"Nothing." Oren spat the word in disgust. I could tell he was disappointed in his own weakness, giving in to Lord Alasdar's probing, although he shouldn't be. Very few would be able to resist for more than a few seconds.

Lord Alasdar considered him, not withdrawing his power yet, as if checking to see if he were telling the truth.

"Very well." He stood with a brusque nod to Izumi. "Then he is of no more use to us."

Izumi drew her sword from her hip.

I lunged forward. "Wait!"

It was too late. Blood splattered across the thick layers of rugs as Izumi drew her blade across Oren's throat in a savage swipe. He gurgled and swayed for a moment, before pitching forward to crumple at a heap on the ground.

As connected as I had been to the magic of the desert in the tent, the sudden extinguishing of his life left me dizzy, a hint of nausea rolling over me. Lord Alasdar turned to look at me, eyes narrowed as if he could sense my weakness.

"It's good that one of you does not hesitate to do what needs to be done." His tone was icy, but it burned just as deep as hot iron across my back.

I owed Lord Alasdar everything I had but failed to carry out his wishes.

"He could have had information on Kelvadan's defenses or been used to feed false rumors to the queen," I pointed out. Even as his blood soaked through the rugs into the sand, and I felt the desert purr at the lifeforce that was returned to her, rage built in my head at the wastefulness of Izumi's actions.

"He would not have known anything you haven't already told me,"

Lord Alasdar dismissed. "Leaving him alive would only have given him a chance to escape, as you did with the exile girl."

I bit my tongue so hard my mouth flooded with copper. Izumi raised her chin triumphantly, standing over the fallen spy with a look of victory that spoke of conquering more than just an unarmed man.

So, this was Lord Alasdar's ploy: to use his disapproval of Izumi to pit her against me, driving her efforts to new heights and punishing me for my failures. My hesitation to make the sacrifice and use brute force to bring the last five clans under our control had not gone unnoticed. Lord Alasdar's message was clear.

I bowed my head. "We are lucky Izumi remained vigilant."

I would do better. I had given up everything for Lord Alasdar to do my duty and save the desert. He saved me from my madness, and I would do whatever it took to help him in his mission—our mission.

CHAPTER TWELVE
KEERA

I bit my tongue to hide the grimace that always threatened to overtake my face at the taste of lyra tea. Still, the muscles in my brow contracted involuntarily, creating an expression that I imagined looked something like polite constipation.

Thankfully, the queen didn't notice, taking a hearty sip from her own cup, completely unperturbed as she read over the scroll in front of her. I hoped it was more information from Oren. We hadn't heard from him in a while, and I itched for more news of Clan Katal—of the Viper. Now that I knew I was to face him in the Trials, he loomed in my mind as a dark and imposing figure.

As monstrous as he felt in my consciousness as I trained, unyielding and inhuman, even more disturbing was the way he appeared in the dark of night. In my dreams, he was unmasked. Calm. In his last nighttime visit, we had sat before a fire as I hummed a familiar tune, as if he wasn't the enemy who haunted most of my waking moments. Resist as I might, my nocturnal self relaxed in his presence, and I woke suddenly worrying if this was a trap to lure me in, like a coiled snake playing at being dead.

I swatted the idea away. They were just dreams, not visions sent by the Viper himself. Nothing more than my unconscious mind connecting my memory of his face with my underlying anxiety of facing him in the Trials.

"Is the tea still helping you contain your magic?" the queen asked.

I nodded, although 'contain' wasn't the word I would use. After drinking the tea, it was as if a wet blanket had been thrown over my magic, the pit of my stomach feeling dampened and slightly empty. At those times, I could approach the well of power, tiptoeing around in my mind as I stacked mental stones around it.

Every time I rode Daiti in the desert or sparred with Aderyn—or woke from a dream of the Viper—I would come back to myself and find my barrier decimated, carefully placed rocks blown aside as if they were blades of arrowgrass.

So contained? No. Muted? Perhaps.

"I'm glad," the queen continued, ignorant to my mental conundrum. "Because I have a favor to ask."

"Anything," I answered automatically.

The queen chuckled. "Never promise a royal a favor before you know what it is."

"Royals aren't common on this side of the mountains. I know little of them," I admitted.

"And I know more of them than I would like, although it still isn't very much," Queen Ginevra said. "That is part of the favor I want to ask you, though."

I cocked my head in curiosity.

"Next week, two ambassadors will be visiting from Viltov and Doran. I'm throwing a bit of a party to welcome them, and I would like you to come."

My mind whirled with questions, but at the forefront was "me?"

After all, my manners still paled in comparison to the queen's and even Aderyn's. I was new to the city, and of no particular political influence beyond the queen's sympathy for my magic.

"You," Queen Ginevra repeated, unperturbed. "The ambassadors are coming in part because of the Trials. Given that they happen only once every twenty years, and they are one of the few times members of all clans are present in the city, they plan to stay for the competition. Given that your victorious emergence from the Trials is a *particular interest* of mine"—she picked her words with all the poised precision of a born diplomat—"I thought your presence might be appropriate."

I considered her in silence as my brain tried to sort through the political machinations of the queen's mind. I knew little of foreigners—very few clansmen of the Ballan Desert knew anything of those from beyond the mountains. While we knew the mountains that bordered three sides of the desert and the sea on the far edge were not the edges of the world, the clans had little contact with anything beyond those boundaries.

Occasionally, members of Clan Padra—who were good at making things from weapons to glass jewelry made from firing the sand that infiltrated every area of our lives—would travel to Kelvadan. Here, goods could be sold to traders from other countries who were bold enough to cross the mountains. Kelvadan kept the clans from having to interface with outsiders who would not be able to locate the clans in the desert as they roamed around between unknowable locations.

Rumor had it that sailors from Viltov had once taken a boat from their country around the mountains to the coast where the desert met the sea, hoping to bypass Kelvadan and deal with the clans directly. But the desert was vast, and with none of them from a clan with her favor, they had likely perished before they even found fresh water.

"Why would foreigners be interested in the Champion of the Trials?" I asked. After all, the Champion of the Desert would be of little concern to those who lived beyond its reaches.

"Because I mean to ask for their help."

I drew back sharply, my small metal chair tipping back onto two legs. A lord of one of the clans would be too proud to ask another—especially one not from the Ballan Desert—for aid. "Their help?"

"They have armies, bigger than anything one city could muster," Queen Ginevra explained, although her polished demeanor failed to fully hide the hint of disapproval in her voice. "Their countries are vast, and their soldiers could aid us if war comes to Kelvadan. Even if they could just pledge us increased food so we are not dependent on hunting and farming the area around the city in the case that Clan Katal lays siege."

Her reasoning was sound, but doubt still gnawed at me. Inviting foreigners into the desert seemed like a violation of her magic. I preferred not to think about what would happen when—if—the Viper defeated me in the Trials. Similar to survival in the wilderness, it didn't help to focus on what would happen to you when water ran out and hunger became too much. You simply had to focus on finding supplies.

A queen, however, had to be ready for any contingency.

"What would you like me to do?" I asked.

"The desert's power runs strong in you, and you will be an asset to Kelvadan's riders. Give them confidence that our city can emerge victorious and that they will not be pledging their soldiers to die for a hopeless cause."

Her confidence gnawed at me, and the magic in my belly stirred, asleep but still uncontained. This was a job for a prince or princess of Kelvadan—somebody with more control and practice, who had spent far more time among dignitaries or people in general than I had. But the queen had asked me, and I owed her my life, so I nodded.

"I will do what I can."

If I had been afraid of feeling like an imposter all dressed up for a royal dinner, I had underestimated Neven's skill. When I had mentioned the occasion at dinner, Neven had immediately jumped to his feet and rushed to his workshop to figure out what I would wear to such an occasion.

When I had frowned and mentioned that I could wear the purple dress from the festival again, Aderyn had shaken her head and smiled fondly.

"Neven enjoys making clothes for his friends more than he likes selling them, and I can only wear so many outfits."

It turned out Aderyn would be coming to the dinner as well, as the commander of Kelvadan's riders, although she already had a trunk of custom outfits to pick from. Now she helped me slip the gossamer red fabric of my dress over my head.

Underneath, I wore a band of golden fabric around my breasts and my hips to keep me decent, although the dark red fabric of the dress was thin and light enough that it left little to the imagination. I need not have worried about feeling constricted in my formal wear—my outfit was as light as air and left me free to move whichever way I liked.

Once the dress was on, Aderyn fetched gold bangles for my wrist while Neven approached me with a pot of gold paint.

"Are you sure?" I eyed it warily. While clansmen regularly wore paint into battle, or inked lines into their skin like Aderyn, citizens of Kelvadan had taken to decorating their skin for aesthetics alone.

"Trust me," he insisted, and he seemed so pleased with himself that I closed my eyes and let him get to work.

The brush tickled my face as he dusted the golden pigment across my cheekbones and the bridge of my nose. Then he proceeded to dot it on my bottom lip before tapping my jaw and telling me I could look.

Staring in the hand mirror he offered, I found the effect more pleasing than I'd expected. The light dusting of gold across the high points of my face reminded me of the way the sun touched my skin when I turned my face up to the sky, and the metallic color was the perfect contrast against my light brown skin. I smiled, and Neven grinned back at me.

The moment settled the nest of snakes churning in my stomach. Perhaps I was not so unprepared to face the ambassadors from Viltov and Doran after all. By the time we reached the palace though, my nerves had begun to jangle again and my palms grew sweaty. I itched for the feel of a saber in my hand or Daiti between my thighs. As it was, I felt as if I were walking into a battle nearly naked. The only armor I wore was the wet blanket over my magic from chugging a cup of lyra tea before getting dressed.

When we entered the palace dining room, we discovered we weren't the first to arrive, a few of the queen's councilors milled about. I caught sight of Kaius among a cluster of them and he threw me an easy wink. The doors to the adjacent terrace had been thrown open, letting in air and offering a perfect few of the ombre sky, ranging from dusty purple to flaming orange as the sun flirted with the horizon. Near the exit to the terrace stood the queen, conversing with two men that could only be the ambassadors.

Aderyn caught my eyes, jerking her chin toward the trio and indicating we should approach. I lifted my chin and squared my shoulders. Somehow, joining their discussion felt less intimidating when I was doing so on an order from Aderyn. After all, she was my commander, and I was one of her riders.

"Ah, just who I wanted to see." The queen graciously opened her arm toward Aderyn and me as we approached, stepping back to let us join their group. "This is Lyall from Viltov," she gestured to the taller of the two, who took me in with an unimpressed expression. "And Hadeon from Doran."

I observed the second ambassador as Queen Ginevra introduced us in turn. He had golden hair and a wide smile that revealed a chipped front tooth, although the flaw did little to detract from his general handsomeness. He wore a light blue tunic with a plush white fur draped over his shoulders from some animal I couldn't possibly imagine. It wouldn't be very practical to wear in the desert, although the evenness of his fair complexion betrayed the fact that he didn't get nearly as much sun as the clansmen or residents of Kelvadan. While people here had a range of skin tones, those with paler complexions quickly accumulated freckles, even if they always wore a hood.

"It's a pleasure to meet you," intoned Lyall with a flatness that indicated he felt nothing of the sort when Queen Ginevra finished introducing us.

"Quite a pleasure," echoed Hadeon with much more enthusiasm. "Although you make me realize I might be a tad overdressed."

I looked between the three women in the group, finding we were all similarly dressed, with bare arms and abdomens, while Hadeon was covered from wrists to ankles. Even the men of Kelvadan, with no need to hide themselves from the rays of the sun as they dined inside, wore belted vests with bare chests beneath and pants that ended just below the knees.

"Out on the sands, it can be nice to protect yourself from the sun with a hood and a robe, but in the protection of the palace it is nice to stay cool," I admitted.

"Not something I would have thought of when preparing for my journey," Hadeon admitted with a grimace. "I didn't realize it could actually get this hot. In Doran, it's cold enough to snow for three quarters of the year."

"Snow?" I asked.

"Why don't we all take a seat so dinner can be served," Queen Ginevra cut in. "And Keera and Hadeon can sit next to each other to talk about snow."

I didn't miss her pointed look over Lyall's shoulder as we arranged ourselves around the table. Frankly, I gladly positioned myself on Hadeon's right with Aderyn on his left, between him and Lyall, who sat next to the queen. Kaius sat on Queen Ginevra's other side, with most of the councilmen across from us.

"Have you really never seen snow?" Hadeon asked as the meal began.

I shook my head. "I've only heard about it," I admitted. Indeed, some tales from my childhood had mentioned the white powder existing high in the mountains.

"I can't imagine," Hadeon said with an incredulous shake of his head.

The first course of the meal passed easily enough, conversation mainly comparing homelands. I learned the pelt on Hadeon's shoulders came from the cold-weather cousins of the fennec foxes we were familiar with. I kept one eye on Aderyn and Queen Ginevra's conversation with Lyall, and although he divulged his country to be an island nation off the coast of Hadeon's homeland, his descriptions were perfunctory, and he seemed much more interest in what Hadeon was telling me.

"Well, I'm excited to witness these Trials," Hadeon said as the second course was served. "You indicated that they are of great importance to your people."

"They are." Queen Ginevra jumped into our conversation, revealing her ability to listen to every conversation happening around her. "Keera will be competing, and none of us here would be surprised if she were crowned Champion."

Nobody here but me, I added internally, for I still harbored my doubts. The queen insisted that the power of the desert in me was a sign that she favored me, likely even enough to be her Champion. Every time Queen Ginevera mentioned the Trials, I swallowed my doubts, knowing that she and Aderyn were counting on me. I was loathe to disappoint them. Still, after training for mere months, I was dubious about my ability to best more experienced competitors, let alone a rider who seemed more myth than man.

"Based on your correspondence, it is imperative that she does win," Lyall interjected. A hush fell over the room at the comment, and the rest of the advisors at the table abandoned their conversations in favor of listening in on ours.

"I had hoped to let you enjoy more of your meal before burdening you with Kelvadan's requests," Queen Ginevra admitted, "but it is true. Our city has much at stake in the coming Trials."

Hadeon looked at her with interest as Lyall stared stonily, waiting for her to continue.

"If one of the competitors from the clans, a rider known as the Viper, is successful, the clans may unite against Kelvadan and attack. With their combined force, a civil war in the desert could spell death for many."

"Civil war?" Hadeon echoed. "Would it really come to that?"

"I'm afraid war is a language the clans of the Ballan Desert speak well," Aderyn answered this time.

"And why should a Civil war concern Viltov?" Lyall asked frankly. "Although we have sailed to the coast on the far side of the desert, we have never made contact with the clans. Their activities do not affect us."

I bristled at his callousness, but Queen Ginevra's placid, diplomatic expression did not slip an inch. "Viltov has traded with Kelvadan since the days of my grandfather. If the city were to fall, Viltov would not be able to acquire goods from the Ballan Desert."

Lyall appeared unmoved by the prospect of loss of trade. "While our wives certainly appreciate your textiles, you've never traded with us the one thing we've tried to bargain for many times."

Queen Ginevra sat up straighter. "Perhaps arrangements can be made in exchange for your help protecting Kelvadan from the unrest of the clans."

"Are you saying you would consider trading your horses?" Hadeon asked, leaning forward in his seat.

Movement in my peripheral vision caught my eye, and I chanced a glance at Kaius, who shifted in his seat. Some of the same discomfort in his movement echoed through my bones. Horses were sacred to the Ballan Desert.

"Negotiations could be opened if Viltov or Doran offered military aid to Kelvadan," the queen answered.

"Then Viltov will stay and consider if military aid will be required," Lyall responded in a non-answer that I was coming to realize was the way of these politicians.

"Hopefully you are as touched by the desert as the queen mentioned"—Hadeon inclined his head toward me—"and it does not come to civil war at all."

"You can't actually believe that the desert choses her Champion with some kind of magic," Lyall retorted.

Hadeon shrugged. "If these people have never seen snow, perhaps there are things here that I have not seen yet."

After that, conversation started up again but remained stilted for the rest of the evening. I focused on eating as neatly as possible, although my fingers still ended up sticky from dates, and I brushed crumbs from my lips hastily with the back of my hands.

My hopes that this meeting would relieve some of the crushing pressure of the Trials sank miserably. Instead of having an alternative to protect Kelvadan should the Viper be crowned champion, all we had accomplished was further scrutiny on the competition. Only weeks away now, it barreled down on us like an out-of-control horse.

As soon as the meal was cleared, Lyall swept from the room, barely taking the time to wish the assembled group a good evening. For the remaining diners, small cups of *laka* were poured, and everybody began to mill about the room once more.

Without thought, I drifted toward the open door to the terrace. As casual as the tone of conversation was, the dining room remained thick with expectations and anxiety of the coming war. The stars called my name from the now dark sky, drawing me out into the open air where the wind smelled of hot sand and freedom.

As I leaned on the railing around the terrace, nursing my cup of *laka* carefully—the queen had warned me that too much could counteract the lyra leaves' effect—a figure stepped up beside me. I turned, expecting to see Aderyn, standing steadfast as ever in support. Instead, Hadeon stopped beside me, looking up at the stars as I did.

"Don't let Lyall bother you. Viltov was never going to send help," he mused.

"They still might," I argued, although I had to agree that Lyall's demeanor had been icy from the beginning. "Why else would he stay for the Trials?"

"To keep an eye on me." Hadeon rested his elbow on the railing, propping his chin in his hand. As he tilted his head to look at me, a strand of his immaculately styled golden hair fell forward across his forehead. Instead of looking messy, I got the impression that he spent hours coiffing it with potions and pomades, so it fell just so when the moment arose.

"On you?"

"Doran and Viltov have been rivals for generations. The islands Viltov inhabits were once part of our nation before they invaded. They have their eyes on the mainland too, already occupying a few coastal cities. However, my king believes that the islands should be part of Doran once more, but he cannot mount an attack on them without losing ground on the mainland. So, we remain at a stalemate." Hadeon illustrated the conflict for me.

"And so why should your kings care about Kelvadan when war already marches on their own territory?" I asked. Realizing my argument was against my own best interest, I snapped my mouth shut.

"Letting one of us get the advantage over the other would be disastrous. So, where an ambassador from one country goes, another must follow." Hadeon spread his hands. "Rumor has it that horses from the Ballan Desert would mount the greatest cavalry in the world. But if one of us were to supply troops to Kelvadan and thin our defenses, it could leave us open to attack from the other. And so, we watch, and we wait."

My head spun with all the political machinations hidden beneath the surface of a polite dinner. Perhaps the clans had it right, and a duel of honor would be simpler. I shook the thought from my head though. The harshness of the clans had led to my exile, and the complexities of diplomacy were the price Kelvadan paid for peace.

"Why tell me any of this?" I asked.

"We're always looking for an advantage over the other," Hadeon said. "Lyall doesn't believe in the power that some say lives in these lands, but I figured there is no harm in being on the good side of the supposed Champion of the Desert. Who knows what help it could bring down the line?"

Hadeon smiled at me, the expression easy and polished. I returned the gesture, glad of his confidence even as the power in my gut let out a sleepy growl. Another bet had been placed on me, although it seemed that politicians gambled with fate, not coin. I squared my shoulders against the weight of responsibility—a weight that seemed to grow heavier with every passing day toward the Trials. For years, my only responsibility had been to my own life, and even then, I questioned whether survival was wise. Perhaps these expectations were the price of belonging—of having a home.

For Kelvadan, for my home, I would carry those expectations, no matter how much they chafed.

"Come. I have something to show you." The queen met me just inside our usual terrace today, cutting me off and heading up the stairs further into the palace, past the levels I had seen before to unknown heights.

I followed her curiously as we climbed and climbed.

The queen's words came out breathy from the exertion as we walked. "I must admit, the logistics of the Trials have become time consuming lately. Organizing all the challenges is quite a task. I regret that I don't have more time to help you, but I think I might offer you another way to learn."

My curiosity piqued, the staircase led around and around until I bordered on dizzy, I assumed winding to the highest spire that crowned the apex of the city.

Finally, we reached a landing facing a set of double doors. I craned my neck to stare at the tapestry above the grand arch. One side depicted a mountain range, and the blue waves of the ocean filled the other edge. Stretching between was golden fabric, the same color as the sands in the midday sun. In the center was the image of a red gemstone emitting rays of light that shot across the tapestry, marked by iridescent threads.

"Breathtaking, isn't it?" Queen Ginevra asked, following my line of sight. "It was made by the craftsman who trained Neven's late master. Kelvar commissioned it to hang over the door to his and Alix's rooms."

I glanced over at her, and she nodded.

"These rooms at the top of the palace belonged to the first King and Queen of Kelvadan. Now though, they serve as a reminder of my family's legacy—and our failures." She stepped forward and laid one hand on the door but didn't push on it. Inches above her fingers glittered a pane of red-black glass, so dark I couldn't see what lay beyond. A matching panel adorned the other of the two doors.

Blood glass.

"Nobody knew as many secrets of the desert as Kelvar, and even he knew frighteningly little. As his moods raged and he became more distracted, he took to shutting himself in these rooms to pore over old scrolls and mutter to himself. These rooms were a haven to him and Alyx, these blood glass panels recognizing only their touch to allow them in." She ran her fingers over the smooth, dark surface of the glass.

"When Alyx fell ill and finally passed, he wouldn't even let anybody see her body or remove her from their rooms. She was still in there when he rode out into the desert, never to be seen again. Now this room is a tomb for Kelvadan's first queen."

I bowed my head in respect as the queen stared contemplatively at the door before her.

"Everybody speaks of Kelvadan being my grandfather's legacy, but I like to come up here and consider Alyx and what she might have done. While Kelvar was the greatest warrior ever known, strong in the magic of the desert, this city would not have come to be what it was without Alyx. She had a way of bringing people together, bestowing peace on all she touched. Even Kelvar, who was more storm than human sometimes. The desert gifted her with healing magic, letting her heal Kelvar's horse and start their love story."

"She sounds incredible," I admitted, wondering at the dead queen who lay beyond the thick stone doors, likely no more than bones at this point. The city might not bear her name, but it had been built for her.

"She calmed Kelvar's madness for years, it only overtaking him when she was gone and he was blinded with grief," Queen Ginevra's voice got very quiet. "I've always wanted to be like Alyx, but I failed a long time ago." She took her hand from the door and turned to face me. Her eyes were overbright, but she held her chin high. "When I saw you, troubled by the same power that plagues my family, I knew the desert was giving me a chance to set things right. If I could help you, I would be redeemed."

"You don't need redemption," I said with a shake of my head.

"I wish I could offer you the same wisdom that Alyx would, but I'm going to offer you the next best thing," the queen told me. "While the rarest and most precious texts Kelvar had remain locked in his chambers, the rest are down one level in the Royal Library's private collection. I encourage you to read anything you can. Hopefully the same wisdom that Kelvar sought can help you."

I blinked in shock before remembering myself and tapping my brow with my knuckles in respect. "It would be an honor."

"I'm not sure a bunch of dusty tomes and scrolls are an honor, but my knowledge can be yours now." The queen smiled kindly as she led me to down one flight of stairs to a small room filled with shelves. It looked much like her private study down many floors, but the air was mustier, speaking to the age of the books and how often it laid undisturbed.

I lingered there, thumbing through paper as fragile as the skin of an onion, until it grew so dark, I couldn't make out the figures on the page. I hadn't made it very far, and I cursed the slowness of my reading.

While I had been taught as a child, reading was a skill that fell by the wayside as I scraped a living out of bare sand. Now, I itched to unravel the legend of Kelvar that might be hidden in these texts and cursed at the way I had to pause and decipher every third word.

From what I could gather, many of the scrolls and books related to one of the most common tales told among the clans: the first crossing of the desert. While it was often told around the Clan Padra firepits in my youth, I pored over it now with renewed intensity.

Crossing the desert had granted the first clan lord the ability to call this wild land his home and the magic that now ran through its people's veins—the Heart of the Desert. It seemed that Kelvar had become obsessed with uncovering the source of the power that drove him mad. Was the answer to controlling this magic in its origin?

If Kelvar could not figure it out in all his years, then I doubted I would either. Following the trail he left was the best chance I had, though.

Aderyn pursed her lips and stared up at the arched entrance to the city before her. She had pulled her hood low over her face, but I could still see the concern in her gaze.

"Kelvar built this entire city in a day and couldn't be bothered to give us a gate?" she asked nobody in particular.

"I'm not sure a gate made of stone would be very practical," answered Dryden anyway from where he sat on his horse on my other side.

"It would have made me feel better," she grumbled. "At least it is the only way in and out of the city, easily defended from the top of the walls." She raised her voice now, gesturing to the guards walking along the edge of the wall for all the trainees to see. Aderyn decided to take us with her as she prepared the city's security for the upcoming Trials, the trip outside the walls giving us a chance to practice riding in the open space. It also served as a tour of the city's defenses.

"We could build a gate," I pointed out.

"I could ask the queen to commission one, but it would take time to build such a structure." Aderyn shook her head. "Besides, I doubt she would allow it. The lack of gate has always symbolized how Kelvadan is open to all. It would hardly fit with the tone of diplomacy she's adopting for the Trials." The tone of her voice indicated she didn't see diplomacy ending in success. Aderyn was the type to perform negotiations with one hand on her sword.

Still, the queen held on to hope that the Trials could prevent a war. She planned to give places of honor to Lyall and Hadeon, the two diplomats, at the celebrations. By her estimation, just seeing them might show that Kelvadan would not stand alone against the clans of the desert, persuading some of the lords to rethink their allegiance to Lord Alasdar.

"While the clans certainly aren't afraid of battle, they won't risk their riders in a war they know they won't win," the queen had commented the afternoon after the failed dinner. "Perhaps if they see an attack on Kelvadan as hopeless, Lord Alasdar's troops will melt around him."

"We don't have a promise from Viltov or Doran to send aid though," I argued, unsure.

At that, Queen Ginevra smiled tightly. "What people think often ends up being more important than what's actually true."

Aderyn clearly wasn't putting all her faith in the idea of Lord Alasdar's forces disbanding. Night and day, she talked about security for the Trials, spending every second she wasn't preparing for them training the riders in the case that war came fast on their heels.

Stopping before the gate, Aderyn wheeled her mount around to face us. "Pair up and survey the walls for any weaknesses Clan Katal could exploit on an attack of the city. Dryden, Keera, you start from the eastern edge where the wall meets the cliffside and work back toward us. Nyra, Kyler, you head east from here until you meet them."

As Aderyn directed the others to the far side of the wall, Dryden shot a grin at me, eyes squinted against the midday sun. "Race you to the end of the wall?"

Before I could answer, he kicked his mare into a gallop, disappearing in a cloud of dust. Despite the gravity of recent events, I found myself smiling too as I urged Daiti forward with the squeeze of my thighs and a murmured command. He leapt forward with an eagerness I would have expected if I hadn't exercised him outside the wall in a week.

As the wind of our hectic ride pushed back my hood, tendrils of hair pulled free from my twist, as if the desert wanted to play with them, running her hands through my silky strands. The sounds of Aderyn's voice were drowned by the pounding of Daiti's hooves in time with the beating of my heart.

We quickly caught Dryden and his mount, a laugh tearing itself from me as Daiti plunged past them, the muscles in his neck flexing in time with his extended gait. I let myself revel in the feeling of lightness that filled me out here on the sands with no walls to hold me. As much as Kelvadan had become my purpose, the closest thing I ever had to a home, I missed the feel of the sand beneath me and sun above me, the horizon stretching as far as the eye could see in every direction with equally endless possibilities. Riding brought me more peace than all my hours of attempted meditation with Queen Ginevra.

Approaching the cliff where the walls joined the mountain, I slowed Daiti to a trot. I looked over my shoulder at Dryden, still galloping to catch up with me. As he pulled astride and slowed his own mount, he shook his head, the look of defeat on his face too exaggerated to be genuine.

"You wound my pride. I hope the Trials this year don't have too many riding events, or I'll be eliminated early." Dryden panted.

"On the contrary, I'm hoping for many riding events." I had spent many sleepless nights trying to puzzle out what the Trials might entail, but Aderyn and the queen remained tight-lipped throughout the preparations. Despite their desire for me to win, they refused to share any details for the planned events, worried that accusations of cheating might hurt my credibility or have me ejected from the tournament.

So, I had tried to puzzle through what challenges might await me, apart from the duels that were the traditional final event. I didn't mind my loss of sleep, as I had been visited by another troublesome dream as I rested two nights ago. This time, the Viper sat across from me in a small tent, a plate of dates between us.

As he ate one, I wrinkled my nose. "I've eaten too many dates in my lifetime."

At that, the Viper let out a truncated sound startlingly close to a laugh for somebody so fearsome, although his laughter didn't strike me as odd until after I woke. "Are you even allowed to live in the Ballan Desert if you don't like dates?"

"I don't dislike them." I shrugged. "There were just too many times where they were all I had." I stared at the plate, and the fruit transformed into oranges in the helpful way things sometimes do in a dream.

The Viper frowned. "I was enjoying them."

"Well, I prefer oranges."

We reached out for the plate at the same time, and our hands collided. While everything around me remained hazy and out of focus, his hand against mine was jarringly solid, a jolt of reality in a nighttime vision. The warmth of his touch had jerked me from sleep.

I woke with a gasp and returned to considering the Trials and avoiding odd dreams of the man I would compete with for the fate of the desert in a matter of days. Perhaps the dreams were just my mind's attempt at puzzling out the masked Viper. After all, I had been hoping for more word from Oren on my competitor—who he was under the mask or how he came to have such a position of power—but Queen Ginevra's spy had remained silent. From the worried crease between the queen's brows whenever I asked if Oren had sent a falcon, the lack of information on the Viper concerned her too.

Dryden brought me back to the present by speaking. "I guess I'll have to hope we don't race each other on horseback too early on."

I nodded and patted Daiti's neck, turning toward the wall to do as Aderyn had bid. I scanned upward, still in awe of the solid sheet of rock that surrounded the city. Before I could ensure this section of wall was without fault, a rustle sounded behind me.

Dryden's yelp split the air, followed by a terrible howl. I wheeled around. A red wolf flew through the air at Dryden whose mount sidled out of the way, eyes rolling in her head. The dodge kept the wolf from unseating Dryden as it might have, but it still caught his arm in its jaws.

A scream tore from Dryden's lips as several smaller wolves approached from the far side. I reached for my sling in my belt instinctually, heart skipping a beat when I came up empty. Dryden grunted in pain as he tried to shake the wolf loose, serrated teeth ripping the sleeve of his robe, now stained crimson. He didn't see the predators approaching from the other side.

The wildness in my chest from my gallop, which had not quite dissipated, rose again, overtaking my mind in the space of a breath. I felt the wolves, their hunger, the panic of the horses and the dunes in the distance that would lead to the sea.

I threw my hand out with a yell and a crack like thunder split the air. I blinked to clear my vision from the white spots that had overtaken it, eyes finally focusing on the shapes of four wolves, all limp on the ground.

I lifted my gaze to check on Dryden, only to find his horse's back empty. In a panic, I slid off Daiti, knees nearly buckling as my feet hit the ground. Among the slumped forms of the wolves, whether dead or unconscious, I did not know, lay Dryden face down in the sand.

I rolled him over only to be overcome by a wave of nausea. A spreading line of blood crossed his shoulder. It wasn't a rough tear from teeth or claws that rent his flesh, but a clean slash—like the magical cut I had just used to dispatch the wolves.

I had done this.

The tan fabric of his tunic soaked through as I watched, and he blinked open bleary eyes. I reached out to press on his wound, anxious to stem the bleeding but when his gaze focused on me, he flinched back. I tried again, but he shied away, panting in pain, his eyes wide and full of an all too familiar emotion: fear. It was the look in my parents' eyes after I split the earth at my feet—the look that haunted me in the darkest hours of the night.

A bared my teeth at the burning behind my eyes, untying my hood from around my head. I ignored Dryden's expression, using the fabric to tie around his arm, putting as much pressure as I could muster on his wound.

"Can you stand?"

He nodded, but as he tried to move, he wavered unsteadily. I helped him up with an arm under his good shoulder.

"We have to get you back to the gates."

He nodded again, but his dark skin had taken on an ashen undertone. I didn't trust him to keep his seat on his horse, but I didn't have time to negotiate with him to ride double with me or with Daiti to let him clamber onto his back. Instead, I let him use me as a human ladder to climb his own mare. Then I led her forward, walking alongside her in case Dryden slipped off. He didn't seem far from it as he lay heavily over her neck. Daiti immediately followed, coming up to flank Dryden on his other side as if sensing the same unsteadiness I did.

The walk back to the gates was short but felt like it lasted eternity, Dryden using the little strength he seemed to have to shoot wide-eyed looks at me.

I opened my mouth several times but bit my tongue, eventually hard enough to taste copper in my mouth. There was no good apology for what I had done—no easy explanation. Dryden knew I had lost control before, but nobody had been hurt. Maybe it had just seemed like a fun novelty when nobody had been killed, but my abilities had an ugly side. I had been working for months to gain command over the power that resided within me but only seemed to be worse than when I started. I was a failure. After all Kelvadan and the queen had offered me, I couldn't even keep them safe from myself. No matter how kind Aderyn and Neven were to me, it had been unrealistic to hope Kelvadan could be my home. I was a menace to her people, even as I tried to save them.

Seeing us approach, the group by the gates immediately saw something was wrong. Aderyn galloped up, Nyra and the others hot on her tail.

"What happened?"

Dryden shot a fearful look at me but didn't speak.

"Wolves. We took care of them." Guilt and fear mixed in my chest as I said it. Soon, they would find out what I had done, and everybody would look at me with the same horror that Dryden did.

Aderyn nodded but looked between the two of us with discerning eyes. "Nyra, help Dryden to the healer. Kylar, you go ahead and tell them to expect him."

They sprang into action, while I stood frozen, toeing the sand with my boot. Dryden whispered to Nyra as she began to lead his horse away, and they both looked at me over their shoulders. Nyra's eyes narrowed.

"I'll go investigate. Make sure there aren't any more," Aderyn declared. "And Keera... I'll see you at home."

She rode off, but I stood there with a lump in my throat for a few moments before trudging back to the city. Daiti trailed me with his head hung low.

I heard the front door open and sprung up from the couch where I was sitting, squeezing my hands together before me. I had spent the past hour thinking of something I could say to Aderyn, but I still didn't know where to start.

She walked into the room and looked at me, raising one brow before sitting down to pull off her own boots.

"You really did a number on those wolves," was her first comment as she shook the sand out of her shoes.

I resisted the urge to stare at the floor. "Why do you let me stay here?"

It wasn't what I had planned on saying—I had rehearsed everything I could think to say about how I would fail Kelvadan in the Trials—but all of a sudden it seemed like the most pressing question. She had taken me into her home without protest and let me stay even when I had proven myself a liability on multiple occasions. She had given me a purpose, when even my own clan couldn't extend me a home.

"Did you have somewhere else to go?" she asked.

"I made it on my own for a long time."

She gave me a long look, leaning forward and propping her elbows on her knees. "I've made some of my best friends by taking in strays."

"I'm not the first?"

"No." A smile quirked the edge of her lips. "Neven was the first."

I furrowed my brow in question. She leaned back with a sigh and gestured for me to sit.

"Neven was a member of Clan Tibel. He was given his horse when he came of age, but training to be one of the clan riders...well, it wasn't for him. He always wanted to be a craftsman, but his parents were both warriors and hunters, and they tried to force him to follow in their footsteps. One day, when the clan passed close by the city, he left. He rode into Kelvadan looking just as lost as you did.

"I was the guard at the gate that day and decided to help him. Now he weaves the best cloth in the city, and traders from across the mountain consistently come in search of it. And us..."

Aderyn shrugged, but her meaning was clear.

"Neven seems less likely to accidentally cut your arm off though," I grumbled.

"Dryden isn't going to lose an arm," Aderyn snorted. "He's just shaken up. Doesn't really have a warrior's disposition."

"What if I can't win the Trials? What if I end up hurting more people than I help—if people would be safer if I left?" My heart hurt even as I said it. Kelvadan was the closest to belonging I had ever felt, even if I occasionally felt homesick for a place I couldn't even picture. It certainly wasn't the oasis where I struggled to survive, even more trapped than I felt when entombed in the stone of the mountain. Here, I had Aderyn and Neven, who included me in conversation easily every night, even if I didn't contribute much to the proceedings. I enjoyed being part of their family.

Something flickered in Aderyn's eyes—something looking suspiciously like hurt. She looked away, not meeting my gaze as she spoke low, as if confessing to a grave misdeed.

"I knew somebody who struggled the same way you do once. I lost them many years ago. I hoped—I still hope—that helping you might be a way to set things right. And I still believe you came to Kelvadan for a reason."

I tilted my head. The queen had said something very similar when she explained to me her family's fraught history.

"Stay through the Trials," Aderyn proposed. "I believe you are more likely to win than you are to hurt anybody."

I nodded my agreement. It was the least I could do for one of the first real friends I had ever had, even if I didn't fully understand her faith in me.

The plains outside the city had been transformed, now almost as lively as the streets inside the walls. Rows of tents lined walkways through an encampment larger than even the one of Clan Katal I had escaped from months earlier. The large tents of prominent families mixed with the small dwellings of single riders. Flags of every color hung at the entrance flaps, signaling the presence of all the tribes, although I gave tents sporting the maroon scorpion of Clan Padra a wide berth.

The whicker of horses and the smell of meat roasting over fire filled the air as all the competitors for the Trials arrived. They had been trickling in for days now, more and more coming as we approached the opening feast, which would be held this evening.

I walked among the tents in awe of the number of riders ready to test their skills. Perhaps I would be eliminated by some other skilled rider before I even encountered the Viper, or perhaps the Viper would lose to somebody else. The thoughts swirled in complicated eddies that I couldn't fully keep track of as I pondered the competition.

Dryden wouldn't be able to compete at all after his injury. When I went to apologize to him, he waved me off and told me the feasting and dancing interspersed with the competition would be the most fun part anyways. Something about the way he said it told me he was just trying to avoid upsetting me. The tinge of fear in his eyes, perhaps of how I might react if he enraged me, hurt the worst of all.

It was part of the reason I explored the temporary encampment alone now. Aderyn had appointed herself as the queen's additional bodyguard for the duration of the Trials, and Neven was busy running a stall to sell his textiles to the many visitors who would be using the Trials as a time to buy goods from the city. There would be plenty of time to do business as the Trials were scheduled to last a full month, with time between the events for competitors to recover and celebrate.

While Dryden, Nyra, and the other trainees would certainly be enjoying the events too, I couldn't bear the sidelong glances they had shot me ever since Dryden's injury.

The sun creeped toward the horizon, staining the whole camp in crimson and gold as the underlying buzz of excitement built. Competitors emerged from their tents or left their campfires as dusk approached, moving toward the main thoroughfare of the camp.

I joined them, waiting for the appointed hour when the queen would arrive and all competitors would declare their intentions to join the Trials. We crowded into the wide street created by two lines of tents leading straight toward the archway into the city. I tried my best to stay on the fringes, where the bodies crowded together less densely.

My reluctance to push into the crowd found me carried to the back of the queue of fighters, ready to pledge their intention to the queen. While I stood above almost all the other female riders in height, the taller men still made it difficult to see as Queen Ginevra emerged, standing in the archway, outfit glimmering in the light of dusk. I could just spot Aderyn, standing off her shoulder with a hand on her dagger, glaring at each warrior who stepped up to the queen and knelt, swearing to fight honorably in the coming Trials.

The queue inched forward, and I ran over the words Aderyn had taught me as the ceremonial request to compete for the honor of being named Champion. So engrossed was I in my mental rehearsal that I almost missed when a hush fell over the competitors around me. The entire rear quarter of the line turned to stare at the figure who fell into the very back of the queue. I turned to see what they were staring at, and my heart froze in my ribcage. Standing alone, black silhouette outlined by the setting sun, was the Viper.

CHAPTER THIRTEEN
THE VIPER

The riders waiting their turn to kneel before the queen gave me a wide berth. I did nothing to dissuade them, leaving my hand resting on the hilt of the dirk shoved into my sash. Many of those assembled came from the tribes already united with Clan Katal, familiar enough with my methods of persuasion. The riders from the remaining five tribes feared what I might do to bring them into line. While tales of the Viper might not have reached the citizens of Kelvadan, my appearance and the whispers from other warriors were enough to inspire uneasiness.

I almost snorted in wry amusement at the thought that I was more easily recognized with my face covered than without. Still, with my mask, they recognized me only as a figure to be feared—the snake of Clan Katal. I preferred it that way.

My teeth creaked in my head from grinding them as the line inched forward. My skull felt tight as the whispers of the desert in my mind turned to insistent murmuring with every step forward, as if they were anxious for me to reach the front of the line. I had plenty of time to conquer my conflicted feelings about kneeling before the queen on the way here. If it was necessary to achieve our purpose, I would put aside my pride. After all, a sword had no pride, it only did as its wielder commanded.

Something about the coming encounter made the desert stir though. I caught sight of the queen's form, much as I remembered it, although still touched by the passage of time. Her silhouette was softened by the decade since I had seen her, but her upright posture was rigid as ever. I halfway expected the murmuring in my mind to turn to shouts upon seeing her, but they remained an insistent tether at the base of my skull, pulling me toward an unseen goal.

It seemed like just a moment, lasting an eternity, until it was only me standing in the thoroughfare before the entrance to Kelvadan. I didn't look at the queen's face as I stepped forward and dropped to one knee in the hardened sands a few paces in front of her.

"By the sands, I pledge to test my blood against all others in the Ballan Desert, using only the strength of my body and the iron of my will."

As I repeated the same words as all those who had knelt before me, a sharp intake of breath came from the queen. While my mask limited my peripheral vision, I saw the shadow of movement from the woman beside her, most likely an instinctual grab for a weapon.

I finished my pledge and raised my head, meeting the eyes of my mother for the first time in ten years.

Sounds of boisterous conversations and revelry drifted through my tent flap. I sat cross-legged on my sleeping mat, sharpening my saber. I wouldn't be able to use it in the combat event's coming Trials, instead switching it out for a blunted version, but my hands moved through the motion out of habit. Just as my forms brought me some semblance of peace in their familiarity, caring for my weapons soothed the whispers of magic in my mind.

I needed all the peace I could find tonight. My magic surprised me by continuing to test my control. I focused on the stinging of the blistered lines on my back to ground myself, but it was almost healed, only paining me when the sheath of my saber rubbed over it. Perhaps I should have let Lord Alasdar burn another line into my skin before I left for the Trials, but I hadn't thought the occasion would test my control. My confidence in my skills left me without fear I could accomplish my goals, and even my confrontation with my mother had passed without incident.

While her face had paled, and she'd paused for a moment before accepting my entrance into the tournament, she had not treated me any differently than the other competitors. From the spy, Oren, she would have known to expect the Viper's entry to the competition, and my goals in coming here. She would have come to terms with her inability to deny me entry without turning the clans further against her and had schooled herself into neutrality toward me—until she'd heard my voice. No doubt she remained unsure if it was really me. With my face covered and my voice deeper than it had been when I left—barely a man and still growing into myself—I would be difficult to recognize. I had even left my sword with Alza, on the off chance she would recognize it and change her mind about denying me entry to the Trials. Considering she had thought me dead, she likely questioned herself, though she clearly found me familiar.

Footsteps stirred the sand outside my tent, and I lifted my head just in time for the tent flap to open. A woman pushed in without invitation, glaring at me with her arms folded. I met her dark gaze from behind my mask and cocked my head at the familiar aggression in her stance, trying to place her.

Aderyn.

Her eyes darted back and forth between my mask and the saber in my lap, and I tensed. She would recognize it as having belonged to my great-grandfather, gifted to me on my sixteenth birthday, and the only thing I had taken with me when I left Kelvadan in the dead of night. Longer than any other I had ever seen, with curved quillons decorating the cross-guard hilt, there would be no mistaking it.

She looked harder than she had when I left, not that she had ever been soft. Her hair had been shaved off to show a tattooed stripe across her head. It gave me pause, as such a style was a mark of the clans from when the desert had first been crossed, and I wouldn't expect it on somebody dedicated to Kelvadan as she was.

"Erix." She made the one word sound like a question and an accusation at the same time. I didn't respond, although my eye twitched. Even Lord Alasdar never called me by my name, and he was one of the few people who knew it.

"I knew it was you. You can take off the stupid mask. It won't hide your identity," she continued.

I ignored her comment. "Why have you come?"

"Why? Why—why did you let Ginevra think you were dead for ten years? Let her–us– think we failed you for so long?"

I slid my saber back into its sheath with snap.

"You did fail me. And you continue to fail this desert."

Aderyn's eyes flamed in her stony face. The familiarity of that expression stirred something within me, but I stood firm.

"You can't do this to her." Her voice was a murmur, but still carried clearly over the noise of the opening celebration outside. "We know what will happen if you win."

"Are you saying you won't let me compete in the Trials?"

Aderyn shook her head. "Queen Ginevra won't change her mind about that."

"Then we have nothing more to say. I will be named Champion of the Desert, and then I will leave Kelvadan again."

"I wouldn't be so sure," she argued, but backed toward the exit anyway.

I shrugged. Even if she herself competed, and she had been the closest to beating me in training before I left the city, I had improved tenfold since then under Lord Alasdar's training. I could best her.

Grabbing my dirk to sharpen it as well, I waited for her to leave.

"Erix." She looked over her shoulder with her hand resting on the tent flap. "If you violate the peace of the Trials, I won't hesitate to stop you. By any means necessary."

"You have nothing to fear in that regard," I promised with actual sincerity and without doubt that Aderyn would do everything in her power to end me if I engaged in foul play. "I cannot cheat for the same reason you can't. The people must believe in their Champion for the desert to be saved."

"And the people will believe in Kelvadan's Champion." She disappeared into the night, and I paused, wondering who she'd laid her faith in. Perhaps if we had been able to question Oren, I might have known who my fiercest competitors would be. It hardly mattered now though. I was here, and I would do what I had to.

I finished sharpening my dirk before laying down on my mat to rest. I pulled my mask off, setting it just off to the side next to my saber, both within easy reach. The Trials would start in the morning, and I would emerge victorious.

The line of competitors, mounted on their horses and standing shoulder to shoulder, stretched farther than I could see. Not that I bothered searching the faces of my adversaries. We stood with our backs to the towering city, watching the sky turn from black to gray to pale orange as the sun prepared to crest the horizon.

Alza pawed the ground and flicked her ears back toward me, as if asking what we were waiting for. I patted her neck, having very little patience of my own to share. I itched to get through the first event, announced as we gathered here before dawn. It was a hunt. We each had to return with a clean kill by midday or be eliminated from the Trials. I was impatient to move on to something more difficult. Even more than that though, I itched to ride out into the open sands and away from the shadow of Kelvadan. Something about the densely packed crush of life, intensified by all those drawn in by the Trials, turned the whispers of the desert in my mind from an insistent nuisance to an inexorable demand that I do... something. I wanted to peel off my skin, but I was unsure what it was my magic wanted from me in exchange for a moment of stillness. The only battles to be had for the next weeks would not end in bloodshed, making the opportunity of a reprieve from my madness seem slim.

While the Trials had a brutal and bloody history, deliberately killing a competitor had been outlawed since the founding of Kelvadan, Kelvar being the last Champion to behead his final enemy and emerge victorious from the duels. Now, the duels were performed with blunted blades and foul play was frowned upon. I was equal parts relieved not to have to dispatch all my opponents and enraged that the importance of the Trials had been undercut in such a fashion. Unfortunate riders still perished every Trial though, whether through accident or the will of the desert. I guessed it was one of the purposes of the opening hunt: to weed out those who were too young or incompetent before the events became truly dangerous.

Finally, the edge of the sun came into view and the line of riders broke, green warriors galloping off hectically while more experienced competitors carefully picked a direction to ride in. I nudged Alza to head east, away from the majority of riders who headed to the plains dotted with arrowgrass where herds of Oryx would roam.

The rules of the opening hunt hadn't specified what kind of game one needed to bring in, only that you must cleanly slay a creature and present it at the central fire of the encampment by the time the sun reached its zenith. While many would aim for slower and more plentiful oryx, the number of hunters tracking them would spook and scatter the herds. Taking down a predator like a red wolf or a caracal came with more risk, but I would avoid the inexperienced and enthusiastic hunters driving off my kill.

The sounds of other hoofbeats indicated a handful of riders following my lead, but quickly dispersed until Alza and I were alone among the dunes. Zephyr slept in my tent, head tucked under one wing. I would leave him behind during all the events, despite how valuable he would be on such a hunt, unwilling to risk anybody saying I did not follow the terms of the Trials to the letter. After all, such complaints were why Lord Alasdar was not welcome in Kelvadan anymore.

Alza's ears pricked, and I pulled her to a halt, listening for what she heard. In the distance, in the direction of a formation of golden rocks, quiet yips signaled the presence of a caracal. Hopefully they were hunting in small numbers so I could make quick work of my kill.

Reaching across my back, I pulled out my short bow and several arrows, looped around my shoulder. My saber wouldn't be very useful on this hunt, but I never rode out without it.

Alza slowed as I nudged her toward the rocks. She seemed to sense my need for quiet and placed her hooves gently. It might be more difficult to sneak up on the caracal this way, but I was in a better position to give chase on horseback, and it would give me the advantage against a larger group of them.

We approached a bend in the rock, the sound of yips and growling growing louder, echoing against the stone. I leaned forward to peek around the edge, seeing a single caracal bent over a small carcass, likely an unfortunate jackrabbit or rock squirrel. It had a successful hunt, and now I was about to have mine.

Nocking my bow, I took advantage of the animal's distraction to take careful aim. I inhaled the scent of the earth and the blood of the dead animal on the ground, calling on the desert to guide my arrow. I wasn't as practiced of an archer as a swordsman, but the desert had never let me go hungry while I served her, and my arrows flew true on a hunt.

The threads of magic snapped taught in my mind, like an untamed horse pulling on its lead, just as I let the arrow loose. Before it could meet its mark, a hooded figure dropped from the short rocky cliff above the caracal, where I had failed to see it crouched. It landed squarely on the caracal, who yelped before suddenly cutting off.

My arrow ricocheted on the rock over the figure's head, having missed them by inches. Their head snapped up and I was pinned by a pair of golden eyes. For some reason, I felt as if I couldn't move, bow still held ready at the side of my face.

She, for I could now see the figure was a woman, sprang to her feet and drew the saber from across her back, leaving her short knife embedded in the caracal's neck just below its skull. It had been a clean stab, severing the caracal's spinal cord and killing it neatly.

"I thought it was against the rules to engage with other competitors on the hunt," she accused, although the way she held her blade didn't seem to speak of any reluctance to fight.

"I was shooting at the caracal," I admitted. I didn't need to explain myself to her, but something familiar in her voice took me off guard and left me more focused on placing it than the contents of our conversation.

"Well, this kill is mine." She sheathed her saber with a snap and stepped over the felled animal without turning her back to me, clearly distrustful. Probably rightly so.

She yanked her smaller blade free from the caracal, revealing it to be only a few inches long, before wiping it on her pants and shoving it into her belt. She seemed utterly unperturbed by the blood now smeared across her thighs and belly, a sight that stirred something odd in me.

"That's a rather small knife for hunting caracal with," I pointed out before I could stop myself. I should be off to find other prey, but my legs were frozen at Alza's side, refusing to nudge her away. My mount didn't seem inclined to move of her own accord either.

"It works better than a sling. Besides, I knew it would be distracted with the dead rock squirrel I planted."

My brows furrowed, rubbing up against my mask as I frowned. "If you had already caught the rock squirrel, then why bother with the caracal?"

The glare she fixed me with knocked something lose in my head, and I was brought back to the last time I had stared into those eyes—my blade at her throat and magic crackling through the air. It was a glare that had haunted my dreams too often in the past months.

"Keera," I breathed involuntarily, cutting off whatever answer she had been about to give. It had been months since she had told me the name I hadn't even meant to ask for, but I had woken with it echoing in my mind more times than I cared to admit. The fact that she escaped that night irked me, and the fact that I had let her grated at me even more. Even though I had hesitated to slit her throat twice, knowing the last person to see my true face lived ached like a healing brand. Still, I had turned away to douse the burning tents while she dashed off into the night. I thought it likely that she died, despite how often she visited me in my sleep, seeing it as my subconscious reminding me of the shame of my failures. Now, Keera crouched before me looking utterly transformed. Where her hair had been matted and dark before, it was now a mass of curls that shined the darkest brown in the sun. Her cheeks had filled out to accentuate her heart shaped face, deep set eyes under a bold brow, giving her a look of proud strength. The difference in her appearance made it clear why I hadn't recognized her immediately, but she wore the same defiant expression I remembered.

She sprang to her feet and drew her saber once more, the silver blade a blur as she whipped it out before her in defense.

I lowered my bow and raised my hands. "I plan to abide by the rules of the Trials. You are safe from me...for now."

She didn't sheath her weapon, but the tip lowered a few inches. She clicked her tongue a few times and the sound of hooves signaled her approaching mount. As a golden stallion rounded the bend, I nearly choked on my own tongue.

Lord Alasdar's warhorse, Bloodmoon, calmly approached the woman, although I didn't miss his dark eyes flicking over me and imagined they held distaste. I'm sure my gaze held no less contempt, as he had certainly left me with broken ribs from a savage kick more than once. I supposed I should have guessed Keera took him in her escape, but it seemed more likely to me that he had run off during the lightning storm. After all, he was only a few degrees shy of completely wild and liked nobody, not even Lord Alasdar.

Things seemed to have changed though, as Bloodmoon thrust his nose into Keera's chest, completely ignoring her drawn sword and searching for affection. She kept her glare on me but patted him on the nose. The last time I had tried to touch him, I nearly lost several fingers to his vicious teeth.

I slung my bow back across my shoulder and stifled a sigh. Whoever this woman was, every second I spent in her presence left me more off balance than the last. I couldn't afford to lose focus with so much riding on the Trials.

Now that my weapon was away, Keera seemed a little more at ease and hoisted the caracal off the ground with one arm, hefting it across her mount's back. She followed it, making the leap up onto his significant height easier than I might have guessed.

"I don't know what you're doing, but you won't get away with it," she announced as she kneed her mount around. "I know what you have planned for Kelvadan, and we are ready. I won't let the city fall."

With that, she kicked her horse into an easy canter and headed back toward the mountains in a puff of dust. I squinted after her for a few moments before realizing how bright the sun had gotten.

I had wasted far too much time talking to the woman, and I still needed to have my own kill back to the encampment by midday.

CHAPTER FOURTEEN
KEERA

The ride back to the walls passed quickly, but I wished it hadn't. The pounding of Daiti's hooves and the hot wind in my face was a balm to my swirling thoughts after my encounter with the Viper, who haunted my steps, both awake and asleep.

After his dramatic appearance at the opening of the Trials yesterday, rumors had swirled amongst the members of the other clans. They shared stories of his ruthless efficiency as Lord Alasdar's enforcer with the citizens of Kelvadan, who were all curious about the man who had garnered such a stiff reaction from the queen. Not wanting to spark any interference in the Trials, she had kept the stakes communicated to her by Oren between her close advisors and the ambassadors.

The rumors told about the Viper by other competitors from the clans spanned from unsettling to outrageous: he killed anybody who opposed him without hesitation; he drank the blood of his enemies to gain their strength; nobody who saw his true face lived to tell of it.

I kept silent as I heard the last one. I remembered his face more clearly than I would have expected, considering the brief glimpse I had gotten of it months ago. Perhaps his proud features had seared themselves into my memory as I'd expected them to be the last thing I ever saw. Or perhaps it was his expression—not the one of bloodthirsty rage I would have expected of somebody about to snuff out my life, but an odd smoothing of his brows in something like surprise.

Now I sat back, pressing my sits bones into Daiti's back to slow him to a walk as we passed into the outskirts of the encampment. It was still quiet compared to last night, with most of the riders out on the hunt; only their families and a few spectators gathered to see who would be bringing back fresh kills.

Most citizens of Kelvadan, and those who had travelled to watch the Trials, were likely still sleeping off the excess *laka* as the opening celebration had lasted well past midnight.

At the open circle in the middle of the encampment I dropped off my kill in the small pile of oryx and red wolves, alongside the occasional jackrabbit, from those who had returned before me. I glanced around to see if Queen Ginevra or Aderyn were present but found no sign of them.

Aderyn and the queen had disappeared last night as soon as the competitors had finished declaring their intent to participate in the Trials. They had seemed shaken by the appearance of the Viper, although we had known he would come. Perhaps, like me, they found the reality of him in person more foreboding than they had anticipated.

After the volunteers marked my name on their lists with a checkmark, indicating that I would be competing in the next round of the Trials, I joined the spectators for a while, curious how many would be joining me in moving forward.

After a frustratingly short amount of time, my eyes darted to the horizon, where the dark silhouette of a rider approached. I knew from the tall black mount and the feeling in the pit of my stomach that it was the Viper.

It was not as though I had expected him to fail in the first round, but I had hoped he would arrive more than a quarter hour after me, considering I had stolen his first kill. The small amount of hope that had been lit within me, that perhaps he wouldn't be crowned Champion after all, was dampened by his quick appearance. Before he could enter the encampment, I turned and led Daiti away toward the arched entrance to the city. There was only to be one event today, as the Trials would grow in intensity throughout the weeks, and this was just the first day. I wanted to make sure Daiti was safe in his stall with a bale of arrow-grass before I returned to the encampment to help Neven with his stall for the remainder of the day.

When I arrived at the stables where the Kelvadan riders and their recruits kept their horses, the air was static, most mounts still on the hunt. It wasn't until Daiti was in his stall, and I was brushing over his coat again, even though it already shone like burnished bronze, just because he seemed so pleased with the sensation, that I heard voices.

The voices were growing in volume, enough that I could now hear them through several walls, as they were coming from the large stall that marked the end of the long, narrow building.

"—dead. He has been for a decade, and I can't keep watching the horizon, waiting for him to return."

The first voice was gruff and unyielding where it normally held laughter: Kaius.

"You would give up on our son so easily?"

I almost gasped and threw a hand over my mouth to stifle the sound. The poised tone was unmistakably Queen Ginevra, although I had never heard her mention a child before.

"It's not giving up to face the truth."

"You weren't there. You didn't hear him. He sounded like Erix. Older, but still Erix."

There was a pause and a rustle. I leaned closer to the wall of Daiti's stall, not wanting to miss a word. Part of me nagged that this conversation clearly wasn't for my ears, but the notion of a son in the royal family intrigued me. After all, didn't I bear the same burden as their bloodline?

"Do you really remember the sound of his voice?" Kaius's voice was quieter now, and I strained to hear. "I think I do, but with each passing day, it gets dimmer, as if the sun is bleaching it out of my mind like dye from cloth. The only thing I know I remember anymore is the way he rode a horse, as if he could outrun time itself."

"He's still out there. The Viper in the mask—I swear it's him. Why else would he conceal his face?"

"And even if it is?" Kaius's voice rose sharply. "Is Lord Alasdar's snake really our son anymore, even if he wears Erix's face? He's not the same person. Not after all they say he's done. Not after how we failed him."

My chest tightened, Daiti's coat blurring before my eyes as I subconsciously leaned on him for support. He tossed his head and pawed the ground, and I stood upright again, my head spinning.

The man in the mask—the one who had delivered me to my doom, only for me to find a new purpose for my survival—was Kaius and Ginevra's son.

Erix.

It felt odd to give him a name, when for months he had existed as more symbol than man in my head. A faceless figure in black and a nameless threat to Kelvadan. A danger I trained to stand against.

But I had known he was a man under the metal, as I had met those bottomless eyes under the moonlight and felt the warmth of his hand at my throat, sensation heightened by the knowledge that I was about to die. That gaze had visited me in my dreams more times than I cared to admit in the past months, although likely because he was the first person I met after so long in isolation—and because I feared what his victory might mean for Kelvadan.

"Erix," I mouthed quietly. It felt right to know the name of the person who was the first to know mine, even if the knowledge felt strangely like a weapon.

"We have to try." Queen Ginevra's voice came once again, slightly pleading this time. "If we just—"

The stable door slammed open to let the sounds of laughter and carefree joking tumble in. More hunters must have returned. There would be no more eavesdropping on this conversation, although it already had my mind swirling.

I slipped out of the stables, only sparing the other recruits a nod as they bragged about their kills or bemoaned their bad luck at not moving on in the Trials. As I considered the coming weeks of competition, the knowledge of who I truly faced in this competition sat heavy in my belly.

The next day held no competitive events, giving all the visitors to the city their first uninterrupted chance to peruse the stalls of the temporary market. Sitting dumbly in Neven's stall, barely processing his requests as I folded and moved bolts of cloth, I was glad for the reprieve. My arms were as leaden as the stone of the city wall, and I didn't think they would be much good with a sword today.

It wasn't yesterday's exertion that weighed them down, but the heaviness of my thoughts. Despite knowing I would need my rest for the coming events, sleep had not found me easily last night. Every time I closed my eyes, I snapped them open again, fearing I would find the face of the Viper in my dreams again. His nighttime visits had been disconcerting before, but knowing the man I had been sharing strangely intimate conversations with was the queen's son left me with an odd hollowness in the pit of my stomach. Anger threatened to fill that hollowness at the thought that the Viper had run away from such a home, only to fight for its destruction and steal away my only hope for belonging.

I had the thought that I needed to come to a decision before facing him again, but I had no idea what that decision might be. I knew I had to face him in the Trials and emerge victorious, no matter who he was under the mask. But the image of him flickered in my mind's eye when I thought of him now oscillated between a faceless warrior—larger than life with hands soaked in blood—and the man I knew lived underneath, whose mother just wanted to believe he could come home.

"I asked for the blue silk, Keera, and unless the heat is getting to me, that's red." Neven gestured to the bundle of fabric in my arms. I looked down to find that he was right.

"Sorry," I mumbled, hurrying to grab the right bolt of silk.

Neven narrowed his eyes at me, not unkindly, as if he could see through my skin to the whirling thoughts beneath. He opened his mouth, but before he could pry, a familiar voice cut him off.

"Keera!"

I turned to find Hadeon standing in the makeshift road between rows of stalls. He luckily had traded out his snowy furs for a light robe in the style of the clansmen that protected his fair skin from the sun.

The tunic he wore underneath remained unlaced at the neck, revealing a smattering of light hair on his sternum.

I found myself smiling, despite my earlier consternation. "How are you finding the Trials?"

His attention set off a fluttering under my sternum, mixed with a healthy dose of hope. Perhaps his warmth toward me was a sign that he could be swayed to Kelvadan's cause.

"Hot," he admitted, fanning himself with a rueful smile. "Lyall has decided to remain in the palace and out of the sun unless there are competitive events to watch. My curiosity got the better of me today though, and I had to come see what the clans had to offer. Care to show me around?"

I glanced at Neven, ready to tell Hadeon that I needed to stay and help at the textile stall. However, Neven's eyebrows were raised with a smile toying at the edge of his lips. "Go ahead and take a break, Keera. You deserve to enjoy the Trials, considering you're competing in them."

I nodded in thank you, quickly stepping around the bench laden with textiles to join Hadeon in the dusty thoroughfare. With a friendly grin, he gestured for me to lead the way, and we began strolling down the wide row between vendors. I imagined Neven's gaze heavy on the back of my neck, but when I glanced behind me, he was helping his next customer already.

"What are these?" Hadeon paused next to a low table laden with handmade jewelry. The violet banner flying from the peak atop the stall marked the vendor as a member of Clan Vecturna, and the allegiance was echoed in their work, much of it bearing the emblem of a hunting dog.

I looked at the object Hadeon pointed at, a large flat circle of silver emblazoned with the snarling face of a dog. The eyes glittered darkly as though with fire from deep within the earth, and as I leaned in to find that the sparkle came from tiny gemstones.

I looked at the stall keeper, who gave me a nod, before picking it up and turning it over in my fingers, revealing a sturdy clasp on the back of the disc.

"It's meant to clasp your hood in place," I explained, although I had never worn such an ornament myself. Most clansmen simply tucked the end of their hood over their face to further protect them from the sun, but some wore decorations for special events, or if they were given one as a gift.

"That one is very special," chimed in the shopkeeper, reaching forward a wizened hand covered in sunspots to tap the engraving. "The eyes are genuine blood glass."

"Blood glass?" Hadeon echoed curiously, leaning in to get a better look.

As he peered over my shoulder, Hadeon's hand came to rest on the small of my back, pinky finger just brushing my skin in the gap between my cropped vest and pants. My muscles tensed involuntarily at the touch of bare skin in such an unexpected place, but Hadeon didn't seem to notice, his eyes glued on the clasp before him. With a steadying breath I managed to release my gripping muscles and return my focus to the conversation. I couldn't afford to alienate Hadeon by overreacting to his advances when so much rode on gaining his support.

"It's one of the most valuable materials among the clans, made from the sand of the desert mixed with blood before it is fired. These specific pieces were made using the blood of Clan Vecturna's very own warlord. They're harder than diamonds and wearing it the amplifies the desert's magic and grants her favor," the shopkeeper explained in a hushed tone, as if she were sharing a great secret with us. "The Champion's circlet that will be awarded to the victor at the end of the Trials is adorned with several pieces of blood glass, cut into the shape of gems. They are said to have been made from the blood of the first lord to cross the desert."

I tilted my head, trying to remember stories of blood glass. The lord of Clan Padra had possessed a saber with a piece of blood glass in the hilt when I rode with them. Stories whispered around the fireside during my childhood claimed it had given her the power to defeat the former lord and assume leadership of the clan.

Two planes of blood glass, the largest I had ever seen, also adorned the locked entrance to Alyx's tomb at the top of the palace.

"They look just like dark rubies to me," Hadeon commented with a shrug.

"I don't think I'm in the market for amplified magic right now," I commented as I put the clasp down.

"What are you in the market for?" Hadeon asked, removing his hand from my back to pick up another bauble and inspect it. The rest of the tension melted from my body, but I found I didn't feel the sudden relief I normally did when somebody stopped touching me. Perhaps I was finally getting used to the close quarters I now lived in. Or perhaps it was Hadeon's easy manner that made it hard to feel on edge around him.

"How about a pair of earrings?" Hadeon held up a pair of silver drops beside my face, as if seeing how they would suit me.

I thanked the sun for my already darkened cheeks as blood rose to my face. "I'm not really the jewelry type," I admitted. "Besides, I haven't had my ears pierced."

"Maybe you just haven't found the right thing yet," Hadeon continued, undeterred. Next, his fingers landed on an arm band, gold and wrought in the shape of a curling snake. He slipped it onto my left upper arm, nestling it neatly into the divot between my biceps and shoulder muscle.

"I think it suits you," he commented, admiring his handiwork. "I noticed that gold complimented you well that first night we met."

I glanced at him curiously. The dinner with the ambassadors had been many weeks ago, and I had nearly forgotten the dusting of gold power across my cheek and lower lip, even though it had taken nearly a week to scrub off all traces of it.

Hadeon seemed unperturbed, turning to the shopkeeper. "How much?"

Before I could balk at the amount of coins the jeweler asked for, Hadeon had produced them from his belt and plunked them into her outstretched hand. I still hadn't quite mastered the use of coins or how much they were worth, but even I could tell he had just handed over a small fortune to the stall owner. She had likely expected him to haggle, as was the way in the clans, but he turned to me with a broad smile as if he hadn't nearly been robbed for a shiny, completely unnecessary, trinket.

"Why would you buy it for me?" I asked, right hand coming to rest over the piece of jewelry, already warming to my skin.

"The proper response is *thank you*," he said, already starting to drift toward the next stall and leaving me to trail in his wake. "And as I said before, there is no harm in being on the good side of the Champion of the Desert."

"I'm not the Champion yet," I argued as fell into stride with him again. "I've only just made it through the first round of competition. Who knows if I'll even make it through tomorrow's challenge."

"I meant to ask you, do you have any idea what the challenge may entail?"

I shook my head. "None of the competitors know. It is supposed to keep the Trials as a fair test of the riders' skill and the deserts favor if nobody has the chance to prepare."

"Well, that's a shame, I should have liked a hint," Hadeon commented, his tone light although he did sound disappointed. I myself had been pointedly avoiding dwelling on what challenge might face me tomorrow, the competitors only having been told to report to the city gates at dawn. Now my worries returned full force, like a blow to the gut at the reminder.

"What smells so good?" Hadeon asked, looking around and seemingly blind to my sudden consternation.

Raising my head, I caught the whiff of a sticky warm sweetness laced with spices that made my nose twitch. I pointed to a nearby stall, the heat from a clay oven out front making the air dance and shimmer.

We approached curiously, and the sickly-sweet smell became oddly familiar, although the spices added an element I wasn't accustomed to.

"Stuffed dates?" offered the man working the oven.

Hadeon nodded. "They smell incredible." He quickly turned over the requested amount of coin for a small stack of the glistening fruits.

He held them out to me in offering as he popped one in his mouth. I automatically reached out to take one, not in the habit of turning down food when it was offered. As I bit into it though, and spices dripped down my fingers to my wrist, I was reminded that I didn't care for dates. After too many days where they were my sole source of nutrition, I would be all too happy to never see them again.

Hadeon remained blissfully unaware of this and smiled widely before taking another one. "These are incredible."

I nodded in agreement as I dutifully chewed and swallowed. He would have no way of knowing that I disliked dates. Only once had I told anybody of my aversion, and that had been in a dream.

At that thought, a prickling awareness rose at the back of my neck. I turned around just in time to see the metal mask of the Viper, looking at me from a few stalls away, before he turned and stalked off down the row and out of sight.

I took another date from the offered pile and chewed it furiously, letting the sticky sweetness drive the vulnerability of my nighttime conversations from my head.

CHAPTER FIFTEEN
ERIX

I ground my teeth and tried not to pace in my too-small tent.
Zephyr had taken to squawking in disapproval at my antics as
they'd woken him from his nap. Still, these days of rest between
events grated. My sword was so sharp it could cut through a single hair,
and Alza's coat shone so brightly it could blind me, but still there were
many hours left in the day before it would be time to sleep.

The gaps between events were a tradition, giving the clans time to
converse and trade in addition to cheering on their riders, but with the
state of the desert they seemed a foolish pursuit. I couldn't be the only
competitor restless to have a sword in hand and a horse beneath me
again.

Zephyr trilled, letting me know my restlessness could be felt even as I
knelt on my sleeping mat trying my best to meditate on my purpose in a
desperate bid for patience. With a grunt, I pushed to my feet and stalked
from the tent, pushing my way out through the flap. Even though I had
been alone, I had put on my mask already. The physical shield gave me
some sense of separation from the hubbub of nine clans' worth of riders
in the encampment with me, although it didn't feel like nearly enough.

I had planned to walk away from the encampment, into the sands
where I might get some distance from the amplified whispers at the base

of my skull, which crescendoed as I drew near the city walls. Instead, my feet unconsciously turned toward the most densely populated area where a temporary market had been set up for the duration of the Trials.

There was nothing I could want there. My saber was my most prized possession, really my only personal belonging outside of my mask, so the fine weapons sure to be on display were of no use to me. I wore the same gray clothes every day, and I wouldn't take off my mask to eat any of the foods that drew in many who wandered the encampment with their mouthwatering scents.

Still, my steps carried me toward the crowded thoroughfare, and my mind hurried to justify my direction. Perhaps there was something to be learned about the clans that Lord Alasdar would soon command by mingling with them, or maybe I could discern a weakness of Kelvadan I had not thought of before.

Thankfully, I traversed the crowds easily as I walked, shoppers stepping aside the moment they looked up to see my masked face and leaving a clear path for me. I huffed through my nose, realizing I was unlikely to discern anything about the people around me if conversation continued to die as I passed. Shifting my weight, I prepared to turn around and head out into the open desert as I'd originally planned when I saw her.

Keera stood with her back partially to me before a stall boasting platters of stuffed dates, their scent thick despite the mask shielding my nose. I frowned at the sudden memory of her sitting across the fire from me a world away, telling me she didn't like dates, but that had been a dream. Still, as she popped the treat into her mouth—my gaze unconsciously tracking the way her lips closed around her fingers to catch the spiced juice—I imagined a crease between her brows and a slight wrinkle to her nose.

Then she smiled at her companion, my attention turning to the fair man that had offered her the treat. He certainly didn't look to be from the desert or the city. He must be an ambassador or a prominent trader, as they were the only people who regularly crossed the mountains to visit the city. A knot of magic in the base of my skull pulled tight as I wondered what the former exile would be doing with an ambassador.

Just then, Keera turned, looking straight at me as if I had called her name.

Spinning on my heel, I stomped back in the direction I had come before I could see her reaction. A long walk in the quiet of the wilderness would help me manage the swirling in my head. I didn't envy Keera spending her downtime entertaining ambassadors, however that had come about. A small voice in my mind chimed in that it was a glimpse of the life I might have had if I hadn't left Kelvadan nearly a decade ago. It wasn't a life I desired.

Noticeably fewer participants lined up before the city walls than had for the hunt, but the line still stretched dozens of riders from the end where I sat atop Alza, as well as several horses deep. This time, we had not been told what our task would be before we arrived, the only instruction given the night after the hunt for the remaining riders to come at dawn with their horses and blunted blades.

Several figures emerged from the arch in the city walls, my gaze snapping to the shortest of the silhouettes. I instantly recognized the queen's posture, as much as I thought memories of her had been scorched from my brain. I tore my eyes from her to see several others carrying a large pot, the way they leaned toward it telling me the contents were heavy. The last figure was unmistakably Aderyn, and although I couldn't see her expression clearly, I imagined her eyes darting up and down the line of competitors, alert for any possible threat to her queen.

"Riders!" The queen raised her arms to draw the competitors' attention, as if the gathered participants hadn't collectively held their breath the moment she emerged, awaiting her instructions. Despite her stature, her voice projected clearly, years of practice allowing her to command the attention of groups easily. "Today's event will be a test of not only your individual skill, but your cunning and ability to cooperate."

I shifted my weight on Alza's back. The Viper didn't cooperate. The Viper commanded.

"You will be divided into five teams. Each team will be tasked with retrieving one of the four flags that have been placed at an undisclosed location in the plains beyond the city. Each flag will belong to the team that is the first to capture it. All the riders in the team that fails to claim a flag will be eliminated from the Trials."

An inaudible ripple ran through the assembled riders as the queen finished explaining the challenge. It was not unheard of for the events of the Trials to be set up in a manner that rewarded cooperation amongst competitors, but this degree of reliance on others had me—and many others, I was sure—bristling.

"Each of you will come forward and pick a stone from the basin." Aderyn spoke this time, gesturing to the earthenware pot at the queen's feet. "The color of the paint on the stone will determine what team you are on."

She waved, and we all shuffled forward into a rough queue. Each rider dismounted and drew a small flat rock from the basin before shuffling off to let the next competitor decide their fate with a splash of colored paint.

When I approached the front of the line, I dismounted from Alza with the weight of the queen's gaze heavy upon me. I didn't look up at her, for some reason loathe to afford her the opportunity of catching sight of the slightest silver gleam of my eyes, even though they wouldn't be a surprise to her. It seemed like she was searching for hints of her son in my posture as I bent to retrieve a stone from the shadowed innards of the pottery vessel. She would see my eyes as a sign that the Erix she remembered was only separated from her by a thin sheet of metal, but she would be wrong. Erix of Kelvadan was dead and buried along the distant trek across the desert to the sea.

My gloved fingers closed around my stone, and I pulled it forward to reveal a splash of red across the flat gray surface. I nodded at it as if in some agreement before vaulting back onto Alza's back and joining the milling competitors all waiting to see who would join their team.

As dozens of riders repeated the process, I, at first, tried to keep track of who the painted rocks sorted into each team. A stocky rider from Clan Tibel pulled a blue rock, a woman from Clan Otush joined me with a red one. Eventually though, I gave up the pursuit, instead idly twisting Alza's mane between my fingers. It didn't matter who rode on my team or who stood against me. I would retrieve the flag for my team and move on to the next round—I had to.

Against my will, my gaze drifted up as a familiar blood bay stallion stopped before the queen. The figure dismounted with grace despite the significant distance from her horse's back to the ground. My fingers froze in Alza's mane as Keera bent down and pulled a stone from the basin.

A flash of red in Keera's hand—a sudden tensing of her muscles, and my heart stuttered.

Keera lifted her head to look at Queen Ginevra, although her expression was partially shielded from my view by the end of her hood.

After a moment of stillness, the line moved on, and Keera joined the crowd of waiting riders, lost from my sight in the crush of horseflesh. I was glad of the momentary reprieve as magic whirled in my throat, threatening to bring my mind along with it. With an iron grip, my fist squeezing around the hilt of my blunted saber until it cut a line in my palm through the gloves, I shoved it down. As before, who was on my team made no difference. I would succeed, and that would be the end of it.

As the last competitor drew their stone, Aderyn shouted for the riders to sort themselves into teams. I found myself on the edges of the red group, and volunteers from Kelvadan quickly distributed strips of fabric to tie on our arms to designate our team membership. I fastened mine around my bicep as my gaze flickered unconsciously to Keera, who was doing the same on the far side of the loose circle.

"You have five minutes to coordinate as a team, and then the trial will begin," the queen announced.

Muttering ran through all the groups in a wave, snippets of plans and ideas murmured to teammates within the circle. The teams quickly dissolved into smaller factions discussing the best way to go about acquiring a flag. I ground my teeth. A quick count of my teammates revealed about two dozen.

"Trios," I said, not a shout but a clear statement that rang out from behind my mask, silencing the disjointed conversations around me. "We will divide into groups of three to cover the most ground, while not leaving any riders alone if we should face opposition from the other teams."

In a moment of stillness, the riders silently weighed my command. In the twisting magic around us, the battle between the need to cooperate and the resistance to my leadership was palpable. Then, a shuffling broke out as riders sorted themselves out, gathering into clusters of three and introducing themselves to their temporary allies.

A knee bumped against mine, and I started, looking up only to be pinned by a golden gaze. Keera had pulled Bloodmoon up alongside Alza, who seemed as if she wanted to edge away at the memory of the warhorse's violent temper. If Bloodmoon recognized my mare, he showed no sign of it.

"You certainly seem used to giving orders," Keera observed, her tone biting, as the red team sorted themselves out as I suggested.

"How convenient, as you are likely used to following blindly as a rider of Kelvadan." The words were out of my mouth before I could school myself into neutrality. My personal opinions about the Great City didn't need to be shared for me to fulfill my role in Lord Alasdar's plans and emerge as Champion.

"I belong to no one." Keera's tone was defiant, but some uncurrent of sadness in her statement nearly gave me pause.

"If you would suggest a different plan, be my guest." I gestured to the team before me, assembled groups of three already beginning to pick directions in which they would search for a flag. It was a blatant challenge, daring her to try and overturn my authority.

She surprised me by shaking her head. "No, it's a good plan. I'm just joining your trio. Somebody has to keep an eye on you."

I blinked, the muscles in my jaw tightening in frustration, although my magic whispered in excitement. Maybe it would be a good thing to have her near—an exile who had clearly ingratiated herself at Kelvadan shockingly quickly and seemed determined to stand against me. Maybe the power in my skull was just pleased by the prospect of violence, facsimile as it might be.

"We need one more to be a trio." I looked around, finding most had backed away from where Keera and I stood, as if a well of tension around us was palpable. One rider from Clan Otush inched forward.

"I'll join you," he offered, his voice almost too casual, as if he were expending great effort to seem unperturbed by the idea of riding with us.

Keera and I only nodded in response, and we lapsed into a fraught silence.

"I'm Axlan," he introduced in a bid to break the tension.

"Keera," she offered before glancing at me.

I didn't bother to introduce myself. They would both know me as the Viper already, and that was the only name I used.

A shouting voice cut off any further attempts at conversation. "Time is up, riders! Capture a flag for your team or be eliminated from the Trials."

With that, the queen rang a small gong one of the attendants had brought. The thunder of hooves filled the air, drowning out the reverberations before they could fully fade.

Without waiting for the other members of my team to decide on a direction, I rode out diagonally away from the city, choosing an angle between the mountains and where the sun had crested the horizon in the distance.

I would let the desert guide me to my victory. It would be on Keera to keep up if she truly wanted to keep an eye on me.

The beat of heavy hoofs to my right indicated that she followed.

"No consultation on which direction to take? You really don't take orders from anybody else," she prodded.

The itchiness of healing blisters on my back reminded me that I followed orders more than she knew, but I kept that to myself.

"Do you object to the direction I chose?"

I wished I could observe her ponder the answer out of the corner of my eye, but my mask blocked my peripheral vision, and I wouldn't signal that I was watching her by turning my head. It was a subtle test though, to see if she could hear the whispers of the desert guiding my direction. If the desert spoke to her at all, then she might continue to be a worthy adversary in the Trials—somebody to keep an eye on myself.

"It's as good a direction as any," Keera answered noncommittally.

We lapsed into silence, keeping our mounts at a brisk clip as the pockets of competitors fanned out over the empty ground.

After a while, Keera turned to look over her shoulder. "Axlan is falling behind."

Alza and I didn't slow our pace. "I don't need him to handle any trouble we might encounter."

For a moment, Keera fell back in hesitation until she urged her stallion up alongside me once more. I swallowed. Hopefully her presence wouldn't be too distracting. I tried to block out the physical awareness of her next to me and reach into the interwoven web of the desert, searching for the thread that might lead me to my goal.

Instead of a tapestry of barren life spreading around me as I usually felt, the fibers around me pulled in a tight tangle. It was as if I stood at a magical nexus of sorts, and picking out the way to go next was nigh impossible. The unintelligible voices rose in my head, drowning out the sound of Alza's hooves.

I shook my head trying to clear it, but the maddening cacophony continued until a much for physical voice cut through, like morning sun through a gap in a tent flap.

"There." Keera pointed at the horizon.

I swung my gaze in the direction she pointed, and sure enough a splotch of crimson mottled the horizon, oscillating gently like a flag flapping in the breeze.

Without a word, I nudged Alza into a gallop, but she was already accelerating, eager to keep pace with the stallion next to her that had already surged forward. We plunged across the dunes, Keera clearly as unconcerned with my ability to keep pace as I had been with Axlan's.

Admittedly, if I were any less of a horseman, with any less of a mount, it might have been a struggle. Keera rode like she had been born to it, and the warhorse under her surged with unbridled power.

I leaned forward over Alza's neck, resting my hands on her muscled shoulders. Magic stirred beneath my breastbone, as it always did when I let Alza gallop, but like this, it wasn't some unpleasant thing to be tamed. As we chased down the larger horse, the whispers in my mind amplified, a joyous undertone to their cacophony. The tail of the stallion whipped across my mask, and for a brief moment, I wished I could feel it across my face.

My eyes snagged on a cloud of dust to the left, and the rare quiet in my mind that accompanied the chase shattered. We had competition for the banner.

I nudged Alza toward it, moving to intercept. Keera sat up straighter for a moment, looking around until she appeared to catch sight of our competitors too and followed my course.

As the distance closed between us and the other group, I counted five of them, a flash of green marking each of their arms. Keera and I appeared to be faster, but they were already closer to the target. Pulling the blunted saber from across my back, I prepared to engage them, hoping I could keep all of them busy enough to keep one from getting away and snatching the flag.

Seeing me approach, they reached for their weapons, but it was too late. I held out my saber to the side, swerving Alza at the last moment to duck behind a green rider's horse and strike him flat across the chest. I heard his collarbone snap as the momentum threw him from his horse, but I did not pause.

I wheeled around, engaging up close with the next rider as they had all been riding in a tight group. I swung my sword in a large arc, distracting him with the motion. While he got his own weapon up in time to block my blow, I took advantage of the moment to hook my foot around his. With a heave, and help from Alza as she recognized the maneuver, I dumped him unceremoniously from his horses back.

I turned to find my next opponent, and my eyes caught on two green riders still galloping toward the flag at breakneck pace. Before I could pursue, the fifth rider moved to cut me off.

Keera, however, leapt into action. She and her golden stallion had veered off when I attacked, following the two charging toward the flag. Her saber remained sheathed, but she didn't seem to intent on using it anyway as she took a flying leap from her mount's back. Landing on her opponent's horse, she wrenched her arm across his shoulders, tearing him from his seat to tumble to the ground in a heap.

I looked away from her for a moment to take on my own opponent. To his credit, he parried several of my blows, only for a punch from my unarmed hand to catch him across the jaw. He slumped forward, unconscious over his horse's neck, before listing sideways, and slipping slowly to the sand.

I looked up again only to scream internally. The fifth green rider continued charging toward the banner unhindered. Meanwhile, Keera remained on her opponent's horse, running horizontally.

Sands, what was she doing?

Then, I saw it: a sixth rider with a red arm band. Axlan had followed Keera and me, but she was heading as if to cut him off.

It hit me with the force of a stampede of addax. If our team lost the challenge, I would lose my chance to be crowned Champion, and Keera knew it.

With a wordless shout, I urged Alza to join the chase to where all four of us were converging on the flag. The prize that would mean winning the challenge stood on the top of a dune, and as we drew closer, I saw protections had been erected to increase the challenge. Stones formed a ring, piled high enough that only a skilled rider would be able to jump it. The terrain was littered with sharpened spikes, driven into the earth, and pit traps that could easily be overlooked if distracted by a competitor. All of us were forced to slow as we approached the obstacles, dodging around them.

I trusted Alza to pick a safe path as I kept my eyes on Keera. She was nearly to Axlan, although he and the green rider were both several hundred meters from the flag—much closer than me. Alza was fast, but I wasn't sure if we could make up distance that quickly.

Axlan was my best chance of the red team reaching the flag first, as long as Keera didn't get in his way. I had to stop her.

Alza was nearly level with her mount's nose when I saw it—a patch of differently colored ground that marked sinking sands to those who knew how to spot them. All rational thought flew from my brain aside from Keera and how I needed to stop her.

I threw myself from Alza's back, the full force of my body weight crashing into Keera. My arms tangled around her torso as my momentum carried us both over the far side of her horse and into the sinking pit.

She let out a raw screech as we tumbled, thrashing in my hold, and managing to flip us over, but I held fast. I hit the sands first, her weight driving me down as she was pulled partially in with me.

Immediately, I let go of her, leaning back and spreading my arms as I kicked my legs back and forth to avoid sinking further. I had already been submerged up to my shoulders. Trapped in the sand together, Keera's back pressed flush up against my front. Despite the threat of panic at the edge of my consciousness, something in my brain went oddly blank. Like there was space in my mind there hadn't been before.

I struggled to form coherent thoughts as magic swirled within me, although it didn't seem to offer up a way to get me out of the sand, just warming and twisting in my skull.

Keera's shouting cut through the sudden swell, threatening to pull me under as thoroughly as the sucking sands. "Daiti!"

Keera shifted before me, her arms not yet trapped like mine, her fall having been broken by me. Then her torso pulled away. I craned my neck forward, just able to make out the golden silhouette of her stallion, leaning over the edge of the sand and helping Keera haul herself free of the pit.

Hopefully I had slowed her enough that she wouldn't be able to interfere with Axlan capturing the flag. I opened my mouth to yell for Alza's help, unsure of how I would pull myself free without my arms, but it was too late.

The last thing I saw before the sands engulfed me fully was Keera's scowl as she crouched at her horse's hooves.

Chapter Sixteen
Keera

If I did nothing, in a matter of seconds, the Viper's threat to Kelvadan would be over. Even if Lord Alasdar and Clan Katal remained set on seeing the Great City fall, the heaviness at the base of my neck from knowing facing down the Viper was inevitable would be gone.

As the tips of his black gloved fingers dipped below the quicksand, I glanced toward the banner. The green rider and Axlan were engaged in a skirmish to see who would emerge with the flag and advance their team in the Trials. I grabbed Daiti's neck, ready to haul myself on to his back and run for the flag. If the Viper was gone, there was no reason I couldn't hope for the red team to emerge victorious and continue in the Trials.

Before I could stand, the Viper's mare caught my attention, prancing at the edge of the pit of sinking sands. The screams of distress at the disappearance of her master tugged at my gut, a wave of nausea rolling over me.

I froze, glancing back and forth between the fight on the horizon and the earth where the Viper had disappeared moments earlier. It looked like Axlan was gaining the upper hand in the fight. In a split-second decision, I began unwrapping the long fabric of my hood from around my head and shoulders.

"*Sands.*" I was really doing this. May the desert forgive me.

With deft movements, I tied one end of the fabric strip around Daiti's neck. Then the other end looped around my left palm several times before also being knotted off, somewhat clumsily with the use of only one hand to maneuver. I wished I could tie it around my waist, but the fabric of my hood wasn't quite long enough for that, and this would have to do.

"Don't let me die in there," I muttered to Daiti, my heart attempting to leap up my throat as I stared down into the pit in front of me.

Daiti stamped and snuffled, as if insulted by the suggestion that he would ever let me meet my end while he had anything to say about it.

Before I could second guess myself, I took a deep breath and jumped.

The sands sucked me under with a crushing pressure. It swallowed me much faster this time as I had gone in feet first, with less surface area to slow my descent. My world went dark, and I thrashed around clumsily, movements slowed by the gripping sludge around me as I tried to locate the Viper.

I had done my best to land right next to where I had seen him disappear. All I felt around me though, was the suffocating pressure of wet sand. A blinding fear started bubbling up, and I had to remind myself not to open my mouth to scream.

Just as my thrashing turned from searching to panic, I encountered something solid. I reached out and traced the solid limb up to a thick torso. I had found him. As I reached out, wrapping my right arm around his broad chest as tight as I could, a newfound strength filled me.

The desert would not claim me today.

I tugged sharply on my left hand, gripping the fabric connecting me to Daiti in my fist. At my signal, a tug began on my arm, Daiti using his considerable bulk to pull us free.

The sand around us resisted, as if sentient and gripping us tighter with the thought of our escape. I strengthened my hold around the

Viper as he began to slip away, straining to keep his considerable bulk with me. As it was, the tension between the weight of the Viper and Daiti's insistent tugging threatened to pull my arm straight out of its socket. My shoulder screamed as loudly as my lungs after holding my breath for so long.

Try as I might, the Viper started slipping from my grasp. I squirmed, trying to grab on to him with my legs as well. Then he surprised me.

Apparently still conscious, his arms came to wrap around me, clutching me with surprising strength. In a few seconds that stretched forever as my enemy and I wrapped ourselves around each other, my head crested the surface. I gasped for air, my lungs demanding oxygen even as I coughed around the sand in my mouth. As Daiti backed up inexorably, I crested the edge of the pit, blinking away the grains that clung to my lashes, as hopeless as the idea of ridding myself of the sand covering me was.

Seated on the edge, I used my elbows under the Viper's arms to continue pulling him free, as he was too busy coughing and regaining his breath to be able to climb out himself. With a sudden slurping sound, like the quicksand was protesting relinquishing its prey, he fully emerged from the pit.

Without the sand pulling him down, the Viper lurched forward, knocking me back and pinning me beneath him. I froze. While his broad shoulders dwarfed me, he seemed strangely fragile as coughs continued to shudder through his frame, hunching over me weakly.

I took a deep breath despite the sand in my nostrils, ready to quell the uncontrollable swell of quivering magic that accompanied even a small amount of human contact—it was sure to be devastating with the Viper's whole body pressed against me.

The wave of mind-rending awareness never came though. My magic only gave the slightest quiver, like a hunting caracal completely tense but totally still. Instead, the scent of sweat and metal, and underneath it all salt and sandalwood, overwhelmed my senses.

The moment shattered as the Viper rolled to the side, removing the pressure that grounded me in place. He turned his back to me, hunching over as gloved hands scrabbled at his hood, yanking it off and pulling at the straps that crisscrossed the back of his head. Seeing his bare head in sunlight, I realized his hair wasn't black as I'd originally thought, but a dark brown that might even shimmer with streaks of chestnut if allowed to bleach in the sun.

A shuddering gasp, followed by enthusiastic spitting, told me he had removed his mask, having been suffocated by the sand it trapped against his face. A sudden urge to grab his arm and wrench him around struck me—to look into those unnerving silver eyes and demand to know why he was doing this and why we kept tangling together.

Instead, I turned away, squinting at the horizon to determine the fate of this challenge. A wave of numb acceptance rolled over me as Axlan sat proudly on his roan mare, brandishing the large red flag over his head in victory. Both the Viper and I would be moving on to the next round of the Trials.

I gritted my teeth in frustration; the fact that I had cast aside this chance to eliminate the Viper from the Trials once and for all was tinged with annoyance at myself for not being entirely disappointed that I would be moving forward as well.

"You saved me." The measured voice of the Viper snapped me from my musings, although his tone gave away neither surprise nor thanks.

In a long moment of silence, I searched my mind for some explanation to give him as the Viper's black mare snuffled through his hair in search of injury.

"I did," was my only response. There was nothing else to say.

Drumbeats filled the air outside the city walls, pounding into my skull and forcing my heart to beat in time. Although tonight's celebrations spilled between the tents and into the large open area in the center of the encampments, making it considerably less crowded, more people danced and drank than had been present at the Kelvadan festival months before.

I could still taste the bitterness of the lyra leaf tea on my tongue that I had swallowed hastily before heading out, and I let it reassure me that all would be well. My magic twirled sleepily in my gut, hazy and distant.

For now, I stood at the edges of the circle of tents, watching both competitors celebrating their victory and those drinking to forget their elimination. No other members of the green team had been successful in capturing a flag, and so their time in the Trials was over. The next event wouldn't begin until the day after tomorrow, and so people threw themselves into the only logical pastime: drinking *laka*.

As if summoned by the thought, a brimming glass was shoved against my palm with such enthusiasm that some of the *laka* within spilled over my fingertips. I looked up to meet a friendly grin on a handsome face. Hadeon's eyes looked oddly flat as he handed me the beverage, but I blamed it on the backlighting of the braziers and lanterns at the angle we stood. I shook off the cold shiver that washed over me at his expression, blaming it on the difficulty I still tended to have reading people's expressions. He had never given me any indication of anything but kindness and warmth.

"You live to fight another day!" Hadeon congratulated as he raised his glass to me.

"And so does the Viper," I added silently, but I peeled my lips into a smile and toasted back.

"It was a close call," I admitted as I drained half my glass in a single gulp. The burn of alcohol crawled down my throat as I swallowed back a wince. Drinking too fast was a habit I had yet to break after a lifetime of scarce liquids.

"Well, I do appreciate a flare for the dramatic, and you easily stomping the competition wouldn't be good entertainment," Hadeon said. "Besides, I dare say it's given you a little adrenaline to work off at tonight's festivities."

"More like too much sand to wash off before I was in any shape to show up," I grumbled. I had stood under the trickle of water in Aderyn and Neven's bathroom for what felt like hours, until my teeth chattered from the cold, but the rough chafe of sand still lingered on my skin. A buried part of me rejoiced at the feeling after months of relative cleanliness in a world of polished stone. Some twisted part of me missed the constant grit and the headachy feeling from squinting too long in the sun.

"Well, you cleaned up more than admirably." Hadeon's eyes drifted appraisingly over my outfit, my current posture pushing my leg out of the long slit in the side of my pants that hung loosely apart from where they gathered at my waist and ankle. I didn't miss the way he smiled at the snake armband that I had thrown on at the last second.

"Finish your drink," Hadeon ordered. "Then we'll dance."

"I don't really dance," I admitted, although I was already taking another large swallow of my *laka*.

"I'll admit, this is very different from the dancing I'm used to back in Doran, but I'm sure we'll figure it out together." With that, he whisked away my empty glass before pulling me out into the center of the circle. His fingers on my bare wrist caused me to jolt as always, but his touch was warm and not altogether unpleasant. I clasped my hand in his in return.

Then we were dancing, and Hadeon smiled at me brightly as he bobbed disjointedly. I nearly laughed at his awkwardness. He clearly hadn't been lying at festivities in his home country being different.

His grin turned sharp. "Are you laughing at my lack of coordination? I'll have you know that I'm much more used to dancing with a partner."

"You have a partner." I gestured to myself as I swung my hips back and forth to the beat. While an odd effervescence filled me, it didn't threaten to overwhelm me as it had the last time I danced. I could do this.

"I meant like this." Before I could register his words, Hadeon's hand circled my wrist once more and tugged me against him. I nearly stumbled as the front of my body pressed flush against his. My focus zeroed in on where my bare skin touched him—my hand that had come up to grab his shoulder in surprise. The bare inches in the gap between my pants and my cropped shirt pressed against his belly.

"Much better," he commented, seemingly unaware of the sudden rushing in my mind at the contact as he started to sway. I joined him, helpless to stop as I tried desperately to quell the rising sensation in my gut. The sleepy feeling surrounding my magic was all but gone, burnt away by *laka* and Hadeon's hand encircling the arm band he had bought me against my skin.

I opened my mouth to tell Hadeon that I needed to take a break, but as I breathed in, my mouth filled with the hot scent of smoke and spices, and I became too overwhelmed to form words. This was nothing like the stillness I had experienced when pressed chest-to-chest with the Viper just this morning. Perhaps I wasn't as in control as I had thought, and now I would lose it again.

A sand slide barreled through my mind with the force of galloping horses, and I shook my head trying to clear it before I hurt the dense crush of people around me. I wanted to leave, but I couldn't make my mouth form words. Hadeon's eyes narrowed at me, and his grip tightened around my arm—perhaps to support me, but it only made things worse.

It was a matter of seconds until I would explode, and I opened my mouth scream out a wordless warning.

A hand landed on the nape of my neck, and everything fell still. It was as if I were a kitten grabbed by the back of the neck, frozen but calm.

A familiar voice drifted over my shoulder, and I knew who the hand belonged to.

"Sorry to cut in."

CHAPTER SEVENTEEN
ERIX

Finally, I understood. The restlessness of the desert since I had arrived—since I had plucked this exile from the sands—had not been my own magic, but Keera's. The supernatural lightning storm that reminded me so much of the ones I had summoned as a child with nightmares were exactly that. A symptom of panic and uncontrolled emotion from the woman before me.

Through my hand at the base of her skull, I wrapped my ironclad control around her mind, containing the sudden swell that had threatened to rend the air around us just moments before. I grit my teeth in surprise at the strength with which her power thrashed, but it calmed quickly at my touch. Meanwhile, my own power perked up at the use, as if I had signaled it to ready for battle.

The man Keera had been dancing with—the one I had pegged as a diplomat a few days ago—frowned up at me. His expression seemed disgruntled, but I didn't miss the way his gaze darted over me, as if taking stock. I didn't bother to stand up taller or square my shoulders.

"I'm not sure—"

"It's fine." Keera cut him off.

After a moment of hesitation, the diplomat backed up and melted into the crowd, although the weight of his gaze remained heavy upon us even as I lost sight of him. I ignored it, keeping my attention on Keera, who still hadn't turned.

I debated pulling my hand away now that she had calmed, but I could feel the softness of the hairs that escaped her braid tickling my fingers. I don't know why I had touched her in the first place. While it helped with using magic on somebody, I was surely powerful enough to do without.

My pinky finger drifted back and forth in infinitesimal movements.

Instead of turning away, I stepped forward into Keera's space, standing close enough that we could have passed for dancing if we swayed. I could have sworn she shivered at my proximity. It seemed the press of people around her had triggered the near loss of control—something I could understand too well—but her magic remained contained despite the fact that I stood close enough to feel the heat of her body radiating off her.

"How could you tell?" she murmured, quietly enough that none of the dancers around us continuing in their celebrations would be able to hear her question.

I chewed my tongue before answering. The truth was, I had been watching her. I planned to stay in my tent and avoid the celebrations altogether, but something urgent in the beat of the drums had driven me out—pulled me toward the revelry at the center of the encampment. Lurking in the shadows, I watched the twirl of dancing bodies and breathed in the air fragrant with woodsmoke and spiced food—wishing for the clean smell of hot earth and horseflesh.

My gaze had snapped to Keera as soon as she entered the crowd of revelers, and the magic within me twitched as she began to sway. The moment the diplomat pressed her against him, I was weaving through the dancers toward where they stood. It must have been the swell of her magic, pulling me inexorably toward its source.

Keera began to turn to look at me, but I tightened my grip on the back of her neck to stop her, realizing that she was waiting for an answer. Even though she couldn't see my face, I oddly didn't want the weight of her stare.

"It's hard not to feel your lack of control." My words came out unusually harsh, as if I spat them out with great disgust.

Keera stiffened. "If you just came to insult me then..." She began to step away.

"You need help," I cut in before I could stop myself. "I—I could help."

"Your *help* is the last thing I need." Before any more unwise words could tumble from my mouth, she stormed off through the dancers, not stopping as she reached the edges of the celebration but continuing on toward the gates of the city.

My attention returned toward the celebration around me. I realized now that I stood at near the center of what served as the dancefloor, the rhythmic movement continuing around me and giving me a slight berth as I stood stock still. I was a dark rock in the bubbling of a spring, blocking its cheerful flow.

I turned and stalked back to my tent, breathing heavily through my nose. It had been unwise to go to the party, and even less well thought out to offer Keera my help. She stood between me and the Champion's circlet—the fall of Kelvadan—and would be eliminated like every obstacle that faced me.

Still, the more I thought on it, the less I regretted my offer. I couldn't afford a slip in my restraint now. Even when I had been leagues away, her turmoil had threatened my control, tugging at the strings of madness that always hovered at the edges of my awareness. This close, combined with the unease from sleeping in the shadow of Kelvadan, the uncontrolled waves of her magic threatened my very sanity.

The encampment at my back was quiet, everybody still asleep after the dancing and feasting had lasted well into the night. While food for many of the clans had been scarce recently, the yield of the opening hunt had provided ample meat. Despite the sleepiness of the clans and the city behind it, the desert was awake, and I let the feeling of the hidden life stretching beyond the horizon fill my bones.

I sat on the ridge of a dune a way out from the encampment, the sun just a threat of light below the horizon while the sliver of moon shown bright overhead. I always rose before dawn, but I had been unable to sleep long under the canvas roof of my tent and ventured out even earlier than usual. Zephyr fluttered back from wherever he had been hunting, landing at my side and pecking at the lizard he'd caught himself. I watched him with envy, wishing I too could fly away as I wished.

The shifting and squeaking of sand underfoot signaled somebody's approach from the encampment, but I did not turn. I knew it was Keera, and wondered for a moment how she knew where I was, but concluded quickly it was the same way I could identify her footsteps at this distance in the dark. After all, who else would be coming to see the Viper in the dark of night? And surely nobody else pulsed so strongly with power that the strings at the base of my skull tugged insistently in response.

Her feet swished quietly over the sand as she approached, stopping beside me. I didn't look up, keeping my arms folded loosely across my knees. She paused for a moment before sitting off to the side, mirroring my position as she too gazed at the horizon. Out of the corner of my mask, I could just spot her toes digging into the sand, apparently having walked out here barefoot. She sat far enough away that several more people could have fit between us, and it struck me as painfully close as well as awkwardly distant.

"Why?"

I stayed silent. She could have been asking me any sort of question, but I knew she was asking about my offer to help her. If she was here though, sneaking out of her comfortable bed somewhere in Kelvadan, I knew she was considering it for the same inscrutable reason I had offered. Ever since I happened upon her in the wilds, we were like two hawks circling above our prey, encountering each other at every turn, but inexorably drawn to the same target.

She huffed at my lack of answer. "Why should I trust you?"

"You shouldn't," I said, voice low with warning. "But I'd bet whatever the queen is trying to teach you is only making your situation worse."

It was an educated guess, but the long pause before Keera responded confirmed my suspicions. Her power would not have escaped the queen's notice and could likely be credited with her finding a place in

Kelvadan so quickly, but I did not envy her. I could still taste the lyra leaf tea on my tongue sometimes, and in the darkest hours of the night, I felt the weight of the mountains pushing in around me, an oppressive silence filling my mind as I was cut off from the desert. The silence disturbed me even more than the hum that made me want to tear my skull open to let it out.

"Wouldn't it be to your advantage for your adversary to not be able to control their magic?" she asked.

"Maybe once I show you the truth power of you wield, you won't be my adversary anymore."

"Unlikely," she shot back without hesitation.

"Besides," I started, chancing a glance over at her, as if I could see the magic dancing off her skin instead of feeling it with the odd sense that lived at the nape of my neck, "you're throwing off so much turmoil that I can feel it halfway across the desert. It makes it hard to get anything done."

"How do you know it's from me and not your own turmoil?"

I barked out a humorless laugh, and Keera jumped at the noise.

"I've become familiar enough with the feeling of my own madness over the years to know that this is not mine. At first, I thought I was losing control, but after tonight, I'm sure you were the source of the disturbance."

Keera turned to look at me too, narrowed eyes glinting in the moonlight. "You're just telling me this so I'll agree to whatever trap you've concocted."

"Today you lost control when you were crowded in a large group. Maybe it has happened like that before," I mused out loud. "It was at the Kelvadan festival, wasn't it? I was sitting in my tent that night and I could feel it all the way at Clan Katal's encampment."

Keera's shoulders slumped, and I knew I was right. I was glad, and yet somehow wished I wasn't.

"Fine."

My brows rose. I hadn't actually expected her to agree to anything. "Fine?"

"You can try to teach me, but it doesn't change anything else. I won't let you win the Trials, and I won't forget that you tried to kill me."

"You were trying to rob me in my sleep," I pointed out.

She ignored me. "And I'll only talk to you at night. Nobody can see us together."

"Of course. It wouldn't do for that handsome diplomat to see you consorting with the Viper." The retort came out more bitter than I'd hoped, but I knew she was right. I doubted Lord Alasdar would be pleased if he heard of me giving any aid to one who so clearly sided with Kelvadan. Keera was a distraction from the mission, but the whispers of the desert in my mind nudged me toward her insistently. First at the oasis, and again and again during the Trials. I got the overwhelming impression that her power was something important, and with the desert tearing itself apart at the seams, I couldn't afford to ignore any signs.

"Then I'll see you tonight, after most of the encampment is too drunk to notice me slip away."

With that, Keera stood and marched back the way she came. Zephyr let out a low crow beside me as I watched her go. What had I gotten myself into? The voice of the desert in my head muttered in anticipation.

Keera's approach broke me from the focus of my meditation, but I didn't move right away, remaining kneeling with my fists clenched tightly on my knees. I took the opportunity to observe the writhing turmoil that sprouted from her in magical waves, amazed that I had been able to overlook it when I first encountered her. Perhaps it had grown wilder and more untamed, as mine had whenever Queen Ginevra insisted I suppress it.

I nearly snorted at the thought of anything about Keera being more untamed and feral than she had when I first met her. As if to prove my point, she lightly kicked sand at me and huffed noisily at my lack of acknowledgement.

"Saber forms," I said as I stood with no other preamble.

Keera crossed her arms. "I already know saber forms. If this is just a trick to rob me of my sleep so I'm tired in the Trials, then I will march right back to the city."

I ignored her accusation. "How do you feel when you practice your forms?"

Keera narrowed her eyes at me. In the dark of night, her face was mostly inscrutable, but the stars still caught in her golden eyes. "Better," she admitted.

"The desert appreciates action. Practicing fighting, even on your own, can help calm your magic," I explained.

She tiled her head in consideration but did not argue.

"Do the first form with me, and focus on how the magic inside you reacts, not just the movements," I ordered.

I settled into the opening stance, feeling slightly off in the position without my saber in hand, but it wasn't uncommon to train the movements empty handed. I hadn't brought my sword, fearing if we were discovered with our swords drawn against each other, the incident would be twisted into foul play that ejected me from the Trials. As it was, I was taking an unconscionable risk by doing this.

After a moment of stillness, Keera settled into the stance next to me. We began to move, and after just a few breaths, Keera was already a few beats ahead of me. Perhaps she was surprised by how slowly I moved through the forms, many thinking that completing the exercises quickly was a sign of competence. For this purpose though, slower was better, and she soon fell in time with me.

By the end of the first form, when we both stood in the final position, our hands folded, palms facing down. Magic pulsed in the air. Maybe it was the reaction of my own power to her, but it seemed to ripple in time to my breaths.

"What did you feel?" I asked. The question sat oddly on my tongue, perhaps because such prompting was never how Lord Alasdar had taught me. Given our situation though, Lord Alasdar's methods of pain and brutal discipline in teaching were not an option.

"I feel... good."

Keera's answer was simple, but I felt the truth in it.

"The magic responds well to an outlet of aggression and anger, although forms are a relatively controlled way of doing it."

Keera stiffened before the words were out of my mouth. "I'm not aggressive." She nearly hissed the words in a manner so at odds with her statement that I let out a snort of disbelief.

"You're a feral little fighter," I argued, although the insult came out less derisive than it sounded in my head.

She tilted her chin up in a set of defiance. "Maybe, but I'm not cruel like you."

"I'm no crueler than the desert in which I live." My tone held a growl of warning. "And you can lie to yourself about that if you like, but I know better. You almost let me die in that sand pit. Go ahead and reassure yourself of how noble you are at saving the life of your enemy, but I know you considered leaving me. Your spy told your *queen*"—the word came out as a curse—"that my winning the Trials would lead to the clans uniting against Kelvadan, and letting me die could have solved that problem."

Keera's shoulders pulled toward her ears with tension, and her nostrils flared when I mentioned the spy.

"What did you do to Oren?" she demanded.

"Me? Nothing," I admitted. "But Izumi drove her saber clean through his chest. He gave himself away by trying to cut a deal for information with one of the clan's best riders."

A series of emotions flitted over Keera's face—shock, anger, guilt— but it settled into a flinty anger. Her expression was so hard she might have been the one wearing the mask.

I pushed forward, strings of my magic tangling unbidden in the swell of power around Keera, pulling conflicted emotions out of the swirl without a thought. "But despite but what Oren did tell you, and the fact that you had a chance to put an end to my time in the Trials, you're glad we weren't eliminated. You want to fight me again. And you want to be crowned Champion because that will mean you aren't a disappointing exiled...nobody anymore."

It was Keera's turn to growl, her teeth bared in a snarl as her eyes flashed. "Stop trying to pretend that we are the same. That you understand me."

She turned on her heel and marched back toward the city gates, a lone dark silhouette across the moon-bleached sands. I bit the inside of my cheek until it bled, focusing on the sensation to yank my magic free of hers and shove it back into the confines of my skull. Despite Keera's wishes, I understood her better than she thought.

CHAPTER EIGHTEEN
KEERA

Daiti pranced happily, in perfect juxtaposition to my sour mood. Exhaustion tugged at me, as I had hardly slept the night before, dwelling on what a mistake I had made in following up on the Viper's offer to train me. It was one of many mistakes I had made lately.

Every time I tried to close my eyes, tossing and turning to get comfortable in my rooftop nest, Oren's face would appear on the back of my eyelids. I had only met him once, but I was responsible for his death, just as I was for the clansmen that had been swallowed by a gaping chasm at my feet. I had pointed Oren toward Izumi, thinking she was kind, and all she had given him was a blade through the heart. I clearly wasn't a capable judge of character. I wouldn't be sneaking out to see the Viper at night again.

At least Daiti seemed pleased today by the opportunity to venture out further after so long exploring only the plains around Kelvadan. Despite the simmering anger from my encounter with the Viper, I too found my mood lifting the further we rode.

All remaining competitors for the Trials had been instructed to prepare for a two-day journey, as we would be heading a day's ride out of the city for the next event. Although we wouldn't find out what the event was until tomorrow morning, it apparently required us to be able to spread out more than was possible just outside the walls of the city.

By now, it was late afternoon, and we had been riding since dawn. Horses less well-bred than Daiti were starting to flag, and the mountains beyond Kelvadan were just jagged peaks on the horizon behind us, the city itself invisible to the naked eye.

I rode at the front of the caravan, near Aderyn, who led the pack out of the city. Sitting tall upon Daiti's back, the hairs at the nape of my neck prickled. Although I knew the Viper rode at the rear of the pack, where all the other competitors gave him a wide berth, I imagined the weight of his gaze on me often.

Finally, Aderyn held up a closed fist, and the group ground to a halt.

"We will camp here for the night," she announced.

I looked around, but there appeared to be no distinguishing landmarks indicating this was a predetermined location. Then again, predetermining the location of anything in the Ballan Desert was nearly impossible, with distances morphing and shifting depending on her whim. Perhaps the only stipulation had been that the next event be held a day's ride out from the city gates.

Everybody dismounted and began staking out a patch of ground in which to set up their camp. Nyra, one of my fellow riders in training at Kelvadan, had not yet been eliminated from the competition either, and I spotted her lifting the bundle that was her small tent from her mount's back. I started picking my way toward her, but as if she sensed my approach, she looked up suddenly, stiffening as she met my eyes.

I stopped, biting my lips. I doubted she would feel comfortable sleeping near me after what happened with Dryden, despite her being one of the faces I recognized among the remaining competitors. Just as I was about to give up and slip to the edges of the make-shift encampment, a familiar green sash and a hesitant smile caught my gaze.

It was Axlan from my team in the group event. The cautious friendship in his gaze told me he hadn't entirely noticed my intent to knock him from his saddle and eliminate our team from the Trials, which was likely for the best.

I led Daiti over to him, and he offered a nod of welcome as I began to unload my supplies.

"What do you think we are doing out so far?" he mused as I pulled my small number of packs off Daiti's back. They held little more than a spare hood and my sleeping mat.

"I couldn't say," I admitted.

After that, we lapsed into silence, like the rest of the competitors scattered around the area. While the encampment had been brimming with excitement for the last two nights, the clans and the city dwellers taking the opportunity to trade and drink, now everybody stewed quietly in apprehension. While the Trials were far from over, most of the riders that had entered for nothing more than the right to say they had competed were eliminated. Everybody left sized each other up out of the corner of their eyes, wondering in what ways we were to be set against each other next.

By the time everybody had claimed their square of sand and pitched their tents, Aderyn hovered over a fire in the center of the circle. Around it bustled the two dozen citizens of Kelvadan that had accompanied the riders to aid in the organization of the next event. Notably, the queen had not come. Perhaps she was loathe to leave the city unattended at such a time.

All the competitors drifted toward the fires over which volunteers stirred pots of fragrant stew. We had been instructed not to bother with bringing food in our supplies as we would be fed from the communal fires. A few fruits and a strip of dried meat had still made their way into my saddle bags as I slipped through the kitchen though.

We all ate quietly from the portions that were dished out to us. While some lingered in the common area making stilted conversations, most drifted back to our own areas to eat and contemplate what might be waiting for us. Across the camp, my gaze caught on the dark figure of the Viper ducking into his tent with his bowl, presumably to uncover his face where nobody could see.

Maybe everybody was worried about being well rested for whatever awaited us in the morning, or maybe it was to escape the palpable nervousness in the camp, but everybody began retiring quickly after dinner.

My belly pleasantly full, I laid back in the sand where I sat, jaw cracking with a wide yawn. I would get in my tent soon, but for a moment, I wanted to stare up at the unhindered sky before it was hidden by a canvas roof. The quiet out this far into the sands was deeper, the darkness thicker. It fell over me like a blanket, soft and comfortable. There was nothing but the scent of horses and the dryness of the rapidly cooling air whispering over my skin, peacefully beckoning me toward sleep.

The overwhelming crush of loneliness woke me. Before I even opened my eyes, something told me I was completely and utterly isolated. It was apparent in the frantic pounding of my heart and the swish of the desert's magic in my core as no life around competed with its hold on me.

I opened my eyes to the thin light and rising heat of late morning. Sitting upright, I clapped my hand to my forehead as my brain tried to batter its way out of my skull. It was the feeling of having drunk too much *laka* but amplified. I pushed that sensation down in favor of standing and turning in a circle, trying to get my bearings.

There were no bearings to get.

All that stretched around me was golden sand. No indentations marked this as a place dozens of riders may have camped last night. None of the others were in sight. Absent was the comforting wicker of horses nearby, and I couldn't make out any sort of irregularity on the horizon that could signal the mountains. Even Daiti was gone, my first real friend in a decade.

Hot sand scraped my palms, but I didn't remember falling to my hands and knees. One word echoed in my head in time with the pounding of my heart.

Alone. Alone.

Fear rose like bile in my throat, choking me even as I swallowed rapidly, hard won survival habits resurfacing. I'd had a taste of companionship in Kelvadan, and even if I hadn't quite found my place among others yet, it still made the renewed threat of exile worse in my heart. I couldn't go back to living like that.

I was startled from my panic by a shifting of sands too rhythmic to be from wind alone. I whipped around, rolling from my hands and knees into a crouch. I squinted at the shimmering heat over the next dune, which formed itself into a man. The first thing I recognized was a green sash.

"Axlan?"

I had fallen asleep next to his tent last night, and although the camp was gone, now he stumbled over the dunes toward me. A look of relief crossed his face, and he quickened his pace toward me as I stared in confusion. He stopped just before where I sat.

"Not how you expected to wake up either?" was his greeting.

I shook my head, hand drifting to my own sash warily, only to find my weapons had abandoned me too.

Axlan raised his hand in a gesture of peace. "I'm not here to harm you. I think this is the next challenge. A test of our survival skills."

I glanced around. If Axlan had woken up the same way I had, it seemed likely that the other riders had too.

"The stew," I thought out loud. We had all eaten from the same pots, and never before had I fallen asleep so quickly I hadn't even remembered it. "They must have drugged us."

Axlan rubbed the heel of his hand against his forehead. "It would explain the hangover."

"So, what do you think we are meant to do?"

He peered around, squinting in every direction. "I would guess we're meant to make our way back to the city."

I nodded while contemplating the task. Not knowing how far out we might be, and with those who abandoned us not sure how long of a journey it would be for us either, my first priority needed to be supplies. Water was my first need. As well fed as I was these days, I could likely make it a couple days before hunger overwhelmed me. I wouldn't say no to a weapon either. The sash around my waist and a few stones would be a passable makeshift sling.

Axlan's feet shuffling in the sand reminded me that I had been staring sightlessly at the horizon for a while now.

"I'm going to pick a direction and start walking." He cleared his throat awkwardly and his meaning was clear. I was still his competitor, even though we had been on the same team in the last challenge. He was hesitant to ally with me, and as much as I had feared the isolation just a moment ago, I wasn't anxious to put trust in a near stranger. I had survived a decade on my own—I could do a few days.

"Good luck." I nodded to Axlan as I stood, brushing off my clothes as best I could.

He hesitated. "There is a hidden spring just over that rise." He pointed toward the direction he'd come. "I just drank from it, but it might be a good place to start."

I tapped my knuckles to my brow in a heartfelt thank you. He returned the gesture, and we walked our separate ways, me toward the rising sun, and him away. I would likely follow in that direction, considering the sun normally rose in the direction of the sea, not the city, but water was my priority now.

The acrid stickiness in my mouth took over my thoughts as I trudged in the direction Axlan had indicated. It served as a reminder that I was still working whatever drug had made me blind to the world out of my system. Any potential side effects would also be a concern in surviving the next few days.

Cresting the rise, I caught sight of a patch of green scrub, signaling I had found my target. I hurried toward it, finding a sluggish spring bubbling up from beneath the earth giving the plant life the moisture it needed.

I bent, using my cupped hands to gulp down water. I grimaced at the sulfuric taste that coated my tongue, but only hesitated a moment before swallowing another mouthful. While I had been lucky that the oasis where I resided was relatively free of the minerals that laced water from underground wells, it was not uncommon for desert springs to have a distinct taste.

Despite the mineral taste of this water being cloying strong, I downed steady sips that wouldn't make me sick but would keep me well hydrated for the miles to come. I couldn't afford to be picky.

I stood from the spring, taking a moment to take stock of my surroundings. Some small stones scattered around the edges of the small, bubbling pool. I toed through them, looking for some that might fit my makeshift sling. It wouldn't seriously injure any larger predators, but a well-placed stone could serve as a persuasive deterrent. Once I had a suitable collection, I shoved them into my pockets.

Turning to the barren shrubbery, I put my hands on my hips in contemplation. While the wizened plants didn't appear to bear any edible fruit, I was loathe to turn down any possible advantage. Perhaps if I could hack off one of the larger branches it could be used as a club or a small walking stick.

With a sigh, I set to work, yanking at the waist height bushes. After a minute of fruitless tugging, I pulled off my long leather vest and wrapped it around my hands, my palms already raw from my efforts.

A splintering sound signaled my progress. With pride, I observed a split at the base of the thickest branch. A few more solid tugs and it would come free. Then it would only be a matter of cleaning off the prickly twigs so I could hold it more comfortably.

Before I continued though, I paused to rub at my chest. Despite the heat of the sun suffusing my whole body, the skin there was filled with an awful burning. I clawed my hands, using my nails to scratch at it more determinedly. Still, the itch did not abate.

I glanced down to find tiny red dots adorning my bare skin. It was as if I had been pricked my hundreds of pins across the entire surface of my chest. I frowned as I scratched at it again, but the sight didn't change except maybe to get even redder.

Perhaps I was sensitive to the shrubs, although it seemed an awfully inconvenient time to find out. I had lived among this flora and fauna my whole life and had never had such a reaction. I would just have to be careful to touch as little of my skin as possible to the leaves.

I turned to my work again, and the branch fractured further, hanging on to the main plant by the barest splinter. Before I could fully detach it, the itching came again, now spreading down my arms. I unwrapped my vest from my hands, finding the same odd red markings on my palms.

Heat flushed through my body as if I were suffering from dehydration even though I had just drunk my fill. More worrying though, was the taste of copper that coated my tongue. I brought my fingers to my mouth, bringing them away to find them coated in blood. I was bleeding from my gums.

Dizziness followed the heat, and I swayed. I would have toppled if not for the bush, which I grabbed as gravity threatened to bring me to the ground. Unfortunately, my hand closed around the branch I had been working on and it snapped after just a few moments of supporting my weight.

My breath came in short, frantic pants as I lay at the edge of the spring. Try as I might, I couldn't slow it down to clear my head and figure out what could possibly be happening to me. Maybe it was a delayed reaction to the drug in my dinner the night before. No matter what had happened though, the outcome was the same. Unless I could recover quickly, I would die out here.

I needed a plan. My eyes slid shut. Maybe if I just rested for a moment and gathered myself, I could figure out what to do.

CHAPTER NINETEEN
THE VIPER

I trudged doggedly up the side of another dune, the sun hot on my back. Sweat dripped down my temples, pooling at the edges of my mask and soaking my tunic. I was without my leather pauldrons as I hadn't been wearing them when I slept last night, although I was glad I had left my mask on despite the privacy of my tent. If I had gone without it, I might be facing this challenge bare faced—a thought that made my stomach churn uncomfortably.

Still, the heaviness of my clothes, damp with perspiration, reminded me of my most pressing issue. The constant need that plagued all who called the desert home.

Water.

I might have an option if the situation got too dire, but for now I would suffer on, hoping to find an oasis or a spring. I trudged on for what felt like hours. Cramps began rippling through my thighs and I gritted my teeth against them.

As they spread up toward my back, I paused, taking a deep breath in. On the exhale, I focused on all that pain, trying to think back on Lord Alasdar's lessons on accepting agony and letting it strengthen me.

The pain crashed through my body as I turned my attention to it, like one of the waves of the distant sea. I refused to let it pull me under.

My magic responded in the way I had hoped, focusing in my skull to a hard a lethal thing.

That is what would carry me through to survival.

Bolstered by the hard edges of my power, I soldiered on. Finally, a splotch of green on the horizon ignited my hope that water was imminent. I hurried toward it only to hesitate as I grew close enough to pick out individual shapes.

Huddled among the smallest patch of greenery was a human form. I crouched down quickly, not wanting to draw attention to myself if it was another rider in the Trials. While it was forbidden to kill another competitor in the Trials, nothing was stopping any of the other riders from trying to hinder me. If they stood against me, I couldn't guarantee that they wouldn't get hurt by my resistance, and I couldn't afford a misstep.

After a minute of tense stillness, the slumped form hadn't moved. I inched closer, curious. Perhaps they had not yet awoken from their drug-induced slumber, although it seemed unlikely given how long I had been alert.

Drawing closer, moving with less caution as it was clear the person was numb to my presence, my stomach did an odd lurch. Eyes closed, face tipped to the side, I stared full into Keera's face.

"*Sands,*" I spat, wondering how we had managed to find each other in the vast expanse of the wilderness once more. Even as I said it though, I frowned at her appearance. Blood trickled sluggishly from one nostril and an odd rash decorated her skin. The rise and fall of her chest was rapid, indicating that she was alive and unwell.

I fell to my knees beside her. At least if I found out what had befallen her, I could be sure to avoid it myself. Looking closer, my gaze caught on where more rivulets of blood leaked from cracks at the corner of her mouth and coated her teeth. My breath hissed out harshly through my teeth.

I had seen this before.

Such uncontrollable bleeding was a symptom of a poison made from the distilled venom of pit vipers. It was a horrible death, blood leaking slowly from more and more orifices until the victim was completely exsanguinated or suffocated on the fluid filling their lungs over a course of days.

It was a favorite poison of Lord Alasdar's—a slow and horrible death for those who stood against him or a torture as he withheld the antidote until somebody acquiesced to his requests. Even though I had stood stoically at his side as these sentences were carried out, even hunted the vipers needed for the poison, the sight of the bleeding victims haunted me more than I cared to admit.

Now, they wore Keera's face. But how had she been poisoned?

I looked around, but the only notable features of our surroundings were a bubbling spring and a handful of stubborn bushes clinging around the edge. I approached the spring and leaned in cautiously. Instead of the slightly mineral scent of fresh well water, a stronger, sharper scent of sulfur wafted over my face. I pulled back with a grimace. I wouldn't be drinking here.

My attention drew back to Keera as a weak cough shuddered through her. I scowled. Once again, she was complicating what was once the straight-forward task of winning the Trials.

Maybe if I left her here to die, she would stop visiting my dreams. Or maybe her face would still fill my sleeping hours, but now with blood dripping from her mouth and eyes. After all, she had not left me behind when it would have been all too easy to do nothing. Besides, somebody had clearly tried to poison her, and given my reputation, it would be all too easy to pin such foul play on me, which I couldn't afford.

These were the reasons I repeated to myself as I bent down and hoisted her off the ground and draped her over my shoulders. I grunted —she weighed noticeably more than when I'd once slung her over Alza's hindquarters.

In truth though, my magic curled like a hunting dog happily around its master's feet as I began to carry Keera along. Letting her die would be a waste, just as Lord Einil's and Oren's deaths had been foolish. Magic filled Keera's being to the brim, and even if she could not control it yet she could make a fearsome weapon.

If only I could convince her to help Lord Alasdar and me heal the desert, instead of blindly following Kelvadan's folly.

I bit my tongue as my knee hit the ground with a painful thud. It wasn't the first time I had stumbled in the past hour. The bolstering of my magic with pain seemed to have lost its effectiveness, my power more interested in the woman draped across my back than the ache of my muscles.

With a sigh of defeat, I lowered her to the ground, sitting heavily beside her. We hadn't been lucky enough to happen upon another water source since we left the poison spring in our wake. I rubbed at the tunic where it stuck to my shoulders and my fingers came away wet with crimson.

Looking at Keera I found that the rivulets of blood dripping from her mouth and nose came faster now. Peering even closer, I spied the red shadow of blood in her ears as well. She wouldn't make it much farther without the antidote, and neither of us would survive long without water.

I glanced around, but no signs of salvation lay in sight.

Then again, nobody was around to see me use my last resort. I chewed the inside of my cheek as I stared at my unconscious charge. As she inched closer to death, I doubted she would remember many of my actions when she woke. Still, I had decided to save her to ensure that my record in the Trials was spotless as it could be, considering I had already thrown Keera and myself into a pit of quicksand. Then again, she couldn't very well say anything about that without admitting she had been attempting to sabotage her own team as well.

Despite all this, doubt gnawed at me at using my magic so dramatically in the Trials. I was supposed to overcome these challenges using the strength of my body alone.

If I didn't though, I might fail, and the desert would continue to shred at the seams. And Keera would die.

Slowly, I pushed to my feet, letting my bare hands play through the sand as I levered myself up. For once, I was glad to be without my gloves, the unfettered connection to the earth helping awaken my connection to the desert around me. Standing now, I turned my face up to the sky and began unspooling the knot of power at the base of my skull.

The whispers of the desert in my mind, quiet as I had carried Keera, grew in volume until I could see them—taste their mad power. I grit my teeth to not get lost in the mad tangle of life and death intermingled in the desert around me, instead grasping on to the fabric of nature.

Holding my arms out before me, I clenched my fists and *ripped*, rending through the stillness of the air around me.

A crack of thunder. A flash of light behind closed eyelids.

I snapped my eyes open, not even realizing I had closed them, just as the first drops of rain began to fall. They pinged off my mask and were quickly soaked up by the dry sand at my feet. Within moments, fragile green tendrils pushed through the baked earth, long dead roots of plants awakening in sudden rearrangement of the universe.

But I stood frozen in place. The power still coursed through me, my sense of self having tangled in the loose fibers of the fabric I tore. The sound in my skull was not voices but a long, unending shriek, and I was helpless to fight against it.

I screamed along with them, staring up at the sky, paralyzed by the same storms that had taken hold of me as a child. If I just had my knife, I could stab it into my thigh to give myself a sensation to ground on to, but I had nothing.

I buckled to my knees and pitched forward dangerously. Then, my palms landed, and the world tipped sideways. The screaming was gone, although the rain still pattered around me. Whatever madness had held me hostage though had released me from its clutches.

Staring down at my hands, I jolted at the sight that greeted me. My left had unknowingly landed on Keera's bare arm, her flesh fevered and soft under my fingers. Just as when I had tightened my hand at her throat, my magic zeroed in on the point of contact, shivering in still anticipation.

I stared for a long moment before coming back to myself. When the light rainfall began to soak through my hood to my hair, I yanked my hands away, reminded of my purpose.

Casting around me, a looked for a way to collect the water gently pattering from the sky, but I did not have a skin or a basin. There was only one thing on either of our persons that was not made of fabric.

I turned away from Keera and raised my trembling fingers to my face. With slow, even motions, I pulled the mask off and turned the metal contraption up to the sky. It could only hold a small amount of rain before the water began leaking out the eye and mouth holes, but it was enough.

Again and again, I let it fill with a few mouthfuls of water before gulping them down. Once my throat no longer felt glued shut and my lips stopped threatening to crack with dryness, I hesitated.

Keera needed to drink too, and she needed the antidote to the poison.

I shifted on my knees, turning toward her, and reminding myself that she could not see me, unconscious as she was. Shuffling forward, I tipped a few drops of water from my mask into her open lips. Her tongue darted out to lap at them eagerly, despite her blindness to all else around her.

The light rain had rinsed away some of the blood clinging to her, but the odd red rash and the rasping of her breath remained. Already, the rain began to slow, even the magically induced storm as short as the ephemeral showers of the rainy season.

Quickly, I raised my mask to the sky one last time, letting as much water as I could pool in the recesses. Setting it carefully on the ground, I cast around for the plants I had felt shivering life beneath my feet minutes earlier.

Sure enough, one of them was adenium, one of the few flowering plants that dotted the occasional green area of the desert. I plucked the petals, rubbing them between my fingers before dropping them into the small amount of water.

While the pit viper poison destroyed the essence of your blood that allowed it to scab a cut and prevent bleeding, the petals of this flower could restore it.

With as steady a hand as I could manage, I tipped the paste of crushed flowers and water into Keera's parted lips. I watched her throat work as she struggled to swallow the antidote, but as thirsty as her body was, it complied. Even her tongue darted out to lick at the last drops clinging to her bloody lips.

Normally, the antidote was to eat a whole flower, but I doubted I could persuade Keera to chew in her current state. This would have to do. I would find out in a few hours whether the antidote had taken hold. For now, I hoisted Keera onto my back again and continued to march on.

The sun was low in the sky, inching toward the mountains I could now see in the distance, when Keera shifted on my back. It was the first sign of life besides shallow breaths and a light cough.

I paused, lowering her to the ground. Something tight in my gut loosened when I saw that no more blood leaked from her nose and mouth. The adenium had worked. She would survive, which meant it was time to part ways. I had saved her from the foul play of another rider to save my own name, but she was still my competitor.

Staring down at her, I took a moment to contemplate what I had done. She still might not make it back to Kelvadan, but if I had ever owed her any sort of debt for my life (a tally I did not like to keep), it was now repaid. She could simply be my enemy once more, even if she was a nuisance that pulled at my magic.

Her eyelids fluttered as if waking were not far off, and I jumped. I had lingered too long. With long strides, I walked off toward the mountains and the city at their base, away from the woman sprawled in the sands.

I tried not to dwell on why I chose to sit on the fence at the edge of the horse's enclosure on the outskirts of the encampment as I sharpened my saber. After all, Alza had missed me as we had been separated for the better part of three days, and I wanted to make sure she was well. I preferred to take care of my own mount, and something about the Royal horse master being charged with Alza while I trekked through the wilderness irked me. Although I knew all too well that the Royal horse master cared for horses better than almost any other.

My lingering at the edges of the encampment had nothing to do with the slow trickle of competitors limping toward the gates of Kelvadan as they made their way back from the wilderness.

Once night fell, riders would set out and sweep the sands for any competitors that remained lost, although they would be eliminated from the tournament. Still, some would not return at all.

My saber was so sharp I could have used it to shave by the time a familiar figure crested the horizon. Although all the riders were crusted in sand and slumped with exhaustion, a certain stubbornness in her stumbling gate gave her away.

Keera had made it.

Before she could reach the city gates, I turned and made my way back to my tent. Zephyr fluttered to my shoulder as I walked, apparently pleased to have company again.

Meanwhile, I needed to prepare for the next event. I could not afford any more distractions. No matter how far that feral sand cat made it, I would defeat her in the duels and be crowned Champion of the Desert.

CHAPTER TWENTY
KEERA

My saber weighed heavy against my sweaty palm in the afternoon sun, the feeling of the grip foreign in a way that set my teeth on edge. In a few short months, I had already gotten used to the saber I trained with for the guard, and the blunted standard issue version passed out for the next challenge of the Trials brought me a sense of discomfort, the balance just off.

Still, I was glad this challenge would not involve drugging me and leaving me to die in the desert, instead providing me with an opponent I could face with a weapon in hand. I remained unsure of just how I had made it back to the city alive, although perhaps it was because a chunk of time was missing from my memory as I wandered in a fevered fugue. Whatever had caused my illness had worked its way from my system though, and I had woke up shivering and nowhere near the spring in the dead of night.

Neven and Aderyn had insisted I see a healer when I returned to the city, but they found nothing wrong with me outside of exhaustion and dehydration. It was nothing that a few days of rest between events couldn't fix. Neven credited my miraculous recovery from my illness to the desert's favor. I wasn't so sure.

Now, I pulled my hood higher over my head to protect my face from the sun beating down from above. The searing brightness could be used as an advantage against my opponents if I positioned myself right, and I thanked the sands for the line of black paint Neven drew across my eyes before I reported to the encampment for the competition. It would absorb the worst of the sun's rays.

The last of the competitors filed into the large, flattened area, marked off for the fight and surrounded by spectators. The herd had been thinned considerably, but I estimated about fifty competitors filled the arena.

A hush fell over the crowd as Queen Ginevra climbed the steps to the temporary dais at the far end of the arena.

"We challenge all the remaining competitors to a melee. Those who are hit should leave the arena. The last sixteen participants will move onto the remainder of the competition," she proclaimed grandly, raising her arms. Light glanced and scattered off a series of gold bangles at her wrists. "Fight honorably and bravely with the spirit of the desert."

The fighters all shifted on their feet, hefting weapons and sizing each other up out of the corners of our eyes. Sixteen competitors remaining would mean it was time for the final duels. While I was squarely in the middle height wise, most of the competition still outmatched me in muscle, even with me eating Aderyn and Neven out of house and home for several months.

As the judges positioned themselves at regular intervals around the edges of the arena, spectators crowded in close, jostling against each other for the best few. Coin purses jingled with people placing the occasional bet on who would emerge victorious.

I raised my saber in a ready position above my head, point facing forward with my free hand extended in front of me. The competitors took a collective breath, followed by a stretched moment of stillness.

Clang.

Queen Ginevra rang the gong, and I sprang into action. Immediately, the clash of blunted steel and grunts of exertion filled the air, punctuated by the occasional yelp. My first lunge carried me into a fighter with a blue hood at a speed that surprised even me. He moved to parry my swing, but I ducked the tip of my sword beneath his blade and caught him squarely in the breastbone.

He clutched his chest with a soft *oomph* as the air rushed out of him. He raised his other hand in surrender, but I didn't wait to watch him leave the arena. Turning to the next opponent, I swung before I even zeroed in on my target.

My limbs moved of their own accord, my dissatisfaction with my weapon completely forgotten. While both the forms and sword drills had come to me more easily than my general fitness, the feeling of muscle memory that wasn't mine grew as I fought. Perhaps fueled by adrenaline, or the freedom of my first time fighting with true abandon, my mind grew fuzzy as I landed blow after blow. A feeling of static; the sound of wind whispering through the dunes filled my head as I nearly slipped out of my body.

I watched my arms swinging my sword with more force than I knew I could muster, slapping one opponent upside the head before hitting one behind her knee, causing her to crumple to the ground. The rushing feeling in my head threatened to overwhelm me, dragging my ability to think coherently under, panic rising as my breath came faster.

Not again, I couldn't lose—

Before I could finish my thought, my gaze caught on the flash of light off a blade. A dirk tucked behind a man's back, glinted menacingly, certainly not dulled like the rest of the competitors' weapons. I jolted at the sudden danger, the sight of the dirk pulling me from my fugue. He approached a tight knot of fighters, all gathered around a dark figure cutting a shadowy splash across the sun-bleached landscape.

The Viper faced off against a half dozen fighters, all coming at him together. Despite them teaming up against them, he held them off admirably, parrying an overhead strike from a fighter to his right while stepping back to avoid the blow from a man directly in front of him.

The man with the dirk tucked behind him approached from his unguarded left side. I lurched forward, feet pounding across the sunbaked earth without my direction. The sun glinted off the sharpened blade as the man raised it overhead.

With a clang, it flew out of his hand, spinning through the air before burying itself sharpened point first in the trampled ground. My saber swept through the air from where it had knocked the blade out of his hand to catch the would-be cheater in the shoulder, a blow that would have taken his arm off if my weapon weren't blunted.

The Viper's head snapped in my direction, and I caught the briefest glimpse of wide metallic eyes before I spun back to the fight at hand. Between the two of us, the remaining fighters in this knot of combat were taken out quickly.

He eliminated nearly twice as many as me, but soon, the combat around us had thinned enough that our attention drew toward each other. As fiercely as I had leaped at other competitors, I backed off a step, circling around the Viper cautiously. He needed to be eliminated for the sake of Kelvadan, but the speed at which he had dispatched his other enemies left me hesitant. Doubt creeped into the edges of my mind. He was the superior saber fighter.

To my surprise, the Viper didn't circle at all or advance, instead standing perfectly still with his blade in a forward guard. It might have made me think he was unprepared to block a sudden blow, but my mind rang with alarm bells. A Viper could strike with no warning.

I debated trying to take him off guard with an uppercut from my off hand but dashed that idea. He seemed like the type who had thrown enough mad-cap right hooks in his life to see it coming.

Sensing my hesitation, the Viper cocked his head to the side, and with a deliberate motion raised a hand to crook a finger at me. A deliberate challenge.

My blood boiled and a snarl ripped from my throat. I crouched ready to spring forward sword first.

The gong rang out across the arena, and all fighters raised their hands in unison, blunted sabers falling to the ground in a clatter. The set number of fighters had been eliminated, and the melee was over.

My breath came in quick pants, and I ripped my gaze from the Viper's expressionless mask to the raised platform where the gong rested. I blinked, finding Queen Ginevra already descending the steps and approaching the line of stones that marked the edge of the arena.

She picked between the fighters who deferentially made way for her. At first, I thought she was heading toward me, and I shrunk back. Perhaps she was going to berate me for not taking the opportunity to eliminate the biggest threat to Kelvadan from the Trials. I wouldn't blame her, and she didn't even know how I had pulled him from the sinking sands.

Her course turned to the side though, and she approached an open patch of ground, marked by the dirk I had knocked from a fighter's hand. She plucked it from the sand, and all the remaining fighters in the area remained preternaturally still as she examined it.

She ran her finger across the edge, and we collectively hissed as a line of red marked her flesh. Blood welled and dripped to the sands at her feet, soaking the gold to a deep crimson.

The blade had been intended to end a life during this melee.

The queen grabbed her skirt, wrapping her hand in the fine linen, seemingly unperturbed by the stain the blood would leave on the pale green fabric. With the other hand, she pointed the offending blade at the at the competitor who had wielded it, standing at the edge of the arena with the rest of the eliminated fighters. He clutched his shoulder where I had struck it, and I tamped down the odd swell of pride that filled me at the sight.

"Seize him. He has violated the sacred agreement of the Trials and tried to unfairly injure a competitor."

City guards rushed forward and grabbed him. He didn't resist, his eyes trained somewhere over my shoulder on the battlefield. I turned to see what he stared at, only to be greeted by the retreating form of his intended target. The Viper didn't look back, walking off the field, his broad shoulders harshly silhouetted by the afternoon sun.

I turned back in time to see the Kelvadan guards wrenching the fighter around, his hood falling from his face in the process and revealing a stony expression. His gaze held no trace of remorse, only defiance as he was turned away toward the city walls.

"Keera."

I started, heart leaping into my throat as the queen said my name.

"Walk with me," she instructed, already striding back toward the city as well.

I swallowed thickly as the gazes of the remaining competitors weighed heavily on me. They made my skin itch—a far cry from the invisibility that came with my life of isolation not so long ago. Still, I squared my shoulders and marched obediently after her.

I caught up with her quickly, my long strides carrying me farther than her much shorter legs. I fell into pace at her left, while Aderyn materialized at her right, a protective shadow.

We walked in silence through the city, climbing the levels to the palace at the top. Our steps echoed through the uncharacteristically empty courtyard—most of the usual inhabitants were still mingling in the encampment on the plains.

I looked up at the mounted statue, as I always did when I entered the palace, and finally placed the jolt of familiarity that shot through me. While Queen Ginevra certainly bore similarity to Kelvar, the proud cheekbones and delicate nose were the same as those of the man in the mask.

Erix.

Kelvar's great-grandson.

I wondered if Erix ever smiled like Kelvar did, full of mischief that would have looked like arrogance if not for the softness of his eyes.

Queen Ginevra and Aderyn were almost to the palace doors, and I wrenched my eyes from the statue, lengthening my strides to catch up with them.

"Dispatch a rider to the lord of Clan Tibel. The punishment of his rider for breaking the agreement of the Trials will fall to him," Queen Ginevera instructed Aderyn.

"You don't wish to pass down judgement yourself?" Aderyn asked.

The queen shook her head. "Dealing out punishments that should belong to another lord would not help my case if the clans are uniting against Kelvadan. I do not seek to usurp their power, only to offer a place where the clans can put forth a united front to the rest of the world, and a safe haven to those who do not agree with clan life."

I chewed my cheek as I remembered the words Lord Alasdar had used to whip the combined clans into a frenzy against Kelvadan. I didn't think this soft response to a crime would ingratiate Kelvadan to those who thought the loss of the old ways was tearing the desert apart.

This conversation was between Queen Ginevra and Aderyn though, so I stayed silent. They did not keep me around for my understanding of the nuances of politics. I was a blade and a sometimes-unpredictable source of power.

"I would speak to the rider though, before he is sent back to his clan," said the queen.

"They will have him held in the cells near the guard quarters. I will dispatch your message while you speak with him, so it will precede him to his clan." Aderyn bowed her head with her fist on her breastbone before heading off toward the stables.

I hesitated, shuffling my feet as I debated whether I should follow Aderyn or not. I still wasn't sure why I had been summoned.

"Come," the queen commanded again, answering my unspoken question. Still, she didn't speak as she led me toward area where the guards without their own homes in the city stayed.

It was only when we reached the room with the cells, and I cocked my head curiously at the wooden structures, did she speak.

"Kelvar had the foresight to make many things when he hewed this city into the mountainside, but a place to hold criminals wasn't one of them. It turns out he was a touch optimistic." She wore a wry smile at the thought.

Indeed, it was odd seeing wooden cells when I had become accustomed to everything from walls and stairs to benches being seamlessly integrated into the rocky city.

We walked to the end of the row where the fighter from the melee sat cross-legged. His head remained bowed as we approached.

"The Trials are supposed to be a time of unity," she began without preamble, her voice icier than I had ever heard it. I straightened my spine at the total lack of her usual warmth.

"They were not always so." The man still did not look up.

"It has been hundreds of years since the Trials were a fight to the death. Twenty years ago, the last time somebody tried to spill blood at the Trials, I did not tolerate it. I will not tolerate it now." Her tone was sharp as a saber.

"And yet the one you exiled is the one who sends his snake after us now, spilling our blood so we might march on your city and restore the desert's good will," he ground out, finally looking up, eyes still as defiant as when he had been marched away.

"Lord Alasdar chose exile when he resorted to lethal force in his efforts to win the title of Champion," Queen Ginevra argued.

"And now he sends the demon in a mask to bring the clans together and purge the weakness of the city that sent him into exile for his determination. The man I tried to kill, the one she stopped me from killing" —he inclined his head toward me—"is the one spilling the blood of my kin. Yet you would deny me my justice."

"You say I was wrong to exile Alasdar and call me weak for punishing murder. Yet you also seek to kill the one who serves Lord Alasdar," the queen pointed out.

"You can both be wrong," he said with a shrug. "Besides, I'm not the first one to attempt murder in these Trials."

The queen took a step forward, and for all her posture appeared calm, her knuckles whitened as she clasped her hands tightly with each other. "Who is interfering with the Trials? Tell me and I will urge your lord to be lenient."

The prisoner ignored her, his attention swinging toward me instead. I raised my chin against his casual perusal.

"I'm surprised to see you made it back from the survival challenge."

I stiffened, pieces clicking together in my head.

"You... you poisoned me!" I accused.

He had the gall to smile. "I was too busy trying to kill the Viper to worry about you, but that doesn't mean I wasn't offered a great price to see that you didn't make it back to the city alive. I'm sure somebody else took it."

"Who asked you to do this?" The queen's voice was sharp enough to cut stone, but the man just leered.

"And why would I tell you?"

"To uphold the tradition of the Trials, the Ballan Desert's most sacred tradition," the queen said imperiously.

"The desert's most sacred tradition is spilling blood, and you are too much of a coward to do so even when it would save us a war. Kill the Viper, and Lord Alasdar and the clans who wish to march against Kelvadan will be crippled."

The queen shifted next to me, and a moment of silence echoed through the stone room. Her lack of response weighed heavy, settling like a blanket over us.

"You will be allowed to return to Clan Tibel, but your lord will be informed of your actions. He will decide your punishment, whether it is to be exile or worse," she finally said, her voice dangerous and soft.

I suppressed a flinch at the thought of his exile. It was not a fate I wished on any.

At this, the man's stony façade shattered, and he tipped his head back and laughed. "You think I will be punished for trying to kill the Viper? When he is the one responsible for the death of Lord Einil of Clan Ratan, my lord's cousin." The fighter shook his head with a broad smile that did not reach his eyes. "His only disappointment will be that I did not succeed."

"You will be escorted from the city and beyond the encampment by the guard. If you should try to return, they will use all necessary force to stop you," Queen Ginevra declared. With that she turned on her heel and strode away in a swirl of green linen.

I stood stunned for a moment, head swirling, before my mind caught up with my body, and I turned after her. I chanced one glance behind me before leaving the room, but the man was back to staring at his lap, sitting just as he had when he entered.

The queen stormed up the stairs, clearly angry but somehow managing to maintain her dignity in the process. It wasn't until we stopped on a balcony overlooking the city and the encampment beyond that I cleared my throat.

"What did you want me for?"

Queen Ginevra sighed, leaning her forearms on the railing. For the first time, the silvery hairs at her temple made her look weary.

"You saved a man's life today," she answered.

I stayed silent, but she didn't continue, so I thought she might be waiting for a response.

"I would have done it for anybody." For some reason, I bit back the admission that I had saved his life in the team challenge as well. Then I would have to dissect why I kept going out of my way to save a man who was supposed to be my mortal enemy.

"But it wasn't just anybody. He is your greatest enemy in the Trials and to Kelvadan."

I clasped my hands tightly behind my back, waiting to see where she was going with her speech.

Queen Ginevra looked me over carefully "You would have good reason to want him dead, and I must thank you twice over for not letting him be killed." She took a deep breath as if to plunge headfirst into a pit of sinking sand. "I've never told me about my son."

I blinked, but apparently my expression didn't convey adequate surprise to convince her of my ignorance.

"You knew?"

"I'd heard you had a child," I admitted.

"He died—or at least we thought he had—ten years ago. He was... troubled. So intensely powerful that we feared he would suffer from the same madness as Kelvar. Even as a baby he was hard to calm, a whirlwind of emotion in human skin. We tried our best to help suppress his power, but the desert spoke to him so strongly, he lost control often. One night, he snuck out of the city and wandered into the desert. We searched and searched, but never found him. We assumed he faced the same fate as his great-grandfather.

"But I then I heard his voice behind that mask, and it was like seeing a ghost. I've prided myself on my diplomacy my whole life, and for the first time, I've been disarmed by my opponent."

"I'm sorry." It was a horrible thing to say, but it was the only thing there was. After so many years with only myself to talk to, poignant sentiments were beyond me. I could only hope to help through action.

"And I'm sorry to saddle you with this burden, knowing you will likely have to face him in the duels." For the first time ever, the queen looked tired. A few hairs in her perfectly braided crown slipped out as she scratched her head, and something heavy and uncertain settled in the pit of my stomach.

As the Trials went on, the simple charge of emerging victorious became more fraught. It reminded me of my apparent brush with death in the survival challenge.

I cleared my throat. "When we were stranded in the desert..."

The queen's gaze sharpened—the heart-aching exhaustion was gone, only to be replaced with the fierce political observation once more. "Somebody tried to kill you?"

"I thought I had an adverse reaction to the drug that was used on us, but the rider of Clan Tibel's words make me think that I was poisoned," I admitted. "I fell ill after I drank from a spring."

"Was anybody nearby that could have poisoned it?"

My heart skipped. "Axlan of Clan Tibel. He pointed me toward the water when we happened on each other."

The queen summoned a guard.

"Find Axlan, and bring him here."

I shot to my feet when a commotion sounded at the entrance to the terrace where the queen and I sat drinking lyra tea, rejoined by Aderyn who was not partaking. The reason for the noise became clear as four guards dragged not one, but two struggling figures before us.

My mouth fell open, but the queen beat me to the gasp of recognition.

"Hadeon?"

Gone were the dancing eyes of the man who had urged me to dance at the feast almost a week earlier. Instead, the expression that met me was the calculating gaze of a man appraising a horse.

"We found the two of them meeting together in Hadeon's quarters," one of the guards explained. "They had this."

A second guard stepped forward and presented Aderyn with a vial filled with a viscous black liquid. Aderyn popped the cork off and took a delicate sniff before drawing back and blinking rapidly.

"Pit viper venom." Aderyn's tone was grim. "It would cause the bleeding Keera described when she returned."

I whirled back toward Axlan and Hadeon, the former of which at least had the decency to look ashamed. Fury boiled in my veins, and if not for the lyra leaf tea I had just finished, my magic would surely be bubbling up beneath my skin. As it was, it frothed discontentedly in my belly. It didn't matter that I was too angry to speak though, as the queen stood from her chair. No matter that she was the shortest in the group, everybody shrunk back a step.

"You come here as ambassador and enjoy my hospitality, only to turn and interfere with one of my land's most honored traditions? Even when you knew what rested on Keera emerging as Champion?" she demanded.

Axlan shrank back but Hadeon stood tall.

"It was your mistake admitting that Kelvadan might fall if the Viper were to win the Trials," Hadeon commented as if discussing the weather and not the fate of the entire desert. "It was too good of an opportunity to pass up, when all it would take was a subtle push to set the fall of your Great City into motion."

"Opportunity?" I spluttered finding my voice again.

He leveled me with a gaze full of condescension. "For two hundred years, Kelvadan has stood between the rest of the world and the desert. This city is the one entrance point that would need to be overcome for Doran to invade through the mountains. With the city gone and all the clans fighting for themselves it would be all too easy for our armies to march in and take what we want by force: the horses of the Ballan Desert."

This time, it was Aderyn who cut in, her voice dangerously calm. "You think it would be so easy to subdue the clans?"

"Nothing but ragtag savages with swords," Hadeon sneered.

"I thought you were on my side," I snarled. All his talk of how he wanted to be friends with next Champion of the Desert. The feeling of his hands on my skin, one of the first times I had allowed even a casual touch on the arm. The golden armband he gifted me.

"A means to an end." Hadeon shrugged and my skin crawled. "I had hoped that I could charm my way into your bed where I could knife you quietly in your sleep without having to get anybody else involved. Due to unforeseen interruptions, I had to recruit some help."

I swallowed bile. This marked twice that a man had shown romantic interest in me since I arrived at the city. Instead of feeling desired, or like I belonged though, I just felt sick. Dryden's interest had abruptly ended when the truth of my power had been exposed. Hadeon had only feigned interest in me for my power. Either way, the magic that I couldn't control defined me.

"And Axlan, why would you agree to violate the peace of the Trials?" Queen Ginevra demanded.

Axlan's eyes flicked back and forth between the queen and me. I stared him down with all the rage that simmered below my breastbone.

"He offered me a place in Doran—a way out of the desert." Axlan's voice was halting but did not shake. "No matter the outcome of the Trials, the desert shudders at the seams. I was there when a bone spider attacked my clan. We will not survive if we stay in the desert, and I have no desire to die to a creature of legend."

My heart sank. A bone spider. The desert had moved beyond sandstorms and thinning herds. Now, creatures that had not been seen since the desert had been crossed were rising again.

"Well," the queen said tersely, "you shall both get your wish. You are to depart for Doran immediately."

Axlan's eyes widened. "I am not going to be punished?"

"This is your punishment. You wanted to leave the desert, and so you will never see it again. You are stripped of your clan and your horse."

The moment the weight of his choice hit him, Axlan's face crumpled. The desert was harsh, but it was home, and to those who rode with a clan, their horse was their life.

The guards began to pull the men away, ready to send them on a perilous journey through the mountains. Before he was dragged away, Hadeon managed to sneer, "Doran will be watching, and we will be waiting for the desert to fall."

As the group retreated into the palace, Aderyn released a long breath. "Are you sure we should let them go?"

"I'm sure of very little anymore." The queen shook her head. "But imprisoning or executing an ambassador is asking for a war we cannot afford right now. Keeping the Trials fair so Keera can become Champion is still our best hope for peace."

They turned to look at me, and my pulse pounded harder than Daiti's hooves against baked earth.

"After all, you're almost there. Only one more challenge faces you before the duels."

Chapter Twenty-One
The Viper

I felt more than heard the presence outside my tent. An itching at the base of my neck made me look up from where I was feeding Zephyr strips of raw meat.

At first, I thought it was Aderyn come to visit again after the scene at today's challenge, but when the form didn't enter, I knew it wasn't. Aderyn would never wait for an invitation. With a grunt, I pushed to my feet and walked toward the flap. My muscles were stiff after the fighting today, having had most of the competition take the fight as an invitation to swing at me with little finesse. Still, I relished the soreness of my limbs, knowing I was one step closer to achieving my goal. The final duels were nearly upon us.

I pushed the tent flap open, and the figure there jumped back in surprise, nearly tripping over their feet and falling backward in the sand. They managed to right themselves with surprising grace.

"You," I said, meeting Keera's golden glare.

She opened and shut her mouth a few times but did not speak, and I took the opportunity to get a good look at her. She still wore the black stripe of paint from temple to temple, accentuating her narrowed eyes, making their molten color stand out even more.

"Why are you here?" I asked, as she continued to stare at me wordlessly. I knew she couldn't see beyond my mask, especially as shadowed as my eyes would be now that the sun had set. Still, her gaze was as heavy as though she physically touched me.

"I don't know," she admitted.

I exhaled heavily through my nose. We stared at each other for a few more moments before I made as if to go back into my tent. She had made it clear after my last misguided offer to train her in control that my form of aid was not appreciated.

"I did save your life today," she blurted out before I could push the tent flap aside.

"Are you expecting thanks?" I thought about throwing back at her that I had saved her life in return, but I kept that information to myself. If I admitted to it, I would have to explain why.

"No," she shrugged. I tracked the movement of her shoulder, and the way the moonlight shone off her deeply tanned skin. "But I wanted to know, why are you here?"

"The same as you. To win the Trials."

"And if you do? Will you and Lord Alasdar really march on Kelvadan?" she asked.

I cocked my head. "Why should it matter to an exile?"

"I'm not an exile anymore." She raised her chin defiantly. "I'm a citizen of Kelvadan."

The noise in my skull crescendoed, having been quiet for most of the conversation. The image of her following obediently behind the queen's billow of green linen today as she left the melee snapped to the front of my mind. This girl who had been nobody just months ago now filled the role of Kelvadan's favorite champion. My throat tightened.

"Then you shall die alongside the rest," I snapped.

Keera drew back as if I had slapped her, and my lips pulled up into an invisible snarl. She shouldn't be surprised, as I had tried delivering her to her death before.

"Why do you want to destroy the city that is the beacon of peace in the desert?" she argued, eyes flashing.

"The peace of Kelvadan is a lie," I spat back. "There is no peace to be found among the sands, only the strength to survive or the release of death."

She blinked at me, and I turned away to storm back into my tent. I felt magic boiling under my skin, aggravated by her presence. I bit my cheek until salty copper flooded my mouth, the pain distracting me from the odd whirlwind brewing inside me.

"Erix."

I froze in my tracks. My name on her lips made my heart skip a beat. I had heard it spoken twice in the past weeks, but this time, it was as if a spell had fallen over me. The storm within me dissipated, and I felt... still. In the odd silence in my body, it almost felt as if I floated a few inches above the ground.

Then the world came crashing back in. The whicker of horses and the sounds of the encampment pushing in on me, making my skin itch with awareness of every living thing.

"I am not Erix. I am the Viper, and you would do well to remember it," I growled. I pushed into my tent without looking behind me. I stopped just inside, and it was several long minutes before Keera's footsteps carried her away and into the night.

Alza pranced proudly, as if she could sense that the time for her to show off was near. I let her preen, looking up and down the row of sixteen assembled riders. None compared to my mount, her black coat like molten obsidian in the morning sun. I had cut my forms short this morning just to spend a few more minutes brushing her coat and braiding her mane.

The only other horse in the line-up that matched Alza stood at the end of the line, as far from me as possible. Lord Alasdar's former warhorse stamped at the ground moodily while his rider looked so determinedly away from me that I knew she was avoiding me on purpose.

I frowned and looked away as well. After she left last night, I had laid awake on my bedroll for far too long, the defiant set of her jaw filling my mind every time I closed my eyes.

Now, Queen Ginevra climbed the wooden stand at the end of the line that demarked the start of the horse race. While Aderyn had declared when the challenge was announced that no riders would be eliminated from the competition here, the results would determine the rankings for the final stage of the Trials: the duels.

I kept my eyes straight ahead on the horizon, toeing Alza up to the starting line. While most of the riders were packed tightly enough that their knees brushed, the competitors on either side of me gave me as much room as possible, as if I would knock them off their horses if given the chance.

With Alza beneath me, I had no need for such trickery.

"Riders ready," called a familiar, imperious voice.

I drew in a deep breath and held it, letting it fill my lungs as I relaxed into my seat, loose but tense at the same time.

Alza leaped forward at the gong, faster than an arrow loosed from its bow. I leaned forward over her neck, resting my hands on her muscled shoulders. The riders on either side of me disappeared as Alza pulled away, and the wide swath of competitors narrowed into a single file. As the herd thinned out, and we came toward the first turn in the track that ran around the entire encampment, only one rider remained in front of us.

Keera.

Her golden warhorse's hooves pounded the earth in a rhythm that thudded in my chest as we tailed her. As we sped around the curve, she was several horse-lengths in front of me. We hit the straight away, and I murmured encouragement to Alza under my breath.

Approaching the second bend, we started to pull even with Keera. She spared me a glance out of the corner of her eye, and I couldn't help but look back. The wind had pulled dark tendrils of hair from the braid down her back and whipped them around her face, hood thrown back in the thrill of the chase.

Even though Keera had the inside on the turn, giving her the advantage, Alza continued to gain ground. While the stallion had the greater power off the start, Alza's slighter frame had the better endurance.

Nobody could beat us in a sprint to the finish.

Turning onto the last straight away, I loosened the leash on the magic in my mind that connected me all living things in the desert— especially my horse. With Alza and I moving as one, her head bobbing

as she lengthened her stride to reach impossible speeds, we pulled
ahead.

The finish line came into view, and the soaring feeling that only
came with riding full tilt lifted my soul. With the competition of Keera
and her stallion galloping just off my shoulder, the sensation intensified.
For a flash, I could swear I was the wind whipping through Keera's hair.

Then the finish line flew by, and the assembled crowd roared. I had
won by less than half a horse-length. I let Alza slow to a trot, patting her
sweat-soaked neck and wheeling around to let her cool down. Keera
pulled up next to me doing the same, and I couldn't help but look at her
as she tipped her face up to the sun. Her eyes were closed, and the look
on her face wasn't quite a smile, but I knew she felt the same joy I did
echoing through her from the race.

A smile curved my lips of its own accord, and the muscles around
my mouth protested at the uncommonly used expression.

As if she could sense me looking, Keera's eyes flew open, gaze
shooting to me and pinning me with a glare. The beginnings of my
smile were extinguished just as fast, along with any remnants of the
exhilaration from the ride.

She wheeled away and trotted off, leaving me to wonder how I had
forgotten it was a race, if only for a moment. I couldn't afford to lose
focus when the fate of the desert was on the line.

I was not alone in my tent that night. A warm form pressed against me
on my sleeping mat, comforting in the dry chill of the desert night. My
arm draped over a soft curve, and I tightened my grip, pulling my
bedmate closer.

Her response was a feminine sigh and a subtle wiggle, as if she itched
to get closer as well. As her round ass pressed up against me, I grinned in
pleasure at the closeness. Something sleepy and muted in my head
wondered at the contact—didn't I always sleep alone?—but I pushed it
aside in favor of basking in the comfort of a warm body against mine.
Unsurprised that I was already hard, I ground my length against the

small of her back. How could I not be aroused with hair that smelled of sunshine and larrea flowers tickling my nose?

As I relieved some of the pressure in my cock by thrusting gently against her ass, I let my hands wander, drifting between her breasts and down her stomach where I flattened my palm, pulling her more firmly into me.

She let out a shuddering breath in response and threw her head back to rest on my shoulder. The movement pushed her dark hair out of her face, and I bent over as if to press a kiss to her neck. Before my lips could touch her skin, I caught sight of her face and froze.

At my stillness, her eyes snapped open, and I looked in horror into the deep molten pools of Keera's eyes staring straight at my bare face.

I woke with a moan dying on my lips, the warmth of the dream chased away by the icy fear in my veins. My hands flew up to touch my maskless face, and a few moments of staring at the canvas above me reminded me of my solitude. No one was here with me.

I growled at the warmth of arousal still echoing in my core. Why would I have such a dream about the woman who had made these Trials so complicated? She had seen my face once, and it already haunted me, yet my mind continually assaulted me with images of us in increasingly vulnerable positions—with her seeing more of who I was than just my bared face. It was like my subconscious mind wanted to torment me with things I could never have by the light of day.

I rolled and pushed to my feet, ready to go practice my forms. No matter how much longer I laid in my tent, I wouldn't be getting any more sleep tonight.

Chapter Twenty-Two
Keera

A hand landed on my shoulder, and I jumped before realizing it was Neven. His warm gaze was a welcome sight to my frayed nerves. I had spent the remaining rest days of the Trials firmly ensconced in his textile stall, not trusting myself to join in the festivities after my last social liaison had apparently been a ploy by a would-be assassin. While I worked with Neven, fetching and carrying or making change, he never brought up the coming duels or tried to pry details from me about the prior challenges. If he made conversation at all, it was idle gossip about the other stall owners, and I appreciated him making space for me in the normalcy of his life. For the last weeks, my nerves grated, and increasingly disturbing dreams about the Viper haunted my sleep. The last one had echoed the first dream of intimacy I had when arriving at Kelvadan, but this time my companion wore the Viper's face. I woke from that dream with an overwhelming rush of both heat and cold washing over my skin. The time spent in Neven's stall was a safe haven from such confusing dreams and the speculation of the Trials.

Now, Neven held out a pot of black paint and gestured to my face, offering to help me apply it across my eyes. As the individual duels were fought starting in the afternoon, moving into evening, it would be all too easy to be blinded by the sun.

I turned away from the fight currently underway, glad for the distraction. Watching the competitors only made bile rise in my throat at the thought of my own impending duels. I had never truly expected to make it this far in the Trials, and the volume of the audience's cheers with every clash of blunted sabers jangled my nerves.

I shut my eyes and focused on Neven's cool, damp fingers tracing a stripe across my face.

"I'm glad you don't have to fight in the first round after placing so highly in the race." Neven made casual conversation as he worked. "It'll keep you from being as tired in the later rounds."

"You say that as if I'll be fighting in the later rounds," I grumbled, half under my breath, but he seemed to hear me none the less.

"You've made it this far."

"I'm still not sure how that happened. I've only been training for a few months," I pointed out. Even though Aderyn and the queen had put their faith in me to win the Trials and prevent war in Kelvadan, standing here facing down the final duels held the strange blurred quality of a dream. Perhaps I was still lying in the empty sands, drowning in my own blood and having fevered visions of what being in the final round of the Trials would be like. Still, the visceral sensations in my body told me this was real. Perhaps the desert really had chosen me, and I would defeat the Viper to save Kelvadan—and finally earn a real home here in the Great City.

Or maybe, I would fail the queen, despite all her efforts to help me.

Nerves jangled my belly, making the fruit I had eaten for lunch churn uneasily. I swallowed my nausea down, unwilling to waste the food by retching it up.

"You act as if keeping yourself alive in the desert for years wasn't any sort of preparation." Neven finished up and wiped his hands on a cloth tucked into his belt. "Besides, the Trials are where the desert picks her Champion, and she is never wrong. People who have trained for years for the Trials have lost to those the desert deemed worthy."

"Some people in Kelvadan seem to think that the chosen of the desert is nothing more than a myth," I pointed out. Even more believed that being crowned Champion was a sign of some great destiny, but that didn't seem to fit me right now either.

"Every myth comes from some truth."

I opened my mouth, but my response was drowned out by the crescendo of the crowd. Turning toward the ring, I peered over the heads of those in front of me to the ring where the duels took place. The two competitors were caught in a grapple. One man had the other's blade arm trapped by his side, essentially disarming him. The fighter didn't give up, grabbing at his opponent's sword.

The crowd gasped as the pinned man wrenched his competitor's saber free, hitting its previous wielder over the head with the pommel. He stumbled back, tripping over his own feet, stunned by the blow. In a flash, his adversary had both sabers crossed at his throat.

The gong rang out above the cheers and hollers of the crowd.

"Silas moves on to the next round."

The victor offered his hand to his opponent and helped him to his feet. They clasped forearms, and the loser rapped his knuckles to his brow in respect.

"The next match will be Badha of Clan Otush and Keera of Kelvadan."

My lunch threatened to reappear again, but the feeling was drowned out by the leaping of my heart at the announcement—I was a citizen of Kelvadan. I was fighting for this city that had welcomed me with open arms when nowhere had ever felt like home.

I unsheathed my blunted saber and marched into the ring, the eyes of the crowd weighing heavily on my back, but I raised my chin. My opponent bore a green sash, the color of Clan Otush, and raised her arms boldly in the air as she entered the ring. The hollers and cheers told me that she was a favorite of the spectators, and she seemed to revel in it. I avoided looking to either side, instead focusing on my opponent.

She sprang forward with a flurry of attacks as the gong sounded, driving me back. I quickly changed my momentum, moving to the side so she wouldn't coral me into the edge of the arena where I would have no room to maneuver. My mind raced, trying to recall the words of wisdom Aderyn had about fighting opponents so fast and nimble.

In a flash, a strike came at my unprotected side. Before it could slash me in the ribs, I turned, lifting my elbows over my head, and catching the blade in a hanging parry. The force knocked the saber off course, and I moved the momentum into an overhead strike.

Badha's eyes widened as I pressed the advantage, only just missing her shoulder with my downward blow. I couldn't remember any of the drills Aderyn had put me through, but it didn't seem to matter. My body did.

Time blurred, and the whistling of wind filled my mind. In a matter of moments, or at least that's what it seemed, my opponent had her empty hands in the air, my saber at her throat.

I lowered my weapon quickly, uncomfortably familiar with the feeling of a saber point at my throat and loathe to subject anybody to it, even if it was blunted. Badha clapped me on the shoulder with a rueful but friendly smile as we made our way out of the ring.

I stopped at the edge of the ring, crestfallen as strangers offered me smiles and pats on the back. My arms hung limply at my side, tip of my practice saber dragging on the ground. Standing among the crowd and accepting their congratulations felt like belonging—something I had craved for so long it felt carved into my identity. Now though, it felt oddly as if it were happening to somebody else.

The next few fights passed as I stood dumbly among the crowd, but I was pulled from my reverie as a familiar figure, broad shouldered and imposing, pushed into the ring. This time, the onlookers didn't cheer but were overtaken by a sinister hush.

With the mask on, I couldn't see the Viper's expression, but his body language gave away nothing. He simply swung his sword back and forth in a few passes as if to loosen up, the whistling noises it made carrying across the ring.

The blood drained from the other fighter's face as he took in his opponent. I couldn't say I blamed him. Even though I had technically bested him in the hunt, everything I had seen from the Viper spoke of terrifying competence, from the effortless way he had kidnapped me and lugged me across the desert, to the swathes of competitors he had eliminated during the melee. The man who had pressed a gentle hand to the nape of my neck and offered to help me contain my magic was nowhere to be found.

I hadn't even registered the gong ringing, and the Viper's adversary was face down in the dirt. The onlookers barely had time to react, a stilted rumbling instead of a cheer filling the arena.

"The fighter from Clan Katal wins the match!"

The Viper stood in the ring over his opponent. He didn't offer his hand, but he hesitated. His fallen adversary scuttled away on his hands and knees and scurried out of the ring, clearly unwilling to take the assistance up even if it were offered.

A shiver ran up my spine despite the heat of the late afternoon as the next duelists were called forward. If that ruthless efficiency won the Viper the title of the desert's Champion, peace would no longer be an option for Kelvadan.

My next fight passed in much the same way as the first, my enemy felled by my body before my mind could process what was happening. It might have been Aderyn's training, embedded in my muscle memory, and letting my instincts be the guide, but the sensation was unnerving. By the time I found myself in the semi-final match, my skin itched as if too tight, and the chatter of the crowd, growing in pitch and excitement, felt like dozens of flies swirling around my head.

The fights grew more brutal, competitors putting more force behind their blows, with each passing match. The only person besides the Viper I recognized that had made it to the duels was Nyra. I blinked in surprise as her name was called, not having realized another fresh trainee was still in the Trials.

I straightened as her fight began, only to slump again almost immediately. Her opponent parried her opening move easily, knocking her blow aside and rapping her firmly on the wrist. The blow caused her to yelp, and her blunted sword dropped to the sand. I grimaced. Aderyn had used that move on me enough that I knew it caused your hand to go numb, your grip useless.

Nyra retrieved her sword and shuffled from the ring as her opponent was declared winner. I fully expected her to brush past me as she left, but she paused, touching two fingers to my elbow.

"Good luck," she murmured. Then, she melted into the crowd at my back.

It was the first time any of the trainees had acknowledged me since the accident with Dryden. Even those who disliked me were counting on me. My heart hammered.

But every time my name was called, "Keera of Kelvadan," it served as a balm to my fraying nerves. I represented Kelvadan, and it was a responsibility at which I would not balk. Not when they had given me more second chances than my own parents. After all, I had promised Aderyn I would fight in the Trials, and she had never been anything but kind to me. Even as Aderyn hovered off the queen's shoulder across the arena, Neven stood stalwartly and silently at my back.

My feet carried me into the ring for the semi-final match. With a quick feint I baited my opponent to parry. Then I ducked my blade under his and drove it forward into his sternum. He raised his hand in defeat. With a single and anticlimactic trap, I had won, moving on to the final match.

The cheering of the crowd at my swift victory clashed with the growing sense of unease.

I watched the Viper fell enemy after enemy, each with so little fanfare, it was if he didn't find any of his opponents worth any extraneous movement. The woman he had just defeated limped out of the arena after taking a harsh but fair blow to the leg ten seconds after the gong had sounded. Despite whatever luck—will of the desert or otherwise—that had brought me this far, despair began to rise in my throat. Nobody could stand against the Viper's skill.

"The fighter of Clan Katal will fight in Keera of Kelvadan in the final match!"

The hum that rose might have been from the crowd or the rush of noise in my head. Somehow, this ending had seemed inevitable since the race this morning, but my mind had shied away from the reality of what was coming. There was no way I would make it to the final round, yet here I found myself, walking into the packed dirt circle on numb legs. Now that I was here, I was certain this was as far as my newfound skills would take me.

Neven patted me on the shoulder as I passed him to enter the ring, and I forced my chin up. Even if I walked toward defeat, the people of this city had given me so much more than I deserved. I wouldn't sentence them to war without a fight.

By now, the sun hung low in the sky, the long shadows lending a dreamlike quality to the affair. Or maybe the feeling of floating while weighing more than Daiti was from the odd way sounds filtered through my ears to my frazzled brain, warped as if I were underwater.

All I knew was that my gaze locked on to the figure who entered the ring across from me, not actually that much taller than me, but larger than life in the way he haunted my thoughts since the day he had first said my name.

Silence hung thickly in the air, and then the gong rang. This time, I leaped off the start, opening with a series of quick slashes. The Viper parried easily, knocking my blade aside, but not throwing any attacks back. We circled each other for a moment, and my gaze darted over his shoulders and chest, looking for any hint of the next attack. I found none.

An overhead cut crashed down on me, and I threw my block up just in time. Unprepared as I was, the force of the blow drove me to one knee. I teetered backward. He raised his hand to strike again while I was off balance, but I let my momentum carry me, rolling backward over one shoulder as his weapon struck the sand where I had knelt just a moment before. As I sprang to my feet, I kicked at his weapon, throwing a horizontal slash, but he was too quick. Reversing the momentum of his blade to knock mine off course.

He circled once again, and frustration bubbled in my throat, the strangled sensation of a repressed scream. He was fast enough that he should have been able to land a blow while I was on the ground, but he hadn't. The Viper had the audacity to toy with me, even when the fate of the Ballan Desert rested on the results of this fight.

I leapt at him with a flurry of blows, increasing the force behind them until my muscles strained. He matched them, strike for strike. My blade skittered along his, and sparks flew through the air before we separated. I panted, winded from my attack, but if my opponent was tired, he showed no signs.

Now he advanced on me, twirling his blade in an arc I could barely follow. I dodged his strike, but only just, the wind from his sword brushing my cheek as it swished past. He drove me back, attacking in earnest now. I stopped at the edge of the ring, attempting to hold my ground, and our blades locked.

He pressed the advantage of his greater size, bearing his weight down into me. My knees shook as he pushed forward, the blank mask of metal over his face hovering inches over my own. My legs gave out, and I fell to my knees again but refused to let me guard drop and surrender. Still, it was only a matter of seconds before he would overpower me.

The sand beneath my knees shifted, and the shouts of encouragement from the crowd at my back became garbled and overwhelming. I was going to lose. I was going to fail Kelvadan, after I had found my purpose to survive once more in saving the city from this war. All those who had put their trust in me would be lost, and I would be alone again.

A familiar yet unwelcome sensation washed over me, and magic bubbled beneath my skin. The last thing I saw before magic erupted forth from me was widening silver eyes behind a sheet of metal.

Chapter Twenty-Three
The Viper

Screams tore through the air, the sounds whipped away by the unnatural storm, centered around me and Keera. Lightning danced through the cloudless sky, striking somewhere nearby, making every hair on my body stand on end. Footsteps pounded as people fled, but my gaze was fixed on the woman before me, the epicenter of the chaos.

Her eyes were screwed shut and she vibrated with energy, although she remained motionless. If she was aware of the world around her, she showed no signs of it, likely wrapped up in the deafening cacophony that poured in when one opened themselves to the magic of the desert with no filter.

I had known she was powerful the moment I felt her magic threaten to tug mine until it snapped earlier, but this—she was just lightning trapped in human skin. Even now something soft and unfamiliar washed through me at the recognition of what it was to barely feel like you owned your own body sometimes.

I pushed forward to where she knelt, fighting against the whipping winds that pulled at my clothes and flung sand at my face. Without thinking what I was doing, I reached out for her, prying her clenched fist open to entwine her fingers with my own gloved hand.

The touch seemed to bring her back to her body some, and the pitch of the wind's howling lowered, but thunder continued to rumble far too close. I squeezed her hand and after a moment's hesitation, she squeezed back.

I closed my own eyes, opening myself up ever so slightly to the flow of magic around us, an overwhelming torrent that would have carried me away were it not for years of discipline and Lord Alsadar's training. Instead, I followed it back to the woman before me and traced it down to the one thing planting her in reality: my hand in hers.

Still caught up in the flow of the desert around me, I pulled on that connection, growing it as much as possible, trying to give her something to latch on to. A guide to follow back to her own body when she couldn't even remember where she was.

The howling of the wind stopped, and the world became quiet, the air still in the way it is only after a terrible storm. I peeled my eyes open to find that I had knelt down before Keera and pulled her into my arms. I clutched her to my leather tabards, arms tight around her trembling form. Her eyes were still closed, her face tipped up toward mine, but her arms wrapped around my waist in return, clutching on to me as a lifeline.

Her eyes fluttered opened, and for a moment neither of us moved. Then, I stiffened and jerked out of her grasp, pulling my arms back. Golden eyes, that had held something intensely soft upon opening, narrowed in confusion before shuttering.

I sprang to my feet, backing up a few steps, but she stayed on the ground, shrinking in on herself as if she wished she could sink into the sands beneath her knees. I looked away, rubbing my gloved hands harshly on my arms, as if it could scrub clean the fact that I, the Viper, had held my opponent just moments ago.

Turning my attention to the chaos around me, it appeared that not many had noticed my antics, fleeing as they had been from the epicenter of the storm where Keera and I knelt. Now, the guard who had been announcing the duels stood in close conference with Aderyn and the queen, whose hair had been ripped from its elaborate twist by the storm. Beams from the wooden scaffolding that had been erected for the announcer lay splintered and scattered across the windswept ground.

With the air calm once more, the spectators inched forward, murmuring quietly among themselves. Finally, Queen Ginevra nodded grimly and walked away from the group into the center of what had once been the fighting ring. She raised her arms, and the crowd went quiet. It was a moment I had once dreamed of as a child, standing in the dueling ring of the Ballan Trials as the queen announced the next Champion of the Desert.

The grim look of resignation she wore was a far cry from the look of pride I imagined on her face as a boy, but I knew what it meant now.

"Keera of Kelvadan has forfeited the duel by using magic after pledging to win only through the strength of her own body. The rider of Clan Katal will be crowned the next Champion of the Ballan Desert."

While I sat far from the main bonfires of the encampment, the celebrations sounded subdued. The climactic end to the Trials seemed to have left the revelers unbalanced, but I was sure once the *laka* was flowing, the feasting would quickly turn into dancing and storytelling of Trials past. Parents would recount the Trials of their youths, while younger competitors would bemoan their losses or brag of their victories. Although this year, the revelry would be stilted by the threat of looming war. Even if the significance of my victory wasn't common knowledge, the tension in the air was clear to all.

Even though I had won, fulfilling my mission and bringing me one step closer to healing the desert, I did not feel the urge to celebrate. Kelvadan must fall for the desert to survive, and it would bring me satisfaction to see the walls crumble as the lies of the city were unraveled. But thinking of the coming war brought me no joy. Instead, a heavy weight lay over my shoulders, making me hunch down and seek out solitude.

I sat on the ridge of a dune a way out from the encampment. The flickering of braziers, only an orange glow at this distance, did little to chase away the thick dark of night or dull the stars. Zephyr fluttered back from wherever he had been hunting, landing at my side and pecking at the lizard he caught himself for dinner.

A dark silhouette broke from the edge of the tents and made its way across the sands toward me. Part of me had wondered if Keera would seek me out, but my heart still jumped as she approached.

She stopped before me, but I made no move to greet her or turn her away. The magic of the desert danced between us in the silence.

"Why?" Her voice was quiet but steady.

She could be asking me any number of things, but something told me she was asking why I had helped her when we stood on opposite sides of an inevitable war.

"I had already won anyway," I responded, evading the question.

She exhaled loudly through her nose in what might have been frustration. The silence stretched between us, a tangible thing.

"I don't know," I finally admitted, although it was a half-truth. In the moment, I hadn't had a reason when I reached out and grabbed her hand in the middle of the storm. The whispers of the desert in my mind had left me no choice.

I had realized as I sat here in the dark though, that I recognized something in that confused outpouring of power. It was the same frightening madness that had driven me out into the desert when the walls of Kelvadan closed in around me as a child. The rush of power that made everything in my old bedroom burst into flames in a moment of frustration. The same overwhelming sensation that led me to Lord Alasdar's tent to burn another line on my back just to drown out the deafening roar.

"And now you will unite the clans and march on Kelvadan." It was a statement, but Keera's voice rose at the end like a question.

"Yes." There was no point in lying to her.

"I'm surprised you haven't ridden out yet, now that you got what you came for."

"I'm waiting to be crowned," I admitted. I had originally planned to leave without waiting to receive the Champion's circlet, but I was sure news of the circumstances of my victory would spread to the clans. I didn't want to leave any doubt that I was the true Champion when I went to claim their allegiance for Lord Alasdar. If I could present the Champion's circlet, adorned with the blood glass of the first man to ever cross the desert, there would be no denying me.

"So, you're going to sit here and sulk in the dark through all nine nights of feasting?"

"I hadn't noticed you joining in on the festivities."

"The last time I let loose in a crowd of people, it ended a lot like this afternoon," she admitted in a quiet voice.

"My offer to help you find control still stands." Now that the Trials were over, her outbursts costing me my own restraint was less of a concern. Still, the same impulse that led me to draw her into my arms when she lost herself to the desert during the duels made itself known in my quiet offer.

"You've already told me I shouldn't trust you," Keera said.

"And if I were trying to trick you, I wouldn't have told you that," I argued. "Maybe learning the true nature of your power will convince you of how wrong Kelvadan is."

"I doubt it."

Without another word, Keera turned and marched back to the encampment. With a slight shudder, I realized she hadn't flat out refused me.

CHAPTER TWENTY-FOUR
KEERA

It wasn't hard to tear myself from the festivities of the encampment on the second night of feasting after the duels. Shoulders jostled me as I walked between the tents, and stories were recounted at increasing volume at every fire. I had listened curiously to tales of the past Trials at first, but the longer I sat around the braziers, the more I felt an outsider watching the festivities.

The queen and Aderyn weren't at the celebrations either, having retreated to the palace the moment the Viper had won the Trials. I assumed they were already preparing for war, but I was not invited. I didn't blame them for excluding me. I had failed them by losing my final duel—why would they trust me to protect the city now?

The day before, I had been introduced as a citizen of Kelvadan—a title I bore proudly. Now, when I sat down on a bench, the people on either side of me would inch away, even as they pressed shoulder to shoulder with other clansmen and city dwellers. All had seen my outburst at the end of the Trials, and I recognized the wary look in their eyes as they offered painfully polite smiles.

Every time I caught somebody glance at me with fear, I saw my parents' faces. The chances of Kelvadan being the home I dreamed of faded away like water soaking into the sand.

It was a relief to slip out into the dunes, where the only noises were the swish of the breeze over sands and the low hoot of a nearby burrowing owl. I headed in the same direction as I had the night before, toward where I knew the Viper would be.

Erix, my thoughts whispered in correction, but I pushed against the name. Despite my odd nighttime imaginings, my opponent had remained firmly planted as the Viper in my mind through the challenges of the Trials. Something had shifted though after the duels, when I slipped back into my body to find strong arms around me, not making my skin crawl but grounding me.

When I thought of him as Erix, I would only picture his proud, shocked face and the feeling of his hand on my bare skin. He had made it clear he was the Viper, and it would be ill-advised to drop my guard around him. Still, thinking of him as Erix made me feel less like I was doing something incredibly foolish by stealing away in the darkness to meet him.

I wasn't sure what had brought me to him that first night after the duels, but the feeling of his arms would not leave me. While too often, the touch of others threatened to send me into a spiral of uncontrollable sensations, his embrace had given me something to hold on to in the maelstrom of the desert. My mind screamed at me that I walked into a trap, but as I thought of the fear with which people looked at me, I knew I had no choice.

The queen's methods of suppressing her son's magic had failed, but he had mastered his power since he disappeared. If there was a way for me to master this storm within me and serve the Kelvadan riders without endangering those around me, I had to take it. Even if it meant fraternizing with the one who would see the Kelvadan fall. Maybe this was my one chance to gain the control that would redeem me in the eyes of the queen and her city and soothe the gnawing guilt of failure.

I started as a falcon fluttered up to me, flapping around my head as if investigating.

"Zephyr," called a stern voice, and the bird backed off, instead flying to Erix where he stood in a dip between dunes and alighting on his shoulder. I had seen the falcon the night before but didn't remember him having it when I first came upon him at my oasis.

"You came," Erix said. His voice was flat, giving away neither surprise nor disappointment.

I shrugged. It was the only real explanation I had.

Erix nodded once. "Come." He gestured toward a pile of rocks, ranging from the size of my fist to a boulder the size of me. "It's time you learned how to use your power."

I froze, balking. "You said I could learn to control my power; you said nothing about using it."

"The magic of the desert doesn't take kindly to sitting idle," Erix argued. "Like a horse, it must be exercised, or it will turn volatile and restless."

I shook my head, backing away a few steps. This was a mistake. I had reminded myself of that last time, and all we'd done was practice familiar forms together. This was something else entirely.

"What does your magic do whenever you try to close it in?" Erix asked before I could turn away. I hesitated and took a few steps back toward him. He stared at me in silence, and I wished I could see his expression.

"Throw the rock," he ordered.

I frowned and took a step forward, but he threw out an arm, stopping me.

"With your magic."

I looked at him with what I'm sure was an incredulous expression.

"It's a part of the desert. You should be able to manipulate it just like the wind and the lightning." He demonstrated, flicking out a hand as if swatting at a fly; one of the mid-sized rocks flew off the pile and landed in the sand a way away with a dull thud.

"How?"

He stilled, and I got the distinct feeling he would be frowning if I could see his face. "The part of you that feels all the desert crashing in around you when you lose control. Try pointing it at the rock and opening up a little bit."

I opened my mouth to snap that his instructions were impossibly vague, but I paused. Somehow, they made the tiniest bit of sense. Deep in my core, dwelled a twisting, living thing—one that snapped and growled when I found myself closed in by the mountain around me or the writhing crush of people in the city. Even now, I felt it whirling inside me, drowsy but very much still there.

Experimentally, I nudged its attention toward the smallest rock in the pile. I tried to do as Erix said and roused it just a bit, but my mind clamped down around the efforts. I screwed my eyes shut, seeing scared faces behind my eyelids: Dryden, the queen. My parents.

A crack rung through the air, and my eyes snapped open. A boulder, once standing as tall as Erix, fell in two separate directions. It split cleanly down the middle as if hewn in half by an incomprehensibly large saber.

I stared in dumbfounded silence before stumbling back a few steps.

"This was a mistake," I murmured. I turned and hurried back up the dune toward the distant noises of laughter and conversations that I was not a part of. Erix didn't call after me, but I felt his gaze heavy on my retreating back.

I returned the next night. When I woke in the morning, I was resolved not to seek out Erix again. He brought out something wild and untamed buried deep within me, that I could not afford to unleash.

But as the shadows grew longer, and my restlessness with them, I found my feet carrying me out across the dunes. My opportunity to learn would be gone in a matter of days, and I would not let my fear stop me.

Fear was an old friend of mine, keeping me from wandering too far from my oasis in exile, and compelling me to count how many dried strips of meat I had left a dozen times over. I could live alongside fear easily enough if it would eventually free me from the burden of this power.

I found Erix with his saber in hand, moving through motions I knew by heart myself now. Something twisted within me at the thought of both of us practicing our forms, both on the opposite sides of the desert, and the looming war, but moving through the same patterns.

I stopped a short distance away, sure Erix could sense my presence, but he did not stop his flowing movements. He finished one set and moved straight into the next without pause. I glanced down at my feet, feeling oddly as if I were intruding on something private, but found myself looking up again quickly. After all, we had done these movements together over a week earlier, but I hadn't had a chance to really watch him then.

The proficiency with which he moved through the positions, a dance of strikes and parries with no enemy, spoke of the deadly efficiency I had seen in his duels. Despite there being no wasted movements though, the pattern of his limbs moving through space was oddly mesmerizing—a dance as deadly as it was enthralling.

When he still made no move to stop, I decided to join him in his practice. After all, with Aderyn still busy with the extra security around the temporary encampment, there had been no training sessions for the new recruits.

I fell into my stance where I was, and while there was the slightest hitch in Erix's movements, he didn't say anything. I moved through the same form he did, trying to match the pace of his movements, once again slower than felt comfortable, and with grace I wouldn't expect from someone rumored to be a ruthless butcher.

As I flowed through the poses, although not nearly as gracefully as my counterpart, an odd sensation started to inch through me, beginning low in my core and spreading out toward my fingers and toes. The rhythm of my breath was no longer mine, but the rhythm of the desert. It was the breath of Erix next to me and the wing beats of his falcon off somewhere on a hunt. My blood rushing through my veins was the rock squirrel scurrying through its tunnel and the water pulsing deep underground from a hidden well.

I felt the edges of my awareness blur before I gasped, snapping back into my body and standing stiffly. My hands curled into fists so tightly that my forearms shook, as if I could hold myself in my body with the strength of my grip.

Erix had stopped moving as well, masked face turned toward me. Maybe I was imagining things, but I sensed curiosity in his gaze. He didn't say anything though.

"How do you manage it, when you feel your control slipping?" I had gathered enough from Queen Ginevra to know Erix must have experienced such things when he was younger. More than that though, something in his posture, in his very offer to train me, spoke of understanding.

"You must find something, a sensation or an anchor, to ground you in your body."

I remembered his arms around me—their warmth and solidity the thing that brought me back to my own body. I shook the thought from my head. I somehow doubted that he would offer to repeat the embrace, or that such displays were how the Viper managed his power.

"What anchors you?" I asked.

"Pain."

I blinked once. Twice. "You hurt yourself on purpose?"

"When the occasion calls for it. In a fight, letting yourself sustain an injury can work if you are running out of options." He shrugged, as if having to injure himself to maintain control was no issue. "Pain cuts through the awareness better than any other sensation, impossible to ignore and utterly physical. If you hurt yourself badly enough, it's impossible to lose yourself in the consciousness of the desert, even if you wanted to."

"That's barbaric," I argued.

"The desert is not a soft mistress. Those who cannot do what it takes to survive the elements are shown no mercy," he retorted. "Her magic is no different."

"There has to be another way."

He tilted his head. "I suppose other strong sensations might do as well, but pleasure is a little harder to deploy on a battlefield."

His tone was so even that I couldn't be sure, but I got the impression it was the closest Erix came to a joke. It was equal parts humanizing and unnerving, thinking that the faceless figure before me, wielder of unfathomable power, was being sarcastic.

"Well, you won't know if you don't try. It might unnerve your enemies."

His shoulders stiffened, as if he hadn't expected me to play along. Then the moment passed, and he stomped over to the same pile of rocks we had used the day before, unmistakable from the cracked boulder at the center.

I didn't manage to move any rocks today, but none broke either.

On the third day, when I crested the dune that hid where Erix and I met from the encampment, I found him kneeling, sat back on his heels. He would have looked completely relaxed if not for the tight squeeze of his fists resting on his knees. So tense were they, I was surprised I couldn't hear the creak of his black leather gloves.

"Today, we will meditate," he said, not moving as I approached.

I turned on my heel, ready to walk right back to Kelvadan and take Daiti out for a ride. Meditation was a strategy I had tried and failed more times than I could count. I wasn't about to spend another hour pretending to focus on containing my magic just to avoid the inevitable outburst.

"Not like the queen would have taught you," he added before I could take more than two steps away.

I hesitated before turning. Doubt that any sort of sitting quietly would help slithered through my mind, but I found myself loathe to leave. More than anything Erix had said so far helping me, it was more the feeling that he understood what I felt, in his own twisted way.

The storm that raged within me sometimes made me feel more alone in Kelvadan than I had when isolated at my oasis in the desert. How odd it was that the man who had ripped me away from my solitude in isolation was the first to face my power without fear. Even the way the queen tried to help me left an aftertaste of apprehension in my mouth.

I knelt in front of Erix, sitting back on my heels, mirroring his pose. Our knees were a few inches apart, and the warmth from his body seeped through my loose linen pants. I wondered how he could stand to be covered so completely from head to toe in the beating sun.

"Picture the origin of your power within you," Erix instructed once I had settled.

"Aren't you going to tell me to close my eyes?"

He shrugged. "I prefer to meditate with my eyes open, but I suppose it doesn't matter."

I let my eyes flutter shut. I didn't think I was going to be able to focus on anything staring straight into his metal mask.

"Now, focus on your purpose. The drives that decide all your actions and the passions underneath them."

Surprisingly, I found his tone soothing as I turned my attention inwards. His voice was a smooth tenor that lost its hard edge when he wasn't trying to be menacing. I internally shook myself, remembering his words.

My purpose.

"To protect Kelvadan." He hadn't asked me to say it out loud, but it felt right.

He huffed in derision but didn't comment. "Now think about the emotions that drive that goal."

I dug deeper within myself, tunneling down into my psyche.

Of course I wanted to protect the city that had been a symbol of hope for me through years of exile. How could I not, when even my own clan had turned me out, but Kelvadan had found a place for me? Even if I didn't feel like I belonged there just yet, I could prove my worth. I could...

At the bottom of the well of my magic lay something dark and pulsating. I reached out a mental finger to poke it, only to have it snap and snarl at me.

It was angry.

The feeling slapped me in the face like a sandstorm. Hidden deep within me lived the resentment I felt for being left to die alone in the desert when I was barely more than a girl. There was the rage at the needless death of my horse and the fury that I couldn't just live without fear of myself like everybody else. There was anger at myself that I still felt alone even when surrounded by a city's worth of people.

"Good."

I jumped, nearly having forgotten about Erix's presence.

"Let that anger be a funnel that siphons the power out of you, even as it feeds it."

My eyes snapped open. "No."

Erix tilted his head.

"It was working, wasn't it?"

I didn't answer his question, scowling at him instead. "I won't do things your way if it makes me like the Viper."

"I wasn't the one who looked within myself and found anger. That was all you." He sounded satisfied, and my hackles rose.

"And what is the purpose you meditate on? To destroy your own city—your own family?"

"The peace of Kelvadan is a lie." His smooth voice had transformed into a menacing growl.

It was the second time he had said something similar, and I found myself springing to my feet.

"Says the one that would bring war to his own people. I was wrong to think that you could teach me about anything but violence and betrayal."

I spun on my heel and set off into the desert. Wishing for the strength of Daiti beneath me, I pumped my arms, my soft soled boots churning up the sand beneath me as I ran. I knew Erix didn't follow, but I felt compelled to put as much distance between us as possible.

I ripped off my hood, wanting to feel the wind in my hair and the sun on my face. The desert was my one constant companion throughout the years— the one who looked on me without judgement. I ran until my lungs screamed and my legs turned to fire.

Falling to my knees in the sand, I panted, gathering my breath before turning my face to the sky and letting out a feral scream. It was a wild noise, the type of thing that felt natural in exile, but I held in within the walls of Kelvadan.

The sound of pure frustration was swept away across the open plain by the wind. I could run away from the Viper, but I couldn't outrun the anger I found inside myself.

I led Daiti out of the arched opening to Kelvadan, the flanking guards looking at me curiously as I turned in the opposite direction of the encampment. I wasn't in the mood to join the feasts tonight, even though I had no intention of joining Erix again. Now, I only wanted my horse and the open sky for company.

I swung up onto Daiti's broad back, relishing the solidity of his body between my thighs and the silkiness of his mane as I let it wash over my hands. He pawed the ground and tossed his head, obviously pleased to be out of the stables himself.

Wasting no time, I urged him into a canter, riding straight out, away from the cliffs. I didn't worry about getting lost when the spire of Kelvadan could be seen for miles.

The desert looked different in the moonlight, less harsh in the silvery light of night. Where the sun leeched the landscape of its colors, now the sky looked so rich and velvety that I imagined I could reach out and touch it. Still, the desert was no less alive in the dark, a burrowing owl swooping overhead as it looked for its next meal and a family of sand cats darting by in search of water.

Some semblance of peace had just started to wash over me when the quiet was shattered by a shout.

"Rider!"

I wheeled Daiti around, looking for the source of the sound.

"Rider!"

I spotted a woman, stumbling over the sands, waving her arms desperately for my attention. With a murmur, I urged Daiti toward her, hand on the hilt of my saber. As I approached, I released the weapon. The woman was so haggard, clothes torn and barely on her feet, that I knew she posed no threat to us.

"Please, I need help." She tried to clutch at Daiti's side, whether for support or to keep me from riding away, I couldn't tell. My mount tried to snap at her hand, but I slapped at his neck in a silent command to stand down.

"What's wrong?" I frowned down at her, wandering the desert without a mount. Perhaps another exile.

"Clan Otush, we're under attack," she gasped. Her voice came out rough, as if she hadn't had anything to drink in hours.

I unhooked my skin from my belt and handed it to her. "From another clan?"

She gulped greedily before answering, shaking her head and wiping her mouth with the back of her hand. "No, the clans are in a truce until the results of the Trials reach us. It's a creature... a lava wyrm."

I frowned, shaking my head, even as a slither of fear crawled up my spine. "It can't—"

"I know what I saw." Despite her obvious exhaustion, the woman's voice came out strong.

My blood ran cold despite the warmth of the night. Lava wyrms existed only in legends—stories of old told around clan campfires of how they could only be felled by the greatest riders. They hadn't been seen since the desert had been crossed and tamed by humans nearly a thousand years ago.

The woman staring up at me, determination palpable in her gaze, convinced me otherwise.

"Get on," I ordered, scooting forward to make room behind me on Daiti's back. He huffed as if annoyed that I would let somebody else mount him, but stayed still as I glared between his ears, begging him to behave.

We set off toward the encampment, my mind racing as fast as Daiti over the baked earth. Perhaps the desert was really tearing itself apart if creatures of legend were terrorizing the clans once more. This would only make the lords more desperate for a solution—one that Lord Alasdar and his Viper were all too happy to supply.

But if Kelvadan came to their aid, perhaps the clans would think twice about turning on the Great City.

The encampment came into view on the horizon, and we didn't slow until we approached the center circle of the tents. By this time, the fourth night of feasting was in full swing, and dancing spread through the open area. Revelers jumped aside as we skid to a halt before the low table where the queen sat with Kaius, presiding over the celebration. Aderyn stood over her shoulder, a watchful shadow, while Neven sat at the table a couple seats down.

Whispers darted around the crowd, hidden behind hands as I dismounted, helping the woman from Clan Otush down after me. I shrugged off the weight of judgmental gazes, trying not to worry that I was making a spectacle of myself for the second time during the Trials. This was too important to spend time worrying about the opinions of others.

"Queen Ginevra," I addressed her, rapping my knuckles against my brow in respect. The woman next to me echoed my action. "I found this woman crossing the sands with dire news."

"Clan Otush needs aid. A lava wyrm is terrorizing our encampment, eating horses and killing our hunters. We're afraid to even try to pack up and move, for fear of leaving ourselves exposed."

Murmurs skittered through the assembled crowd. The queen's eyes widened, and Aderyn took a step forward as if she was unaware she was moving.

"A lava wyrm? Can you be sure?"

The woman raised her chin, unwilling to be cowed by the doubt clearly displayed at her fantastical tale.

"This wasn't just some hunter's tale. I saw it with my own eyes. I was sent for aid as the fastest rider, and out in the desert alone, it accosted me. I lost my horse, Yessenia, to the lava wyrm, watching as its molten breath melted her flesh from her bones. I only managed to escape as it was distracted, feasting on her flesh."

Something hot smoldered in my stomach at the thought of a noble steed meeting such an end. It felt far too similar to the anger I had reached into yesterday. I ignored the sensation.

"If what you say is true, and the beasts of the desert rise again, then we must all be vigilant," Queen Ginevra declared, pushing to her feet. She shook her hands free of her billowing sleeves, held to her wrists with silver bracelets. "Aderyn, see to moving all within the city walls where they can be defended. Send out riders to comb the area and report back on anything unusual they might come across. Tell them to stay together in pairs."

"My clan—" the woman at my side started.

"You will be safe here." The queen reassured. "All are welcome within the walls of Kelvadan."

"But my people..."

"The warriors of your clan are strong and will protect your people, just as I must protect mine." The queen's words were bitingly harsh, even as her tone was soft. I itched to shout, to argue with her on the woman's behalf, but the devastated look in Queen Ginevra's eyes told me it would be futile. This wasn't a decision she made in the absence of compassion, but to protect her people. Still, the well of anger in my core boiled more insistently. The people of the clans needed protection too.

I felt more than heard the shuddering gasp of defeat wracking the frame of the woman beside me. She began to sway, and I hesitated before reaching out to grab her. I itched to help, but that form of easy contact still came so slowly. Before I could act, a figure stepped out of the shadows where I hadn't seen them before.

"I will ride to your clan to fight the lava wyrm." Erix's words cut through the nervous chatter of the encampment, though he had barely raised his voice. My chest stuttered with something like relief that I could not place, an odd feeling in response to the otherworldly way the flickering light from the brasiers danced over his mask. The effect, combined with his sudden appearance and imposing frame, gave him the air of a demon materializing from the night.

The woman stiffened next to me, clearly fighting an internal battle. The Viper and the whispers that followed him would not be unknown to Clan Otush, but right now, he was the demon who offered her people salvation.

"I've been to Clan Otush's encampment. I'll ride there to face the wyrm while you recover in the city. I can set out immediately."

The woman hesitated only a moment before nodding in agreement. Queen Ginevra's face paled, her lips thin from being pressed together so tightly.

"Come," she commanded, reaching her hand out. "We will find you accommodations to rest after your harrowing journey. I'm sure you're hungry and tired."

The queen turned toward the city, already murmuring instructions to Aderyn who trailed her. The woman hesitated, staring at Erix for a long moment, before rapping her knuckles to her own brow in respect. Then she hurried away toward the promise of food and a safe bed.

I stood frozen, now alone in the middle of the encampment. The jovial atmosphere had dissipated faster than the occasional eerie morning mists that clung to the hot earth. Everywhere people were scurrying around disassembling tents, anxious to get behind the safety of the walls or back to their own people in the face of such a legendary threat.

At the center of the vortex of activity, I remained rooted to the ground, looking between Erix and the retreating back of his mother. He tilted his head to the side as if waiting for something, but I remained unsure. Then I turned and raced after the trio of women walking towards the city.

When I caught up with them, Queen Ginevra was giving instructions to an attendant to find quarters in the palace and draw a bath for their new guest. Aderyn had a knot of guards around her who were listening to her instructions regarding increased security for having so many visitors inside the city walls.

I waited for them to disperse before stepping into her line of view.

"You can't leave Clan Otush to face the lava wyrm alone," I began without preamble.

Aderyn sighed, looking intensely weary for all her unyielding posture. "There is no other choice."

"Of course there is. There's always a choice, even if it is a difficult one. You could send riders to help. I would—"

"I have been charged with the protection of this city, a vow I will not betray until my dying breath," Aderyn snapped, fire replacing exhaustion in her eyes. "Do not ask me to put her in jeopardy when her peace already hangs so precariously in the balance."

I drew back as if she had slapped me. While I had grown used to Aderyn's brusque manner, I had never felt true hostility from her. Now the idea that she would leave innocents defenseless against a terror straight out of myths left me unbalanced.

The queen approached as I stood stunned, but my brain started thinking again, travelling down another path.

"If the captain from Clan Katal aids them, that would only cement their loyalty to him," I pressed. "But if Kelvadan were to send aid, they might be reticent to attack the city on Lord Alasdar's behalf."

"Based on what we heard from the rider of Clan Tibel, Clan Katal will already have united all the riders of the desert based on the Viper being named Champion," the queen pointed out. "This very well may be their attempt to draw our riders out of Kelvadan and attack when we are defenseless."

I blinked, not having thought of that. A growl of frustration itched in the back of my throat, but I swallowed it down. I could not let my anger rule me—would not let it shred my control.

"These decisions are the reason I do not relish being queen," she continued more quietly, "But it is final. My great-grandfather built this city to be a beacon of safety, and I will see it remain as such at all costs."

I looked down at my feet, nodding deferentially even as my heart sank. There would be no changing these women's minds when they were set down a path. It was something I respected in them, even as the storm in me raged against this decision, the thought of an innocent horse being swallowed by lava seared into my brain. I did not change my mind when it was set on something either.

"I'll bring Daiti to the stables and then report back to help with security," I volunteered.

Aderyn nodded her approval and Queen Ginevra offered me an encouraging, if sad, smile. I left them to further discuss their plans as I headed through the wide arch into the city, remaining on foot instead of mounting Daiti. I didn't want to draw any more attention to myself after the spectacle in the encampment.

Once inside, I didn't turn up the winding climb toward the palace but took the road toward Aderyn and Neven's home. Upon arriving, I left Daiti outside with a pat on the nose and a whispered assurance that I'd be right back.

I slipped through the door quickly, ready to head for the kitchen and yelped in surprise when I nearly ran headfirst into Neven. He raised his brows at me questioningly.

"I ah—Aderyn sent me... she needed—"

Neven shoved a pile of bundles into my arms, effectively silencing my attempts at explanation. "You'll need these."

I looked down at them curiously, picking out what appeared to be a bedroll and several other bulging packs.

"I'm not sure how far Clan Otush's encampment is, but it should be enough when supplemented with your hunting skills," he explained.

I opened and shut my mouth twice before settling on tilting my head instead of asking a specific question.

Neven shrugged sheepishly. "I've been married to a stubborn

woman for long enough to recognize the look in your eyes. It's the one Aderyn has when I know she is going to get her way, no matter what."

"You don't agree with her that I should stay and protect the city?" I asked.

"I agree that the city needs to be protected, but so do the clans. Aderyn may have been born and raised here, but I grew up riding the sands. As much as Kelvadan is my home, I know many who call the clans home." Neven paused, something in his eyes examining me like some of his weaving that wasn't quite laying right, searching it for the tiniest snag. "I've seen the way you look out at the horizon. As much as you love Kelvadan, I know you miss the freedom of the desert. If anybody should ride out to protect it, it's you."

I nodded, not sure of what I could say to possibly thank him. Instead, I asked a question. "Do you ever miss the adventure of the desert?"

One corner of his lips pulled up in a wry smile. "Being married to Aderyn offers me all the adventure I could ever need. Now go, before anybody notices you're missing."

CHAPTER TWENTY-FIVE
THE VIPER

A flutter of wings and a stutter of magic warned me of Keera's approach. I didn't look up from where I latched my bundled-up tent to Alza's back, but something inside me loosened and tensed simultaneously. Even as I realized that leaving now to aid Clan Otush would mean I wouldn't be able to receive the Champions circlet, it hadn't been a hard decision to ride out. Aiding the clans would win me more loyalty from them than a ceremonial piece of metal.

What had been a harder realization was that I would be riding away from Keera sooner than I had expected.

I found my gaze darting toward the encampment often, hoping to see her dark silhouette approaching our usual spot. An odd tightness formed beneath my ribcage when the sands remained empty, but I was unsurprised. I wasn't even sure why I wanted her to come. Perhaps I had found her a welcome distraction from the monotony of waiting through the feasting to be awarded the Champion's circlet. I couldn't deny any longer that I found her fascinating—a tangled-up knot to be unraveled.

From the one time my bare skin had touched hers, the power inside her, the same power that lived in me, had called to my magic, quieting it. We were the two people possibly most connected to the magic of the desert, and I could feel her life like an echo at the base of my skull. The odd surges of raw power I had felt in the past months were likely shadows of her own loss of control.

The thought soothed me as much as it terrified me.

I shoved that thought away violently as I yanked a knot tight on my packs. Alza snorted in protest, and I breathed a measured breath out through my nose. The Viper did not feel fear.

Keera didn't speak as she stepped up beside me. I peeked out of the corner of my eyes and nearly snorted to see packs tied to Bloodmoon. He had never suffered such treatment before, carrying only his rider when we moved encampments, while Lord Alasdar's belongings were carried by another.

"You certainly have an eye for horseflesh," I commented by way of greeting.

"I think Daiti chose me as much as I chose him."

"Daiti?" I asked, realizing she must have renamed the stallion.

"He carried me swiftly across the sands and deserved a name that said as much."

I finished loading my packs and turned to face them fully. "He's never let anybody mount him besides Lord Alasdar. He was caught wild, and I would say that Lord Alasdar was the one who tamed him, but that would be an overstatement."

Keera's narrow eyes widened to an almost comical degree as she looked between me and the fearsome stallion currently nosing at her pockets as if they might contain treats. "Lord Alasdar? Well, that would explain why he nearly took off Kaius's fingers."

My spine stiffened as if shocked by lightning at the name of my—at the name of the royal horse master. I squeezed my hands into fists so hard the leather of my gloves creaked. "It's a miracle he hasn't taken a bite out of you yet."

Keera shrugged, patting Daiti's nose as if she hadn't noticed my tension at the mention of Kaius. "I like wild things."

Of course she would. The woman had been half feral when I first came upon her, and even now, clean and well-fed, she had the air of something untamed about her. I looked away.

"I take it you're coming with me?"

"Yes."

I nodded and swung up onto Alza's back and Keera did the same. Without another word we set off across the moon drenched sands and into the unknown.

Keera was a better travel companion than I had hoped. I had anticipated being irked by having company, accustomed as I was to traveling with only Alza for companionship. Keera didn't fill the air with chatter though, seeming to be as comfortable with the quiet as I was. Instead, we both surveyed the horizon, taking in the subtle but undeniable life of the landscape.

If one didn't know better, our surroundings would seem devoid of life, isolated and leeched of color by the harsh sun. The magic around me betrayed the fennec fox in her den and the mice scurrying through the dry looking brush. Zephyr circled overhead, looking for his next meal.

I forced my eyes back between Alza's midnight ears as I had found them drifting toward my quiet companion again. Keera tipped her head back to watch the falcon wheeling above us, the sun turning her deeply tanned skin golden. Alza's muscles twitched beneath me, signaling that she could sense my tension.

I just wasn't used to having company.

Seeing a formation of rocks ahead, I pointed. "We can stop there and wait out the hottest part of the day in the shade of that cliff."

Keera nodded. "How far of a ride do you think it will be to Clan Otush?"

"The last time I visited, the desert showed me to my destination in four nights. If she is so angry though that lava wyrms have begun to roam, then I wouldn't be surprised if it took longer."

"I hope we can make it there in less than that," Keera admitted. "I wouldn't want to leave the encampment to face the wyrm alone for so long."

"You seem awfully keen to defend the clans for an exile," I pointed out.

"I'm a citizen of Kelvadan now," she argued.

"And yet here you are, riding into the wilds with one who would see the Great City fall."

A frown creased her dark brows, accentuating a full lower lip as she glared. I had the urge to make her frown more, the look in her eyes so reminiscent of the wild defiance she wore when we first met.

"Why were you exiled?" I asked, the words out of my mouth before I could ask myself why I cared.

"The same reason you left Kelvadan, I would guess."

I stiffened in my seat. I had known she knew of my identity after she called me by name that night during the Trials. I shouldn't have been surprised that Queen Ginevra or Aderyn had told her, but it wasn't something we had openly acknowledged. Her mentioning my past now was like plucking at a loose string that would unravel the fabric of our tenuous peace.

"The magic of the desert isn't an easy burden to bear," I settled on as response. "Still, it must have been useful in keeping you alive when you were in exile."

Keera's frown deepened, taking on a puzzled cast. She shook her head. "It didn't. All the years I spent alone it just... slept. I thought the desert had abandoned me as punishment for what I'd done, for losing control. It didn't wake again until... Until you."

She looked over at me, dark gaze boring into me as if it could penetrate the protective shield of metal on my face. I looked away.

By now, we had reached the short cliff of jagged rock, sticking up from the otherwise flat landscape as if a giant piece of stoneware had fallen from the sky to shatter on the ground.

We both dismounted in the shade, the slightly cooler air a welcome respite from the baking sun. Sweat collected between the fingers of my gloves and at the nape of my neck, but I dared not take them off. Something about being around Keera left me exposed, no matter how many layers I covered myself in. It was as if the title of Viper wouldn't quite settle right when she looked at me. She had seen under the mask.

"My horse died."

I blinked, confused by her sudden statement. She kept her eyes on

Daiti's golden mane, weaving her fingers through it absently as she spoke.

"After she broke her leg, our horse master slit her throat. I felt her slip away, and the next thing I knew, everybody that stood within twenty paces of me was dead. Swallowed whole by the ground splitting open." Her shoulders rose up toward her ears, as if in protection. I was struck by the momentary urge to rest a hand between her shoulder blades, to soothe the ache I knew she harbored deep in her chest as I felt it echoed in my own.

I balled my hands into fists instead and offered the only sentiment that seemed to fit. The motto that carried me through many fitful nights. "The desert gives, and it takes."

"What did it take from you?" she asked, glancing over her shoulder.

"Everything."

We made camp that night out in the open. Fresh water had not presented itself to us. Tomorrow, we would have to hope for better luck.

As I set up my tent, Keera rolled out a sleeping mat on a soft patch of earth.

"You didn't bring a tent?"

She shook her head. "I prefer to sleep where I can see the stars."

I nodded before looking back at my tent, considering joining her, even if it meant I would have to sleep with a mask on. Looking back at her, setting sun glimmering off her skin, dark hair curling around her heart-shaped face, I shook myself. I already felt unbalanced enough around her, I did not need to give my mind over to unconsciousness with no semblance of a barrier between us.

I would need to exhaust myself thoroughly to find any sleep tonight.

"The horses need to rest, but it's still early. Do you want to train?" I offered.

Keera narrowed her eyes at me, and I shrugged. "It's what we were going to be doing if we were still at Kelvadan. And I think we might be more productive without such a raucous party happening over the next ridge."

Sucking on her cheek in contemplation, Keera looked around. "I don't see any rocks around for us to practice with."

"You call down storms when you're upset, and you think your magic is only good for... throwing rocks?" I quirked my brow at her in incredulity, even though I knew she couldn't see it.

"Well, it's what we had been working on," she defended, a flush rising in her cheeks. I found myself mesmerized by the fact that I had pulled such an expression from her.

I turned away, surveying our surroundings. "It can be convenient, but it's hardly the most advantageous use of magic anyway. Why throw rocks at an opponent when you can slice off their head?"

"Maybe I'd rather knock my opponents down than kill them," Keera argued, folding her arms.

I huffed. "That's not how you fight."

Her brows drew down, and she bared her teeth, rewarding me with another one of her many expressions.

"And how do I fight?" she demanded.

"Like me."

In truth, I had been testing her when she faced me in the Trials. I had planned to dispatch all my opponents as neatly and efficiently as possible, becoming Champion with as little opposition as possible. But watching Keera with saber in hand, striking out at her opponents like a snake defending her nest, I had grown curious. When she came at me with her opening flurry, reckless but somehow deadly precise, I wanted to see more. For once, I faced an opponent who matched me in ferocity, even if her skill hadn't caught up yet.

Not even Izumi gave me a fight like that. Where Izumi was all technical precision, Keera was a force of nature, unshaped but powerful.

"If I fought like you, you wouldn't have been able to toy with me." Keera was clearly unhappy with my answer.

"Like me doesn't mean better than me."

She wrinkled her nose. "Well, if we're not going to throw rocks, what are we going to do?"

"How about fire?"

Her eyes widened.

"Being able to light a fire with nothing more than your hands is a good skill for survival," I pointed out.

Keera chewed her lip. "You've seen what happens when I lose control. I'm not sure fire is the best idea."

And all of a sudden, the warrior that came with me a snarl on her face wore the face of vulnerability I recognized all too well.

"That's why you have me to help. I'm as powerful as you, and I can reign it in if things go awry." It was potentially an exaggeration. From what I had seen, Keera was the only person I had met whose power was my equal. My own magic might not be able to negate hers, but I had pulled her back to herself once before. The more accustomed I became to her magic, the ebb and flow working into my mind with each hour we spent together, the more convinced I was I could lead her back to the center of her power once more.

"We'll start with just controlling the fire, not lighting it."

We combed the area for dry brush to fuel the fire, arranging it into a small pile that wouldn't burn too intensely but would give Keera enough to work with.

"I'm going to light the fire. See if you can feel my magic as I do it, so you'll be able to emulate it yourself later," I instructed.

I held my hand over the fuel, reaching into the knot of threads at the base of my skull, preparing to pull one loose and unleash a lick of power to initiate the flames. As I did, a flow, like a trickle of water, poured over my mind as Keera reached out hesitantly. At the cool touch, caressing a part of me that most people couldn't even see, I shuddered.

Lord Alasdar, with his gift for sensing magic and touching others' minds, reached into my power often, but it didn't feel like this. Where his touch was clinical, running hard fingers over the knots of power in my mind, Keera was curious, testing them with a flow of magic that held hidden depths.

I ignored her, pulling on a string and letting fire flare to life under my palm. The brush caught instantly, building to a small but merry crackle.

"Now, see if you can push and pull the fire a little," I instructed.

Keera reached out a hand, and I didn't miss the way it trembled. I clenched my fists. Fear of oneself was something I understood all too well.

I opened my mouth, ready to tell her to bite her tongue to ground her if she needed to, but the words stuck in my throat. There was another way to ground her that I knew would work for her from experience.

"Here," I laid a still-gloved hand on her outstretched forearm. She jumped but didn't pull away. Even through her sleeve and my leather gloves I could feel her warmth. My head felt light at the contact—a being that wasn't my horse not recoiling from my touch—but I pulled my attention back to the rushing current of power that Keera's skin failed to contain completely.

"Pull the fire to you."

Taking a deep breath, Keera did as I asked. A gasp escaped her as a tendril pulled toward her fingertips, like a snake charmed by a melody.

"This is easier than rocks," she murmured.

"It's because fire is almost alive, just like the desert," I explained. "See if you can shape it into a ball."

Keera turned her palm upwards, twisting her forearm under my touch. Eagerly, the fire jumped toward her waiting hand, the tendril starting to curl up into an orb. I chanced a glance at Keera's face. Her brow furrowed in concentration, and a hint of pink tongue poked between her lips. Warmth swept through my traitorous body—probably from the fire—and I turned my attention back to her handful of flames.

A perfect ball of fire now hovered a few inches above her fingers.

"Good. Now, see if you can make it ebb and flow with your breath."

She took a deep breath in, holding it for a few seconds before releasing it. The flame didn't respond. She shook her head, and a few tendrils of hair brushed against my shoulder. I hadn't realized I had moved so close, my body nearly encircling hers, although our only point of contact was still my hand on her arm.

"It's not working."

"You only tried once," I pointed out, nearly smiling at her desire to master this right away. Still, I sent a tendril of my power to brush against hers. "Try again, and I'll help."

Keera took another breath, ribs expanding to nearly brush my own chest. I breathed with her, letting my mind meld into her power. Tracing up the stream of her essence, I encountered the problem nearly immediately. A dam held the majority of the limitless well of her magic back, keeping it from fueling the fire she held further.

Matching my breathing to her own, I prodded at it gently, trying to allow her to let more of her power through. I realized my mistake immediately.

Keera shuddered, and her even breaths cut off in a sharp gasp. Instead of widening the gap, her magic flowed through, and the entire dam fractured under the light pressure of my touch. Unthinking, I threw my body on top of Keera, throwing both hands out toward the sudden tower of flames where our small campfire had just been. My shield of power flew up just in time to protect us from the worst of the explosion, a roar of flames rushing over us without touching us.

It died out just as quickly as it had come, and I opened my eyes to find Keera staring up at me with wide eyes. I laid over her, every inch of my body pressed against hers as I had shielded us from the flame. My mind stuttered, and I felt clearly how she was no longer the skin and bones creature I had thrown over the back of my horse, despite the layers of fabric between us. This time, I knew the heat that washed through me was not just from the fire.

I scrabbled backward on the ground, ripping my attention away from Keera to where the fire had been. The fuel we had collected was no more than a pile of fine ash dusting over the pit of sand we had dug. However, fire still crackled merrily where my tent had once stood.

"Sorry," Keera said quietly.

I grimaced. "I prefer sleeping under the open sky anyway."

We didn't practice anymore that night, the furrow of concern between Keera's brows telling me it would likely be counterproductive to push her any further. When it was time to sleep, I unrolled my sleeping mat as far from Keera's as I could without looking suspicious, and I kept my mask on. Still, the metal could not protect me from the memory of how her body had felt beneath mine. Where normally I shied away from the touch of others, I hadn't hated the warmth of Keera's skin a few layers of fabric away from mine. I might have slept better if I had.

Alza sensed my restlessness as we headed out the next morning, flicking her ears back as if in question. I patted her neck in reassurance. Lord Alasdar had helped me build my control, and I would just have to reinforce it. Despite my initial tension though, I found myself relaxing as the day wore into late afternoon, Keera an easy riding companion.

A freshness on the breeze told me we approached an oasis. Alza's ears perked up at the promise of fresh water, as she too lifted her face. It was perhaps earlier than I would have liked to make camp, but I wouldn't pass up the chance to camp near water.

Keera sensed it too. Without warning, she kicked Daiti into a run, dashing toward the patch of brush that was our destination. Before I could settle her, Alza took off after her, taking their sudden acceleration as the sign of a chase.

By the time we arrived at the edge of a small, clear body of water, our mounts panted happily, and a smile split Keera's serious face. If I had been tempted to make her frown earlier, it was nothing compared to the overwhelming urge I had to see her smile more. With her curls escaping their braid and the slight redness of a sunburn across her cheekbones and nose, she was the picture of freedom.

I busied myself dismounting and relieving Alza of her burdens. It was unlike me to be distracted by such things. Spending this much time alone with a woman was affecting me, that was all.

My brain unhelpfully supplied me with the information that I spent plenty of time around Izumi with no such distractions, but I pushed that thought away.

Placing my belongings on a flat rock, I looked up just in time for Keera to begin unwinding the sash that held her vest closed over her tunic. It fell open, and she hastily shucked her layers, toeing off her boots before her fingers moved to the laces of her flowing pants.

"What are you doing?" I asked, heart leaping into my throat.

"Bathing," she responded simply, as if it were perfectly normal to disrobe without preamble in front of somebody who, until very recently, and probably still, was an adversary.

I should have looked away as she pushed her pants down her legs, exposing more tanned skin to the sunlight, turning golden in the late afternoon hour. Her tunic came off next, leaving her in nothing but her skin. I swallowed and tore my eyes away, looking down at my own heavy boots and riding pants. Not an inch of my flesh was exposed.

Splashing reached my ears, and I looked up as Keera plunged beneath the water.

"I missed bathing outside," she admitted, surfacing and dashing the water from her eyes.

I instructed my body to begin setting up camp, but my limbs didn't cooperate, freezing me on the spot like a boulder.

"The waterfalls in the houses of Kelvadan are certainly fun, but nothing beats the open sky." Keera leaned back and spread her arms out to float on the glassy surface of the oasis. From this angle, I could just see the outline of the points of her breasts. My limbs only unfroze themselves when I felt an uncomfortable tightness in the front of my pants, allowing me to whirl around and hide my reaction from Keera.

How odd it was that the woman who had grown up shunned from her own tribe eagerly bared herself to the world, free of all sense of embarrassment. I had grown up a prince of my people—had been told every day of the great legacy I was to fulfill—and I hid myself away from the world, too ashamed to let people look into my face unguarded.

"I'm going to scout around for predators," I said before stalking off. A few hundred yards away stood a pile of boulders. I walked to them without looking back, shoulders hunched.

Once I reached them, I slumped down behind their cover, sitting so I would be out of sight of where Keera swam. I breathed in deeply through my nose and out through my mouth, trying to calm the rushing in my head. It felt like my magic but not—something headier but just as dangerous.

For years now, I had styled myself as a weapon, more monster than man. It served my purpose to be seen as what instead of who I was. Keera had just reminded me in the most visceral of ways though, that I was indeed a man under all the armor.

I hadn't been able to deny that I found Keera a striking woman since I galloped alongside her in the races at the Trials. Now though, that observation had given way to full-fledged desire, coursing through my body and settling deep in my core.

But lust was just another emotion, one that I would conquer like I did every feeling that was too much, too close, threatening the tight grip of my control. I would master this just like I mastered my magic.

That's what I told myself as I undid my belt and lifted my cock out of my pants. I hissed at the leather of my glove as I took myself in hand, repeating in my head that I just needed to master my body. If my mind conjured images of Keera gasping beneath me as I stroked myself fast and hard, then that was between the desert and me.

CHAPTER TWENTY-SIX
KEERA

I squinted at the boulder Erix had disappeared behind, but he did not reemerge. For some reason, his sudden disappearance grated at me, although I should be grateful for the moment alone to gather my thoughts. It seemed like a retreat, but from what, I could not say.

He didn't return until I was out of the water and dressed in the second set of clothes Neven had packed for me. The ones I had worn during the days of riding dried on a flat rock after I washed them.

Erix didn't say a word when he returned, only turning to his bundle, and beginning to set up camp. I chewed my lip, halfway wondering why he didn't bathe while mentally shrugging. He must want to wash his clothes and cool off in the crystalline water, but apparently his insistence on being covered head to toe extended to when it was just the two of us.

For some reason, that irked me too.

I rolled out my sleeping mat on a soft patch of earth, and he did the same. We were both quiet as we went about our evening activities, him sharpening his weapons and me working on mending a rip in my shirt I had acquired when Erix tackled me to the ground the night before. We had been mostly quiet as we rode as well, but for some reason the silence now seemed thicker.

After the sun had set, Erix laid down on his mat on the other side of the fire—I had left the lighting to him—and I squinted at his outlined form. He was still fully dressed, including his gloves and the strange mask. I still hadn't been able to puzzle out its purpose.

"I won't look," I found myself saying.

A rustle sounded on the other side of the fire, but I stared straight up at the sky to prove my honesty.

"At what?"

"If you want to take your mask off, I promise I won't look at you."

There was a moment of stillness, and then a slow, deliberate rustling. I hoped he had taken advantage of my offer, but true to my word, I didn't look over to check.

His words drifted across the fire so quietly that I thought I might have imagined them.

"Thank you."

I rolled onto my side, facing away from the fire, to avoid the temptation to look into those striking metallic eyes of his. Instead, I found them in my dreams.

My eyes fluttered open, and my muscles filled with the languid energy that only comes from a long, restful sleep. I stretched luxuriously, keeping my eyes closed against the pale light that indicated dawn.

Movement that I felt in my bones more than heard made me look around for the source of the flowing energy. A way away along the bank of the oasis stood Erix, flowing through his forms just as I had found him several nights before. I watched for only a few moments before grabbing my own saber from where it had lain at my side as I slept.

He didn't react as I joined him. I fell into rhythm with his movements, breathing his breaths as if they were my own. My movements flowed even more easily than before. Part of me kept waiting for the swell of power within me, a fraying of the edges of my identity, but it never came. Out here in the quiet of the wilderness, kept company only by the light morning breeze, my soul remained calm.

We finished in unison, ending in the traditional pose with our hands clasped on the hilts of our sabers before us, tips pointed directly at the ground. Finally, Erix looked over at me, and we stood together in perfect stillness for a moment.

In an instant of pure instinct, I rapped my knuckles to my brow as I would in respect to Aderyn or another teacher. I froze, but to my surprise, Erix returned the gesture. Then he turned toward our makeshift camp, moving to pack up and tend the horses.

"We should hunt before we go further," he said by way of good morning.

I nodded. In my haste, I had only taken what meager supplies Neven had gathered for me. After months of regular meals, the thought of going without made my heart quicken.

We walked back to our small camp, and Erix grabbed the bow I had seen him use during the hunt in the Trials from his packs. fished out my sling and a pouch of rocks I had gathered. Erix stared at the crude weapon in my hands, but I shrugged.

"Rocks are easier to come by than arrows."

"I'll teach you how to use a bow," he offered.

"Once again, you volunteer to teach a warrior who is to be on the opposite side of a war from you. I wonder if you are as effective as all the tales say," I observed.

"And once again, I say you might end up joining the clans by the time I am done teaching you."

I looked away from him, turning to count the rocks in my pouch. The truth of the matter was that, while I loved Kelvadan, and I found myself missing Neven and Aderyn dearly, being back out in the wilds was a balm to my soul. Under the stars, with Erix the only other human around for miles, I'd slept the best I had in months.

"Let's get hunting so we can move on," I urged, not wanting to continue down my mental path. With that, I tucked my sling into my sash and slung my saber across my back.

We both mounted our horses, Daiti seeming happy to stretch his legs without the chafing of packs tied to his back. Without a word, we set out. We would not have to go far to find prey, as they would be drawn to the water of the oasis, even if we had scared them away briefly with our presence. Erix's falcon joined us, perching familiarly on his gloved arm before flying off in search of small game.

We made our way toward a rock formation where nooks and crannies would give wildlife a place to make their homes. The air here was thick, and an odd earthy scent raised the hairs on my arms. We hadn't gone far when we heard it—an eerie hissing and spitting like a caracal in heat.

I whirled around, but it was too late.

"Keera!"

Daiti reared, turning on his back legs to avoid the black and white blur that leaped from a nearby boulder. I slipped backward but managed to squeeze my legs tight enough at the last second to avoid falling to the ground.

The feline shape skidded to a stop on the far side of me, fixing me with glowing purple eyes, before changing direction with supernatural speed. Before I could draw my saber, a dark mass hurled itself between me and the attacking creature.

Erix charged at the animal, meeting it mid-leap. He slashed his saber where its body soared through the air, longer than any caracal I had ever seen, but it twisted out of the way. A tearing sound ripped the air as its claws raked Erix's sleeve, but if he had been injured, he paid it no mind.

He was already charging again, trying to take the creature off guard while it was recovering from its last leap. As Erix swung his saber in a brutal downward cut, the creature swiped at him with paws the size of palm leaves, claws digging into where his leather tabards draped over his thighs.

Erix's strike slashed the creature across its shoulder. It still managed to pull him from his seat with its massive paws as it reared back with a hiss. Erix toppled to the ground, head hitting the rocky earth with a sharp crack that echoed loudly enough, it might have been my own skull taking the blow.

Breaking free of the surprise that had paralyzed me, a ragged cry tore from my throat. I watched the creature open its maw to take a savage bite out of Erix's shoulder. He lay unmoving on the ground. I flung my hand forward, palm open, power pulsing through me.

A thud and a crack filled the air as the boulder from beside me rammed the creature into the rockface behind it. I panted in the ensuing silence, staring stunned at the rock that was easily the size of me. I had flung it through the air without even a thought. After hours of trying several nights ago, I had been unsuccessful, and here I had done it in a moment of panic.

Erix.

At the thought I slithered down from Daiti's side with no grace, darting to where Erix lay in a heap on the ground. He hadn't moved.

Dread filled my belly at the copper tang in the air. Falling to my knees next to him, I gently lifted his head, fingers coming away wet with blood that had soaked the back of his head. I reached for the end of the cloth that wound around his head and shoulders, but my fingers hovered above the fabric for just a moment. I shook myself. Then I set my jaw and began unwinding the length of gray linen. He could cover himself all he wanted, but I doubted he would thank me for leaving him to bleed on ground without aid.

As I peeled back the layers of his hood, I revealed a mess of dark waves, ones I had only seen hints of peaking around the edges of his mask. I had the sudden urge to plunge my fingers into them, but I focused on the task at hand. Turning his head to look at the back, I found his hair matted down with blood. The source seemed to be underneath one of the leather straps holding his mask in place.

My fingers danced over the buckles for a moment of indecision before I started unfastening them. With the straps loosened, the mask fell to the ground with a clang that felt far too heavy for its size. I carded through his hair to find his wound, the strands silky against my fingers even as blood soaked as they were.

I located the cut quickly and found it to be shallow, although it bled profusely as cuts to the scalp often do. It seemed like his hood and mask had cushioned most of the blow, and his skin was merely split. The bump under my finger indicated nothing more sinister than a bruise.

With that, I turned his head back, letting it rest in my lap. Even though it felt like a strange violation, I looked my fill at his face.

Before me were the features I had looked at so often in the statue of Kelvar, a strong brow over high cheekbones. Long lashes rested against cheeks pale enough that it was easy to believe he hadn't removed his mask in the light of day for years, even though he would probably tan well. Even as the features were the same as the statue's, I catalogued small differences, from the slight indent in the center of his chin to the hair that waved and curled where Kelvar's had been long and straight. Unconscious like this, Erix's features were smooth, and the realization that he appeared to be a man that hadn't even reached his thirtieth name day ran through me with a jolt.

Without a thought, I reached out, running my fingers in a featherlight touch over his temple and down to his square jaw. I felt, more than heard his breath catch before his eyes fluttered open, fixing me with a bottomless stare.

CHAPTER TWENTY-SEVEN
THE VIPER

My blood rushed under my skin with a frightening intensity, even as my chest refused to expand with my next breath. I was completely at the mercy of the woman who cradled my head in her lap. She rested her fingers on my cheek so lightly, it was as if she thought I might shatter.

She might not be wrong.

The first time we had ever touched, skin to skin, was my hand on her throat. It was the first time in too long that I had felt any sense of stillness within me. I had thought it was some anomaly, the shock of human contact, but now I knew I was wrong. That same stillness ran through me now, although now that I was paying attention, I could feel that quietness undercut with a slight vibration. I was a bowstring pulled taught, ready to leap forward, if only at Keera's command.

I opened my eyes, gaze finding hers instantly.

Her fingers started to pull away, and without warning, my own hand darted out, grabbing her by the wrist. I had the flickering thought of wishing I wasn't wearing my gloves. Even through them, I could sense her pulse fluttering rapidly beneath her skin.

She didn't resist as I pulled her hand to my face once more. This time she flattened her palm, letting the entirety of it rest against my cheek, cupping my face. I breathed in slowly through my nose, holding it before letting it out to brace against the feeling of my soul flying out of my body.

"Why do you wear it?"

The words were quiet in the tenuous silence between us, but they echoed as loud as a gong.

"Because it's easier to pretend there is nobody underneath the mask."

The words rang truer than they had any right to.

"I see you," was Keera's only response.

"That's what I'm afraid of."

My sanity was slipping out of my grasp like the frayed end of a rope at the continued warmth of her skin on mine. I was admitting things I shouldn't, but I couldn't think straight with another human—with Keera—touching me with an intention other than to injure. It needed to stop. I wanted more. So much more.

I turned my head away, breaking the contact, and the spell was broken. I groped around on the ground next to me, and Keera handed me my discarded mask without my asking. I slipped it back on, feeling equal parts like I was replacing an integral part of myself and that I was losing something valuable.

"Your head," she started.

I waved her off. "It's fine. Just stunned me more than anything."

In all honestly, a dull throb had settled in my skull, but I could barely focus on that when I still felt her hand on my face, hotter than any brand Lord Alasdar had ever burned into my back.

"The Sichat?" I asked, looking around for the creature that attacked us.

"A Sichat? But those are just myths."

"Just like the lava wyrm we are on our way to fight and the bone spider I encountered a few months back," I pointed out. "What happened to it?"

"I threw a rock," Keera admitted sheepishly.

"With your sling?"

"With magic."

I looked around curiously and found a boulder lying on the opposite side of our horses. She hadn't been able to move the smallest pebble in our hours of practice, but in the moment I fell from Alza, her magic had cooperated. The earthy smell of unleashed power still lingered on the air. I distracted myself from the train of thought that might lead me down.

"So, I am a good teacher," I said instead.

Keera's lips quirked in the slightest smile, and she stood. She reached her hand out to me to help me to my feet, and I took it, letting her haul me up, once again marveling at how strong she had grown in such a short amount of time.

I had spent the last several months feeling as if I had been training double, and here she was halfway a warrior when I had found her frail and feral at that oasis. I shoved that information away with the rest of the thoughts that I didn't want to dwell on right now.

Keera walked over to the fallen Sichat and stared down at it. Just like the last one, the creature was large and vaguely feline, all black but for the patch of silky white fur on its chest in the shape of a star. Dull purple eyes stared lifelessly up at the sky.

"I'd say we had a successful hunt, but..."

I knew what she meant. Waves of distinctly unfriendly magic came off the corpse, a distinctly visceral reaction rolling through me at the thought of eating the creature.

"Leave it. We will see if Zephyr found some smaller game."

Back at camp, Zephyr had indeed been successful at catching two black tailed jackrabbits. I let him tear into one, while Keera picked up and efficiently began skinning and cleaning the other with a practiced hand.

She was quiet as she did so, which wasn't unusual for her, but I sensed a turmoil in her silence that distinguished it from what we had established as our normal companionable cooperation.

I observed her out of the corner of my eye as I built the fire on which to cook our meat. Eventually she paused, bloody knife hovering above the skinned carcass.

"Why are the sichats and lava wyrms returning? They disappeared after the desert was conquered."

I hesitated, not sure how much to divulge to somebody that might still be an adversary. But my own words, partially in jest before, played back to me with a ring of truth. Perhaps she would no longer be my enemy if I taught her what I knew.

"The desert is angry and rises against us. Kelvadan is an insult toward the way the clans have lived since the first rider crossed from the mountain to the ocean and won the right to call the Ballan Desert home.

"The desert values strength and survival above all else, and the clans embody that. The strong rise to power, and the weak fall. Their warring ways offer the desert death and blood in exchange for the life she gifts us. But Kelvadan... the peace brought by the city is just weakness by another name. Even worse, the city looks beyond the borders of the Ballan Desert, welcoming those to our home who don't respect or even believe in her power."

I started with the part that Lord Alasdar told the clans to win them to our side. But there was another layer to the story he did not share.

Keera frowned. "Kelvadan is my home." She said it almost too firmly, as if it was something she was telling herself as much as me.

"My great-grandfather's legacy is one of failure as much as victory." I couldn't help the bitterness in my tone as I thought of the burden I had been yoked with, both from his successes and his sins.

Keera stared at me, tilting her head in curiosity as she waited for me to continue.

"Kelvar was the Champion of the Desert, more powerful than any could remember. He carried within him the power to shape the desert to his will, and he did. That type of magic comes with a cost though."

"It drove him mad," Keera murmured. Her eyes held something soft and vulnerable that I didn't dare place. I plunged on with my story.

"It did, and worse. The legends say that the Heart of the Desert should be conquered by whoever crosses her from the mountains to the ocean. If you survive the tests that journey would pose, then the magic is yours to command."

"That's how the first lords of the clans tamed the sands and were the first to harness the magic of the desert so that it might be a place where we could live," Keera volunteered, as if it were a line recited from rote. It was a tale all clans people would have heard around their fires, engrained in their heads from the time they were born.

I shook my head. "It's not just that though. While Alyx herself carried strong magic within her, it wasn't on the scale of Kelvar, and she began to sicken with age before him. Despite all the power within him, he could do nothing to stop it. As the madness slowly took him, he devised a plan. If he could claim the Heart of the Desert—then he would have the power to keep Alyx alive.

"So, he crossed the desert and stole her Heart to bring back to Kelvadan. But he was too late, and Alyx had died while he was gone. Now the desert is without her Heart, and she shreds herself apart."

Keera frowned. "The Heart of the Desert isn't something you can steal. Besides, Kelvar wandered into the desert after Alyx died and was never seen again."

"Have you been to the doors to Kelvar's rooms?" I asked.

"Yes."

"Then you will have seen the tapestry above the entrance, showing the Heart. The red gem that grants all the magic of the desert to whomever should possess it."

Doubt began to creep into Keera's eyes where they had been sure before.

"Maybe Kelvar went after the Heart, but we don't know if he succeeded. He wandered out into the wilds, never to be seen again," she argued.

"I know he succeeded because I have crossed the desert myself, and I have seen the empty temple where the Heart should be."

Keera dropped the knife, sitting back on her heels and looking up at me. She rested her bloody hands on her knees, seemingly uncaring of the stains she was leaving on her pants.

"So why wage war on Kelvadan?"

"Because the Heart of the Desert is locked in the rooms at the top of the palace, and I intend to restore it to its rightful place. Only with Lord Alasdar's help can I open the chamber and retrieve the Heart. Just as

Kelvar's madness is mine to bear, so are the consequences of his legacy, and I must set things right."

"Then restore the Heart." Keera's hands balled into fists on her knees as she stared up at me. "But Kelvadan doesn't need to fall for that to happen."

"The monument of Kelvadan is a lie!" I snapped. "Everybody calls it a testament to everlasting love that Kelvar built for Alyx, but that same love is what drove him to risk the destruction of everything we know. Kelvadan needs to fall, to protect everyone for repeating the sins of the past."

Keera stayed silent, but I hadn't wanted a response anyway. I turned around and stormed toward Alza, leaving her kneeling in the bloody sand.

Chapter Twenty-Eight
Keera

I couldn't help but watch Erix as we rode, my head swirling. A rational voice in my mind told me not to trust him. Why should I believe the words of one who had tried to kill me on several occasions? It would be to his advantage to have me join his cause.

The memories of his saber point at my throat were overshadowed though by the image him throwing himself between me and the sichat just this morning. Stronger than the feeling of cold steel at my throat was the warmth of his arms around me as he pulled me back to myself when the current of my magic threatened to pull me under.

Erix's mare, whom I had heard him call Alza when he murmured to her under his breath, led us as we walked single file along rocky cliff face. I stared so hard at the back of his head that I imagined I could crack it open, understand the thoughts that swirled within, and know if he was trying to mislead me. How could I trust one that killed so indiscriminately for his cause that he had earned the name the Viper?

His words from earlier echoed in my head.

It's easier to pretend there is nobody underneath the mask.

Perhaps the Viper was also a mask, one he wore to hide the truth of his motives.

So engrossed was I in my thoughts that I didn't notice the rising swirl of dust on the horizon until Erix pulled his mount to a stop before me. I started, pulling up short as he pointed out to our left, the opposite direction of the cliff-face.

"Sandstorm. We need to find cover."

Indeed, a wall of tan, practically solid in its density, raced over the ground toward us, swallowing the landscape whole. In unison, we kicked our horses into a gallop, searching for an alcove or cave that could protect us from the desert's wrath.

Wind howled, beginning to pick at my clothes as the storm barreled toward us. It was less than half a mile away now, and we were running out of time. We charged on, still exposed against the rock.

"Up ahead!"

The wind threatened to carry Erix's voice away from me as we ran, but I saw him gesture to a gap in the rock. We hurtled toward it at breakneck speed. As we reached it, the horses skidded to a stop, their hooves kicking up loose pebbles. Erix jumped down from his mount, and I moved to follow him. We urged the horses forward, getting them into the gap of the rock. They disappeared inside, indicating a cave or open area beyond. The low rumbling of the storm grew to a deafening volume, but before I could look behind me at the wall of dust almost upon us, a blow between my shoulder blades drove me forward into the cave.

Sand blasted my back, rough against my skin even through my clothes. It sought out every gap in the fabric to get at my skin, scratching and burning. Still, I whirled around, pulling the loose fabric of my hood over my face.

"Erix!"

He wasn't inside the cave yet, caught outside in the blinding swirl of sand. So thick was the flying debris that I couldn't even see him through the gap in the rock, as close to it as he must still be.

I shoved my hand through the gap, groping into empty air even as the storm chafed my bare skin raw. A few seconds that felt like an eternity later, my hand met a solid form. I grabbed at the fabric and dragged Erix through the narrow opening into the shelter of the rocky alcove.

As the storm howled outside, we stood face to face in the protection of the cave, so close that our chests brushed as we panted. Erix's formerly dark clothes were crusted with dust, the color underneath nearly imperceptible under the coating of sand.

"Thank you," I said, voice quiet enough that it would be hard to hear over the howl of the wind if he wasn't standing close enough that I could see my breath fog the metal of his mask. For the briefest moment I appreciated its existence, as it probably protected his face from the worst of the elements outside. Still, now that I had seen his eyes in the light of the sun, I itched to be rid of the barrier between us.

We stood like that for a long moment before the whicker of a horse behind us broke the stillness. Erix brushed past me to go check on our mounts. Luckily, they had been beyond the shelter of the ridge when the worst of the storm broke over us and only seemed mildly spooked.

We led them further into the shelter; it turned out to be not much larger than my room at Aderyn and Neven's house, big enough for us all to fit comfortably but not enough for us to spread out.

Getting settled in to wait out the storm, Erix brushed fruitlessly at his clothes, as if that would be sufficient to clean them. Instead, he only left streaks through the tan crust on his dark robes.

"You'll need to change and clean those at the next oasis."

Erix hands hovered, unsure for a moment, before reaching for the length of fabric around his head and shoulders. He turned his back to me as he unwound it. I should have looked away, but I couldn't bring myself to. After seeing his face again this morning, I found myself itching to see more of him, to touch more of him.

His mask fell to the ground, followed by those damned gloves. The belt unwound from his tapered waist, letting him shrug off his vest and tabards before reaching for the bottom of his tunic. As it passed his shoulders, the curiosity and growing warmth I felt at him disrobing turned to icy horror.

Row upon row of neat scars, each a raised red line, marched along his shoulders. The ones near the base of his neck were well healed, but the ones at the bottom were red and angry, the very last few still bubbled with blisters.

"What..." I spluttered, unable to articulate my question. Instead, the well of rage deep in my core bubbled ominously.

"Remember how I told you that pain is the best way to control your magic?"

"You did this to yourself?"

"Lord Alasdar did it, but yes."

My vision went white, a rushing noise overwhelming my ears. I only returned to myself at the warm press of a hand over my sternum. My eyes cleared to find Erix standing before me, still unmasked and bare chested. Thankfully, I could no longer see the marks of pain along his back.

"Why would you serve a monster who would do such a thing to you?" I demanded, voice low and rough.

"Lord Alasdar saved me," he insisted.

"Mutilating you is not saving you!"

"He found me in the desert when I was lost and alone!" Erix snapped, drawing his hand back from me suddenly. I was left cold and reeling, but he ranted on, as if the tether keeping him in check had been cut.

"My own parents refused to love me for what I was, making me shove down my powers until I thought they would explode—drugging me when that didn't work. They wanted me to be the perfect heir to Kelvadan, Kelvar come again in both appearance and power, but I knew the second part of that birthright. I was expected to live up to the legacy while carrying the weight that someday it would drive me mad.

"So, I ran... away to the desert where at least my rage and the feelings that I pretended didn't exist couldn't hurt the citizens of the city I was supposed to protect. Lord Alasdar found me among the dunes, starving and delirious and waiting for death. He showed me that my power could be wielded. Even if I was destined to be destructive, my destruction could be managed.

"What's more, he showed me the truth of Kelvar's legacy and gave me a purpose. I would be his sword as he set this desert right once more. It is the burden of my bloodline, and he gave me a way to escape it."

Erix's eyes shone in the dim light of our shelter and tension ran through the tendons of his neck and the set of his shoulders. As he panted, as if the admission had taken great effort, I saw clearly what lay under the disguise of the Viper.

He was just a young man, saddled with the power to shake the foundations of the desert, and drowning under the weight of the sins of his family. Lord Alasdar must have seen it too.

"He's using you," I murmured, voice as soft as if I were trying to soothe a wild horse.

"I know," Erix admitted. "But being a sword frees me from the weight of being its wielder. The blade is not responsible for the blood it spills, but the one who swings it."

I swallowed thickly, heart wrenching in my chest. "You're not a sword though. You're a man."

"I haven't wanted to be. Not until—not until I met you."

I stepped forward, unable to stop myself even if I wanted to. I reached up to cup Erix's cheek as I had before. This time he leaned into the touch.

Chest to chest with him, I stood on my toes, using my hand on his face to pull him down to me. Ever so slowly I lifted my face until I could press my forehead to his. A full body shudder racked his frame, but he did not pull away. Time stretched and compressed as we stood there, breathing the same air. This close, I could sense the salt and sandalwood scent drifting off his bare skin.

Magic swirled between us, although I couldn't tell who it belonged to. Still, as our heartbeats fell into synchrony, it settled to a pleasant pulse running from the top of my head to the tips of my toes. The ragged sound of our breaths filled the space, and I realized the world had gone quiet around us.

The storm that raged outside had calmed.

CHAPTER TWENTY-NINE
ERIX

The next two days passed in the same rhythm, thankfully absent of more storms or mythical creatures. Every morning we flowed through our forms together, riding until evening when I would help Keera practice with her magic. It seemed to be coming to her easier by the day, rocks and fire leaping to life at to her command. If she noticed that I took the practice as an opportunity to lay my hand on her shoulder or the small of her back, knowing that it helped her access her power with less fear, then she didn't comment on it.

On the third night, we set up our camp in the divot between two dunes. We had leftover meat from our hunt that morning and Keera produced two pieces of fruit from her pack, making a fire or another hunt unnecessary.

I grabbed my sleeping mat and rolled it out a few feet away from hers. I sat down on it, cross legged, and unsheathed my saber. Keera looked up at the metallic slide from where she was devouring her meal with a single-minded efficiency. Fruit juice dribbled between her fingers, and she licked them clean.

The jut of her hipbones and shoulder blades against my arm as I tied her across Alza's back all those months ago flashed through my mind. I made a mental note to send Zephyr out to hunt for us again. I would not let Keera go hungry.

Methodically, I ran the whetstone across the length of metal in my lap. I hadn't used my sword today, but it was a habit I couldn't break. I cared for my saber every night, and sleep would not come for me if I left the task undone.

"I'm a little sad I didn't succeed in stealing that from you," Keera said around a mouthful of orange.

"It was Kelvar's," I admitted. "It's the only thing I brought with me."

Keera looked at it curiously. On a whim, I offered it to her hilt first. She stood and walked over slowly, wiping her hands on her pants. Cautiously, as if it were a snake that might strike out at her, she reached for the hilt.

Upon taking it, she took a few stances with it experimentally. I knew from experience that there was no weapon as balanced or deadly, longer than any other sword I had ever encountered. I had never let another wield it, but it looked right in Keera's hand.

"It seems like Kelvar was trying to compensate for something," Keera commented wryly as she ran through a few stances.

"I wouldn't know. Strangely enough, the statues and paintings in Kelvadan are all of him fully clothed."

Keera chuckled, and I reveled in the sound, mixed with the swish of the blade as she swung it experimentally. Pausing, she pointed the tip of the weapon at me, tip angled straight toward the base of my throat.

I let her, not moving to defend myself. It wasn't lost on me how we had been in this position before, roles reversed.

"Why didn't you kill me?" she asked. She didn't need to elaborate.

"The whispers of my mind... the madness that threatens to engulf me when I'm not spilling blood on behalf of the desert—something happened when I touched you. I felt still."

Keera nodded, as if she understood without further explanation. "With your hand at my throat, I felt alive for the first time since my clan left me to die. I had been fighting to survive, but I didn't know why until something awoke in me. It took you holding your blade to my throat for me to realize that I still had a reason to be alive."

How odd that I had awoken her while she had settled me.

"Why don't you kill me now?" I asked.

The saber tip inched forward, resting against my collarbone. It wouldn't be such a bad way to die, looking up at the one person whose power might be able to match mine. Still, I found myself hoping she wouldn't. After so long being ambivalent about my own existence beyond my purpose in restoring the Heart of the Desert, it was a heady feeling.

"You know me," was Keera's simple answer. She let the saber point drop and handed it back to me. I set it at my side.

Hesitantly, giving Keera a chance to pull away if she wanted to, I reached out to where her hand dangled at her side. Instead, she met me halfway, our fingers intertwining. It was the first time I had initiated contact between us without the guise of training, and something I didn't know had been tight in my chest loosened as she responded.

Before I could react, she stepped forward and fell to her knees in my lap. Her thighs bracketed mine and the sudden warmth of her pressed against me initiated the same reaction as before, as if Alza and I were galloping at full tilt but also, I was sitting completely still for the first time in too long.

Extricating her hand from what had become a death grip on my part, she slowly reached up toward my mask. She gave me the same chance to pull back as I had when I reached for her hand. Like her, I let her continue.

Her fingers found the leather straps at the back of my head, fumbling a bit as she undid them. I didn't move to help her, instead focusing on keeping my breath even as I voluntarily let somebody see my face for the first time since Lord Alasdar had given me the mask ten years ago. It was my most important piece of armor, and I was letting this wild, gorgeous thing in my lap peel it off with her gentle fingers.

It fell to the mat beside my saber with a gentle thud. This time, Keera traced her fingers along my hairline, toying with a curl that fell onto my forehead. Over the initial shock of human contact, I found myself wanting more than her fingers on me. I wanted to rub my face on her cheek and at the crook of her neck. Between her breasts.

As if she had heard my thoughts, Keera's gaze snapped to mine from where she had been engrossed in the examination of my hair. Slowly, hesitantly, her gaze drifted down to my lips, tracing the same path with her fingers. Gently, but without hesitation, she pressed her thumb against my bottom lip, parting them slightly. As my increasingly ragged breath tickled her fingers, I found myself itching for the same thing she was clearly considering. Her touch had unlocked a torrent of want within me, and I exercised all my control to hold myself still as she made her decision.

Her lips collided with mine, and my blood surged when I found out she kissed just like she fought and rode a horse. There was nothing tentative in the way her mouth moved against mine. She was wild and hungry and utterly untamed. Both of us were clumsy and unpracticed, but the smell of sun-warmed skin and the comforting earthiness of the desert engulfed me.

Her fingers plunged into my hair, and a noise I would never admit to being capable of tore from my throat as her blunt nails raked my scalp. I took it as permission to touch in return, and a hand drifted to her face before tracing the tendon of her neck with my thumb. I found my other hand at her hip of its own accord.

A low growl of pleasure rumbled through me at the feeling of soft flesh over taught muscle, a far cry from the boniness of the woman I once captured. She had been beautiful even then, though I hadn't been in a mind to see it, and it warmed me to know she was no longer at risk of starving to death.

Keera squirmed in my lap, causing a shudder to run through my whole body. The taste of her mouth overwhelmed me. I knew I could kiss Keera for hours without complaint, but the friction of her hips against mine made me hunger for more. I walked my fingers inwards from her hip to the front of the waistband of her pants, waiting for permission. She responded by rolling her hips against mine enthusiastically.

I slipped my fingers beneath the linen, inching downward until the leather of my gloves slipped against the slickness already gathering between her legs. I groaned, realizing what a travesty it was that I couldn't feel this with my own flesh.

I withdrew my hand and pulled back from where her lips and

tongue had begun an enthusiastic perusal of my jaw and ear. She made an angry noise of protest that made my pants tighten even further, but I shushed her in a tone I normally only reserved for Alza.

"I want to feel you," I admitted, before pulling the fingers of my gloves off with my teeth. My eyes nearly rolled back into my head as I tasted her on the leather, my tongue seeking out the flavor of honey and musk.

I wasted no time getting my hand back to her core, anxious to feel her soft slickness against my bare skin. When I did, Keera ground against my fingers, seeking her own pleasure determinedly. I pulled back to look at her face. The rising flush against her golden skin as she panted, tendrils of dark hair clinging to her sweaty temples, sent a frisson of pleasure through me. She wore my hunger reflected on her face.

She threw her head back with a shuddering groan when I stroked a particular spot, and it suddenly became a goal of mine to make her react like that as often as possible. I repeated the motion relentlessly.

"Erix." My name escaped her lips in a breathy shudder. It was a name I had distanced myself from as much as possible, but I would relish being reminded of it every day if it was in that voice.

"I want to see you lose control," I murmured.

A husky laugh escaped Keera as she continued to ride my hand in my lap. "I haven't been in control since the moment I met you."

Neither have I.

Unable to help myself, I palmed my own hardness through my pants with my free hand, not willing to deny Keera her pleasure for even the moment it would take me to untie my belt.

I stroked myself in time to the high whimpers and cries from Keera. As much as she didn't fill silence with meaningless chatter, she didn't shy away from vocalizing her pleasure. As her volume increased, the sands began to dance around us, and I couldn't say whether the magic was mine or hers. I was too overwhelmed with the red-hot pleasure that had taken root at the base of my spine and the way the sunlight shone off Keera's sweat-soaked skin.

I felt the moment Keera came apart, in the shudder of power that ran through me as much as the rush of wetness dripping along my wrist.

So fixated was I on the woman in my lap, I didn't even recognize my own pleasure bearing down on me until a bolt of lightning ran up my spine, and I gasped my release against Keera's neck, gulping down the earthy scent of her warm skin.

Sands, I was utterly lost.

CHAPTER THIRTY
KEERA

e both slept under the stars that night. With Erix's help, I coaxed a fire from the dry scrub we found in the area with my magic. It shielded us from the chill that swept over the sands in the absence of the sun as we laid on our mats with it as a barrier between us.

Neither of us spoke of what had happened between us, but I didn't get the sense that we were ignoring it either. It was simply that words would not suffice to say anything more than our actions already had. Out here in the wilderness, the lines between us blurred as if they had been traced in the sand only to be scoured away by the wind. When we returned to civilization, we would have to redraw them once more, but for now, we were more similar than we were enemies.

The next morning dawned bright and clear, and we set out immediately after practicing our morning forms together. We flowed in unison the same as before, yet differently, as if the magic that flowed between us had been heightened by our intimacy. I wondered at it out loud as we rode.

"You say that you can feel my magic across the whole desert when I lose control. Now that we've ridden together for a while, I can feel yours too. Why do you think that is?"

Erix shrugged. He wore his mask again as we rode, but he had left it off during our morning exercise. "I had never met anybody nearly as powerful as me before you. Only Lord Alasdar came close, although his power has a different nature. Perhaps being the two most magical people in the desert makes us more aware of each other."

I hummed in thought for a moment, sensing something beneath the surface of his statement. "It's more than that isn't it though?"

Erix looked over at me from Alza's back, remaining quiet for a moment—so long that I thought he wasn't going to answer me.

"I don't understand it," he admitted quietly.

I swallowed thickly. "When I started training with the Kelvadan riders, and Aderyn taught me the saber forms, it was as if my body already knew them. I improved as a saber fighter far faster than I had any right to."

I watched Erix carefully as I spoke, but his only visible reaction was the tightening of his fists where they rested on Alza's shoulders. My face momentarily heated at the memory of how he had licked every trace of me off the fingers of his gloves after touching me. I shook that off in favor of continuing to prod him.

"I think you awoke more than magic in me when you touched me for the first time."

"Let's hope for the sake of the desert that I didn't."

Before I could ask what he meant, a sharp whinny that didn't come from either Alza or Daiti split the air. My head snapped toward the horizon where a lone rider stood, waving both arms in the air to get our attention.

Erix and I both urged our mounts into a canter toward the figure. While my hand inched toward the hilt of the dagger in my belt, it seemed unlikely that we would be greeted in such a way by an enemy. After all, the stranger drew no weapon as we approached. Erix seemed to have similar thoughts, his posture alert but not combative.

"Are you of Clan Otush?" Erix asked once we were within earshot.

The man hesitated upon seeing Erix, shying back a bit at the sight of the metal mask. He had clearly heard the tales of the Viper, but the desperation in his gaze was clear as he asked, "Have you come to help us?"

"Your rider told us of the lava wyrm. We have come to face it," I responded.

The man looked dismayed. "Only two of you?"

"It will be enough," Erix stated, and his tone brooked no argument.

The rider's expression revealed that he was still unsure, but he nodded anyway. "I'll take you to our encampment, and we can tell you what we know of the creature."

We followed him over the next rise, after which the close drawn tents of Clan Otush came into view.

"I thought Clan Otush had joined with Clans Padra, Tibel, Vecturna, and Jal to camp together," Erix asked. I glanced at him side-long as we rode.

"We had united to resist..." The man shot a glance at Erix and recon-sidered. "We had banded together for a time, but game became too scarce in any one area to feed all the clans. We split up to cover more territory, hoping to ward off famine but not overhunting any one stretch."

My mouth grew dry at the mention of famine. While the desert was harsh, it teemed with life if one knew where to look. Now, it seemed to be withering if even clans with capable hunters struggled to feed their own. I thought of what Erix had said about the missing Heart and frowned. Even more, most of the texts in the private collection of the Royal Library—texts collected by Kelvar—had focused on the first crossing of the desert and how it won the Lord the Heart of the Desert.

The rider of Clan Otush led us toward his encampment. As we crossed the dry and cracked earth, our mounts picked their way around strange formations of black rock. They looked bubbled and warped, unlike any stone I had seen shaped by the relentless forces of nature. I frowned as Daiti skirted a large patch almost as big as he was. The clansman said nothing, but his expression was grim.

Drawing closer to the encampment, the root of his desperation was clear. Where encampments normally teemed with life—the laughter of children and the barking of hunting dogs—this one frayed at the seams. Tents bore signs of fire and violence, some with obviously patched rips and others sporting blackened char marks on their canvas. The few chil-dren in sight were held tightly by their parents so they couldn't run off, and there didn't seem to be enough horses in the enclosures for the number of people.

We headed for the center of the encampment, faces appearing from behind tent flaps to look at us as we passed, expressions equal parts hopeful and apprehensive.

When we reached the grandest tent, our escort dismounted, shouting, "Lord Dhara!"

In a matter of moments, the tent flap opened, revealing a woman armed to the teeth with a hard glint in her eye. A bow and full quiver of arrows were thrown over her shoulder while a row of curved daggers lined her belt. A gold ring glittered in one nostril, almost as brightly as her keen eyes as she took us in.

"They've come to face the lava wyrm," our escort declared, tapping his knuckles to his forehead as he bowed to his clan's lord. I echoed the gesture from where I still sat astride Daiti, but Erix made no such movement.

"Does Lord Alasdar's pet snake come to save us or to threaten us?" The lord crossed her arms over her chest in defiance. "We told you, our clan would not be threatened into bowing to Clan Katal."

"You struck a deal that you would join our cause if I was victorious in the Trials, and I have returned to you as Champion of the Desert," Erix announced, loud enough that all those in the small crowd that had gathered around the clearing could hear.

"You do not wear the Champion's circlet," Lord Dhara pointed out.

"Your rider reached us with news of your plight before he could be crowned," I found myself volunteering before I could think better of it. I bit my tongue hard enough to taste copper in my mouth. Erix looked at me sharply.

"Is this true?"

"It should not matter if I wear the Champion's circlet or not," Erix countered. "If lava wyrms rise again, you must see the wisdom in uniting the tribes to restore the desert. She tears herself apart at the seams because of the sins of Kelvadan. We must fight together to save our home."

The assembled clansmen broke into scattered whispers, and I caught snippets of agreement.

"Something has to be done."

"Lord Alasdar should have been crowned Champion at the last Trials."

"Clan Katal will save the desert."

I saw the truth of Clan Otush's struggles in the too-thin faces of their women and children and the absence of so many young riders. They struggled to survive in the desert as it was now—a struggle I knew all too intimately. That desperation drove them toward what they saw as a common enemy, and I couldn't say I blamed them.

A voice in my mind argued that Kelvadan wasn't the right enemy. How could it be when it was home to Aderyn and Neven, who had become like family before I could even realize it? It couldn't be the source of this turmoil when the spires were a beacon of hope and peace for so many—when the queen was fair and kind and had offered a lost exile a home and her husband had such a gentle way with horses.

I pictured the tapestry over the locked doors to Alix's tomb and held my tongue. I couldn't be sure of much right now, but I was certain that these people needed our help.

"My companion and I will distract the lava wyrm while the clan escapes," Erix instructed. The lord obviously chafed at being given orders but could see the wisdom of his words and nodded in agreement. "While we fight the beast, you can ride for Clan Katal where you will be safe among the united clans."

"We will prepare to move while giving you a place to rest and recover for tonight. Then we can strike out in the morning," Lord Dhara agreed.

At the decision that we would not be riding out today, Erix and I both dismounted. Clansmen moved forward as if to help us with our packs and horses, but I shook my head. Daiti didn't take kindly to strangers, and I wouldn't risk these clansmen earning a hoof-shaped bruise for their kindness.

Erix waved off those who approached him as well. "I prefer to tend to my own horse."

We were shown to the enclosure where we could leave Daiti and Alza with the rest of the clan's horses. It seemed almost wrong to have them mingle, our mounts' shining coats and proud posture a sharp juxtaposition to the patchy coats and worn-out gait of the other horses. It threw into painful relief just how much these people suffered.

"We'll set up a spare tent for you to use tonight," explained the man who had shown us around.

With that, we found ourselves at loose ends for the afternoon—an odd sensation after days of hard riding. Not accustomed to sitting idle, I looked around the camp. There certainly wasn't a lack of work to be done to get the fraying tribe ready to depart the next day.

I turned to Erix, mouth already open to say we should offer to help, when I found him gone. Looking around, I spotted him drifting toward the far side of the horse enclosure. There, a man and woman were fussing over a horse, the mare appearing to be in distress.

I trailed after him curiously.

Erix stopped a few paces away, but his stance was tense, as if he wanted to approach but didn't know how. I stopped beside him, eyeing his fists clenching and unclenching out of the corner of my eye.

Meanwhile, the mare paced restlessly, tail swishing in irritation. She pulled her upper lip back, kicking her rear legs as the pair tried to calm her.

"What's going on?" I asked, stepping a little closer. Erix hovered just off my shoulder.

The woman looked up, blinking a few times before recognition dawned.

"Keera, right?"

It was my turn to stare in confusion before I realized where I had seen her before. Then, I recalled her clapping me on the shoulder in congratulations after besting her in the Trials. Still, I didn't remember her name. "Yes..."

"Badha," she offered without judgement. "I'm sure you bested too many competitors that day to remember every name."

"I should still do better to remember anybody as good with a blade as you," I said.

She offered her hand to me. I took it, and we clasped each other's forearms.

"What's going on with this mare?" I asked again.

Badha's smile faded. "She's my brother, Koa's, horse, and it's about time for her to foal. He swears something doesn't feel right, but our horse master—the lava wyrm has cost our clan many lives."

Now that I looked closer, I could see the mare's rounded belly, teats already straining, showing her delivery was just around the corner. She paced away from us, swinging her head side to side before turning back.

"I can help," Erix cut in.

I glanced over my shoulder at him, and he stepped forward, reaching a hand out to the mare. She blew a breath at him for a moment, but then nudged forward and let him pat her nose. I remembered that Erix was not just Ginevra's son, but Kaius's too.

"Are you sure?" the man hovering nearby and wringing his hands asked—Badha's brother, Koa, I assumed. "This isn't just tending to a warhorse."

Erix nodded, continuing to pat the horse soothingly, muttering nonsensically under his breath before answering. "I've... worked closely with the best horse master there is. I've helped with many difficult foalings."

Koa glanced at his sister, who looked at me, as if waiting for my judgement on the matter. It felt odd for her to look to me for guidance, but I nodded encouragingly.

"Erix is good with horses." If he had learned even half as much as Kaius knew, then I had confidence in him. Even in the short months I spent in Kelvadan, I had seen everybody in the city seek out his help for all sorts of equine ailments, and he handled them all with patience and expertise. Based on how well Erix treated Alza, I had a feeling he followed his father's teachings.

"Then I would appreciate any help you can give us," Koa said. "I just—something's wrong. I can tell."

"Your magic serves you well," Erix responded.

I blinked. Reaching out with the barest lick of magic, I reached past the beacon of power that was Erix, nearly drowning out all else in the desert, to find a delicate bond between Koa and his horse.

Koa snorted. "It does very little but cause me to spoil my horse rotten."

"It shows," I chimed in. "She's a beautiful animal."

It was true. As much as all the mounts of Clan Otush looked like they had seen better days, as did its people, her thick, if dusty, coat and strong muscles spoke to years of good care.

"I'll need bandages to get her tail out of the way, and some fresh water."

"I'll go," Badha volunteered.

I followed her, planning to help carry water and supplies. She led me to a well dug in the center of the encampment, and I began turning the crank to bring up the bucket. I sensed her eyes on me as I worked. I itched to shrink away, uncomfortable with the scrutiny.

She eventually broke the silence. "I didn't expect to find you riding in such company."

I glanced over, finding her expression open, not holding the judgement I would have expected.

"To be honest, neither did I. But Erix..."

"You call the Viper by his name? I thought nobody knew it. I wasn't sure he even had one."

I chewed my lip, not wanting to unintentionally give away more of Erix's secrets. It felt like a violation of trust, although I had made him no promises.

Badha shook her head at my silence. "I will not tell anybody if you don't wish me to. I suppose his name doesn't really matter. I just didn't expect you to join him after the way the Trials ended."

I winced at the memory of my loss of control. "I wish you hadn't seen that."

"I will admit, I was cheering for you in that fight. I knew that Clan Otush would have to join Clan Katal, and like our lord, I don't relish bowing to others. I rode out right after that fight to tell my lord what had happened. But I did see your power, and you were certainly fearsome to face in a fight... I guess I can see why the two of you might have something in common after all."

"Erix is... complicated."

Badha shrugged as I pulled the bucket from the well. It was heavy with water that I was careful not to slosh over the sides. "If he can help Koa's horse and save us from the lava wyrm, I don't think I would mind following him after all."

At that, I nodded. It was my sentiment too. Out here in the desert, where survival was the ultimate law, the barriers that had been erected between the clans and Kelvadan seemed both less important and looming more imposing than ever. After all, the clans blamed Kelvadan for the suffering they endured.

"Let's get this back to Erix and Koa," I said.

I lugged the heavy bucket back to the enclosure while Badha hurried to grab some cloth from one of the tents. When we arrived back at the horse enclosure, Erix took the bandages and neatly bundled up the mare's tail out of the way of her hind quarters. Then he shucked off his gloves and pushed up his sleeves and used the water to cleanse his hands and arms up to the elbow.

"Try to keep her still, I need to see what position the foal is in," Erix ordered us, voice full of all the calm seriousness of a war-hardened veteran. As all three of us jumped to obey without a second thought, I understood why Lord Alasdar put him in command of the combined clan's riders.

Koa took the mare's head, comforting her and whispering reassurances while Badha and I stood at her sides, keeping her from shuffling away as Erix stood at her rear. Between the three of us, we managed to keep her in place as Erix examined her, but I couldn't help but frown at the sweat coating her sides.

"The good news is that the foal appears to be coming front legs first, so we don't have to worry about it suffocating before its face comes out. The bad news is that it is upside down, with its legs up toward her back," Erix said as he pulled away.

The creases of worry across Koa's brow deepened, and he stroked the mare's nose even as she panted. "What can we do?"

"If we get her to lay down and stand up several times, it should correct itself. If not—well, we'll just have to do our best to help her deliver as is."

Koa's expression took on a determined set. "Tell me what to do."

For the next half hour, Koa and Erix gently coaxed the mare around the enclosure, patiently encouraging her to lay down before prodding her back up again. Badha and I did our best to help, mostly getting Erix whatever he asked for.

By the time the mare lay down on her side, refusing to get back up again, sides rippling with contractions, a small audience had formed around the enclosure. While clansmen hurried around, getting the encampment ready to move at first light, many paused as they walked by. Just like myself, they couldn't seem to take their eyes off the masked man, supposedly the fearsome Viper, with his sleeves rolled up, helping to gently coax a new life into the world.

Badha and I joined Erix and Koa at the mare's side as she showed signs of beginning to strain. Carefully, Erix reached up the birth canal to check the foal. We collectively held our breath, and all those hurrying by outside the enclosure paused to hear the verdict as well.

"It's turned. She should be able to deliver nearly on her own from here."

Koa let out a shuddering breath, and I felt myself echoing the sentiment.

In a matter of minutes, delicate front hooves came into view, followed by a pink nose. Erix carefully removed blood and humor from the foal's nostrils so it could breathe, and the mare continued to push, Koa continually murmuring encouragement.

As the foal's shoulders began to emerge, Erix nodded me over.

"Help me pull gently as the mother pushes. She's beginning to tire."

I laid my hands over his on the foal's front legs, doing as he asked. Together, we applied gentle traction as the mare's sides shuddered and heaved. In moments, the front half of the foal appeared already started to squirm.

"Stop," Erix instructed me. "If we keep pulling now, we might fracture its ribs."

With one final heave, the mare birthed the foal, a bright new colt coming into the desert in the middle of the downtrodden encampment. Koa exclaimed in joy, and murmurs of excitement ran through those who paused by the enclosure's edge.

Incredulously, I reached out my magic, feeling the spark that lived in every horse in the Ballan Desert, small but steady in the foal. He was already proving to be a feisty one, trying and failing to push to his feet only minutes after birth.

An hour later, I sat on the makeshift fence at the edge of the enclosure next to Erix, his arms scrubbed clean and gloves firmly in place.

Together, we watched the foal nurse, already walking around on thin legs that were less wobbly by the minute. Our silence was companionable, and when I reached out a tendril of magic toward Erix, I imagined I could feel a sort of contentment rolling off him that I hadn't felt before.

"I didn't know you knew so much about horses," I said.

Erix shrugged, but the way his face turned to follow the foal wherever it roamed belied his indifference. "Growing up, riding was one of the few times I felt peace. It still is."

I remembered the way Farren felt beneath me—how we would gallop under the stars in a pell-mell race to nowhere when my thoughts became too much. It was yet another sentiment we shared.

"Kai—Kaius tried to help me in his own way." The horse master's name seemed to catch in his throat, but I didn't press Erix. It was the first time I had heard him speak of his parents in a way that was less than hostile, and I feared shattering the moment. "Seeing how much I liked to spend time around the horses, he would bring me to the stables to help him when he could. It was never enough but...it did help."

We fell into silence again. A figure strode up next to us, resting their forearms on the fence next to us. I looked over to find Lord Dhara surveying the foal as well.

"I'm glad we won't have to worry about Koa's mare giving birth as we travel. We hope to make it to the safety of the encampment as quickly as possible," she said.

"The foal will still be slow," Erix pointed out.

Lord Dhara shook her head. "It will already be slow going. Many have lost their horses to the lava wyrm already and will have to take turns riding and walking. Still, with your help we might just make it."

While the lord's voice still held the hardness of a commander, it was laced with a little more gratitude than it had been when we first arrived.

"Come to my fire and get some food tonight. You have more than earned your keep today," she said before striding off toward the center of the encampment.

That evening, we found ourselves sitting around one of the larger fire pits with Lord Dhara and several of the riders. We were each passed a meager portion of cooked oryx meat, but Erix wordlessly tipped his onto my plate. Apparently, the mask still stayed on around others besides me.

"What can you tell us of the lava wyrm?" he asked as I was busy licking hot grease off my fingers. I didn't miss the way his mask darted to me as I made sure not a single dripple escaped me, running my tongue over where the juices dripped down my wrist.

"It first attacked three weeks ago, although we didn't know it at the time," Lord Dhara explained. "One of our hunting parties never returned, and we thought the desert had led them astray or they had been caught in a sandstorm.

"Then a few horses disappeared, only for their charred bones to be found among the sands a few days later. We didn't see it until two weeks ago, when it grew bold enough to attack our encampment at night. We tried to fight back, but it is difficult to get close enough to land a blow when it spits molten rock, turning the ground around it into a burning death trap. We've tried arrows, but they just bounce off its hide. Its underbelly seems unprotected, but the moats of lava it creates around itself when we try to engage it have swallowed any riders that were brave enough to approach.

"We started sending out messengers over a week ago, but the lava wyrm is deceptively fast and sees them as easy prey. I'm afraid that the rider you encountered after the Trials was the only one to get past it alive."

I grimaced even as my stomach sank. If the lava wyrm was really such a formidable opponent, it seemed unlikely that Erix and I would be able to best it. If Erix had any of the same thoughts though, he didn't let them show.

"Do you know where it nests?" he asked.

One of the other riders pointed out in the direction opposite of where we had approached the encampment from. "It normally attacks from that direction, although we haven't ventured out far enough to find where it rests. We've been keeping our riders close, focusing on protecting the encampment while waiting for aid."

"Some aid it's turning out to be," his companion muttered under his breath, but I could still make it out over the crackle of the fire.

I opened my mouth to defend Erix—to tell them he had volunteered to come alone even when all those assembled for the Trials shied away, but Lord Dhara beat me to the punch.

"Are you volunteering to face the beast then?" she asked, her tone icy.

His eyes bellied his cockiness, but the rider raised his chin. "Why should we trust help from one who just months ago threatened to raze our clan if we didn't follow his demands? Or some random girl we know nothing of?"

"Do you need to know anything other than she comes to your aid?" Erix asked in return, his voice controlled, but I sensed the tenuous thread of anger at the base of his tone. To my embarrassment, it sent a thrill up my spine.

The fire crackled violently in the middle of the circle, but to his credit, the rider didn't back down in the face of Erix's expressionless stare.

"Where do you come from, rider?" Lord Dhara asked me.

I swallowed thickly as all eyes turned to me.

"I'm Keera," I responded, letting the silence after my name stretch. While I had been proud of being declared a citizen of Kelvadan just a week ago, I questioned the wisdom of claiming as much in present company. When they joined with Clan Katal, I would be an enemy.

"And what clan do you ride with?"

"Keera needs no clan." Erix's tone was a threat. The rider either didn't notice or was in the mood for a fight.

"I'm supposed to accept being rescued by a filthy exile?"

I had barely processed the insult in his words when a horrible choking noise filled the air. The rider scrabbled at his throat as if strangled but an invisible noose. Erix held out a hand lazily in his direction, head tilted in a predatory manner.

"Perhaps we don't need Clan Otush's help to march on Kelvadan, if your riders are such cowards," he observed, his voice a low growl that might not have been audible if the whole encampment hadn't gone silent except for the desperate gasping of the man held in the grip of Erix's power.

The anger of his magic simmered under my own skin as he pulled at the threads connecting the desert, the tension palpable in the air and pulling at my own well of darkness in the pit of my belly.

I reached out and laid a hand on his outstretched forearm. The tension in the air severed, and the rider collapsed forward onto his hands, gulping down air. I didn't look at him though, watching as Erix's face snapped toward the point of contact between the two of us, all attention on where my hand rested on his long leather glove.

It occurred to me that our explorations of touch, something both of us seemed to need so desperately, might not be welcome now that we no longer had the privacy of the wilderness. Just as I was about to pull back, Erix's other hand came to rest over mine, pinning me in place. A deep breath hissed in and out of the holes in his mask.

Abruptly, he pulled away and stood. "We will ride for the wyrm at dawn. Be ready to ride for the united clans." Then he stalked off into the night.

Silence fell over the group, a far cry from the comforting quiet of the wilderness. All those assembled looked at me as if I had an explanation for what had happened—as if I fully understood it myself.

I stood and wiped my hands on my pants, inclining my head toward Lord Dhara. "Thank you for sharing your fire."

Then I walked off in the direction Erix had gone. The tightly wound knot of his magic was centered around the tent we had been given for the night. I hesitated outside the flap, thinking of how much I preferred the prior night's sleep without shelter, but I knew Erix would not take off his mask where the rest of the clan could see him. I supposed I could set up my own sleeping mat outside and leave him to his privacy, but that didn't seem appealing either.

Inside was dark, only lit by a single lantern. The flame waxed and waned in the rhythm of the measured breaths echoing in the silence. Erix knelt in the middle of the small space, fists clenched on his legs. He didn't respond as I stepped into his space and echoed his posture, knees barely brushing his, just as I had when he had offered to teach me how to meditate.

I thought back to that lesson and the well of magic within me. Closing my eyes, I focused on the swell of power around me, following it back to its source, not inside me, but from the man before me. Where my anger had been a dark thing, hidden at the base of my power, his was cultivated, carefully grown and tended to until it wove through every fiber of his being. I pushed my way into the tangled knot that was the base of his power. He flinched but did not push me away, physically or otherwise.

Deep within him, behind the web of darkness, I found something familiar. Something wild. Something bright.

My eyes snapped open with a gasp. I couldn't see Erix's face, but I knew he stared back at me.

"The darkness makes me strong," he murmured.

"I know." It was the same darkness that pooled within me, buried at the root of all the power I couldn't yet control. It exploded out of me to keep me alive in the face of danger—when Clan Katal had tried to execute me. "Will it be enough to defeat the lava wyrm?"

"It will have to be." He sighed, beginning to move around the small space, our tense moment shattered. The sand swished softly as he unrolled his sleeping mat against it. I moved to do the same. "I'm committed to healing the desert, and I won't let its inhabitants die before we have a chance to set things right."

I started at his use of the word 'we' before realizing he meant himself and Lord Alasdar. For a moment, I wished he didn't. I just nodded, setting up my own sleeping mat. With a thump, I laid down, staring up at the stained canvas above me with a frown.

"I hate not being able to see the sky," I admitted.

A shuffling next to me indicated that Erix mirrored my position. Just out of the corner of my vision, I spotted him setting his mask beside him, but I didn't turn to look. I didn't want to draw attention to how easily he showed his face around me.

"I have trouble sleeping indoors too," Erix admitted.

"Why?" We both stared up at the tent, not looking at each other. Somehow, it felt as if words came more easily when I didn't have to meet those clear eyes that held so much while remaining so closed off.

Erix shifted his weight, and for a moment, I thought he wasn't going to answer.

"I have nightmares about being trapped in the rock," he admitted softly. "Sometimes when I wake up and can't see the stars, I think I'm still a boy stuck in the room beneath the palace in Kelvadan."

It was only the third time we'd directly talked about his life in Kelvadan, and I held my breath, not wanting to scare him from saying more. When he didn't continue, I chanced prompting him.

"The meditation room?"

He let out a humorless snort. "If only it was just for meditation. It also makes a pretty good cell. Sometimes, when I was barely a teenager, I couldn't keep my power in check. My emotions were just too big. Always too much. It would break things or cause lightning storms like yours. When that happened, my parents would shut me in that room to try to cut me off from the desert and calm me down. It would work sometimes, but the mountain around me..."

He trailed off, but he didn't need to continue. I had felt it for myself, that oppressive silence. For one as powerful as him, so in tune with the currents of magic running through every inch of the desert, it must have been devastating.

As overwhelming as the feel of the desert in and around me could be, the complete absence of it was akin to losing an arm. It was a sense of loneliness even deeper and more aching than the isolation of my old oasis. I suspected the experience was similar for Erix.

Words came up short when it came to giving him my empathy, but touch was a language he and I were learning to speak together. I inched my hand across the space between us to find his. Warm, callused skin met mine, telling me he'd already taken his gloves off for the night. He jumped, but then interwove his fingers with mine.

"I have a trick for falling asleep inside though," he admitted.

"Really?"

"Close your eyes and focus on the feel of my magic."

I did as he asked, finding the threads of his magic with relative ease, some of them still caught up in the currents of my power after meditating together. Gently, he tugged on them, drawing me out of myself until I was floating. I knew I hadn't completely escaped myself though from the solid warmth of his fingers in the spaces between mine.

Slightly detached from myself as I was, I could feel the phantom of the rapidly cooling night breeze across my face and the vibrations of life that ran through the clansman preparing the encampment around us.

"Like the sun, it's still out there, even when we can't see it."

I squeezed his hand in silent thank you, and after a beat, he squeezed back. I don't know how long we floated together like that, but when I opened my eyes, the pale light of early dawn filtered in through the tent flap, and his hand still gently clasped mine.

CHAPTER THIRTY-ONE
ERIX

The encampment was no more by the time Keera and I mounted our horses. All the tents had been strapped onto the backs of the remaining horses and only marks in the sand from where they had stood remained. Those too would be dusted away by nightfall.

"Wait until we reach the horizon line, and then ride for Clan Katal as fast as you can," I instructed the assembled clan.

Keera tapped her brow in deference to Lord Dhara as she nodded her understanding. To my surprise, the lord echoed the gesture back at us. Lords rarely made such gestures to others. I bowed my head respectfully.

Without another word, we set out in the direction the rider had indicated the night before. Once we were out of earshot, Keera spoke.

"Do we have a plan for attacking the lava wyrm?" she asked.

"I may be skilled in combat, but even I'm not stupid enough to go into a fight with a creature of legend unprepared."

"Thanks for cluing me in," Keera quipped.

A smile tugged at my lips, but I tamped it down.

"We'll use our sabers," I started.

"How will we get close? I'm not sure about you, but I can't walk through molten rock."

"You know how we've practiced throwing rocks?" I asked.

"Yes. Are you going to throw rocks at it? I thought you just said we will use sabers." Keera looked quizzical.

"You're about the size of a boulder."

Keera stared at me as if she expected this to be some sort of joke and she was waiting for the punchline. When all I did was shrug, her eyes widened.

"You're going to throw... me?"

"That was my plan."

"And how is that supposed to help us?"

"If you can get on its back, you can find a weak point without having to approach it on foot. Besides, you stole my kill in the hunt at the Trials just fine by jumping down from above with a knife. We're just going to be using your strategy again."

Her expression was incredulous. "And what will you be doing after using me as a projectile?"

"I'll be the distraction."

She opened her mouth to argue, clearly not keen on the idea of being launched straight at a beast of legend, but it was too late to turn back. Rumbling shook the ground beneath our mounts' hooves, as if threatening to split open. Even Alza, as used to bursts of magic as she had become, pranced, showing the whites of her eyes as they rolled back in their head.

I motioned for us to dismount. This fight would be safer on foot. Neither of us would have attention to spare for spooked horses.

We continued creeping forward on foot. I drew my saber from across my back and a metallic *shink* to my left told me Keera had done the same. As we crested the ridge of a dune, a smoldering graveyard came into view.

Blackened patches of rock led into oozing magma, still glowing a reddish orange. Charred bones littered the ground, the skeletons of horses and humans intermingled. I swallowed and looked away quickly when my eyes caught on a skull small enough to belong to a toddler.

"Sands," Keera cursed under her breath. When I followed her line of sight to where she was looking, I was inclined to agree.

Curled up on a steaming pile of magma was a lizard three times the size of Alza. A long snout rested on scaley hands, each finger tipped with a claw as long as my dirk. As the creature snored, it became apparent where the rumbling in the earth was coming from. Smoke rose from its nostrils as it exhaled, curling into the pale-blue sky and making the normally piercing light of the sun hazy. Its eyes were closed.

"Do you think we could sneak up on it?" Keera murmured, voice little more than a breath.

"I'm all for trying."

Carefully, we crept down the far side of the dune, doing our best not to make a noise. As we got closer, it became more difficult to avoid small bones that would crunch under foot. The scent of charred flesh grew thick as we approached, gagging me.

We halted at the edge of the patch of gradually hardening lava the wyrm used as its bed. I dared not touch it with my boot even to test its temperature, the billowing smoke telling me that it would likely burst into flames. I blinked against the stinging of my eyes.

Keera waved, grabbing my attention. She mimed throwing, and my heart sank. She had apparently changed her mind relatively quickly about my plan being a good one. Standing as close as we were now though, I couldn't see any weakness that she might be able to exploit even if I did get her onto its back. If what Lord Dhara said was true, the only soft spot would be its underbelly, and laying like this, its vulnerability was completely hidden.

Another step closer, and Keera was standing between me and the creature, looking impatiently over her shoulder, as if now that we were here, she didn't know why I would hesitate to launch her like an arrow from a bow. I took a deep breath in through my nose, considering my options, and regretted it immediately. Between the smoke and the burnt carcasses around us, I choked. I swallowed to suppress my cough, but it was too late.

The moment I made a noise, the wyrm's eyelids snapped open, a second translucent membrane underneath blinking away its sleep.

Burning orange eyes without a pupil fixed on us immediately and the creature let out a roar so loud I was sure our horses were fleeing.

Faster than I would have thought possible for a creature that large, a clawed hand shot out, swiping at Keera. I leaped, tackling her to the ground. We rolled in the sand, the creature's claw just catching on my hood and ripping it free from my head. As it fluttered to the ground, we both sprang to our feet.

The wyrm pushed to stand, the squat, angled legs looking too short for the bulk of its barrel like body. Thin, vestigial wings lifted and fluttered from the middle of its back, causing the smoke around it to whirl and eddy in dizzying patterns.

Keera made to dart forward, but the wyrm opened its mouth, releasing a waterfall of molten lava. She leaped back, the red-hot ooze sizzling inches from the toes of her boots. With a flick of my saber and a lick of magic, I sent the nearby skull of a horse flying at the creature. It smacked it just between the eyes with a solid crack, confirming that its scales were hard as bone. Still, its triangular head swung in my direction and away from Keera.

It snarled, showing far fewer teeth than I would have expected on a beast so fearsome. I didn't have time to contemplate as another bout of lava shot from its mouth, this time in a long stream, jetting at my face. I leaped over it, tugging at the strings of the desert around me to heighten my jump. I flipped in midair to land on my feet once more.

Now the creature charged. Swinging its claws at me again, I used my saber to knock it aside. The blow reverberated through the blade and up to my shoulder. For the first time ever, I worried that Kelvar's saber would not hold up to the strength of my opponent.

I took advantage of the creature getting close to me to dart forward, trying to shove the blade down its throat, but it skittered backward at an incomprehensible speed. Clearly threatened, it made a furious hiss before vomiting up a gout of lava, forming a veritable moat around itself.

"Erix!"

Sometime during the fight, Keera had worked her way around behind me. I chanced a glance over my shoulder to find her charging at me full tilt. I only had a moment to realize her intentions before I crouched down.

Her boots landed between my shoulder blades. I heaved upwards with my body, also reaching out to pluck the strings of the desert's magic that clung to her. They were shockingly easy to grasp, and I tugged on them, flinging her through the air with the combined force of her jump and my magic.

She hung suspended in the air for a moment, and I could only watch in awe. Then the gravity defying moment slipped away, and she landed on the creature's back with a thud. She tried to roll upon landing, but the wyrm bucked at the attack, knocking her off to the side. She just managed to grab the base of its wing to avoid plummeting off, saber dangling uselessly in her other hand. Her toes brushed dangerously close to the lava covered ground as she kicked out, trying to climb back on.

The creature bucked again, spinning around, and trying to push itself up on to two legs before crashing down again. I knew I had to distract it if Keera was going to climb atop it. Using scorching lava around me, I pulled on the heat of the desert to shoot a small spurt of flames at the wyrm.

As expected, it was immune to the fire, but its attention snapped to me. Still it continued to spin away from me. I jumped forward, just to be knocked back as its muscular tail swiped a rock the size of a red wolf from the ground in my direction.

Having found a new way to attack, it continued swiping its tail back and forth, knocking rocks in my face. As it managed to send another boulder flying at me, I released a feral yell, unleashing some of my power as I swung my saber down. The rock split down the middle, skidding to a stop on either side of me in a spray of pebbles and ash.

As the dust settled, I blinked my vision clear just in time to see Keera climb astride the wyrm's back. If I thought seeing her ride a horse was incredible, watching her atop a creature of legend was nothing short of awe-inspiring.

Still, I had no time to consider such things as the wyrm resumed its efforts to unseat her. With a roar, I launched the broken half of the boulder at its side. It whipped around to face me, clearly no longer satisfied with swiping at me blindly. As it spat more lava, I darted to the side to escape its deathly breath. I ran out of space quickly, finding myself up against another smoldering patch of black rock.

Its lips pulled back from its strangely toothless gums as if to grin in triumph, clearly winding up to shoot another stream of fiery rock to where I was standing, trapped. I crouched down, ready to launch myself into the air to jump over the attack.

A fearsome cry spit the air, and Keera leaped over the crest of its head, saber held aloft. She landed on the creature's brow, digging her blade into its glimmering orange eye all the way up to the hilt.

Blood spurted out of the wound, soaking her entire arm, and splattering across her chest and face. The wyrm let out a grunting hiss, crumpling to ground in a scaley heap. It twitched violently in its death throws, but Keera drove her saber in deep, twisting it for good measure.

With one final shudder, the creature went limp. Magic still roared in the base of my neck from the fight, wanting to be let loose—to launch more stones and pull at the edges of the desert until I was the one breathing fire. Still, my gaze remained fixed on Keera, hoping she was uninjured.

She pushed to her feet as she yanked her bloody weapon free of the carcass beneath her. As she stood, she looked at me, and her face split into a dazzling smile, brighter than the sunshine starting to cut through the lingering smoke around us. As she shook her hair back from her face, splattered in blood and grinning in victory, my heart stuttered, but my magic calmed.

I smiled back, irritated that she couldn't see my face as I had put my mask on this morning. Without a thought, I reached up and ripped it off.

"I might need a hand down," she shouted from her perch. There wasn't a safe place to climb down where the ground wasn't half molten.

"I don't know. I think you look lovely up there." It was out of my mouth in an instant, and I found myself biting my cheek violently. Even if I could control my magic, the adrenaline of the fight seemed to have left my tongue on a loose leash.

Keera thankfully didn't react to my comment, instead spinning in place and surveying her surroundings. "I can certainly see a good amount from up here." She pointed behind the beast. "It looks like it has some sort of nest over there."

I headed in the direction she indicated, picking my way around still smoldering patches of lava and bones. Keera mirrored me, walking down the spine of the felled wyrm toward its hind quarters before picking her way down its tail. She paused at the end, crouching.

I nodded to her, and she leaped. With a jolt of my power, I helped her fly over the moat of lava to where I stood. I caught her around the waist without thinking, my free arm wrapping around her and pulling her close to break her fall even though it wasn't strictly necessary.

She didn't pull away immediately resting the hand not holding her saber on my shoulder and smiling up at me.

"Let's go check out the nest," she said. "It's not every day that you get to see the lair of creature straight out of legend."

I followed her toward the dense pile of bones she indicated even as I frowned. "I think legends exaggerate. It wasn't nearly as big as I thought it would be."

"Are you complaining that it didn't block out the sun as it reared up and spread its wings, as the fireside tales like to say?"

"No, although its wings were disappointing."

Keera shrugged. "Even in the stories they couldn't actually fly."

By now we had approached the circle of bones that marked the creature's home. Keera vaulted over the waist-height barrier, and I followed suit. I paused, my frown deepening as I took in the sight that greeted me inside.

A large amount of what looked like blackened pottery littered the ground, leading in a trail to a large orb of the same material. It was shattered as if broken from the inside out.

"Is that..."

"An egg."

We stared in twin disbelief, a weight settling low in my belly. It all made sense now, from the creature's size to its toothless gums.

"If it was a baby though..." I started.

Keera finished my thought for me, her grim tone echoing my own thoughts. "That means there must be a mother somewhere."

CHAPTER THIRTY-TWO
KEERA

I rested my chin on my knees as Erix wrote his message with a stick of charcoal, watching the way the flickering firelight played over his features. The setting sun cast a golden light over his skin, and I pondered it was likely the color his complexion would be if his mask hadn't hidden his skin for many years, keeping it unnaturally pale.

Finishing his note, he whistled softly at Zephyr who hopped over obediently. Erix tied the rolled-up scrap of paper to his leg with a loose bit of string.

We had scoured the baby wyrm's lair for signs of where its mother had gone, easily finding a swatch of destruction leading away toward the setting sun. After ensuring that we would be able to use it to track the larger wyrm, we had retreated back over the ridge to set up camp and plot our next move.

"He's more of a hunter than a messenger, but hopefully the desert will see the importance of our mission and guide him to the encampment," Erix said now as he double checked that his note was secure on Zephyr's leg.

"Maybe he'll fly to Kelvadan for help instead," I mused, needling him more out of habit than anything.

Erix shot me a glare, but it held no venom. "Lord Alasdar will send riders to protect the desert from the lava wyrm. Queen Ginevra only cares for her own city."

I tilted my head in contemplation as Zephyr flapped his wings, taking flight and soaring away until he was nothing more than a dark spot against the sunset.

"Why do you follow Lord Alasdar?" I asked.

"He taught me—"

I cut him off with a shake of my head. "Even if he did show you that the Heart of the Desert needs to be restored, I would think you're more powerful than him."

Erix bowed his head in acknowledgement.

"You're also the rightful heir of Kelvadan, and now the Champion of the Desert. Why wouldn't you go to the top of the palace and recover the Heart yourself? Surely you don't think the queen would turn you away if you asked. As it is, you are the one uniting the tribes, not Lord Alasdar. You don't need to serve him."

Erix's face twisted in something like a snarl. "I owe Lord Alasdar my life...my sanity."

His words wrung out my heart like a damp rag. If Erix were to turn against Lord Alasdar, he would have to see the burn marks on his back and the denial of his identity with that horrible mask for what they were. They certainly weren't the kindnesses that Erix made them out to be. I dropped the issue for now.

"How do you expect to get the Heart out of Kelvar and Alyx's rooms? Nobody has been able to open them since they died," I asked instead.

"What do you know about blood glass?"

I blinked at the sudden jump in topic, but I tilted my head, trying to remember the stories. The lord of Clan Padra had possessed a saber with a piece of blood glass in the hilt when I rode with them. The vendor at the Trials had touted its strength and rare properties.

"It's made by mixing blood with the sand of the desert before melting it into glass. It's said to amplify the power of the desert in whoever wields it," I said.

Erix nodded. "But not just in whoever wields it. It responds best to the one whose blood was used. We give our life force to the desert and bind it to her, and in return she shares her power with us. Even though it looks just like reddened glass, it is nearly impossible to break."

I contemplated Erix as he stared into the flames between us, but I stayed quiet, waiting for him to continue.

"The royal chambers at the top of the palace are sealed with two pieces of blood glass, made from the blood of Kelvar and Alyx themselves. They would only respond to them and allow the doors to open. To enter without their permission, it would be necessary to break the twin panels. To shatter one would take an immensely powerful individual. To shatter both at once and open the door, you would need a pair of the most powerful people in the desert."

Understanding dawned, both as to why Erix depended on Lord Alasdar and why Lord Alasdar would risk keeping somebody so close who was so clearly a threat to his power if his abuse were to stop keeping him in line.

"It would take both of you to get to the Heart," I concluded.

He nodded. "It will take two."

My voice was barely above a whisper, but it seemed terribly loud as I responded. "There are two of us."

Erix's eyes darted up from where he had been staring into the fire, meeting my gaze with startling intensity. "I know."

Something like hope began to kindle in my heart. While the walls between Erix and me slowly dissolved over our journey, the threat of war lingered like storm clouds in the back of my mind. The common enemy of the lava wyrm was a temporary reprieve from the battle we seemed doomed to be on opposite sides of. Now though, I saw away around the bloodshed that seemed inevitable.

"Do you think we might be... allies?" I asked.

My stomach turned to stone as he shook his head vehemently.

"No." His voice was sharp. "I don't feel about you the way one feels about an ally."

My breath caught in my throat. "What do you feel?"

"Too much." Erix looked away.

I didn't press the matter, because I was beginning to feel too much for him as well.

"Do you want to spar?" Erix asked without prelude the next morning after we finished our forms.

Internally, I cringed at the memory of the last time we fought and how easily Erix had toyed with me then. I could learn a lot from him.

"We don't have blunted sabers," I pointed out.

"We could practice hand to hand combat," Erix offered.

"I don't really know much hand-to-hand fighting."

Erix's brow quirked in a skeptical expression. It was refreshing to see his emotions so clearly on his face, as he hadn't put his mask on since we defeated the wyrm the afternoon before. Seeing him without it though, I realized how essential it was to his persona as the Viper. He was far too expressive—his thoughts clear on his face—to maintain such an intimidating reputation without it.

"What is Aderyn teaching the riders these days?" he asked half under his breath.

I paused. "You know Aderyn?"

Erix stiffened, looking away. I thought he was going to evade the question, but he surprised me. "We grew up together. Her father was one of the queen's advisors, and when he and his wife died suddenly, Queen Ginevra gave her a home at the palace."

Aderyn had once told me she knew somebody else like me, and it was part of the reason she went out of her way to help me so much. Between her kindness and the queen's training, even when I repeatedly lost control, I had been living on borrowed compassion. That kindness should have belonged to the man in front of me who carried such a heavy burden, yet cared so much for the desert. It left a bitter taste in my mouth. Erix deserved the queen's kindness as much, if not more, than I had. I wanted to hit something.

"Let's spar." I shucked off my outer layers that protected me from the sun, leaving me in only a cropped shirt and light pants held up by a colorful length of fabric Neven had packed for me to use as a belt.

Erix followed suit, unwinding layers of dark gray linen from around his shoulders and shrugging off his tunic, leaving him in only his pants, wide sash emphasizing the narrow taper of his waist from broad shoulders. My face heated from more than just the sun.

"All right, copy my stance," Erix instructed.

I did as he asked, bending my knees, and extending open palms out in front of me. He led me through a series of kicks and punches, the rush of blood through my limbs dulling but not silencing some of the bubbling anger in my core. Still, where my hidden rage had disgusted me before, now it felt like a well of energy as I let it power my strikes. Maybe it was how Erix felt when he meditated, letting his emotions siphon out his excess magic.

We moved into drills against each other, me throwing various sets of kicks and punches while Erix moved through the coordinating blocks. With each blow, I gained speed, hitting Erix's forearms when he blocked harder and harder. If I bruised him, he didn't say anything, eyes only growing brighter.

As the minutes passed, the drills sank into my muscles like thirsty soil drinking up rain after the dry season. We moved on to sparring. Muscle memories coming from somewhere deep within me surfaced until we were a blur, exchanging blows and blocks faster than my brain could keep up with. It was a dizzying, heady feeling, like after drinking too much *laka* or the weightlessness that washed over to me when Erix's hand was between my thighs.

I stumbled in my moment of distraction, and Erix pressed the advantage, tripping me with a swipe of his leg. Sand puffed up around me as I fell on my back with thud, Erix following me down. Now that my rhythm was broken, he pinned me easily, hips pressed into mine, and he held my wrists to the ground.

He stared down at me, eyes glittering with the same energy I felt coursing through me during our fight. I panted, trying to catch the breath that had escaped me when I hit the ground. With the weight of his gaze on me, it was difficult.

He didn't move to let me up, and I didn't move to push him off, a long moment passing between us. I tracked a bead of sweat down the tendon of his neck to where it pooled in the hollow of his throat. Adrenaline still pumping through my veins, I had the ridiculous urge to lick it away.

I unconsciously licked my lips, and Erix's gaze snapped to my mouth. The memory of sitting in his lap, his hand stroking me to pleasure as he palmed his own erection, burned through my mind once again. The heat in my gut grew, not anger now, but want.

Emboldened by our fight, I squirmed a bit, not trying to get away, but just enough to rub up against Erix. A choked noise escaped his throat. A smile tugged at my lips, and I did it again, watching his eyelids flutter. I had been so alone for so long, that now with Erix over me like this, my body could only cry out for more.

He transferred both of my wrists to one hand, letting the other stroke down my hair to land at my neck. The touch was light, more of a caress than anything, but I recognized the gesture. We had been in this same position before, the night he first stumbled upon my oasis. I felt the same spark of life in me now as I had then, this time laced with a burning desire.

He leaned imperceptibly closer, his eyes holding something smoldering as well as something pleading.

"Let me kiss you," he begged, as if he thought I would say no.

I nodded fervently.

The simmering in my gut burst into flame as his lips met mine, hot enough that I was sure Erix could feel it too. I licked into his mouth and groaned at the taste, as if I had been dying of thirst and he was my oasis.

He was just as greedy as me, pressing my hips into the ground. The heat from his bare torso soaked through my light clothing, and I reveled in the way his weight grounded me, even as his kisses made my head spin. He tasted salty like sweat and blood and life. For the second time, I felt his hardness against my hip, making my head spin faster than any *laka*. I ground against him, purposefully this time. He broke away from my mouth with a strangled sound at the friction, but I wasn't done devouring him. My lips and teeth and tongue found his earlobe, tracing down his neck to taste the bead of sweat that had caught my attention earlier.

"Sands, what do you do to me?" he murmured. His hand at my neck tightened, not in violence, but as if he were trying to ground himself.

"The same thing you do to me."

I knew he could sense it, our magic curling together in the inches between us, flaring as he pressed his hips against mine. Erix now traced his free hand down my body, fingers dipping into the hollow at the base of my throat, between my breasts down to my bare abdomen. His fingers danced around my navel, toying with the hem of my shirt as if asking permission. I wasted no time nodding enthusiastically.

It took both of his hands to lift my clothing over my head. I itched to touch him in return, to run my palms over the sculpted planes of his chest and shoulders, but I kept my hands where he had put them over my head. Something about the methodical way he removed each piece of fabric kept me pinned, his gaze catching on each piece of skin he exposed.

Once I was bare from the waist up, he finally let his hands wander where I wanted them. His calluses rasped the underside of my breast, but I didn't care about the roughness as his thumb brushed over my nipple, teasing it to a peak. I arched against the touch, body begging for more in ways I couldn't put words to.

My hands flew to his shoulders, fingers digging into corded muscle. I scraped at his skin with my blunted nails, pulling another groan from him.

He lowered his mouth to me again, his breath hot on my skin as he trailed his lips down my collarbone toward where his fingers toyed with my breasts.

"Do you have any idea"—he paused to drag his tongue across my taught nipple, and I whimpered—"how much you make me want?"

In response, I rolled my hips against his again, and he used a hand to pin me to the ground. Part of me insisted that I should push back against him, but the louder part reveled in having him like this, wanting me like this. He was the only person who could truly see what I was to the very core of me, and yet he still looked at me as if he hungered for more.

"I haven't let myself want anything for so long." His words were pressed into my skin as he kissed down my stomach, fingers pulling at the knot of my belt. I shimmied myself out of my pants with his help, feeling as though I would burst into flame otherwise. The look he gave me when I was completely bare made me think I might just combust anyway.

"I never thought I would care for anything as much as I cared for the desert," he admitted, fingers stroking gently through the curls at the apex of my thighs, "but you are just as wild and twice as beautiful."

I tried to tell him he was beautiful too, but my words caught in my throat as his thumb found my most sensitive spot and traced a light circle over it. He pressed open-mouth kisses over my hipbone then dragged his teeth over the sensitive skin of my inner thigh in a way that made me mewl. Then his mouth replaced his fingers, and it was as if I had been struck by lightning all over again.

"You taste even better like this," Erix growled before licking a hot stripe up my center once more.

Erix explored every inch of my sex with his lips and tongue, as if trying to memorize the feel of me with his mouth alone. I twisted against him, whether to escape the onslaught of sensations or to get closer, I could not tell. He responded by throwing one of my legs over his shoulder, opening me up further to his explorations.

"Sands Keera," he murmured against my heated flesh, "you're so perfect—so wet that I could drink."

He was right. Slick dribbled down the cleft of my ass and coated the top of my thighs, but if the way Erix lapped at it was any indication, he would never have enough. I plunged my fingers into his hair and tugged, causing him to groan against my center. I keened at the vibrations, unable to contain myself from grinding up into him. He didn't seem to mind, devouring me with me with single-minded efficiency. He added his fingers, pushing them inside me, working in rhythm with his tongue.

My climax ripped through me with earthshattering speed. My back bowed off the sand as a long breathless moan escaped me.

"Erix."

He kept licking me as I shook, a growl of satisfaction pulling painfully exquisite shocks of pleasure from me until I laid boneless and trembling. Erix crawled up my body, the achingly gentle way he pressed kisses to by belly, my breastbone, my forehead, at odds with the ravenous way he had feasted on me minutes before.

The Viper, the Prince of Kelvadan, gentle for me, an exile. Yet for all his power he had been just as alone as me.

I traced my fingers up his back, brushing over rows and rows of uniform bumps before bringing my hands to cup his face. His gaze burned into me.

"Erix," I murmured, relishing the way a tremor ran through his body at his name on my lips. "Please, Erix."

He sat back on his heels to untie his belt, pushing his pants down and kicking them off. I watched his face as he undressed, baring all of himself to me for the first time. Once he was completely naked though, I couldn't resist looking down to where he stood hard and proud—for me. My mouth went dry.

When he leaned forward again, resting his elbows on either side of my head, I wasted no time wrapping my arms and legs around him, tilting my hips up to notch us together. He huffed against my neck, sounding equally wrecked and amused at my impatience, my hair fluttering with his breath.

When the head of him slid in, where I was already so hot and aching, I let out a cry, but not so loud that I didn't hear what Erix murmured into my ear.

"Mine."

And that was it. The thing I had yearned for all those years—to belong. Erix offered it to me so earnestly, even as I ripped away his armor to find the man hidden inside who deserved so much yet took so little.

As he slid inside, deeper and deeper until I swore we were no longer separate people, I found my voice enough to moan out my own response.

"You're mine too."

His cock twitched inside me at that, and I shivered at the overwhelming feeling of fullness, of oneness. Then he began to move, pulling out partway and pushing back in torturously slowly. I rippled around every inch of him, and it was as if the very fabric of the desert shuddered with me.

As he began to move faster, I could only think of Erix, of where he moved deep within me, the burning pleasure threatening to consume me as his hips snapped against mine. His name fell from my lips again and again until he silenced me with a deep kiss, tongue sliding into my mouth as if he had to be inside me there too.

Sensation consumed me, and more than just my body. Our magic came alive. Mine flowed into him as the threads of his power bound me to him. Just as the knot pulled taught, I shattered around him with a cry. Erix responded with a roar of his own, pleasure ripping through both of us, his and mine indistinguishable.

As the sand settled around us and Erix wrung the last echoes of pleasure from my body, I knew the reason his touch had awoken something within me the very first time we met. His power and mine were one and the same.

The next morning after finishing our forms, Erix and I both looked around at a loss. There was little to do but wait for reinforcements from the encampment.

A thick sense of urgency permeated the air, but there was nothing to be done at this moment. It left me restless, looking for something to do with my hands and constantly fidgeting. The lava wyrm continued cutting its path of destruction through the desert, but we could not follow until help arrived. Right now, there was no foal to birth or monster to fight. I brushed Daiti until his golden coat shone like burnished brass, Erix looking on with a look of utmost skepticism as the fearsome stallion turned pliant under my hands.

Still, I wasn't able to sit still, as full of energy as I was. The last night, Erix and I had fallen asleep holding hands once more, and I woke with my head tucked beneath his chin, our arms and legs tangled together. It was the best sleep I'd ever had, and now I brimmed with energy.

"Do you want to learn some trick riding?" Erix asked as I went over Daiti's mane for the third time.

I raised my eyebrows at him. "Trick riding?"

"It's one of the few things I know how to do besides fighting," he admitted with a shrug.

"What kind of tricks?" I asked, interest piqued.

He only whistled, and Alza cantered over obediently. He mounted easily and urged her into a trot, making wide circles around where Daiti and I stood. I put my hands on my hips, watching expectantly. Erix braced his hands on Alza's shoulders and shot me a smirk, an expression

I hadn't seen from him before. For a moment, it made him look so uncannily like the statue of Kelvar in the palace courtyard that I had to assure myself that he was flesh and blood and not hewn of stone.

All thoughts of his similarity to Kelvar flew from my head as he leaned forward, heaving his lower body up so all his weight was on his arms. For the briefest moment, he stood on his hands on Alza's back, who trotted calmly as if he did this all the time. Then, he twisted his body in the air, swinging his legs down on either side of his mount so he now rode backward. I blinked at the feat of acrobatics, something I hadn't expected from someone as thickly muscled as Erix.

Seeing my stunned expression, he let out a huff that was as close as he came to a laugh.

I folded my arms. "When is that ever useful?"

"If it leaves my enemies half as stunned as you are, then I think it might be a very beneficial tactic," Erix teased in that dry tone of his.

"I want to try." I swung myself up onto Daiti's back and murmured him into a light trot, mirroring Alza. Picturing how Erix had done it, I put my hands on Daiti's shoulders, shifting my weight forward. Daiti faltered for a moment at my shifting before falling into a more even stride once more.

I swung my legs with all my strength, trying to lift my weight on my upper body. I wavered for a moment before coming to the realization that, as much muscle as I had put on, my arms still had nowhere near the strength of Erix's. They buckled under the combination of my weight and the unsteady jerking of a trotting horse.

As my elbows crumpled, I tried to land on Daiti's back, but my balance failed me. I rolled off his side, landing on the ground with a tooth-rattling thump.

"Keera!"

Erix's boots pounded in my direction. I stared up into the clear blue sky, blinking away the watering of my eyes as I caught my breath. Doing a quick inventory, nothing seemed bruised except my pride. A broad shadow blocked the sun shining down onto my face as Erix leaned over me.

"Are you all right?"

I nodded, no doubt grinding sand into my braided hair. "You made it look easy."

"I've had a lot of practice." He folded his arms over his chest. Before he could take a step back, I rolled, sweeping my legs at his feet, and taking him by surprise. Now it was his turn to be on his back in the dirt, and I leaped on top of him. Smiling down at him triumphantly, I straddled his hips as he looked up at me in surprise.

"I managed to pick up everything else you taught me quickly enough."

At that, Erix tilted his head, some of the playful spark fading from his eyes. "Remarkably fast. Do you think maybe you gained some of my abilities because our magic..." He gestured between the two of us, clearly at a loss for words.

We hadn't talked about what happened yesterday, but I knew Erix could feel the change too. He would pluck gently on the strings of power that bound him to me, as if testing. When I did the same, he would jump, pausing whatever he was doing to glance over at me.

"What is it?" I asked, mentally stroking the flow of magic between us, as if there was any doubt what I was asking about.

"I don't know," he admitted. He looked pensive for a moment, a deep crease forming between his brows as if trying to remember something in the distant past. "In some of the stories, they said that the bond between Alyx and Kelvar ran so deep because they were both blessed with immense magic by the desert, although their powers were very different. Alyx could heal, while Kelvar was a warrior."

"So are you saying we..." I didn't have the words to put to what I thought he might be getting at. It seemed too much, too farfetched to think we had formed a bond like the one that had moved mountains in the short time we had traveled together. Although, a whisper in my mind reminded me at had started before that, when the Viper hadn't been able to put an end to the life one lonely exile.

"Did you..." Erix began to ask, and then seemed like he thought better of it.

"Did I what?" I prompted, too curious to let the question drop.

"Did you have dreams about me? Before?"

I instantly wanted to deny it, but I stopped. It seemed impossible that he could know such a thing. Unless...

"Too many dreams. Did you?"

Erix nodded, the small motion massive in his significance. I tumbled headfirst into a storm of questions—of how and why the desert would link us in such a way.

I looked down at Erix, anxious to unravel the mystery of our shared dreams. Instead, I found Erix squinting at something over my shoulder.

"Look." He pointed to the sky.

Looking up, I spotted a familiar bird wheeling overhead, descending closer and closer to us. Zephyr landed in a rustle of feathers with a light squawk of greeting. My heart sank in disappointment, the heat in my veins forgotten, as I saw the letter still tied to his leg.

"He didn't make it to the encampment," I said.

Erix shook his head, reaching for the bird. I climbed off him so he could sit up properly, and Zephyr jumped eagerly onto his arm.

"This isn't my message." Erix began pulling the scrap of paper from Zephyr's outstretched leg. "It's a reply."

Erix's eyes darted hastily across the paper, face hardening as he read. He must have read it three times by the time he finally spoke, and I found it difficult to sit still with impatience.

"Lord Alasdar won't send aid. He orders me to return to the encampment at once, saying this shows how important it is to move on Kelvadan immediately." He pushed to his feet stalking toward Alza. I sprang up after him, incredulous.

"You can't possibly be obeying him, just like that." I stomped after him, throwing my hands in the air.

"I can't disobey an order from Lord Alasdar." His voice was tight, as if he grit it out between his teeth. "Maybe once I'm there I can impress upon him how important it is to hunt down the lava wyrm."

"And what, I'm just supposed to ride back to Kelvadan?" My voice rose in irritation. After the past few days together, I had hoped that this might have an ending other than us on opposite sides of a war. Erix stomped on those dreams with every step he took toward returning to the combined clans—to Lord Alasdar.

He paused in gathering up his items to look at me. "You could come with me."

"And do what?"

"Fight for the desert," he offered, his eyes pleading. "Join us in conquering Kelvadan and restoring the Heart."

I shook my head, the burning starting at the back of my eyes nothing compared to the burning in my gut where I knew my well of anger lived. I tamped both down. His offer called to me like cold water when I was about to die of thirst, a mirage of a future where I could belong at his side. Where he could give me the belonging I craved.

But he was still bound to Lord Alasdar's side, and there would be no place for me there. If he was intent on returning to Clan Katal, then Kelvadan was still the only place I could find home. I couldn't let him destroy it. The truth of it cut deep, like a blade straight to my heart.

"You know I don't agree that Kelvadan needs to fall," I said. "But even if I did, I couldn't go back with you. I'd follow you, Erix. But if you go back, you'll put that thing back on"—I nodded to the mask currently bundled with the rest of his supplies in his arms—"and become Lord Alasdar's weapon once more. And I won't follow a man who burns brands into your skin and calls it a kindness."

The words burned my throat as I said them, but I forced them out all the same.

Erix's expression remained stony, but the twitch of a muscle in his jaw betrayed that I had hit a nerve. "So you'll fight for a queen that makes you drink poison instead of letting you be what you are?"

It was my turn to flinch, but I stood my ground. I pictured Queen Ginevra standing outside Alyx's tomb, talking of the legacy she had left, and how she had only ever wanted a place to live with Kelvar in peace. Even if I wasn't sure a city of stone was what I dreamed of, the desire for a home was one I understood all too well. I didn't just want to protect the queen. I wanted to protect the ideal of a city where all might find a place. The image of the city Kelvar had before he fell into madness.

"I'll fight for the desert too. The one Kelvar and Alyx would have wanted." I managed to keep my voice steady. "I'm going after the lava wyrm, because I'm not going to let innocent people die while Lord Alasdar is too busy sating his lust for power to be bothered."

I stomped off to gather my own things, frown only deepening when I rolled up my sleeping mat, so close to Erix's that they overlapped. In a matter of minutes, the camp that we had shared was nothing more than a few marks in the sand. In another hour, there would be no trace at all. I paused before swinging up onto Daiti's back, looking at Erix and waiting for him to say something.

Instead, he just lifted the mask to his face, hands moving to strap it on. Seeing his silvery eyes disappear behind the lifeless metal, bile burned the back of my throat. He was going to ride away from me, leaving me behind until he disappeared into the distance, leaving me utterly alone. Just like Clan Padra had. Just like my parents.

My eyes burned, and I turned away, burying my head in Daiti's mane to hide the shame of my tears. We'd started this journey as allies, drawn together by a common cause and knowing that our parts in this war would likely separate us. I shouldn't have been foolish enough to grow attached, but in the shadows of my lonely heart, I had hoped things would be different. That this time I wouldn't be the one left watching somebody ride away.

At that thought, I wheeled around, spinning on my heel to face Erix once more and finding him already on Alza's back.

"So that's it? You're going to leave me too? Run away just like you keep trying to run away from your past?" My face was hot as I shouted, nearly spitting into the sand.

If Erix reacted, I couldn't see, the sunlight reflecting off his mask seeming dull even in the height of the afternoon.

"This isn't the same. This time, I would have you come with me...if you would choose to. This time, being alone is your choice." His voice was sharper than the blade he tended every night.

I squeezed my eyes shut, and a single tear leaked from the corner of my eye, burning a track down my sunburnt cheek. Loneliness was a well-worn path in my mind, etched into my very soul from treading it so many times. It wouldn't be hard to walk it again, and I walked it well.

Dryden had wanted me until he saw my power. Hadeon had only wanted to use me for my power. I had thought Erix was different, but it turns out he just didn't want me enough.

I opened my eyes, half expecting him to be gone, disappeared into thin air. He still sat solidly before me, his dark silhouette on his black horse so stark compared to the landscape that he seemed like a stain on the golden sands.

"No. You're the one choosing this. You're choosing to be a sword, because that's what you think will fix you."

Erix sat back as if stunned but didn't respond. I didn't wait to see if he would formulate a response. Instead, I jumped onto Daiti's back kicking him into a gallop immediately, riding off in the direction of the lava trails.

Old as it was, the lava wyrm's path wasn't hard to follow. Patches of black volcanic rock and charred bones marked an easy trail. I was thankful I didn't have to give tracking much thought, so I could let Daiti gallop. As usual, the wind in my hair and the pounding of his hooves drowned out the swirling thoughts in my head. It wasn't enough to distract me from the flow of power in my belly that tugged incessantly toward Erix, but I refused to reach down that tether to feel him. He had made a choice.

Instead, I tried to focus on what I was going to do when I found the lava wyrm. A baby had been difficult enough to fell between the two of us, but now I knew what to expect. Given that the lava I tracked had fully solidified and cooled, it was likely several days' ride ahead of me.

For any other animal, I might have suspected the mother would be much closer, but the magical creatures that inhabited the desert before it was tamed were said to be vicious beyond compare. It seemed that the wyrm didn't hesitate to leave an unhatched egg behind just to move on to better hunting grounds. Too much like my own parents.

I shook myself at such a fatalistic thought, making Daiti flip his ears back at me in disapproval. The desert had no time for despair, and neither did I if I were to survive my encounter with the lava wyrm. The important thought was the wyrm's significant head start meant I had time to prepare. Maybe if I could collect wood from any date palms I passed, I could fashion javelins.

Far too soon for my liking, Daiti's pace slowed to a walk, and his head began drooping. I had ridden him hard that day, anxious to put as much distance between myself and the place where Erix had made me feel like maybe I was not as alone as I often felt.

Still, the sun was rapidly moving toward the horizon, and we had covered a lot of ground in one day thanks to our breakneck pace. I found a cluster of palms not far from the lava wyrm's trail and dismounted Daiti to make camp for the night. While the stallion rested, I could start on making my javelins.

I was sitting cross legged on the ground, using my dirk to trim the branches to the appropriate length, when Daiti lifted his head and let out a sharp whinny. I sprang to my feet, saber in hand before I even located the cause of his reaction.

When I did, a strange warmth grew in my chest. The tether in my gut I had been pointedly ignoring all day vibrated.

Approaching my camp was a black horse bearing a dark rider. As they came closer, sun reflected off dark curls, uncovered by a hood or mask. Erix dismounted before me, shifting his weight from foot to foot, but not saying anything. I plucked the strings of power between us and received an answering touch.

"I'm making javelins," I said by way of greeting, gesturing to the pile of raw palm wood I'd collected.

"Good idea," Erix said. "I'll help."

Erix set up his camp, laying his bedroll right next to mine as he had the night before.

CHAPTER THIRTY-THREE
ERIX

The silence as we rode was companionable, but Keera and I both eyed the charred remains of horses and other animals warily. The death in the trail of the lava wyrm only solidified my decision to come after her. I couldn't let such a creature threaten all the clans, and I wouldn't let Keera face it alone.

Of course, that meant I was leaving Lord Alasdar and the clans to face Kelvadan alone. I gritted my teeth and tried to force that thought down into darkness with the constant voice of the desert where I could attempt to ignore it. After all, defeating the lava wyrm would help the desert also. I could return to Lord Alasdar after, and we would still restore the Heart.

Then I might be able to convince Keera to come with me, when innocent lives were no longer endangered by the wyrm. I knew though, that I couldn't watch her ride away again. Seeing her silhouette shrink on the horizon had caused an ache in my chest, deeper than the root of the string of magic that now connected us. Another week with her would give me the time I needed to convince her to stand at my side with Lord Alasdar.

"Tell me about crossing the desert." Keera broke the silence, pulling me from my ruminations. I sensed she was trying to distract herself from the trial ahead, and I couldn't fault her for it.

"It took months," I admitted. "I lost count of how many days we had been riding less than halfway through. Lord Alasdar had done it once before, and he insisted I complete the journey too, to see the damage done by Kelvar.

"We followed the legend, setting off in the direction of the rising sun every morning. The tales say that crossing to the sea is the greatest of tests—that it will wear you down and put many obstacles in your path to break you and see if you are worthy to carry the magic of the desert in you. After all, she only deigned to let the clans live here after the first rider made the journey from the mountains and blessed their descendants with their power.

"Along the way we faced predators and storms. I was barely in my right mind to begin with after having run off into the desert on my own, and I was plagued by hallucinations and mirages. In the shifting sands, I saw myself losing control and all the people I had known struck down by my power. I watched the land crack apart before my feet to swallow all nine clans.

"But we kept going, and at last we saw the ocean."

I hadn't meant to say so much, but Keera stared at me as if transfixed. "Tell me."

"It stretches as far as the eye can see, just like the sands except sparkling and bluer than anything you've ever seen. When we got there, my horse splashed straight into it, bucking and playing in foamy waves.

"And right there on the shore stood a temple, beginning to crumble, one corner of the roof caved in. Lord Alasdar said it was worse than when he had first come years ago. Inside was an altar, carved of the whitest stone I had ever seen and cracked down the middle. In it was a slot for a gemstone as big as my fist, and it was empty, the indent blackened as if burned."

Keera looked over from where she rode beside me, a combination of awe and concern on her face. I swallowed thickly, not having shared that tale with anybody before. Lord Alasdar had insisted we keep the truth about the Heart to ourselves, lest any power-hungry lord or warrior try to take it for themselves. Instead, we fed the clans half truths about why the desert unraveled at the seams.

"I want to see the ocean," Keera said, drawing me from my thoughts.

"It's not an easy trip."

Keera shrugged. "I've survived the elements enough already, and after spending so much of my life in one place, I want to see every inch of this land."

I itched to tell her I would cross the desert as many times as she wanted with her, but I bit it back. Only yesterday, I had nearly been drawn away from her by Lord Alasdar's call. Even now, my brain skirted around what would happen when I returned after directly disobeying his orders. The healing scars on my back itched.

"Look, we might be able to make camp there tonight," Keera pointed at a greenish spot on the horizon.

I nodded. The horses could use the oasis, and both Keera and I could afford a bath. We hadn't been able to fully wash since defeating the baby lava wyrm, and the smell of smoke still clung to my hair.

The idea of chasing water droplets across Keera's golden skin with my tongue jumped to the front of my mind, and I hardened in my pants. I shifted my weight, trying to ease the sudden ache even as I looked forward to our bath.

"No," Keera muttered in a disbelieving tone. The undercurrent of distress spilling out of her and stirring the desert around me snapped me from my fantasy. I looked back and forth, searching for the cause of her anxiety, only to find her eyes firmly fixed on the oasis, growing closer with every step.

"What is it?"

"I'm back; it's my oasis."

I squinted, and the shape of the palms and brush with a scattering of rocks off to one side niggled my memory. It was the same clearing I had found Keera in months ago—the first time I felt that calming stillness that only filled me under her touch.

She urged Daiti into a canter, racing toward the unassuming campsite where so much had changed. Alza and I caught up with Keera just as she dismounted near the rocky edge. She picked around it, me following at a distance, not sure if this was a private moment but unable to step back when she was so clearly upset.

On the far side of the rocks, a ripped piece of canvas fluttered in the breeze, torn free of the propped-up stick structure of a lean-to. Keera fell to her knees in the sand, reaching into a gap in the rocks that formed one wall of the ruined structure.

When she sat back, she held a battered pack in her hands. She dumped the contents on the sands, revealing a tattered sling, dented cookware, and a few mismatched pieces of clothing. She brushed her hands over the odds and ends, a sad, stricken expression twisting her face.

"This was where I lived," she said. "This was all I knew."

My knees buckled, hitting the sand next to her. The anger that was always close at hand snapped against its tether. However, the blinding heat was tempered by a bone-deep sadness.

"How long?" I asked.

"Almost ten years."

My hands shook with barely controlled rage at the evidence of how narrowly Keera had survived, barely more than a girl when she was turned out into the desert to survive alone.

"It wasn't the hunger or the thirst or the constant danger of predators that got to me in the end," she said as if she could hear my thoughts, running the nearly disintegrated straps of the sling through her fingers. "It was the isolation. Knowing that there wasn't anybody in the world who cared if I lived or died."

I knew what it was like to feel alone, but it paled in comparison to what lay before me now. I had been isolated by my power and the distance caused by the overwhelming weight of expectations piled onto my shoulders. Out here in the wilderness, Keera had been truly alone.

My arm wrapped around her waist, pulling her to me. She came willingly, turning into me and burying her face in my chest—a far cry from the feral woman I'd encountered at this very oasis. I clutched her to me so tightly, it was as if I could press her shape into my very soul.

"You're not alone anymore," I murmured into her hair, burying my nose in the tangled strands and taking in the acrid smell of smoke that couldn't quite hide Keera's warm earthy scent. "And I cared whether you lived or died the moment you spit in my face."

Keera snorted into my chest but wound her arms around my waist. "I think you landed firmly on the side of wanting me dead."

I shook my head, my lips brushing back and forth over the top of her head. "From the moment I saw you, feral and defiant, you started weaving yourself into my fate. After you rode off into the night, I kept seeing your face in my mind, even if I didn't know why then."

"Do you know now?"

Keera tipped her face up to look at me, reddened from the heat and the sun, and a single tear tracked down her cheek. I cupped her face and wiped that salty drop away with my thumb. "I think the desert was telling me something. Normally, the whispers of power in my head are distracting at best and maddening at worst, but this time, they wanted me to know that you were the one person who could be my equal—who could understand my loneliness and crack through the hardened shell I had isolated myself in."

With a flutter of her eyelids, Keera blinked away the wetness clinging to her lashes. "Let's take a bath."

I drew back at the non-sequitur, and the ghost of a smile tugged at her lips.

"I want to make a good memory here to drown out the bad."

I stood, scooping Keera up into my arms as I went. She looped her arms around my neck and her legs around my waist, only letting go when we got to the edge of the water.

There, she toed off her boots, the rest of her clothes falling to the ground with soft swishes. I had to tear my eyes away from every inch of skin she revealed to turn my attention to my own clothes. I unstrapped my sword from my back, laying it gently in the sand before turning toward the rest of my clothes. By the time I finished undressing, Keera had already started wading into the water, water lapping at her muscular thighs.

I hurried to follow her, stopping only to grab a lump of soap out of my packs. When I joined Keera, she stood in water up to her waist, proudly displaying sun-kissed curves that did nothing to detract from what had quickly become a warrior's body. More than that though, what made my mouth suddenly dry, was the look in her eyes as her gaze raked over my bare chest and shoulders before moving lower. After so long hiding every inch of skin, the intensity of her focus made me dizzy.

She stepped toward me, meeting me halfway before plucking the soap from my fingers, hanging limply at my side.

Then she began to wash me. She dragged the soap over my chest and abdomen, taking her time to run her fingers over every bit of my skin, investigating the dips and valleys of my muscles. I itched to return the favor, but I seemed to have lost agency over my body, overwhelmed at the sensation of being explored so thoroughly. Different than our coupling before, which had been hot and intense and spontaneous, Keera's touch was slow and intentional, leaving me utterly exposed.

She walked around me, continuing her attentions on my back. She worked the soap through my hair, and I shivered as she rubbed her fingers where it curled at the nape of my neck. She moved her lower, her touch heartachingly gentle as it skated over the brands on my shoulders, alternately sensitive and numb where my nerves had been burned away. I began to tremble in earnest.

"What's wrong?" Keera asked, close enough that her breath tickled the back of my neck.

"I'm afraid." I squeezed my eyes shut against the admission.

"Of me?" The warmth of her skin began to pull away. but I shook my head quickly. My hand shot up to trap hers where it rested on my shoulder.

"Kelvar nearly tore this desert apart out of love for his wife. But I—" My breath escaped me in a shudder. "The world will not survive the way I feel about you."

Keera's forehead landed between my shoulder blades and suddenly I needed to be touching more of her. It was agony not to.

I spun around, plunging my hand into her hair to tilt her head back for a kiss. With a splash, the lump of soap fell forgotten into the water at her side. Her mouth opened to me easily, even as her tongue challenged mine. In this fight, as in all others, she was bold and intoxicating. The need to win this battle hit me nearly as intensely as the desire pooling at the base of my spine, and the pressure building in my cock.

I wanted to best her. And I wanted to surrender.

Without breaking the kiss, I walked her backward toward the far edge of the water, bordered by a series of flat rocks. The back of her knees hit the ledge, forcing her to sit as I followed her down, falling to my knees in the water with a splash.

She gasped in surprise as I sat back on my heels, grabbing her thighs and pulling her to the very edge. I looked up at her from between her legs, my fingers trailing up her inner thighs. The muscles jumped under my touch.

"Yes?" I asked, pressing a kiss to the inside of her knee.

She nodded. "It's always yes with you."

I dragged my mouth up her leg, mouthing and nipping as I went. As I moved toward her center, I pulled her legs over my shoulders. Opened up to me like this, her musky, intoxicating scent overwhelmed me, and I could wait no longer.

At the first drag of my tongue up her center, my eyes rolled back in my head both at the taste and the breathy whine it pulled from Keera. I worked her slowly at first, remembering how she liked to be touched, working her up until her hands wound their way into my hair.

When I added my fingers, sliding them slowly inside her, her litany of moans and whimpers raised in pitch. The fingers against my scalp changed from scratching lightly to pulling. Her legs trembled near my ears, and I knew she was close to the peak of her pleasure. I redoubled my efforts, pumping my fingers inside her in time with relentless swirl of my tongue over her most sensitive spot. I craved her release, needed to feel the way I made her come apart.

With the most beautiful cry I had ever heard, she shattered, pulsing around my fingers, coating my tongue in her release. That, combined with the way the flow of her magic shuddered through me, was enough to make me groan, the echoes of her pleasure ripping through us both. I kept licking her through it, so entranced I kept going just to feel it again.

Keera tried to pull me up her body, but I shook my head. "One more." My voice broke as I said it. I had intended to conquer her, but now I was the one begging.

She generously obliged, loosening her grip on my hair so I could lower myself to her center once more. By the time she shook through another release, I was drunk, ready to keep drawing pleasure from her with my lips and tongue until I couldn't breathe.

Keera had other ideas though, pulling me up onto the rock beside her and pushing me onto my back. My mind, already sluggish, skidded to a halt as she crawled on top of me, rubbing herself up and down my neglected cock. I pulsed against her as she coated me in her wetness, grabbing at her hips. My fingers dug in so hard I feared they would bruise her, but Keera didn't seem to care, just lifting to notch my tip into her entrance.

As she lowered herself down with aching slowness, I hoped my fingertips would leave bruises, so I could look at them and know this was real, not just an illusion sent from the desert to tip me over into madness. After all, as Keera began to roll her hips, I felt like a man possessed. I pushed up against her, and together we found a pace that threatened to shred what remained of my sanity.

"This"—I rubbed my fingers around where I entered her, sliding easily through the obscene wetness there—"is going to drive me mad."

At that she tightened around me more than I thought possible, and I nearly swallowed my tongue. Still, I managed to lean forward and growl in her ear. "And I never want to be sane again."

Keera threw her head back as she rode me, and I remained mesmerized by every move that she made, every shudder and twitch that came over her beautiful body.

"Look at you," I murmured, my voice a broken rasp that I barely recognized as I traced my hands up her sides. At that Keera looked down at me, a smile forming on her face even as she looked dazed with pleasure.

"Look at *you*." She pinned me there with her gaze as she rolled her hips with increasing speed, and I was helpless as my release barreled down on me. How could I not be struck dumb by the way she looked at me—like I was something miraculous when that was clearly her?

We came together, her name tearing from me in a roar. Our releases rippled through the magic between us, so intense that I was sure the entire desert could sense the shuddering that never seemed to end. I hoped they did.

When I finally drifted back to my body, Keera smiled down at me, more brilliant than the setting sun behind her. I reached out to push back the dark hair that clung to her sweaty temples. She leaned into the touch, a slight laugh racking her body, the movement making me gasp with aftershocks of pleasure.

"What?" I asked.

"I think we might need another bath."

Chapter Thirty-Four
Keera

I slept better than I might have that night, worn out and sated by Erix's and my explorations. Still, falling asleep to the familiar silhouettes of date palms and rock formations that had been my only company for so long made me jumpy. I woke up many times in the night, squeezing Erix's hand where it interlaced with my own to make sure he was real, afraid I would wake up to find everything to be a dehydration-induced hallucination. I didn't think I could survive being alone again—not now that I had been with Erix, bonded in a way that did more to soothe the ache of loneliness than being surrounded by a city full of people.

When we rode away in the morning, I was glad to put the oasis to Daiti's tail. As we set out, I turned to take one last look at the sight that had been my entire world for too long. The borders of my existence only continued to grow, but the girl that had been trapped here, abandoned by her own parents, lived inside me. She still itched to scream and rage at the injustice of it all, even as she was afraid of the power that had twisted inside her, lashing out before going silent for too long.

Erix paused beside me. "You never have to go back."

I shook my head. It wasn't enough. It would never be enough to undo what had happened to me.

"Step back," he instructed. I looked at him curiously, but did as he asked, urging Daiti away from where he sat on Alza.

Erix reached out toward the oasis and closed his eyes. A tug at my gut made me jolt, Daiti shifting beneath me as the power of the desert coalesced around Erix. A roaring filled my ears, coming from everywhere as well as inside my own head.

The ground trembled and shifted beneath my feet, and a cloud of dust, like a small sandstorm, swept through the oasis before us, blocking it from view. Then, as suddenly as it came, the roaring stopped and the magic trickled away from Erix, like sand running between my fingers.

Swirls and eddies of dust began to settle, revealing nothing but smooth sand. The palms and the pool of water had been washed away, and even the rocks I'd pitched my lean-to against had been erased by Erix's power, as if they had never been there at all. Erix had reshaped the desert for me.

I nodded, not knowing how to show my thanks, but sure Erix could feel my gratitude nonetheless. In reality, I knew destroying the place that had been my prison for so long changed nothing, but a knot inside me loosened knowing it was gone just the same.

I kneed Daiti around and left it all behind me, Erix riding at my side.

Picking up the lava wyrm's trail again was easy, the black patches of hardened lava marring the ground like scars. The massive beast had a head start on us, and seemed to move quickly as we followed its path for the greater part of a week, even though we rode hard every day.

Every morning, Erix and I started the day practicing our forms side by side, the connection between us growing even stronger as our magic flowed together. Each night, the bond between us was blown wide as we lay in each other's arms. Even as we went to face down the most dangerous creature to have been seen in centuries, the mood between us was as light as it had ever been those first few nights.

I couldn't get enough of Erix, exploring every inch of him with my fingers and mouth every chance I got. Erix, while still looking dumbstruck every time I reached out to touch him, seemed to melt into the attention the more I gave it to him. It emboldened me, as if I could rub his salt and sandalwood scent into my skin.

On the second night, I took Erix into my mouth, craving even his taste. Erix shuddered and wrapped my hair around his fist, and I reveled in how it bound him to me as much as I to him. It didn't last very long before he pushed me off him, pulling my hips into the air and driving into me punishingly from behind.

As the nights passed though, the signs indicated that we were gaining ground on our quarry, and the mood became more subdued. The patches of lava we saw now simmered, and the smell of smoke coming off the trail we followed took on the unmistakable stench of decay and rotting flesh.

After a week, we sat around our campfire, using the fire to harden the tips of the javelins we had worked on as we rode. Tonight, I had managed to start the fire without a flint, a spark of my magic jumping forth easily to light the tinder. Now that I could feel the way he channeled the immense power within him through our bond, I learned how to do it myself more easily. I could only hope that the increased use of my power would be enough for us to defeat the lava wyrm. I tried not to think of how many innocent clanspeople would be swallowed by its fire if we failed.

"I think we'll find the lava wyrm tomorrow or the day after." Erix drew a whetstone over his saber in smooth motions as he spoke. The metallic grating had become almost soothing to me as this was a nightly routine of his.

I nodded. The nearby lava trail contained areas that still glowed reddish orange and bubbled lazily.

"Do you think we'll be able to kill it?" I asked.

It was a question that had weighed on both our minds for days. I could tell Erix wondered at it even as he hadn't voiced it, in the way he contemplated the carnage in our path, his mouth set in a hard line.

"We have no choice." He shrugged casually, despite the grimness of his words.

I hugged my knees to my chest and watched his hands work, his movements clean and efficient. He no longer wore his gloves, which stayed stowed in packs along with his mask.

"I think we should use the same tactic as last time," Erix continued. "Even if this one is larger, its weakness should be the same. No matter how thick its scales are, its eyes should still be vulnerable."

I swallowed, remembering how the baby wyrm had nearly bucked me off, the heat rolling off its hide nearly unbearable as I climbed across its back to dig my saber into its skull. Still, if Erix was volunteering to draw the attention of a fully grown wyrm to give me a chance to strike the killing blow, then I would face down the challenge. Clan Otush had suffered enough of the baby wyrm's wrath, and I shuddered to think what would happen if a fully grown adult would do if it set its sights on a clan encampment. Still, I wondered if there were another way to defeat it.

"Couldn't you just destroy it with your magic like you did the oasis?" I asked.

Erix stared into the fire, opening and closing his mouth a few times as if considering his answer.

"I can't usually do things like that," he admitted. "Occasionally though, the whispers in my head tell me to try things that would normally be impossible. I almost feel that the desert wants things... that she lets me do things I shouldn't be able to when it fits her purposes."

A stared, wanting to argue that his explanation didn't make sense, but that wasn't completely true. While some people, like the queen, spoke of the desert like it was a force of nature, powerful but uncaring, it had never seemed that way to me. The desert was a friend and an adversary, and sometimes I could taste her moods and her intentions on the air. I had thought I had given her sentience in my isolation, to make myself feel less alone, but Erix felt it too. The old ways of the clans acknowledged it too, in their belief that the Champion was chosen by the desert, and not just by their skill in a duel.

"I'm glad you're with me," I admitted. While I had set out to fell the wyrm without him, I had to admit it likely would have been a fool's errand on my own, ending in a smoldering grave. It was a mission I had taken despite that risk, for if I could not find acceptance among the desert's people, then I could at least die for them. This still might be my end, but with the immense power Erix held in the tips of his fingers—

magic that he showed me how to use more and more every day—we had a chance.

"I'll be with you, for better or for worse," Erix murmured.

"It might be for worse."

"I knew that when you spit in my face the first time we met, but here I am anyway." Erix's smile was small, but it bolstered my courage all the same.

The mood was solemn as we set out the next morning. Even the horses seemed to sense the tension in the air, Daiti forgoing his usual show of displeasure when I loaded our supplies. As we mounted, Erix and I both checked that all our weapons were within easy reach. Both of us carried our sabers across our back and dirks at our hips, along with a supply of javelins lashed to the horses' backs.

By midday, all the trails of lava we passed were red-hot and liquid, some still trailing in treacherous streams. The horses picked their way across the dangerous terrain, slowing our progress.

The magma became more and more prevalent, making it difficult to make headway, until we came across a patch of molten rock the size of the pool at the oasis. The surface boiled ominously, the stillness of the desert broken by the thick *plat* of bubbles popping on the surface of the viscous liquid.

Erix squinted, raising a hand to his brow to peer to the other side of the fiery pond. I mirrored him, only to find that beyond the expanse of lava lay only unmarked sand.

"The trail just... ends."

I frowned, looking around. Off to either side spread pristine golden earth, not even disturbed by variation in the sand to tell us where our quarry had gone.

"It can't be injured or dead," I mused. "We would notice a body that big."

Erix's brow twisted in thought. "I know the legends say their wings are too frail to support them but... it didn't fly off, did it?"

I opened my mouth to say that anything seemed possible at this point, but a bone-rattling rumbling cut me off. Even though I screamed for Erix to watch out, it was too late. A roar split the air and the magma before us rippled and writhed before exploding out. A giant blackened form burst forth from the center of the pit, the lava wyrm's blunt, triangular head cresting the surface before rising up and up into the sky on an impossibly large body.

Daiti screamed in terror. So fixated was I on the beast before me, erupting forth from a lake of its own lava, that I didn't have time to grab on to my mount's neck as he reared. I slid from his back, hitting the sand, and rolling. By the time I got to my feet, he was already running away, the black shadow of Alza hot on his heels. Any hope of using our javelins against the wyrm was lost with them as they retreated. Either Erix had dismounted more gracefully or had just recovered faster as he was already crouched, weapons drawn.

The wyrm before us stood up on two hind legs, spread its membranous wings, and shook itself, sending gobs of fiery rock spraying everywhere. I raised my arms against the spray, and a few droplets landed on my sleeves, burning through to scorch my skin beneath.

An invisible hand shoved me to the side, a brush of Erix's power helping me leap out of the way just in time for the wyrm to crash down onto all fours. Its head now between Erix and me, it swung back and forth, maw opening wide to show teeth nearly as long as the saber that I unsheathed.

One glowing pupilless orange eye fixed on me, and it swung toward me with a snarl. Its breath gusted over to me in a choking cloak of sulfur and smoke. I took the opportunity to try to sashay to the side, hoping to skirt around it and rejoin with Erix where we could execute our plan.

The wyrm had other ideas, vomiting up a gout of lava as it spun, creating a half circle of fire around it that effectively separated me from Erix. I heard him shout on the far side of the beast, catching its attention. A clang of metal on hardened scales signaled that he had attacked while I distracted it, and the wyrm whipped around, faster than I would have thought possible for a creature ten times the size of Daiti.

I threw myself backward, just in time to avoid the club of its tail, the end of which was decorated with wicked blackened spikes that the young wyrm had lacked. As the appendage whistled by, hot wind whipped my face, as if I had leaned too close to a fire while cooking. Where the young wyrm's flesh had been uncomfortably hot to touch, I knew the scales of the adult would burn and blister my skin on contact. Still, I had a job to do.

The creature scuttled forward and away from me, apparently advancing on Erix. I unconsciously tugged the tether between him, finding his power knotted tight and strong on the other end as he fought. The feeling reinforced my resolve. If he wasn't there to throw me atop the wyrm's back, I would have to launch myself.

My feet churned in the sand as I pushed myself forward into a run, pumping my arms and pushing myself as fast as possible to gain momentum. I reached for the power of the desert flowing around me, through the well in my gut, in Erix, even in the wyrm before me, where the magic tasted rotten and blackened. As I gathered my strength in my thighs to leap into the air, I threw myself into a current of power. I flew through the air, breath catching in my throat as a few threads of Erix's power tugged me even higher. Then gravity grabbed me once more, and I plummeted toward the wyrm's broad scaley back, poised to land right between its shrunken wings.

I landed in a crouch, a scream tearing from my throat as the heat of its scales melted through the soles of my boots in a split second. Unconsciously trying to avoid the heat, I lost my balance, pitching sideways toward the ground below.

I flung out the arm holding my saber, hoping to stab into the wyrm's flesh and stop my fall, but it skidded across flesh as hard as any armor. The blade screeched against scales, throwing sparks into the air as I dropped.

I landed flat on my back, forcing all the air from my lungs and turning my vision white. A shout from Erix warned me just in time for me to roll blindly away, a foot tipped with deadly talons crashing down where my torso had been just a moment before. However, I wasn't quite fast enough, and the wyrm's weight came down on my shin instead.

My scream drowned out the crunch of my bone as it gave way under the beast's massive weight.

"Keera!"

Erix's shout cut through the haze of pain, the fibers of his magic pulling taught and shuddering with tension as he raged against the wyrm. I blinked against the watering of my eyes, finding myself still halfway under the creature, the flesh on its belly a sickly white color.

It's underbelly—the only place besides its eyes where it was unprotected by scales.

Clangs and cracks, along with the rage pouring down the bond from Erix, told me he had the creature thoroughly distracted. Rolling onto my front, I used my elbows to drag myself forward, further beneath the wyrm to where I hoped housed its vital organs. My one leg dragged behind me uselessly, twisted at an odd angle, but I grit my teeth against the white-hot sensation.

The body above me heaved as the wyrm prepared to spit lava at Erix. Before it could, I shoved my sword up hard. Boiling blood dripped down my arm as I drove my blade in all the way to the hilt. I screamed but didn't let go, twisting savagely as the wyrm roared in agony. The form shuddered and convulsed.

When I was sure I had hit my mark, I let go of my sword, trying to crawl out from beneath the dying beast. I was too late. Partially twisted onto my side, I threw up one arm to shield myself from the massive form collapsing atop me.

Erix's screaming filled my head as searing heat engulfed me.

Chapter Thirty-Five
Erix

My eyes were screwed shut but I could still see the Keera disappearing beneath the hulking form of the lava wyrm as it convulsed in its death throes. My hands clenched into fists, yanking at the fabric of the universe as I howled my rage at the sky. As it so often did, battle had loosened my control, and there was no Keera smiling down at me triumphantly to calm my blood.

Wind whipped around me, tugging at my clothes with unnatural force as the storm of my fury closed in around me. I forced my eyes open, determined to get to Keera, to hack the fallen lava wyrm off her bit by bit if I had to.

I was greeted by the sight of swirling ash, the lava wyrm disintegrated by my rage, its massive body now no more than dust on the wind. I wanted to curse the desert for letting me do such a thing only now, when a few seconds earlier such a show of power would have spared Keera. Instead, the rage rushed out of me as I lurched forward to a huddled form on the ground. I leaped over the river of lava that had separated us with a jolt of my power, still coming easily after a fight.

In a few bounds, I was at Keera's side. I skidded to my knees, my sword falling forgotten at my side. My throat closed as I took in the sight before me.

One whole side of Keera's body was burnt, still-smoldering clothing melted into her body where the wyrm's unnaturally hot flesh had pressed into her. The angry red skin ran extended from her unnaturally bent leg up to the side of her face, where the hair on that side of her head had been burnt away completely.

I cupped her unburnt cheek in my hand and turned her face toward me. The whimper that tore from her at the movement ripped my heart in two even as it restarted its beating. Keera was alive.

"Keera, stay with me," I urged, patting her cheek.

She groaned and her eyelids fluttered. "Erix."

"I'm going to help you."

I couldn't do it here, on this lava-ridden battlefield, still smoldering and stinking of death. The dust that had once been the lava wyrm still drifted on the air, a gray powder settling into Keera's hair, sticking to her lips and wounds, and turning her a deathly gray. Leaving her out here would likely lead to infection. I had to move her.

With all the gentleness I possessed, I slid my arms under Keera, trying to touch the burned side of her as little as possible. Still, she let out a high-pitched sound somewhere between a scream and a gasp. She tried thrashing against my grasp, despite my murmured reassurances, but only managed to jostle her broken leg. I clutched her to me, trying not to let her fall, but succeeding in digging my hand into the mangled skin of her shoulder.

At that, Keera did scream before going limp in my grasp. Relief and worry crashed through me in equal measure. I bent to retrieve both of our swords before trudging up in the direction the horses had run. It didn't take me long to find them, having been scared but not willing to go too far from their masters. Seeing their forms on the horizon, I whistled and Alza cantered toward me immediately. Daiti trailed behind less obediently but quickened his pace when he saw the bundle in my arms.

The stallion seemed to forget his usual animosity toward me as he approached, snuffling Keera's hair and letting out high pitched whinnies of distress.

"Me too, friend," I agreed, eyeing him.

I needed to get Keera to fresh water where I could clean her wounds and rehydrate her. She was already beginning to lose too much moisture through her burned skin, oozing onto my clothes as I held her. A dangerous predicament in the desert.

She couldn't ride, and I didn't want to tie her to Daiti and risk injuring her further. Alza held perfectly still as I lifted Keera onto her back, as if the mare could sense the gravity of the situation. Once I got Keera settled, I mounted behind her, holding her to my chest and setting off in a direction at random. We had helped the desert today by ridding it of the lava wyrm, and she could repay us by leading me to water.

I rode as fast as I could, trying to balance holding Keera tight enough to avoid unnecessary bumping of her unconscious form while not putting excess pressure on her skin, blisters already bubbling up before my eyes. Some on her shoulder burst as she rubbed against me, coating both me and her in the sticky fluid within—fluid she couldn't afford to lose with the unforgiving sun beating down on us.

Daiti trotted alongside us without my urging, clearly loyal to Keera. It was probably only an hour or two before a herd of oryx appeared on the horizon, but it felt like a lifetime as I held Keera to my chest. She had seemed so strong not long ago, riding and training and fighting with all the ferocity of a wild caracal. Limp in my arms though, with her head lolling back onto my shoulder as her breath came in shallow pants, I was reminded just how much of her life she had spent flirting with the edge of death.

I spotted the oryx, a dark patch on the horizon, and nudged Alza in their direction. Where there were herds, there would be water. As we approached, I tugged on the magical tether that had sprung up between Keera and me. Though I could feel her magic swirling and eddying on the other side, there was no response. A lump rose in my throat, and I swallowed it down.

The oryx scattered as we cantered into their midst, but I paid them no mind, heading toward a dip in the landscape. Sure enough, at the bottom was a crudely dug well surrounded by worn stones, likely dug for a clan's temporary encampment before moving on as they pursued the herds.

I dismounted, draping Keera over Alza's neck so she wouldn't fall as I retrieved my sleeping mat. Only after it was spread out on the ground did I lift Keera down, laying her gingerly on the mat where I could wash her and tend to her. Her lashes fluttered and she let out a cracked groan as I laid her down, but still did not wake.

I used my pouches to gather as much clean water as I could before kneeling beside her to set to work. Keera finally woke when I began peeling her charred and tattered clothes away from her raw skin. As painful as her unconsciousness had been, I soon wished for it as her screams tore through the air. At first, she batted at my hands, fighting and twisting against me as I peeled skin away with cloth.

I tried to subdue her gently, but she fought me like a feral sand cat, hissing and crying out. Only when I did my best to pour calm down the tether between us did she settle, although every stifled shriek she let out cut me like a knife.

The work was slow and painstaking. My world narrowed to my task of undressing and cleaning every inch of Keera's skin. I thought of nothing beyond gently rinsing her seeping skin and keeping a mental hand on the bond between us, gripping on to it as if I could keep her from slipping away even as she stayed delirious, conscious of nothing but the pain.

"Stay with me, love," I murmured into her hair. "I know you're too stubborn to die on me. You've survived so much—don't let this be your end."

I was no stranger to burns, and while none of Keera's skin was the blackened color of flesh that had been damaged all the way to the root, beyond what time could regrow, it covered so much of her. She was losing a lot of fluid and would continue to for days until she healed. It would take a great deal of luck for her to make it that far without infection setting in. I knew better than to trust in luck.

By the time Keera's entire side was bandaged in strips of my spare clothes and her broken leg set in a makeshift splint, the unburnt skin on her left side was ashen where it was normally tan. Her shrieks and twitches had died to whimpers and shivers.

She needed more help than I could give her.

I cast about me as if aid would materialize, but only saw our mounts, hovering nearby with an air of concern. I knew better than to think that the desert would offer salvation. She rewarded those who served her, but she was a harsh mistress. Keera knew it too.

There was one way to ask for her help though.

It was something some riders did before battle or in times of great duress to ask for the desert's guidance. I had seen Izumi do it often, although we never spoke of it. If the desert favored a warrior, they would be granted a temporary rush of power. Some even claimed to hear the desert's voice in their mind, guiding them, giving them new abilities.

I had shied away from the custom, already plagued by the desert's constant voice and power I wrestled to keep contained. Fear of what I might do with such a surge of magic had always made me wary.

Legend had it though, that Alyx's magic had blessed her with the power to heal. I had never given my great-grandmother's legacy much thought, as overpowered as I was by the stories of Kelvar. Now though, I itched for a taste of her abilities, if only to ease the suffering of the woman before me. A woman who had sewn herself into the fabric of my being with her ferocity, not taking no for an answer, until she had stripped away all the armor I surrounded myself in to lay her calloused hands on the beating heart of the man underneath. As rough as her hands were, they had been heartachingly gentle with me, bringing me peace where I had known none before.

A bitter laugh tore from my throat, a broken, hysterical thing that startled the horses. All these years running from Kelvar's legacy, and here I was following in his path—giving my heart to a woman who was destined to be my enemy. I hadn't lost her yet though, and I wouldn't if there was anything I could do.

I staggered to my feet, unsheathing my dirk from where it rested at my hip. The desert chattered in my skull, sensing what came next, although my single-minded focus on Keera had quieted it for a time. I grit my teeth against the noise, unused to it now after over a week of unprecedented stillness around Keera.

I wrapped my free hand around the blade of the dirk, squeezing it in a tight fist. With a savage jerk, I dragged the knife down, slicing across my hand and fingers. I squeezed tighter, blood welling up between my knuckles in dark rivulets and flooding my grasp. With a hiss of breath between my teeth, I opened my hand, letting the liquid drip down my wrist.

I took a bracing breath in through my nose, watching the first drops quiver on my pinkie finger and bone of my wrist. Then, they fell to the sand, my offering of my life force to the desert in exchange for her power —her guidance.

Color exploded behind my eyes, swirling together in patterns I might have been able to make sense of if not for the screaming echoing inside my head. I wanted to claw at my eyes and ears to make the onslaught of sensation stop, but I seemed to have lost all conception of my own physical form. There was only the desert. Magic was all I could see, hear, even taste.

Wading through the influx of information, I tried to make sense of it, only to discover a pattern to the incessant shouting. I strained to listen closer, even as my instincts told me to shy away. There were words among those voices, although they were being repeated over and over by hundreds of voices, out of unison and at different pitches. Still, once I made sense of them, I couldn't stop hearing them.

Take her to Lord Alasdar.

The gritty feel of sand in my mouth was the first physical sensation to return. I don't know how long I existed, outside of space and time, but I found myself lying face down, the sun just beginning to dip below the horizon. Pushing to my hands and knees, I glared at the red stain in the sand accusingly. I had risked my sanity for answers, only to be given one that made little sense.

I crawled back over to Keera's side, leaning close to check on her. Her short and fast breathes puffed hot against my cheek. I contemplated her, feeling more helpless than ever.

Lord Alasdar had found me when I was lost and on the brink of death myself. It was he who taught me to leash my power—direct it toward a worthy goal. Maybe he could do the same for Keera. Maybe the desert wanted her to join us and help us in our battle to restore the Heart.

Most importantly, Lord Alasdar could save her.

The journey took the better part of two days, but for how exhausted it left me, I might have crossed all the way to the ocean. I rode double with Keera, letting her lean back on my chest as I kept her upright. She spent most of the ride unconscious, bouncing limply in my arms, but I dared not tie her to the horse and let the rope chafe her already damaged skin. Not when every bump and jostle drew a whimper from her, each one driving a shard of glass into my heart.

As it was, her burns seeped through the bandages to my own clothes. After the first day, the fluid turned milky and sticky. I leaned down to smell her hair often, take in that sun-kissed, earthy scent that reminded me she still lived, but it began to take on the sickly-sweet smell of infection. Her whimpers turned to mutters and moans.

We stopped to let the horses rest, Alza flagging after going so long carrying a double burden, but she seemed to sense our haste and did not protest our pace. Daiti followed without prompting, never far from his master's side.

I knew I should get some rest too, but sleep would not find me. Every time I closed my eyes, I feared I would open them only to find Keera cold and lifeless. We set off again after only a few hours.

Midmorning on the second day, tents on the horizon caught my attention. Relief shuddered through me. The desert wanted us to rejoin the clans and had made the ride short.

I didn't slow our pace as we pushed into the encampment, riding straight for the center where Lord Alasdar's tent would be.

My eyes snagged on the green banners bearing the fox sigil of Clan Otush in front of several tents, signaling our success, as well as the maroon of Clan Padra and the violet of Clan Vecturna. The rest of the clans had arrived while we had been away.

I pulled Alza to a halt in the clearing before the lord's tent, the point of the sloped roof towering high above the encampment, the black serpent-emblazoned banner of Clan Katal flapping in the morning breeze. Lord Alasdar stepped out without any prompting, as if he had known of my coming. Given the swirling of my magic I had been unable to fully dampen since the lava wyrm fell on Keera, he had likely felt my approach.

His normally cold gray eyes flashed as he took in the sight before him. I didn't miss the way his gaze flickered over his former stallion and the woman clutched tightly to my chest before landing on my face. He visibly stiffened, every harsh line of his body projecting shock.

After a suspended moment of confusion, my heart plummeted.

I wasn't wearing my mask.

While Lord Alasdar had seen my face when he first found me, he had crafted the mask for me on the journey back from the ocean. He handed it to me like a gift, a kind look in his eyes, telling me that it would keep my identity secret. I wouldn't have to worry about anybody from Kelvadan finding me and forcing me beneath a mountain of stone. As the months passed, he told me distancing myself from my past would help me learn control, and letting go of my identity could free me from the burdens of my family's power. He stopped using my name, encouraging me to keep the mask on at all times. It was then I started wearing gloves too, not showing an inch of skin whenever possible. I became the Viper.

Now, Erix sat before him, bare faced, clutching a woman to his chest with ungloved hands.

"What is the meaning of this?" Lord Alasdar demanded.

I swallowed, now noticing the gathering audience. Dozens of people looked at my uncovered face, and I itched to wheel Alza around and gallop away into the wilderness. Instead, I sat tall and squared my shoulders. Keera needed help.

"We defeated the lava wyrm, but she was gravely injured." I nodded to Keera, choosing to put off answering just who 'she' was. "I brought her back here so her wounds could be treated."

Lord Alasdar's eyes narrowed as he took in Keera, her head leaning back against my shoulders, her breath coming in wheezes between lips cracked with dryness. I thought I saw a bolt of recognition in them, but it faded as quickly as it came.

"You were right to bring her. Carry her into my tent."

I hurried to follow his direction, even as I tried to be as gentle as possible with Keera. In his tent, I carried her toward the softest pile of cushions I could find—an opulent nest of rugs and pillows off to one side. The fabric was fine enough that it hopefully wouldn't chafe

Keera's burns too badly. At least it would be gentler than the coarse sand-crusted material of my clothes.

So focused was I on setting Keera down as gingerly as possible, supporting her splinted leg at just the right angle, that I barely heard Lord Alasdar step up next to me.

The whisper of the desert in my mind crescendoed sharply, but I was too late. A hard object connected with my temple, and I crumpled to the ground.

Chapter Thirty-Six
Keera

Panic snapped me out of the fugue of pain that had been my existence for an indeterminate amount of time. However long it had been, I had spent it clutching to the flow of magic between Erix and me, his constant presence rooting me in some degree of sanity. Even though his power was tangled in knots, quivering with intense emotion, they told me I wasn't alone in the fevered landscape of my unconsciousness.

Between one moment and the next, that reassurance vanished. My eyes snapped open, and I tried to scream, but my dry throat only managed a choked gasp. My eyes instantly watered at the searing ache that was an entire half of my body. A tear tracked from one eye, slipping down to a raw cheek where it burned a path so intense, I might have been crying lava.

A low tut from next to me drew my attention. I managed to wrestle my muscles through the pain to turn my head, hoping to find Erix, only to freeze at a familiar but unwelcome face.

Lord Alasdar stared at me pensively, showing as little emotion as he had when he sentenced me to die as a sacrifice at Erix's hands.

"I had wondered why a half-dead exile had been the first person Erix hesitated to kill at my command," he started conversationally. "At first I just thought that he had abominable taste in women to be charmed by a feral thing like you, but I see now that there was more to it than that."

I didn't know what to say, so I glared at him as best I could manage with eyes still full of tears. If I had hated Lord Alasdar before for trying to sacrifice me and his threats to Kelvadan, it was nothing compared to the rage I felt now when I pictured the neat lines of burns across Erix's back. The inescapable agony encasing half my body only gave me more insight into the pain they must have caused.

"Your power might be able to rival mine as well, if you learned how to harness it," Lord Alasdar continued. "I see now that it was you who called down that impressive lightning storm. No doubt Queen Ginevra hoped to be the one to control your power, giving Kelvadan a fighting chance against the combined power of me and my Viper.

"I would be impressed with my Viper for luring you away from Kelvadan if he didn't fall prey to the same weakness as his great-grandfather. It would have been amusing to break you too, have a matching pair of attack dogs, but it seems you have become a weakness for my Viper. No matter, he will purge it as he has purged all the rest."

I tried to follow his words, but it was difficult to remain conscious let alone make sense of his self-important monologue. One phrase stuck in my head though.

My Viper.

Erix had not been the Viper in my eyes for weeks now. My brain wanted to reject that identity, but here I was in Lord Alasdar's tent. Erix must have brought me here after I thought he had turned away from Clan Katal to fight the lava wyrm. I squeezed my eyes shut, tears tracking down my face.

"Erix." The name escaped my mouth unbidden, halfway between a whisper and a sob.

Lord Alasdar chuckled, a sound as rough and dry as a snake rasping over rock. "It's about time he joined our little party I think."

He gestured to a shadowy corner, and I blinked, trying to get my eyes to focus around the blur of tears without turning my head too far. When the form came into focus, my throat clenched.

Erix hung limply, chained between two poles, head resting on his chest. From his flaccid posture, I guessed he was unconscious, but that wasn't what made me itch to tear Lord Alasdar's throat out with my bare hands. While Erix had been stripped of his shirt, bare chest covered with a light sheen of sweat, the metal mask was strapped firmly over his face. Dark curls peeked out around the edges, but I couldn't see his face —his stubborn jaw or those silver eyes I had just managed to coax a teasing sparkle out of.

Lord Alasdar stood and walked over to Erix's vulnerable form, using a hand in his hair to pull his head back. A sound like a growl escaped my throat, and Lord Alasdar chuckled again but didn't look over at me. Instead, he closed his eyes as if focusing, cupping Erix's head in both of his hands.

In a moment, Erix's body snapped with tension, clearly regaining consciousness all at once. He struggled against the chains for a moment, manacles pulling at his wrists and muscles flexing wildly. After a few seconds though, he relaxed again.

"Lord Alasdar," his voice came muffled from behind the mask, confused but with a deferential note that set my teeth on edge.

"You didn't return when I commanded you to." Lord Alasdar kept a hand under Erix's chin, keeping his face directed at him, slightly away from me. With his peripheral vision hindered by the mask, he wouldn't be able to see me like this.

Erix didn't say anything, but a muscle in his shoulder tensed.

"You did well to be named Champion of the Desert. The remaining five clans joined us a week and a half ago, saying they would follow Clan Katal and its Viper into battle, even praising you for coming to Clan Otush's aid. You made quite an impression on them, and they were eager to fight at our side. The time to strike was here, fast and swift before Kelvadan could prepare themselves further, but you weren't here.

"I see now why you were delayed—even why you have struggled to contain your power these past months, despite my training. Your magic has become tangled with another's. For years, I've tried to cleanse you of your family's weakness, but you fell prey to the same vulnerability as Kelvar—a woman."

Metal rattled as Erix went tense again, yanking on the chains, just as he pulled on the bond between us, so hard it would have been painful if it weren't so reassuring to feel him on the other end once more. I plucked at it feebly as he snatched his covered face from Lord Alasdar's grip, searching the tent for me. He stopped with his face toward me, and not being able to see his expression pained me nearly as much as the throbbing in my broken leg.

"You were wise to bring her here so I could help purge you of her influence," Lord Alasdar cooed, as if he were offering comfort instead of chaining Erix up and tormenting him. "I'll help you control your magic so it can be separated from hers, and then we will dispose of her. You will not repeat the sins of Kelvar. She is just another weakness you must be rid of—another test along the way to correcting your family's legacy."

Erix jerked and strained against his bonds. I tried to reach out for him, but a whine pulled from my throat at the way movement stretched and cracked my raw skin beneath the bandages. Erix said something that I couldn't make out from across the tent with a layer of metal muffling him.

Lord Alasdar tutted, shaking his head as if dismayed. "You don't see what she has done to you. Corrupting your purpose. You are an instrument, made to heal the desert, and she has distracted you from our mission to raze Kelvadan and restore the Heart it stole—bring back the old ways and the glory of the clans."

I found my voice, and although it was a dry rasp, Lord Alasdar's face snapped toward me as I spoke. "He doesn't need you to save the desert."

Lord Alasdar tilted his head contemplatively. "Did you perhaps think that together, the two of you could breach the tower in the palace?"

My heart sank at the scornful tone of his words, the very thought I had voiced over a campfire not too long ago.

He laughed at my obvious dismay. "And then what would you do?" He turned back toward Erix, one lip curled in a derisive sneer. "Take the Heart yourself? You only avoid the same madness as Kelvar with my aid. With that kind of power in your hands, you would commit even worse sins—perhaps destroy our home outright. This woman has tricked you into thinking you could do this without me. But you need me to restore the Heart. You lack the control to do it on your own."

Erix slumped, and a sob choked its way out of my throat. After weeks of prying at the vice grip Lord Alasdar held around Erix's mind, I thought he was free. Now, my heart shattered at the realization of just how deep his manipulation ran. The mask was back on, and Erix was slipping away into the Viper once more.

I continued to swallow down shuddering sobs, not wanting to give Lord Alasdar the satisfaction. Still, bile rose in the back of my throat as the older man smoothed Erix's hair back from his mask in a parody of comfort.

"I will help you as I always have, and then you will purge yourself of this weakness."

Erix hung his head in acceptance. I wanted to scream and fight, all teeth and nails as I yelled at Erix to stop—to come back to me. Instead, I just squirmed on the cushions, gasping against the pain in my body and barely managing to lift my head.

"I think it will take more than one line for you to regain your sense of control this time."

Lord Alasdar lifted a hand, summoning a palmful of flame, exercising far more control than I'd hoped to have when coaxing our fires to life, often singing my own fingers in the process. My eyes widened in horror as I realized what was going to happen. Despite my weakness, I tried to launch myself from the pile of cushions, ignoring the agony of my tearing skin, searing as blisters ripped open and a new layer of puss coated my bandages.

"Izumi," Lord Alasdar said without looking up from the fire he coaxed to life in his hand.

A figure I hadn't noticed before stepped out of the shadows at the back of the tent, and a woman grabbed me by the shoulders, stopping my feeble crawl toward Erix. Her grip was strong, and the pain of her fingers on my charred shoulder whited out my vision for a moment. When it returned, I tried to meet her gaze, recognizing her as the woman who had fed me during my time in captivity, to beg her to release me, but she didn't look at me, her hard gaze fixed on the two men before us. I could only watch.

Lord Alasdar clapped his hand to Erix's bare chest, right over his heart. He grunted, and every muscle in his body went tight at the same time, twitching and twisting as if attempting to get away but tensing to hold still. Still, he didn't scream, and I wanted to cry out for him. My throat was dry, but silent tears flowed down my face as the smell of burning flesh filled the space. I threw myself down the bond between us, hoping to comfort Erix or take some of the pain for myself. Instead, I found a wall, as if he had completely detached himself from his magic.

Maybe he was right. You could be in enough pain to completely drown out the call of the desert.

After long seconds, Lord Alasdar pulled away, revealing an angry red brand of his handprint forever burned into Erix's skin. The fingers on my shoulders tightened, and perhaps it was my own trembling, but I thought I felt the Izumi's hands shake.

Lord Alasdar cocked his head expectantly.

"Thank you," Erix rasped, and I nearly heaved, despite having nothing in my stomach. His voice was as hoarse as if he had been screaming, even though he hadn't let out a sound.

Closing his eyes, Lord Alasdar breathed in deeply, as if taking in the fresh scent of the desert after rain.

"I can feel your magic has pulled back from hers." His tone was satisfied. "Are you ready to purge yourself of her influence completely."

After a moment that stretched forever, Erix nodded. In a matter of seconds that passed too fast, Lord Alasdar had unchained him. Erix's hands fell to his knees, and although his wrists were red and raw from straining at his bonds, he didn't rub them. He didn't move at all until Lord Alasdar approached him again, offering him the hilt of a saber— Kelvar's saber.

With a hand that only shook slightly, he took the weapon before pushing to his feet.

"Now, give her blood to the desert and free yourself from Kelvar's mistakes."

Izumi still held my shoulders where I knelt on the floor half collapsed, but she didn't need to. I wouldn't try to run, not that I would make it that far even if I did. The one person who I thought had seen the whole of me and not shied away, only saw me as a weakness. He belonged to Lord Alasdar, not me, no matter what we had said when he moved inside me.

Erix approached with slow measured steps. I stared at his boots as they stopped in front of me. He didn't raise his sword though. At his pause, my gaze trailed up his body, stuttering over the fresh handprint on his chest to stare into the mask of the Viper.

When my gaze met where his eyes should be, he raised his blade, point resting at my throat.

"Do it," I whispered.

My greatest regret would be that I wouldn't at least be able to look into his eyes as I died.

Chapter Thirty-Seven
Erix

Keera stared up at me with the same glare she wore the first time I pressed my great-grandfather's saber to the hollow of her throat—somehow both hopeless and defiant.

"I will be free of my weakness," I insisted. My hand trembled from tension and the adrenaline still coursing through my body after Lord Alasdar's lesson. The tip of my saber scratched Keera's skin with the movement, and she gasped quietly. I could only hope she understood what I meant.

Then I struck, swinging out in a decisive arc at where Lord Alasdar stood behind me. Before my blade could meet his neck, I found myself on the ground, saber clattering to the floor next to me, though I didn't remember dropping it. A scream tore from my lips as Lord Alasdar stood over me, hands outstretched. A commotion beside me told me Keera was fighting against Izumi, shouting too, but I couldn't make out her words against the sensation of Lord Alasdar's magic ripping into my own well of power at the base of my skull.

Where Keera's power was always flowing water, sometimes a calming coolness and other times the raging ocean, Lord Alasdar's magic was lightning. It seared nerve endings I didn't even know I had, pinning me in place.

"Maybe I need to remind you how the people this girl serves tried to control your power," Lord Alasdar sneered down at me.

The flickering orange light of the lanterns in the tent disappeared, leaving me blinking in confusion. My fuzzy eyes could only make out dull gray around me. Lord Alasdar was nowhere to be found. I sat bolt upright, whipping my head around. Keera was gone too.

I was about to shout her name when I realized where I was. Everywhere around me was solid stone—hard and gray and unforgiving. Unlike the last time I had been in the chamber in the heart of the mountain, there wasn't even a door. Just a cube large enough for me to reach out my arms and touch both walls.

I reached for my magic, and while the phantom talons of Lord Alasdar still ripped at my mind, the comforting yet maddening presence of the desert was nowhere to be found. I was trapped and alone. I would die here, never feeling the wind of the desert or riding Alza across the sands again. Without ever telling Keera I loved her. Because I did.

I had loved her the first night when she spit in my face and for every inch she had pushed me after that. Even when I'd pretended I didn't exist, letting the monster Lord Alasdar wanted me to be devour the man I was, the heart buried underneath all that darkness only beat for her. And now my weakness would cost both of us our lives.

I screamed, voice echoing back at me in the close quarters. It wasn't enough to drown out my pain, at being separated from the desert— from Keera—forever.

The desert gives and it takes, and it had given Keera to me only to snatch her away in the cruelest way possible. I pounded against the floor, skin on my fists ripping until blood dripped down my wrists but it wasn't enough. I clawed at my face, trying to pull off the stifling mask and take a full breath, but it had attached itself to my face. I couldn't breathe, couldn't hear, couldn't think.

The stone walls around me shattered, and I lay on the floor, staring up at the canvas of Lord Alasdar's tent.

A soft ping of liquid dripping against my mask drew my attention, and I focused my eyes to see the bloody tip of a saber—my great-grandfather's saber—hovering above my face. It was protruding from the center of Lord Alasdar's chest, a look of utter shock etched onto his face. A single drop of blood bubbled from his mouth, dripping down his chin.

"You don't get to hurt him anymore." Keera's voice was weak but sure. She wrenched the blade from his body, and he crumpled, dead before he hit the ground. Crimson spread from where he lay, staining the rich rugs beneath him. I could only stare at his slack-jawed face, the gray eyes that held so much power over me now empty of life.

My savior and my torturer, my mentor and my jailer, dead at Keera's hand in one decisive strike. Trembling overtook me as I stared at the corpse, relief rushing through me, turned bitter by the grief for what Lord Alasdar might have been for me—the father that I had painted him to be.

I looked up at Keera, finding her panting, complexion ashen, eyes red and swollen from crying so much, and utterly perfect.

She wavered where she stood, balancing on her unbroken leg through sheer will alone, although she trembled with weakness. I lurched forward, but Izumi got there first, helping her keep her balance as if she hadn't just slain the man we'd both had pledged our life to—somebody Izumi had betrayed her clan for. I wanted to ask her why, but it didn't matter right now. Not when Keera was about to pass out.

I struggled to my feet, reaching for Keera. Before I could grab her by the shoulders and press my ear to her chest to make sure she was alive, a crash sounded outside the tent. All three of us froze.

A moment of silence stretched, followed by the sound of screaming. Izumi shoved Keera toward me before rushing from the tent. Clashing metal split the air, but my focus stayed pinned on the woman in my arms as I lowered her back to the bed of pillows.

She whimpered as her skin touched the fabric, and I stroked the remaining half of her hair gently. Reaching up, her fingers trailed down my mask, coming away red from where Lord Alasdar's blood had dripped. Without further thought, I ripped it off, throwing it down on the ground next to Lord Alasdar's corpse.

"You saved me," I murmured in awe.

Keera grimaced, her eyes watery, but I got the impression she was trying to smile at me. "I meant it. You're mine. Nobody gets to touch you but me."

"You saw how broken I am." I shook my head. "I'll happily be yours until the day I die, but I don't think you can fix me."

Keera's voice was thin as she spoke, clearly succumbing to the exhaustion and pain she had battled during the confrontation. Still, every word hit me like a punch to the gut. "You don't need to be fixed. You just need to be loved."

A lump rose in my throat, and I choked around my own words. "And I love you."

Keera's eyes fluttered closed as she went limp in my arms before I even got the words all the way out. I touched my fingers to her neck, finding her pulse to make sure she still lived. It was steady if rapid and thready beneath my fingers. She had just overexerted herself.

Before I could set to work getting her comfortable, a clatter drew my attention to the tent flap. I glanced up to find Izumi, armor disheveled and sword drawn. Crimson glimmered off the wicked blade.

"Kelvadan attacks," she panted.

I didn't respond, looking between Izumi and Keera. To the body on the floor.

"You must fight," Izumi insisted with increasing urgency.

"Lord Alasdar is dead. There is no point!" I spat.

"No point?" Izumi's eyes flashed. "The desert still rips itself apart at the seams, and Kelvadan is still to blame. You might have fought for Lord Alasdar, but I fight for the people of the desert. They now stand against the riders of Kelvadan, unorganized and afraid, and they are the ones who will die tonight."

"Then lead them!" I snapped, turning back to Keera, wanting nothing more than to bundle her into my arms and ride away to somewhere safe. There had already been too much pain and death in this tent.

Izumi stomped over to me, clapping her hand on my shoulder. "You must lead them."

I looked up at her, the sincerity in her eyes taking me aback.

"You are the one they are here for. The Viper was named Champion of the Desert, and he is the one that delivered the clans from the lava wyrm. The lord of Clan Otush arrived and pronounced her clan loyal to you, not Lord Alasdar. They know the power you wield, and they only ever followed Lord Alasdar because of you. Now they have gathered here to serve you, and if you do not help them, their deaths will be on your hands."

I clenched my jaw, looking back and forth between Keera and Izumi. Keera had nearly died fighting the lava wyrm to protect the clans of the desert. She spilled Lord Alasdar's blood for me because she thought I was worthy. Would I be worthy if I let the people she was willing to die for perish during a surprise attack in the night?

"When the encampment is secure, we will help her. She is strong and will survive until the threat is driven away." Izumi's voice was gentle but brooked no argument.

"Sands," I swore.

Moving quickly, I bent to retrieve my saber. I contemplated for just a moment before laying it next to Keera's outstretched hand. I would feel better leaving her with a weapon, and my sword felt like the next best thing if I could not be there to protect her myself. Instead, I grabbed the sword from Lord Alasdar's belt, testing it in my grip. It was shorter than I was used to and the blade broader, but it would do.

Before I could charge from the tent, Izumi reached out, offering me something.

My mask.

I only hesitated for a moment. Then I grabbed it and shoved it back on my face, even as my skin crawled. The riders of the clans knew me as the Viper, the Champion of the Ballan Desert, and now was not the time to change that. If I could be a symbol that saved instead of only destroying, then I could stomach the contraption again.

I chanced one more look at Keera, vulnerable but alive, nestled in a bloodstained nest of rugs and cushions.

"I'll be back," I promised, and then shoved out into the chaos of the encampment.

Alza's muscular body between my thighs dispelled the quivering that had overtaken my limbs since I had woken chained in Lord Alasdar's tent. I charged through the camp, sword held aloft and rallying riders to me. Fighters who had run to-and-fro without direction, dousing burning tents and trying to protect their own clans without a clear chain of command, grabbed their mounts and fell in behind me.

Forces that had been scattered, nine fractured factions fending for themselves coalesced into a solid band. With a cry, I struck out at a Kelvadan rider who had managed to make it deep into the encampment.

With the element of surprise on their side, the riders of Kelvadan had penetrated far beyond our defenses in a matter of minutes. I directed the riders with me to push them back toward the west where they had attacked from.

Swinging my saber in vicious arcs and urging Alza to kick out with her deadly hooves, I positioned myself in the thick of things. As clansman saw the masked rider on the black horse, they shouted and rallied to me, although I did not miss the way some of their gazes flicked to the freshly burned handprint on my still-bare chest.

Meanwhile, riders of Kelvadan began retreating the moment they spotted my mask. The Viper ruled the battlefield, even if I knew he lay dead on the ground next to the corpse of Lord Alasdar. I wore his face, and that was all that mattered.

I savagely attacked any fighters I spotted advancing toward the center of the camp. I had left Keera in the tent there, and I didn't intend to let anybody get near her. At I thought of Keera, I pulled on the magic between us, drawing power.

Soon, the mind-numbing hum of battle washed over me. My sword blocked blows before I even noticed them coming, and Alza followed commands before I could give them, as if she and I were of the same mind.

By the time we had pushed the riders of Kelvadan to the borders of the encampment, the full force of all nine clans were at my back and blood splattered my bare chest. Still, battle raged on outside the line of tents. Horses screamed and the harsh screeching of blade meeting blade filled the air. The metallic tang of blood filtered in through my mask, and the threads of my magic began to tremble, tying itself into knots.

I itched to advance, the bloodlust bred into me by Lord Alasdar rearing its head and urging me to push on until all who opposed us had fallen. Still, a tether in the back of my skull to an unconscious woman behind me held a shred of my sanity intact. We needed to be safe. Lord Alasdar was dead, and we needed a chance to regroup. Still, power danced at my fingertips and the sands began to swirl around me. The desert itched to be unleashed upon those who stood against me.

Those in combat closest around me noticed the change, horses edging away from me as white showed around their eyes. Izumi, astride her piebald to my right, eyed me warily.

"Pull back!" I shouted, holding my hands out before me.

Izumi echoed my order, rallying as many riders to her as possible in a hasty retreat. The battle cries of the Kelvadan riders turned to shouts of victory, seeing the clans turning tail as surrender.

I closed my eyes, letting the cacophony roll over me. The voices of both sides turned into an overwhelming rumble as my awareness dissolved, skittering across the landscape. I was every horse and every rider. Every grain of sand moved at my command even as my sense of self dissolved nearly entirely.

A crack split the air the same time I snapped back into my body. Shouts of victory turned into screams of terror. I opened my eyes to find Alza's hooves on the edge of a gorge, so deep that the bottom was swallowed by darkness. Riders of Kelvadan who had been in the vanguard, chasing the clansman in a hasty rout, plummeted into the chasm, falling to certain doom.

The split in the earth ran as far as I could see in both directions, gently curving around the encampment and effectively splitting it from the attackers. Kelvadan's forces skittered backward, retreating from the chasm as if afraid it would advance and swallow more of them.

Among the retreating riders, I spotted a familiar shaved head, marked by a vertical line of black ink. Aderyn shouted orders and wheeled her horse around. She appeared to be carrying a burden with her, but my vision began to blur.

A hand on my shoulder braced me before I even realized I had slipped sideways on Alza's back, tilting dangerously toward the earth. Izumi pulled her mount up next to me, wrapping an arm around my waist in support.

"It's all right. We're safe now."

At her words, the last of my energy drained out of me. I had scarcely slept for two days since fighting the lava wyrm. After bearing Keera across the desert, torture, the upheaval of Lord Alasdar's death, and a battle that left my mind fizzling with aftershocks of power, I wanted nothing more than to answer the seductive call of unconsciousness. I needed one thing first.

"Keera..."

"We'll take care of her," Izumi assured.

Try as I might, I couldn't stop the darkness from claiming me.

CHAPTER THIRTY-EIGHT
KEERA

A strong hand on my shoulder pulled me from the painless release of unconsciousness. I groaned, twitching and trying to tell Erix to stop touching me, even as I wanted him to crush me to his chest and never let go. Every bone ached and every touch felt like a fresh burn across my skin.

Even on my unburned side, everything felt hot. I must have an infection.

"What have they done to you?"

My eyes snapped open at the familiar but unexpected voice.

"Ad—" I choked around the woman's name, but she shushed me. I had never been so glad to see her, yet so terrified at the same time.

"You're safe. I'm going to get you out of here," Aderyn reassured.

I wanted to protest, but I didn't know what was happening. Where was Erix? Why had he left me?

My hands were still sticky with Lord Alasdar's blood. My eyes flickered to the huddled corpse on the ground. Aderyn's gaze followed mine.

"Did you kill him?" she asked.

I swallowed, managing the slightest nod.

"Well done," Aderyn praised. "Serves him right after what he's done to you."

It wasn't what he had done to me. It was what he had done to Erix that had given me the strength to lunge forward toward the fallen weapon and drive in through his ribs with every last bit of strength I had in my body. With Erix screaming and twitching on the floor, even the woman ordered to hold me hadn't seemed intent on stopping me from bringing Lord Alasdar's life to a swift and satisfying end.

I didn't have the words to say this to Aderyn, the last of my strength having been spent telling Erix I loved him. I clenched my hands into fists, and my fingers brushed something hard and metallic. I glanced over, finding Erix's saber next to my outstretched arm.

Seeing where I looked, Aderyn handed me the weapon, and I squeezed so hard that the leather grip was sure to leave an imprint in my hand. Even if Aderyn didn't know what had happened, she was a warrior enough to understand the comfort of a sword in hand.

"Come on. I have to get you out of here while the riders are distracted. I doubt they'll leave you alive after killing their leader." Aderyn gathered me in her arms, lifting me easily despite being shorter than me.

A pained gasp escaped me. I tried to form words around the agony of being moved, but they didn't come.

"Erix..."

It was all I managed to choke out before darkness took me again.

A stone ceiling greeted my bleary eyes. I tried to remember where I was but the only memories I could locate were agony and the squelch of flesh as I drove a blade through a man's heart. Erix's screaming and the smell of burning flesh.

I ran my awareness along my limbs now, finding the agony had dulled to a persistent ache, coating the entire right side of my body, along with a pounding in my broken leg. The shivering heat and delirium that had coursed through my veins before had abated, telling me any infection was likely cleared. I must have been unconscious for a long time.

Chancing to lift my head, I looked around, finding myself in a long stone room filled with empty beds. It was deserted save for the occupant of the chair beside me, bent over a piece of fabric in his hands, embroidering it with intricate patterns.

"Neven," I choked out.

His head snapped up, and a look of intense relief crossed his face, kind eyes crinkling in a broad smile.

"You're awake!"

"How long has it been?" My voice was thin from disuse, but still stronger than it had been in my last memories.

"Several days," he answered. "You woke up almost as soon as you got here, but we had to sedate you. You lashed out and fought at anybody who came near you, shouting about Erix and burning. You nearly brought the palace down with your magic, and we had to force you to drink lyra leaf tea."

I swallowed, trying to process everything through my sluggish brain. "Erix?"

"You're safe." Neven laid his hand on my uninjured shin. "He really did a number on you."

I tried to shake my head. That wasn't what I was asking. I needed to know where he was. The tether in my belly was fuzzy, as if my magic was hard to reach, and while I could feel its presence, I couldn't reach along the bond to find him.

"I'm—I'm sorry I encouraged you to go with him." Neven's face crumpled, and he looked shattered. "If I had known he would turn you over to Lord Alasdar, I never would have helped you run away that night. When Aderyn told me who the man in the mask was and what he had promised to do, I thought... But I was wrong. Lord Alasdar's influence on him was too great."

"Lord Alasdar... he's dead." The words came out more a question than I would have hoped. Everything felt wrong, like a piece was missing from my mind, making the whole thing teeter uncertainly. Maybe the effects of the lyra leaf tea. I wanted to retch.

Neven nodded gravely. "Aderyn told everybody what you did. Even though the attack was a failure, it was worth it as you managed to take out Alasdar."

"The attack?"

"An informant told us that the clans were united and about to launch their siege, but it was delayed by the Viper's absence. Aderyn and the queen decided to attack when they were vulnerable, trying to save the citizens of Kelvadan from a drawn-out siege.

"Unfortunately, the Viper seemed to have returned with you before Aderyn and her riders got there. The element of surprise almost gave them the victory, but he was too powerful."

My mind spun. "What happened?"

"He ripped the earth open, swallowing dozens of riders. Aderyn barely got you out of the encampment before it happened. You're lucky she snuck into the lord's tent to assassinate him and found you, otherwise I'm not sure if we ever would have seen you again."

"Where is he now?" My stomach sank even as I asked.

"The Viper? He's claimed leadership over the combined clans. Our intelligence is limited, but it is only a matter of time before they attack Kelvadan."

No, Erix wouldn't. He had turned on Lord Alasdar rather than kill me. Half delirious as I had been, I could have sworn he told me he loved me.

Then again, if Neven told the truth, he had led the clans in the fight against the Kelvadan riders. I knew why he wanted to breach the city. The Heart of the Desert still lay locked at the top of the palace, the key to restoring the desert he loved—our home.

My mind ached nearly as hard as my heart at the swirling mass of thoughts in my head. I was still woozy, and the knots of my thoughts seemed loathe to untangle no matter how hard I yanked at them. I reached down to the tether I knew still bound me to Erix, across the desert as he might be. Things had been so simple when it was just the two of us alone in the wilderness. I thought we had avoided standing on opposite sides of an inevitable war, yet here we were. He was the Lord of the combined clans, and I was the hero who'd killed his predecessor. If I could just talk to him, feel him, perhaps I could make sense of this once again.

After all, I hadn't killed Lord Alasdar for Kelvadan. I had done it for Erix.

Erix, whom I couldn't even feel through the haziness in my magic caused by the lyra leaf tea.

I squeezed my eyes shut and a few tears escaped, a breath coming out in a shuddering sob.

"I shouldn't have told you so much—you still must be in so much pain," Neven comforted, picking up a cup from the table beside my bed. He lifted it to my lips, and I wanted to protest, but I was too weak. Days in bed left me unprepared to fight him on anything, even though I wanted to insist he bring me back to Erix and get me out of this close stone room.

My vision swam as I swallowed the liquid Neven offered me, but I caught sight of something on the stand next to me—something that gave me the barest hint of hope and made me feel like maybe I wasn't completely alone.

Erix's saber.

There was so much to explain, and I didn't know where to start. Not when Neven and the rest of Kelvadan apparently believed that the Viper had brought me to his lord to be tortured before I killed him and narrowly escaped.

The liquid I drank tasted herbal and medicinal on my tongue, and my pain began to dissolve—at least the physical aches. As the pain killers quieted the roar of my mind to nothing more than a dull buzz, one thought floated to the surface.

I would heal, and I would find Erix, and together we would restore the desert.

EPILOGUE
ERIX

The lanterns lining the walls of the tent exploded in unison, glass shattering everywhere as the flames within them flared violently at the force of my anger. I didn't care.

Keera was gone.

Only an indent in the pillows and a smattering of bloodstains remained to show where she had been. I rounded on Izumi, and she shied away from the force of my rage. The desert chattered in my head, driving me to distraction, but I couldn't seem to quiet it.

"Where is she?" I demanded.

"She was gone by the time the riders of Kelvadan retreated," Izumi insisted. "In her state, she couldn't have gotten out of the encampment on her own that quickly. One of the Kelvadan riders must have taken her."

Closing my eyes, taking deep measured breaths through my nose. It wasn't enough. I raised a hand to my chest, digging my nails into the burn on my chest through the layers of my shirt and bandages. The pain granted me enough clarity to reach into the tangled knot of my magic.

There at the base was the invisible tether, binding me to Keera. I still didn't know what it was, but feeling it intact did something to calm me.

If she were dead, surely it would have been severed. Still, the flow of her power was sluggish, like a well clogged with mud and clay.

I opened my eyes to find Izumi staring at me.

"We will get her back."

Izumi narrowed her eyes at me appraisingly, and I found my skin prickling under her scrutiny. I hadn't put my mask back on since awakening after the fight and having her read my expressions was new territory.

Seeming satisfied with what she found in my face, Izumi nodded once.

"We'll take her back from Kelvadan and save her along with the desert."

I turned back to the pile of cushions and rugs before me. The tent flap rustled as Izumi left, but I didn't look. Instead, a bent down to pick up a pillow, marked with a bloodstain where Keera's skin had cracked and bled. Unsheathing my dirk, I cut away the strip of fabric with the crimson splotch.

I contemplated it, plucking at the tether in my mind once more. I might have imagined it, but I thought it shivered in response, as if Keera was trying to tell me she was at the other end of the bond, stretched as it was. I drew my saber—the one I had taken from Lord Alasdar—taking small comfort in the fact that Kelvar's sword was gone. Keera must have taken it with her.

With an efficient knot, I tied the bloodstained strip of fabric around the hilt of my weapon before sliding it back into the sheath across my back.

The desert gives and it takes, but it had given Keera and me this bond, something in our blood drawing us together. I would continue to serve the desert and undo the damage of my family's legacy. Kelvar's love for Alyx had nearly destroyed the desert, and I understood it now. Because I would lay waste to Kelvadan and get the Heart he had stolen away, but only after I had Keera safe in my arms.

To stay up to date on S.C. Grayson's future releases or join her reader group, visit her link page at https://linktr.ee/scgrayson

ACKNOWLEDGMENTS

I want to start off by thanking somebody who I realized I have never appreciated in my acknowledgments before: myself. This project, more than any of my books that came before, was a leap of faith. I wanted to take a moment to appreciate the voice in my head that told me to go for it, even when the thoughts of self-doubt kept creeping in.

Of course, the part of my brain that encouraged me to take the leap wouldn't have gotten much traction without the incredible army of supporters I have at my back. My editor, Friel, has been a champion for this project since the first time she laid eyes on it. So many incredible artists have also contributed their talents to this book, and I want to thank all of them for bringing my characters to life with so much care.

I would not be where I am without an incredible network of fellow authors. Lily, you are the author bestie I never knew I needed, until you crashed into my life with a sense of humor that makes every situation better. Megan, Lisa, Stacy, Charissa, Alexis, Erin, and Lilla, you make me proud to be a discordant owl.

My parents and my incredible sister are constant sources of strength. Thank you, Amanda, for being a "logical tan" that can find the faults with almost any plot or magic system, helping me to patch them up before I send my stories out into the world. Thank you, Mom, for supporting me in writing what inspires me, even when it is high fantasy that inexplicably contains no talking mushrooms, despite your strong opinion that they are a staple of the genre.

And lastly, to Rhys. No matter how many novels I write, know that they will never be enough to encompass all my love for you.

ABOUT THE AUTHOR

S.C. Grayson has been reading fantasy novels since she was a little girl, and that has developed into a love of writing and storytelling. She is currently focused on fantasy and paranormal romance. She has written several Gaslamp fairytale retellings, and looks forward to publishing additional epic fantasy, paranormal, and science fiction romances.

When she is not sitting in a local coffee shop writing and consuming an iced americano, Grayson is a nurse researcher, focusing her efforts on breast cancer genetics. She lives in Maryland with her loving husband and their two cats, who enjoy contributing to her work by walking across her keyboard at inopportune moments (the cats, not the husband).

Also by S.C. Grayson

The Talented Fairy Tales Trilogy

Beauty and the Blade

https://books2read.com/beautyandtheblade

Little Red Shadow

https://books2read.com/littleredshadow

The Hood and his Thief

https://books2read.com/hoodandhisthief

Made in the USA
Middletown, DE
14 July 2024

57272316R00243